N

Dear Reader:

A vacation has always been a time of possibilities, a time when you leave the familiar behind and travel into the unknown....

And right now you hold in your hand a guaranteed good time from Silhouette Books: a ticket to three fabulous vacations in one, because a good story can transport you to a different world, take you places you've never been before—all without moving an inch!

Bestselling authors Nora Roberts, Parris Afton Bonds and Kathleen Korbel will whisk you to Greece, Mexico and the Caribbean. Whether you're at work, at home or relaxing on the beach, you'll enjoy traveling with each of the three women described in these stories as she experiences the holiday of her life—and meets the man of her dreams!

Let Silhouette sweep you away....

Yours,

Isabel Swift
Senior Editor &
Editorial Coordinator

D0683451

SILHOUETTE SUMMER Sizzlers

Nora Roberts
Parris Afton Bonds
Kathleen Korbel

Silhouette Books®

Published by Silhouette Books New York

America's Publisher of Contemporary Romance

Contents

IMPULSE

Nora Roberts

Summer

Four years ago this month, I was married. When my soon-to-be husband and I were discussing plans for our honeymoon, there was one place that kept coming to my mind.

Greece. For as long as I can remember, I've dreamed of going to Greece, cruising the Aegean, imagining Adonis and Apollo and Aphrodite. I could picture myself walking near the Acropolis or sitting in a seaside café drinking ouzo. I wanted to walk in an olive grove and see wild goats. To me, Greece has always been one of the most romantic and exotic places in the world.

Well, things didn't work out. For the life of me, I can't exactly recall the reasons we changed our plans and headed to the resorts of Cancun and Cozumel on the Caribbean coast of Mexico. But it was all for the best. Right after we made our new plans, ordered tickets and reserved a hotel, the TWA flight out of Athens was hijacked.

We did have a wonderful time in Mexico. Blue water, gorgeous flowers, exotic music. Instead of Greek gods, I imagined ancient Mayans. We didn't cruise the Aegean, but we snorkeled in the warm, clear Caribbean. I don't remember a single day when the sun didn't shine and the birds didn't sing. Of course, I was on my honeymoon.

We listened to mariachis and danced in the moonlight in the square in the village. We toured the ruins in Tulum, then swam in a lagoon called X-ha. That's where my new husband lost the keys to our rental car.

You don't always think of yourself as a foreigner, even in a foreign country, until you're faced with the language barrier. I could ask important things, like "How much does this cost?" and "Where's the rest room?" But

I didn't have a clue how to explain that we'd lost the keys to our car somewhere in the lagoon and our hotel was an hour away.

But, like a true hero, my husband dived back in. The sunscreen had worn off and lunch was only a fond memory when he found them. But find them he did. I guess the gods look out for honeymooners.

Four years later and he's still my hero. From time to time we toy with the idea of that trip to Greece. I still hope to see Mount Olympus and walk in an olive grove. In the meantime, I went there in my imagination with Rebecca and Stephen. I hope you enjoy the trip as much as I did.

Chapter One

She knew it was crazy. That was what she liked best about it. It was crazy, ridiculous, impractical and totally out of character. And she was having the time of her life. From the balcony of her hotel suite Rebecca could see the sweep of the beach, the glorious blue of the Ionian Sea, blushed now with streaks of rose from the setting sun.

Corfu. Even the name sounded mysterious, exciting, glamorous. And she was here, really here. Practical, steady-as-a-rock Rebecca Malone, who had never traveled more than five hundred miles from Philadelphia, was in Greece. Not just in Greece, she thought with a grin, but on the exotic island of Corfu, in one of the most exclusive resorts in Europe.

First-class, she thought as she leaned out to let the sweet breeze ruffle over her face. As long as it lasted, she was going first-class.

Her boss had thought she was suffering from temporary insanity. Edwin McDowell of McDowell, Jableki and Kline was never going to understand why a promising young CPA would resign from her position with one of the top accounting firms in Philadelphia. She'd made a good salary, she'd enjoyed excellent benefits, and she'd even had a small window in her office.

Friends and associates had wondered if she'd suffered a breakdown. After all, it wasn't normal, and it certainly wasn't Rebecca's style to quit a solid, well-paying job without the promise of a better one.

But she'd given her two weeks' notice, cleared out her desk and had cheerfully walked out into the world of the unemployed.

When she'd sold her condo and then in one frantic week, auctioned off every possession she owned—every stick of furniture, every pot and pan and appliance—they'd been certain she'd gone over the edge.

Rebecca had never felt saner.

She owned nothing that didn't fit in a suitcase. She no longer had any tax-deferred investments or retirement plans. She'd cashed in her certificates of deposit, and the home entertainment center she'd thought she couldn't live without was now gracing someone else's home.

It had been more than six weeks since she'd even looked at an adding machine.

For the first—and perhaps the only—time in her life, she was totally free. There were no responsibilities, no pressures, no hurried gulps of cold coffee. She hadn't packed an alarm clock. She no longer owned one. Crazy? No. Rebecca shook her head and laughed into the breeze. For as long as it lasted, she was going to grab life with both hands and see what it had to offer.

Aunt Jeannie's death had been her turning point. It had come so suddenly, so unexpectedly, leaving Rebecca without any family. Aunt Jeannie had worked hard for most of her sixty-five years, always punctual, always responsible. Her position as head librarian had been her whole life. She'd never missed a day, never failed to do her duty. Her bills had been paid on time. Her promises had always been kept.

More than once Rebecca had been told she took after her mother's older sister. She was twenty-four, but she was—had been—as solid and sturdy as her maiden aunt. Two months into retirement, two months after dear Aunt Jeannie began to make plans to travel, to enjoy the rewards she'd worked so hard to earn, she was gone.

After Rebecca's grief had come the anger, then the frustration, then slowly, the realization that she was traveling the same straight road. She worked, she slept, she fixed well-balanced meals that she ate alone. She had a small circle of friends who knew she could be counted on in a crisis. Rebecca would always find the best and most practical answer. Rebecca would never drop her own problems in your lap—because she didn't have any. Rebecca, bless her, was a port in any storm.

She hated it, and she'd begun to hate herself. She had to do something.

And she was doing it.

It wasn't running away as much as it was breaking free. All her life she'd done what was expected of her and tried to make as few waves as possible while doing it. All through school a crushing shyness had kept her more comfortable with her books than with other teenagers. In college a need to succeed and justify her aunt's faith had locked her tightly into her studies.

She had always been good with figures—logical, thorough, patient. It had been easy, perhaps too easy, to pour herself into that one area, because there, and really only there, had she felt confident.

Now she was going to discover Rebecca Malone. In the weeks or months of freedom she had, she wanted to learn everything there was to know about the woman within. Perhaps there wasn't a butterfly inside the cocoon she'd wrapped herself in so comfortably, but whatever she found—whoever she found—Rebecca hoped she would enjoy her, like her, perhaps even respect her.

When the money ran out, she'd get another job and go back to being plain, practical Rebecca. Until that time she was rich, rootless and ready for surprises.

She was also hungry.

Stephen saw her the moment she entered the restaurant. It wasn't that she was particularly striking. Beautiful woman passed through the world every day and they usually warranted a glance. But there was something about the way this one walked, as if she were ready for anything, even looking forward to it. He stopped, and because business was slow at this hour he took a second, longer look.

She was tall for a woman, and more angular than slender. Her skin was pale, and that made him think she had only just arrived at the resort or was shy of the sun. The white sundress that left her shoulders and back bare accented the lack of color and gave dramatic contrast to her short cap of raven hair.

She paused, then seemed to take a deep breath. Stephen could almost hear her satisfied sigh. Then she smiled at the headwaiter, and followed him to her table, tossing her head back, so that her hair, which she wore arrow-straight, swung away from her chin.

A nice face, Stephen concluded. Bright, intelligent, eager. Especially the eyes. They were pale, an almost translucent gray. But there was nothing pale in their expression. She smiled at the waiter again, then laughed and looked around the restaurant. She looked as if she'd never been happier in her life.

She saw him. When Rebecca's gaze first skimmed over the man leaning against the bar, her automatic shyness kicked in and had her looking away. Attractive men had stared at her before—though it wasn't exactly a daily event. She'd never been able to handle it with the aplomb—or even cynicism—of most of her contemporaries. To cover her momentary embarrassment, she lifted her menu.

He hadn't meant to linger more than a few moments longer, but the impulse came suddenly. Stephen flicked a hand at the waiter and had him scurrying over, nodding quickly at Stephen's murmured request and hurrying off. When he returned it was to deliver a bottle of champagne to Rebecca's table.

"Compliments of Mr. Nickodemus."

"Oh." Rebecca followed the waiter's gaze over to the man by the bar. "Well, I—" She brought herself up short before she could stammer. A sophisticated woman wouldn't stutter over a gift of champagne, she reminded herself. She'd accept it graciously, with dignity. And maybe—if she wasn't a complete fool—she'd relax enough to flirt with the man who offered it.

Stephen watched the expressions pass across her face. Fascinating, he mused, and realized that the vague boredom he'd been feeling had vanished. When she lifted her head and smiled at him, he had no idea that her heart was pounding. He saw only a casual invitation, and he answered it.

He wasn't just attractive, Rebecca realized as he crossed to her table. He was gorgeous. Eye-popping, mouth-dropping gorgeous. She had an image of Apollo and ancient Greek warriors. Thick blond hair streaked by the sun fell over the collar of his shirt. Smooth, bronzed skin was marred—and somehow enhanced—by a faint scar under his jawline. A strong jaw, she thought. A strong face, with the darkest, deepest blue eyes she'd ever seen.

"Good evening, I'm Stephen Nickodemus." His voice wasn't accented, it was rounded, rich. He might have come from anywhere. Perhaps it was that, more than anything else, that intrigued her.

Lecturing herself on poise and image, she lifted her hand. "Hello. I'm Rebecca, Rebecca Malone." She felt a quick flutter when he brushed his lips over her knuckles. Feeling foolish, she drew her hand away and balled it in her lap. "Thank you for the champagne."

"It seemed to suit your mood." He studied her, wondering why he was getting such a mix of signals. "You are by yourself?"

"Yes." Perhaps it was a mistake to admit it, but if she was going to live life to the fullest she had to take some risks. The restaurant wasn't crowded, but they were hardly alone. Take the plunge, she told herself, and tried another smile. "The least I can do is offer you a glass."

Stephen took the seat across from her, brushing the waiter aside to pour the wine himself. "You are American?"

"It shows."

"No. Actually, I thought you were French until you spoke."

"Did you?" That pleased her. "I've just come from Paris." She had to force herself not to touch her hair. She'd had it cut, with trepidation and delight, in a French salon.

Stephen touched his glass to hers. Her eyes bubbled with life as cheerfully as the wine. "Business?"

"No, just pleasure." What a marvelous word, she thought. *Pleasure.* "It's a wonderful city."

"Yes. Do you go often?"

Rebecca smiled into her glass. "Not often enough. Do you?"

"From time to time."

She nearly sighed at that. Imagine anyone speaking of going to Paris "from time to time." "I nearly stayed longer, but I'd promised myself Greece."

So she was alone, restless, and on the move. Perhaps that was why she had appealed to him, because he was, too. "Is Corfu your first stop?"

"Yes." She sipped at her drink. A part of her still believed it was all a dream. Greece, champagne, the man. "It's beautiful. Much more beautiful than I imagined it could be."

"It's your first trip, then?" He couldn't have said why that pleased him. "How long do you stay?"

"As long as I like." She grinned, savoring the feeling of freedom. "And you?"

He lifted his glass. "Longer, I think, than I had planned." When the waiter appeared at his side, Stephen handed over the menu, then spoke to him in soft, quick Greek. "If you don't object, I'd like to guide you through your first meal on the island."

The old Rebecca would have been too nervous to sit through a meal with a stranger. The new Rebecca took a second, deeper sip of champagne. "I'd love it. Thank you."

It was easy. Easy to sit, to laugh, to sample new and exotic tastes. She forgot that he was a stranger, forgot that the world she was living in now was only temporary. They didn't speak of anything important—only of Paris, and the weather, and the wine. Still, she was sure it was the most interesting conversation of her life. He looked at her when he spoke to her, looked at her as though he were delighted to spend an hour talking of nothing. The last man she'd had dinner with had wanted her to give him a discount when she did his taxes.

Stephen wasn't asking her for anything more than her company for dinner. When he looked at her it seemed unlikely that he'd care if she knew how to fill out Schedule C.

When he suggested a walk along the beach, she agreed without a qualm. What better way to end an evening than a walk in the moonlight?

"I was looking out at this from my window just before dinner." Rebecca stepped out of her shoes, then dangled them from her fingers as she walked. "I didn't think it could look more beautiful than it did at sunset."

"The sea changes, like a woman, in the light." He paused to touch a flame to the end of a slim cigar. "So men are drawn to her."

"Are you? Drawn to the sea?"

"I've spent my time on her. I fished in these waters as a boy."

She'd learned at dinner that he'd grown up traveling the islands with his father. "It must have been exciting, moving from place to place, seeing new things almost every day."

He shrugged. He'd never been sure whether the restlessness had been born in him or had been a product of his upbringing. "It had its moments."

"I love to travel." Laughing, she tossed her shoes aside, then stepped into the surf. The champagne was making her head swim and the moonlight felt as soft as rain. "I adore it." She laughed again when the spray washed up to dampen her skirts. The Ionian Sea. She was standing in it. "On a night like this I think I'll never go home."

She looked so vibrant, so alive, standing in the surf with her white skirts billowing. "Where's home?"

She glanced over her shoulder. The flirtatious look was totally unplanned and completely devastating. "I haven't decided. I want to swim." On impulse, she dived into the surf.

Stephen's heart stopped when she disappeared. He'd already kicked off his shoes and started forward when she rose up again. For a second time, his heart stopped.

She was laughing, her face lifted to the moonlight. Water cascaded from her hair, from her skin. The drops that clung to her were the only jewels she wore. Beautiful? No, she wasn't beautiful. She was electric.

"It's wonderful. Cool and soft and wonderful."

With a shake of his head, he stepped in far enough to take her hand and pull her toward shore. She was a little mad, perhaps, but engagingly so. "Are you always so impulsive?"

"I'm working on it. Aren't you?" She combed her hand through her dripping hair. "Or do you always send champagne to strange women?"

"Either way I answer that could be trouble. Here." He shrugged out of his jacket and draped it over her shoulders. Unframed, washed clean, her face glowed in the moonlight. There was a graceful kind of strength in it, to the sweep of cheekbone, the slightly pointed chin. Delicate—except for the eyes. One look there showed power, a power that was still. "You're irresistible, Rebecca."

She stared at him, confused all over again, as he gathered the neck of the jacket close around her throat. "I'm wet," she managed.

"And beautiful." With his hands still on the jacket, he brought her toward him. "And fascinating."

That made her laugh again. "I don't think so, but thanks. I'm glad you sent me the champagne and guided me through my first meal." Her nerves began to jangle. His eyes stayed on hers, journeying only once to her mouth, which was still damp from the sea. Their bodies were close, close enough to brush. Rebecca began to shiver, and she knew it had nothing to do with wet clothes and the breeze.

"I should go in . . . change my dress."

There was something about her. The impulsiveness, the easy flirtatiousness, hid an unmistakable innocence that baffled and attracted him. Whatever it was, he wanted more.

"I'll see you again."

"Yes." She prayed for her heartbeat to slow. "It's not a very big island."

He smiled at that, slowly. She felt, with a mixture of relief and regret, the relaxation of his hands. "Tomorrow. I have business early. I'll be done by eleven, if that suits you. I'll show you Corfu."

"All right." Better judgment and nerves be damned. She wanted to go with him. "I'll meet you in the lobby." Carefully, because she suddenly wasn't sure she could manage it, she stepped back. Moonlight silhouetted him against the sea. "Good night, Stephen."

She forgot to be sophisticated and dashed toward the hotel.

He watched her go. She puzzled him, puzzled him as no woman had since he'd been a boy and too young to understand that a woman was not meant to be understood. And he wanted her. That wasn't new, but the desire had come with surprising speed and surprising force.

Rebecca Malone might have started out as an impulse, but she was now a mystery. One he intended to solve. With a little laugh, he bent to scoop up the shoes she'd forgotten. He hadn't felt quite so alive in months.

Chapter Two

Stephen wasn't the kind of man who rearranged his schedule to spend the day with a woman. Especially a woman he barely knew. He was a wealthy man, but he was also a busy man, driven by both pride and ambition to maintain a high level of involvement in all his projects. He shouldered responsibility well and had learned to enjoy the benefits of hard work and dedication.

His time on Corfu wasn't free—or rather hadn't been planned as free. Mixing business and pleasure wasn't his style. He pursued both, separately, with utter concentration. Yet he found himself juggling appointments, meetings, conference calls, in order to have the afternoon open for Rebecca.

He supposed any man would want to get to know a woman who flirted easily over a champagne flute one moment and dived fully dressed into the sea the next.

"I've postponed your meeting with Theoharis until five-thirty this evening." Stephen's secretary scribbled on a notepad she had resting on her lap. "He will meet you for early cocktails in the suite. I've arranged for hors d'oeuvres and a bottle of ouzo."

"Always efficient, Elana."

She smiled and tucked a fall of dark hair behind her ear. "I try."

When Stephen rose to pace to the window, she folded her hands and waited. She had worked for him for five years, she admired his energy and his business acumen, and—fortunately for both of them—had long since gotten over an early crush. There was often speculation about their personal relationship, but though he could be friendly—even kind when it suited him—with Stephen, business was business.

"Contact Mithos in Athens. Have him telex that report by the end of the day. And I want to hear from Lereau by five, Paris time."

"Shall I call and give him a nudge?"

"If you think it's necessary." Restless, he dug his hands in his pockets. Where had this sudden discontent come from? he wondered. He was wealthy, successful, and free, as always, to move from place to place. As he stared out at the sea, he remembered the scent of Rebecca's skin. "Send flowers to Rebecca Malone's suite. Wildflowers, nothing formal. This afternoon."

Elana made a note, hoping she'd get a look at this Rebecca Malone before long. She had already heard through the grapevine that Stephen had had dinner with an American woman. "And the card?"

He wasn't a man for poetry. "Just my name."

"Anything else?"

"Yes." He turned and offered her a half smile. "Take some time off. Go to the beach."

Pad in hand, she rose. "I'll be sure to work it in. Enjoy your afternoon, Stephen."

He intended to. As she left him, Stephen glanced at his watch. It was fifteen minutes before eleven. There was work he could do to fill in the time, a quick call that could be made. Instead, he picked up Rebecca's shoes.

After three tries, Rebecca settled on an outfit. She didn't have an abundance of clothes, because she'd preferred to spend her funds on travel. But she had splurged here and there on her route through Europe. No tidy CPA suits, she thought as she tied a vivid fuchsia sash at the waist of her sapphire-colored cotton pants. No sensible shoes or pastel blouses. The last shock of color came from a primrose-hued blouse cut generously to layer over a skinny tank top in the same shade as the slacks.

The combination delighted her, if only because her firm had preferred quiet colors and clean lines.

She had no idea where she was going, and she didn't care.

It was a beautiful day, even though she'd awoken with a dull headache from the champagne, and the disorientation that went with it. A light, early breakfast on her terrace and a quick dip in the sea had cleared both away. She still had trouble believing that she could lounge through a morning as she pleased—and that she'd spent the evening with a man she'd just met.

Aunt Jeannie would have tut-tutted and reminded her of the dangers of being a woman alone. Some of her friends would have been shocked, others envious. But they would all have been astonished that steady Rebecca had strolled in the moonlight with a gorgeous man with a scar on his jawline and eyes like velvet.

If she hadn't had his jacket as proof, she might have thought she'd dreamed it. There had never been anything wrong with her imagination—just the application of it. Often she'd pictured herself in an exotic place with an exotic man, with moonlight and music. Imagined herself, she remembered. And then she'd turned on her calculator and gotten down to business.

But she hadn't dreamed this. She could still remember the giddy, half-terrified feeling that had swarmed through her when he'd gathered her close. When his mouth had been only an inch from hers and the sea and the champagne had roared in her head.

What if he had kissed her? What tastes would she have found? Rich, strong ones, she mused, almost able to savor them as she traced a fingertip over her lips. After just one evening she was absolutely certain there would be nothing lukewarm about Stephen Nickodemus. She wasn't nearly so certain about Rebecca.

She probably would have fumbled and blushed and stammered. With a shake of her head, she pulled a brush through her hair. Exciting men didn't tumble all over themselves to kiss neat, practical-minded women.

But he'd asked to see her again.

Rebecca wasn't certain whether she was disappointed or relieved that he hadn't pressed his advantage and kissed her. She'd been kissed before, held before, of course. But she had a feeling—a very definite feeling—that it wouldn't be the same with Stephen. He might make her want more, offer more, than she had with any other man.

Crossing bridges too soon, she decided as she checked the contents of her big straw bag. She wasn't going to have an affair with him, or with anyone. Even the new, improved Rebecca Malone wasn't the type for a casual affair. But maybe— She caught her lower lip between her teeth. If the time was right she might have a romance she'd remember long after she left Greece.

For now, she was ready, but it was much too early to go down. It would hardly make her look like a well-traveled woman of the world if she popped down to the lobby and paced for ten minutes. This was her fantasy, after all. She didn't want him to think she was inexperienced and overeager.

Only the knock on the door prevented her from changing her mind about her outfit one more time.

"Hello." Stephen studied her for a moment, unsmiling. He'd nearly been certain he'd exaggerated, but she was just as vibrant, just as exciting, in the morning as she had been in the moonlight. He held out her shoes. "I thought you might need these."

She laughed, remembering her impulsive dunk in the sea. "I didn't realize I'd left them on the beach. Come in a minute." With a neatness ingrained in her from childhood, she turned to take them to the bedroom closet. "I'm ready to go if you are."

Stephen lifted a brow. He preferred promptness, but he never expected it in anyone but a business associate. "I've got a Jeep waiting. Some of the roads are rough."

"Sounds great." Rebecca came out again, carrying her bag and a flat-brimmed straw hat. She handed Stephen his jacket, neatly folded. "I forgot to give this back to you last night." Should she offer to have it cleaned? she wondered when he only continued to look at her. Fiddling with the strap of her bag, she decided against it. "Does taking pictures bother you?"

"No, why?"

"Good, because I take lots of them. I can't seem to stop myself."

She wasn't kidding. As Stephen drove up into the hills, she took shots of everything. Sheep, tomato plants, olive groves and straggly sage. He stopped so that she could walk out near the edge of a cliff and look down at a small village huddled near the sea.

She wouldn't be able to capture it on film; she wasn't clever enough. But she knew she'd never forget that light, so pure, so clear, or the contrast between the orange tiled roofs and the low white-washed walls and the deep, dangerous blue of the water that flung itself against the weathered rock that rose into harsh crags. A stork, legs tucked, glided over the water, where fishing boats bobbed.

There were nets drying on the beach and children playing. Flowers bloomed and tangled where the wind had planted them, more spectacular than any planned arrangement could ever be.

"It's beautiful." Her throat tightened with emotion, and with a longing she couldn't have defined. "So calm. You imagine women baking black bread and the men coming home smelling of fish and the sea. It looks as though it hasn't changed in a hundred years."

"Very little." He glanced down himself, surprised and more than a little pleased that she would be touched by something so simple. "We cling to antiquity."

"I haven't seen the Acropolis yet, but I don't think it could be any more spectacular than this." She lifted her face, delighted by the way the wind whipped at it. Here, high above the sea, she absorbed everything— the salty, rough-edged bite of the wind, the clarity of color and sound, and the man beside her. Letting her camera dangle from its strap, she turned to him. "I haven't thanked you for taking the time to show me all of this."

He took her hand, not to raise it to his lips, just to hold it. It was a link he hadn't known he wanted. "I'm enjoying seeing the familiar through someone else's eyes. Your eyes."

Suddenly the edge of the cliff seemed too close, the sun too hot. Could he do that just by touching her? With an effort, Rebecca smiled, keeping her voice light. "If you ever come to Philadelphia, I'll do the same for you."

It was odd. She'd looked almost frightened for a moment. Fragile and frightened. Stephen had always carefully avoided women who were easily bruised. "I'll consider that a promise."

They continued to drive, over roads that jarred and climbed and twisted. She saw her first of the *agrimi*, the wild goat of Greece, and the rocky pastures dotted with sturdy sheep. And everywhere, rich and defiant, was the intense color of flowers.

He didn't complain when she asked him to stop so that she could snap pictures of tiny blue star blossoms that pushed their way through cracks in the rock. He listened to her delight as she framed a thick, thorny stem topped with a ragged yellow flower. It made him realize, and regret, that it had been years since he'd taken the time to look closely at the small, vital things that grew around him.

He looked now, at Rebecca standing in the sunlight, her hat fluttering around her face and her laugh dancing on the air.

Often the road clung to cliffs that plunged dizzily into the sea. Rebecca, who was too timid to fight rush-hour traffic, found it exhilarating.

She felt almost like another person. She *was* another person, she thought, laughing as she held on to her hat to keep the wind from snatching it away.

"I love it!" she shouted over the wind and the noise of the engine. "It's wild and old and incredible. Like no place I've ever been."

Still laughing, she lifted her camera and snapped his picture as he drove. He wore sunglasses with amber lenses and had a cigar clamped between his teeth. The wind blew through his hair and chased the smoke behind them. He stopped the Jeep, took the camera and snapped a picture of her in turn.

"Hungry?"

She dragged her tousled hair back from her face. "Starving."

He leaned over to open her door. A current passed through her, sharp and electric, strong enough to make him pause with his arm across her body and his face close to hers. It was there again, he thought as he waited and watched. The awareness, ripe and seductive. And the innocence, as alluring as it was contradictory. In a test—a test for both of them—he lifted a hand to stroke her cheek. It was as soft as her scent.

"Are you afraid of me, Rebecca?"

"No." That was true; she was nearly sure of it. "Should I be?"

He didn't smile. Through the amber lenses she saw that his eyes were very intense. "I'm not entirely sure." When he pulled away he heard her release an unsteady breath. He wasn't feeling completely steady himself. "We'll have to walk a little first."

Confused, her mind churning, she stepped out onto the dirt path. A woman on a simple date didn't tremble every time a man got close, Rebecca told herself as Stephen lifted the picnic basket out of the back. She was behaving like a teenager, not a grown woman.

Troubled by his own thoughts, Stephen stopped beside her. He hesitated, then held out a hand. It felt good, simply good, when she put hers in it.

They walked through an olive grove in a companionable silence while the sun streamed down on dusty leaves and rocky ground. There was no sound of the sea here, but when the wind was right she could hear the screech of a gull far away. The island was small, but here it seemed uninhabited.

"I haven't had a picnic in years." Rebecca spread the cloth. "And never in an olive grove." She glanced around, wanting to remember every leaf and pebble. "Are we trespassing?"

"No." Stephen took a bottle of white wine from the basket. Rebecca left him to it and started rummaging in search of food.

"Do you know the owner?"

"I'm the owner." He drew the cork with a gentle pop.

"Oh." She looked around again. It should have occurred to her that he would own something impressive, different, exciting. "It sounds romantic. Owning an olive grove."

He lifted a brow. He owned a number of them, but he had never thought of them as romantic. They were simply profitable. He offered her a glass, then tapped it with his own. "To romance, then."

She swept down her lashes, battling shyness. To Stephen, the gesture was only provocative. "I hope you're hungry," she began, knowing she was talking too fast. "It all looks wonderful." She took a quick sip of wine to ease her dry throat, then set it aside to finish unpacking the basket.

There were sweet black olives as big as a man's thumb, and there was a huge slab of sharp cheese. There were cold lamb and hunks of bread, and fruit so fresh it could have been just plucked from the stem.

Gradually she began to relax again.

"You've told me very little about yourself." Stephen topped off her wine and watched her bite into a ripe red plum. "I know little more than that you come from Philadelphia and enjoy traveling."

What could she tell him? A man like him was bound to be bored with the life story of the painfully ordinary Rebecca Malone. Lies had never come easily to her, so she skirted between fact and fiction. "There's little more. I grew up in Philadelphia. I lost both of my parents when I was a teenager, and I lived with my aunt Jeannie. She was very dear, and she made the loss bearable."

"It's painful." He flicked his lighter at the end of a cigar, remembering not only the pain, but also the fury he had felt when his father had died and left him orphaned at sixteen. "It steals childhood."

"Yes." So he understood that. It made her feel close to him, close and comfortable. "Maybe that's why I like to travel. Every time you see a new place you can be a child again."

"So you don't look for roots?"

She glanced at him then. He was leaning back against the trunk of a tree, smoking lazily, watching carefully. "I don't know what I'm looking for."

"Is there a man?"

She moved her shoulders, determined not to be embarrassed. "No."

He took her hand, drawing her closer. "No one?"

"No, I . . ." She wasn't certain what she would have said, but could say nothing at all when he turned her palm upward and pressed his lips to its center. She felt the fire burst there, in her hand, then race everywhere.

"You're very responsive, Rebecca." He lowered her hand but kept it in his. He could feel the heat, but he wasn't sure whether it had sprung to her skin or to his own. "If there's no one, the men in your Philadelphia must be very slow."

"I've been too . . . busy."

His lips curved at that. There was a tremor in her voice, and there was passion in her eyes. "Busy?"

"Yes." Afraid she'd make a fool of herself, she drew her hand back. "This was wonderful." Trying to calm herself, she pushed a hand through her hair. "You know what I need?"

"No. Tell me."

"Another picture." She sprang to her feet and, steadier, grinned. "A memento of my first picnic in an olive grove. Let's see...you can stand right over there. The sun's good in front of that tree, and I should be able to frame in that section of the grove."

Amused, Stephen tapped out his cigar. "How much more film do you have?"

"This is the last roll—but I have scads back at the hotel." She flicked him a quick laughing glance. "I warned you."

"So you did." Competent hands, he thought as he watched her focus and adjust. He hadn't realized he could be as attracted to competence as he was to beauty. She mumbled to herself, tossing her head back so that her hair swung, then settled. His stomach tightened without warning.

Good God, he wanted her. She'd done nothing to make him burn and strain this way. He couldn't accuse her of taunting or teasing, and yet...he felt taunted. He felt teased. For the first time in his life he felt totally seduced by a woman who had done nothing more than give him a few smiles and a little companionship.

Even now she was chattering away as she secured her camera to the limb of a tree. Talking easily, as though they were just friends, as though she felt nothing more than a light, unimportant affection. But he'd seen it. Stephen felt his blood heat as he remembered the quick flash of arousal he'd seen on her face. He'd see it again. And more.

"I'm going to set the timer," Rebecca went on, blissfully unaware of Stephen's thoughts. "All you have to do is stand there. Once I get this damn thing set, I'm going to run over so it'll take one of both— There." She interrupted herself, crossed her fingers and ran to Stephen's side in a dash. "Unless I messed up, it'll snap all by itself in—"

The rest of the words slid down her throat as he crushed her against him and captured her mouth.

Chapter Three

Heat. Light. Speed. Rebecca felt them, felt each separate, distinct sensation. Urgency. Demand. Impatience. She tasted them, as clearly as wild honey, on his lips. Though she'd never experienced it, she had known exactly what it would be like to be with him, mouth to mouth and need to need.

In an instant the world had narrowed from what could be seen and understood to a pure, seamless blanket of emotion. It cloaked her, not softly, not in comfort, but tightly, hotly, irresistibly. Caught between fear and delight, she lifted a hand to his cheek.

God, she was sweet. Even as he dragged her closer, aroused by the simplicity of her acceptance, he was struck by—disarmed by—her sweetness. There had been a hesitation, almost too brief to be measured, before her lips had parted beneath his. Parted, invited, accepted.

There was a sigh, so soft it could barely be heard, as she stroked her hands up his back to his shoulders. Curious, simple, generous. A man could drown in such sweetness, fall prisoner to such pliancy. And be saved by it. Beneath the patterned shade of the olive tree, she gave him more than passion. She gave him hope.

Charmed, he murmured some careless Greek phrase lovers might exchange. The words meant nothing to her, but the sound of them on the still air, the feel of them stroking across her lips...seduction. Glorious seduction.

Pleasure burst in her blood, in her head, in her heart, thousands of tiny bubbles of it, until she was straining against him.

The quiet explosion rocked him. It tightened his chest, fuddled his mind. She fitted into his arms as if she'd been born for him. As if, somehow, they had known each other before, loved before, hungered before. Something seemed to erupt between them, something molten, powerful, dangerous. But it wasn't new. It was ancient, a whispering echo of ageless passions.

She began to tremble. How could this be so right, so familiar? It wasn't possible to feel safe and threatened at the same time. But she did. She clung to him while a dim, floating image danced through her head. She had kissed him before. Just like this. As her mind spun, she heard her own mindless murmurs answer his. As freely, as inescapably as the sun poured light, response flowed from her. She couldn't stop it. Frightened by her sudden loss of control, she struggled against him, against herself.

He slipped his hands up to her shoulders, but not to free her, to look at her. To look at how their coming together had changed her. It had changed him. Passion had made her eyes heavy, seductive. Fear had clouded them. Her lips were full, softened and parted by his. Her breath shivered through them. Under his hands he could feel the heat of her skin and the quick, involuntary trembling of her muscles.

No pretense here, he decided as he studied her. He was holding both innocence and delight in his hands.

"Stephen, I—"

"Again."

Then his face filled her vision and she was lost.

Differently. Should she have known that one man could hold one woman in so many different ways? That one man could kiss one woman with such stunning variety? There was gentleness now, as familiar and as novel as the urgency. His lips persuaded rather than demanded. They savored instead of devouring. Her surrender came as quietly, and as unmistakably, as her earlier passion. The trembling stopped; the fear vanished. With a complete trust that surprised them both, she leaned against him, giving.

More aroused by her serenity than by the storm that had come before, Stephen pulled back. He had to, or what had begun would finish without either of them saying a word. As he swore and pulled out a cigar, Rebecca placed a hand on the olive tree for support.

Moments, she thought. It had been only moments, and yet she felt as though years had passed, racing backward or forward, perhaps spinning in circles. In a place like this, with a man like this, what difference did it make what year it was? What century?

Half terrified, she lifted a hand to her lips. Despite her fear, they curved under her touch. She could still taste him. Still feel him. And nothing, nothing, would ever be quite the same again.

He stared out at the rough and dusty land he'd known as a boy, and beyond, to the stark, tumbling rocks where he and other wild things had climbed.

What was he doing with her? Furious with himself, he drew on the cigar. What was he feeling? It was new, and far from comfortable. And it was comfort he preferred, he reminded himself. Comfort and freedom. Bringing himself under control, he turned to her again, determined to treat what had happened as a man should—lightly.

She just stood there, with the sun and the shade falling over her. There was neither recrimination nor invitation in her eyes. She didn't flinch or step forward, but merely stood, watching him with the faintest of smiles, as if... As if, Stephen realized, she knew what questions he was asking himself—and the answers.

"It grows late."

She felt the ache and fought not to let it show on her face. "I guess you're right." She dragged a hand through her hair—it was the first sign of her agitation—then walked over to pick up her camera. "I should have a picture to remember all this by," she said, forcing brightness into her voice. Her breath caught when his fingers closed over her arm and whirled her around.

"Who are you?" he demanded. "What are you?"

"I don't know what you mean." The emotion burst out before she could stop it. "I don't know what you want."

With one jerk he had her tumbling against him. "You know what I want."

Her heart was in her throat, beating wildly. She found it strange that it was not fear but desire that she felt. She hadn't known she was capable of feeling a need that was so unreasonable, so reckless. It was almost purifying to experience it, and to see it mirrored in his eyes.

"It takes more than one afternoon." Didn't it? Her voice rose as she tried to convince herself. "It takes more than a picnic and a walk in the moonlight for me."

"One moment the temptress, the next the outraged innocent. Do you do it to intrigue me, Rebecca?" She shook her head, and his fingers tightened. "It works," he murmured. "You've hardly been out of my mind since I first saw you. I want to make love with you, here, in the sun."

Color flooded her face, not because she was embarrassed, but because she could imagine it, perfectly. And then what? Carefully she leveled her breathing. Whatever impulses she had followed, whatever bridges she had burned, she still needed answers.

"No." It cost her to go against her own needs and say it. "Not when I'm unsure and you're angry." She took a deep breath and kept her eyes on him. "You're hurting me, Stephen. I don't think you mean to."

Slowly he released her arm. He was angry, furious, but not at her refusal. The anger stemmed from the need she pulled from him, a need that had come too fast and too strong for him to channel. "We'll go back."

Rebecca merely nodded, then knelt to gather the remains of the picnic.

He was a busy man, much too busy to brood about a woman he barely knew and didn't understand at all. That was what Stephen told himself. He had reports to read, calls to make and paperwork—which he had both a talent and a distaste for—to deal with. A couple of simple kisses weren't enough to take a man's mind off his work.

But there hadn't been anything simple about them. Disgusted, Stephen pushed away from his desk and wandered to the terrace doors. He'd left them open because the breeze, and the fragrances it brought, helped him forget he was obligated to be inside.

For days he'd worked his way through his responsibilities, trying to ignore the nagging itch at the back of his mind—the itch that was Rebecca. There was no reason for him to stay on Corfu. He could have handled his business in Athens, or Crete, or in London, for that matter. Still, he'd made no plans to leave, though he'd also made no attempt to approach her.

She...concerned him, he decided. To be drawn to an attractive woman was as natural as breathing. To have the attraction cause discomfort, confusion, even annoyance was anything but natural. A taste of her hadn't been enough. Yet he hesitated.

She was...mysterious. Perhaps that was why he couldn't push her from his mind. On the surface she appeared to be an attractive, free-spirited woman who grabbed life with both hands. Yet there were undercurrents. The hints of innocence, of shyness. The sweetness. The complexity of her kept him wondering, thinking, imagining.

Perhaps that was her trick. Women had them...were entitled to them. It was a waste of time to begrudge them their illusions and their feminine magic. More than a waste of time, it was foolish, when a man could enjoy the benefits. But there was more, and somehow less, to Rebecca than innate feminine magic.

When he had kissed her, though it had been the first time, it had been like coming back to a lover, to a love, after a painful separation. When his lips had found hers, something had filled him. A heat, an impatience, a knowledge.

He knew her, knew more than her name and her background and the color of her eyes. He knew all of her. Yet he knew nothing.

Fantasies, he told himself. He didn't have time for them. Leaning a hip against the railing, he lit a cigar and watched the sea.

As always, it pulled at him, bringing back memories of a childhood that had been careless and too short. There were times, rare times, when he allowed himself to regret. Times when the sun was a white flash of heat and the water was blue and endless. His father had taught him a great deal. How to fish, how to see both beauty and excitement in new places, how to drink like a man.

Fifteen years, Stephen thought, a smile ghosting around his mouth. He still missed him, missed the companionship, the robust laughter. They had been friends, as well as parent and child, with a bond as easy, and as strong, as any Stephen had ever known. But his father had died as he would have wanted to, at sea and in his prime.

He would have taken one look at Rebecca, rolled his eyes, kissed his fingers and urged his son to enjoy. But Stephen wasn't the boy he had once been. He was more cautious, more aware of consequences. If a man dived into the sea, he should know the depth and the currents.

Then he saw her, coming from the sea. Water ran down her body, glistening in the strong sun, sparkling against skin that had warmed in the last few days to a dusky gold. As he looked, as he wanted, he felt his muscles clench, one by one, shoulders, stomach, thighs. Without his being aware, his fingers tightened, snapping the cigar in two. He hadn't known that desire could arouse a reaction so akin to anger.

She stopped, and though he knew she was unaware of him, she might easily have been posing. To taunt, to tease, to invite. As drops of water slid down her, she stretched, lifting her face skyward. Her skimpy suit rested low over her boyish hips, shifted enticingly over the subtle curve of her breasts. At that moment, she was totally absorbed in her own pleasure and as un-self-conscious as any young animal standing in the sun. Nothing had ever been so alluring.

Then, slowly, seductively, she combed her fingers through her hair, smiling, as if she enjoyed the wet, silky feel of it. Watching her, he felt the air back up and clog in his lungs. He could have murdered her for it, for making him want so unreasonably what he did not yet understand.

She plucked a long, mannish T-shirt from a straw bag and, after tugging it on, strolled barefoot into the hotel.

He stood there, waiting for the need to pass. But it built, layered with an ache that infuriated him and a longing that baffled him.

He should ignore her. Instinct warned him that if he didn't his life would never be the same. She was nothing more than a distraction, a momentary impulse he should resist. He should turn away, go back to work. He had commitments, obligations, and no time to waste on fantasies. With an oath, he tossed the broken cigar over the rail.

There were times, he thought, when a man had to trust in fate and dive in.

Chapter Four

Rebecca had hardly shut the door behind her before she turned back to answer the knock. The sun and the water had left her pleasantly tired, but all thoughts of a lazy catnap vanished when she saw Stephen.

He looked wonderful. Cool, a little windblown, intense. For days she'd wondered about him, wondered and wished. She felt her pulse skip and her lips curve just at the sight of him. With an effort, she kept her voice breezy.

"Hello. I wasn't sure you were still on the island."

It wasn't really a lie, she told herself. An offhand inquiry had assured her that Mr. Nickodemus hadn't checked out, but she hadn't actually seen him.

"I saw you come up from the beach."

"Oh." Unconsciously she tugged at the hem of her cover-up. To Stephen the small gesture was one more contradictory signal. "I can't seem to get enough of the sun and the sea. Would you like to come in?"

By way of an answer he stepped through and shut the door behind him. It made a very quiet, a very final sound. Rebecca's carefully built poise began to crumble. "I never thanked you for the flowers." She made a gesture indicating the vase near the window, then brought her hands back together and linked them in front of her. "They're still beautiful. I...I thought I might run into you, in the dining room, on the beach, or..." Her words trailed off when he lifted a hand to her hair.

"I've been busy." He watched her eyes, eyes that were as clear as rainwater, blur at the slight touch. "Business."

It was ridiculous, she knew, but she wasn't at all sure she could speak. "If you have to work, I doubt you could pick a more beautiful place."

He stepped closer. She smelled of the water and the sun. "You're enjoying the resort, and the island."

Her hand was in his now, caught lightly. It took only that to make her knees weak. "Yes, very much."

"Perhaps you'd like to see it from a different perspective." Deliberately, wanting to test them both, he lifted her hand to his lips. He grazed her knuckles—it was barely a whisper of contact—and felt the jolt. She felt it, and he could see that she did, so it couldn't just be his imagination. "Spend the day with me tomorrow on my boat."

"What?"

He smiled, delighted with her response. "Will you come with me?"

Anywhere. Astonished, she stepped back. "I haven't any plans."

"Good." He closed the distance between them again. Her hands fluttered up in flustered defense, then settled again when he made no attempt to touch her. "Then I'll make them for you. I'll come for you in the morning. Nine?"

A boat. He'd said something about a boat. Rebecca drew in a deep breath and tried to pull herself together. This wasn't like her—going off into daydreams, feeling weak-kneed, being flooded with waves of desire. And it felt wonderful.

"I'd like that." She gave him what she hoped was an easy woman-of-the-world smile.

"Until tomorrow, then." He started for the door, then turned, a hand on the knob. "Rebecca, don't forget your camera."

She waited until he'd closed the door before she spun in three quick circles.

When Stephen had said "boat," Rebecca had pictured a trim little cabin cruiser. Instead, she stepped onto the glossy mahogany deck of a streamlined hundred-foot yacht.

"You could live on this," Rebecca said, then wished she'd bitten her tongue. But he only laughed.

"I often do."

"Welcome aboard, sir," a white-uniformed man with a British accent said.

"Grady. This is my guest, Miss Malone."

"Ma'am." Grady's cool British reserve didn't flicker for an instant, but Rebecca felt herself being summed up.

"Cast off when you're ready." Stephen took Rebecca's arm. "Would you like a tour?"

"Yes." A yacht. She was on a yacht. It took all her willpower to keep her camera in the bag. "I'd love to see it all."

He took her below, through four elegantly appointed cabins. Her comment about living on board had been said impulsively, but she could see now that it could be done easily, even luxuriously.

Above there was a large glassed-in cabin in which one could stretch out comfortably, out of the sun, and watch the sea, whatever the weather. She had known that there were people who lived like this. Part of her job had been to research and calculate so that those who did paid the government as little as possible. But to be there, to see it, to be surrounded by it, was entirely different from adding figures on paper.

There was a masculine feel to the cabin, to the entire boat—leather, wood, muted colors. There were shelves filled with books and a fully stocked bar, as well as a stereo system.

"All the comforts of home," Rebecca murmured, but she'd noted that there were doors and panels that could be secured in case of rough weather. What would it be like to ride out a storm at sea, to watch the rain lash the windows and feel the deck heave?

She gave a quick gasp when she felt the floor move. Stephen took her arm again to steady her.

"We're under way." Curious, he turned her to face him. "Are you afraid of boats?"

"No." She could hardly admit that the biggest one she'd been on before this had been a two-passenger canoe at summer camp. "It just startled me." Under way, she thought as she prayed that her system would settle. It was such an exciting, adventurous word. "Can we go out on deck? I'd like to watch."

It was exciting. She felt it the moment the wind hit her face and rushed through her hair. At the rail, she leaned out, delighted to see the island shrink and the sea spread. Because she couldn't resist and he didn't laugh at her, she took half a dozen pictures as the boat sped away from land.

"It's better than flying," she decided. "You feel a part of it. Look." With a laugh, she pointed. "The birds are chasing us."

Stephen didn't bother to glance at the gulls that wheeled and called above the boat's wake. He preferred to watch the delight and excitement bloom on her face. "Do you always enjoy so completely?"

"Yes." She tossed her hair away from her face, only to have the wind rush it back again. With another laugh, she stretched back from the railing, her face lifted to the sun. "Oh, yes."

Irresistible. With his hands at her waist, he spun her toward him. It was like holding a live wire. The shock rippled from her to him, then back again. "Everything?" His fingers spread over her back and, with the slightest pressure, moved her forward until their thighs met.

"I don't know." Instinctively she braced her hands on his shoulders. "I haven't tried everything." But she wanted to. Held close, with the sound of the water and the wind, she wanted to. Without giving a thought to self-preservation, she leaned toward him.

He swore, lightly, under his breath. Rebecca jolted back as if he had shouted at her. Stephen caught her hand as he nodded to the steward, who had just approached with drinks. "Thank you, Victor. Just leave everything." His voice was smooth enough, but Rebecca felt the tension in his hand as he led her to a chair.

He probably thought she was a fool, she decided. All but tumbling into his arms every time he touched her. He was obviously a man of the world—and a kind man, she added as she sipped her mimosa. Not all powerful men spoke kindly to those who worked for them. Her lips curved, a little wryly, as she sipped again. She knew that firsthand.

His body was in turmoil. Stephen couldn't remember, even in his youth, having had a woman affect him so irrationally. He knew how to persuade, how to seduce—and always with finesse. But whenever he was around this woman for more than five minutes he felt like a stallion being spurred and curbed at the same time.

And he was fascinated. Fascinated by the ease with which she went into his arms, by the trust he saw when he looked down into her eyes. As he had in the olive grove, he found himself believing he'd looked into those eyes, those rainwater-clear eyes, a hundred times before.

Still churning, he took out a cigar. The thought was fanciful, but his desire was very real. If there couldn't be finesse, perhaps there could be candor.

"I want you, Rebecca."

She felt her heart stop, then start up again with slow, dull throbs. Carefully she took another sip, then cleared her throat. "I know." It amazed her, flattered her, terrified her.

She seemed so cool. He envied her. "Will you come with me, to my cabin?"

She looked at him then. Her heart and her head were giving very different answers. It sounded so easy, so...natural. If there was a man she could give herself to, wholly, he was with her now. Complications, what complications there were, were her own.

But no matter how far she had run from Philadelphia and her own strict upbringing, there were still lines she couldn't cross.

"I can't."

"Can't?" He lit his cigar, astonished that they were discussing making love as though it were as casual a choice as what dinner entrée to chose. "Or won't?"

She drew a breath. Her palms were damp on the glass, and she set it down. "Can't. I want to." Her eyes, huge and lake-pale, clung to his. "I very much want to, but..."

"But?"

"I know so little about you." She picked up her glass again because her empty hands tended to twist together. "Hardly more than your name, that you own an olive grove and like the sea. It's not enough."

"Then I'll tell you more."

She relaxed enough to smile. "I don't know what to ask."

He leaned back in his chair, the tension dissolving as quickly as it had built. She could do that to him with nothing more than a smile. He knew no one who could excite and solace with so little effort.

"Do you believe in fate, Rebecca? In something unexpected, even unlooked-for, often a small thing that completely and irrevocably changes one's life?"

She thought of her aunt's death and her own uncharacteristic decisions. "Yes. Yes, I do."

"Good." His gaze skimmed over her face, quickly, then more leisurely. "I'd nearly forgotten that I believe it, too. Then I saw you, sitting alone."

There were ways and ways to seduce, she was discovering. A look, a tone, could be every bit as devastating as a caress. She wanted him more in that moment than she had ever known she could want anything. To give herself time, and distance, she rose and walked to the rail.

Even her silence aroused him. She had said she knew too little about him. He knew even less of her. And he didn't care. It was dangerous, possibly even destructive, but he didn't care. As he watched her with the wind billowing her shirt and her hair he realized that he didn't give a damn about where she had come from, where she had been, what she had done.

When lightning strikes, it destroys, though it blazes with power. Rising, he went to her and stood, as she did, facing the sea.

"When I was young, very young," he began, "there was another moment that changed things. My father was a man for the water. He lived for it. Died for it." When he went on it was almost as if he were speaking to himself now, remembering. Rebecca turned her head to look at him. "I was ten or eleven. Everything was going well, the nets were full. My father and I were walking along the beach. He stopped, dipped his hand into the water, made a fist and opened it. 'You can't hold it,' he said to me. 'No matter how you try or how you love or how you sweat.' Then he dug into the sand. It was wet and clung together in his hand. 'But this,' he said, 'a man can hold.' We never spoke of it again. When my time came, I turned my back on the sea and held the land."

"It was right for you."

"Yes." He lifted a hand to catch at the ends of her hair. "It was right. Such big, quiet eyes you have, Rebecca," he murmured. "Have they seen enough, I wonder, to know what's right for you?"

"I guess I've been a little slow in starting to look." Her blood was pounding thickly. She would have stepped back, but he shifted so that she was trapped between him and the rail.

"You tremble when I touch you." He slid his hands up her arms, then down until their hands locked. "Have you any idea how exciting that is?"

Her chest tightened, diminishing her air even as the muscles in her legs went limp. "Stephen, I meant it when I said..." He brushed his lips gently over her temple. "I can't. I need to..." He feathered a kiss along her jawline, softly. "To think."

He felt her fingers go lax in his. She was suddenly fragile, outrageously vulnerable, irresistibly tempting. "When I kissed you the first time I gave you no choice." His lips trailed over her face, light as a whisper, circling, teasing, avoiding her mouth. "You have one now."

He was hardly touching her. A breath, a whisper, a mere promise of a touch. The slow, subtle passage of his lips over her skin couldn't have been called a kiss, could never have been called a demand. She had only to push away to end the torment. And the glory.

A choice? Had he told her she had a choice? "No, I don't," she murmured as she turned to find his lips with hers.

No choice, no past, no future. Only now. She felt the present, with all its needs and hungers, well up inside her. The kiss was instantly hot, instantly desperate. His heart pounded fast and hard against hers, thunderous now, as he twisted a hand in her hair to pull her head back. To plunder. No one had ever taken her like this. No one had ever warned her that a touch of violence could be so exciting. Her gasp of surprise turned into a moan of pleasure as his tongue skimmed over hers.

He thought of lightning bolts again, thought of that flash of power and light. She was electric in his arms, sparking, sizzling. Her scent, as soft, as seductive, as a whisper, clouded his mind, even as the taste of her heightened his appetite.

She was all woman, she was every woman, and yet she was like no other. He could hear each quick catch of her breath above the roar of the motor. With her name on his lips, he pressed them to the vulnerable line of her throat, where the skin was heated from the sun and as delicate as water.

She might have slid bonelessly to the deck if his body hadn't pressed hers so firmly against the rail. In wonder, in panic, she felt his muscles turn to iron wherever they touched her. Never before had she felt so fragile, so at the mercy of her own desires. The sea was as calm as glass, but she felt herself tossed, tumbled, wrecked. With a sigh that was almost a sob, she wrapped her arms around him.

It was the defenselessness of the gesture that pulled him back from the edge. He must have been mad. For a moment he'd been close, much too close, to dragging her down to the deck without a thought to her wishes or to the consequences. With his eyes closed, he held her, feeling the erratic beat of her heart, hearing her shallow, shuddering breath.

Perhaps he was still mad, Stephen thought. Even as the ragged edges of desire eased, something deeper and far more dangerous bloomed.

He wanted her, in a way no man could safely want a woman. Forever.

Fate, he thought again as he stroked her hair. It seemed he was falling in love whether he wished it or not. A few hours with her and he felt more than he had ever imagined he could feel.

There had been a few times in his life when he had seen and desired on instinct alone. What he had seen and desired, he had taken. Just as he would take her. But when he took, he meant to keep.

Carefully he stepped back. "Maybe neither of us has a choice." He dipped his hands into his pockets. "And if I touch you again, here, now, I won't give you one."

Unable to pretend, knowing they were shaking, she pushed her hands through her hair. She didn't bother to disguise the tremor in her voice. She wouldn't have known how. "I won't want one." She saw his eyes darken quickly, dangerously, but she didn't know his hands were balled into fists, straining.

"You make it difficult for me."

A long, shuddering breath escaped her. No one had ever wanted her this way. Probably no one ever would again. "I'm sorry. I don't mean to."

"No." Deliberately he relaxed his hands. "I don't think you do. That's one of the things about you I find most intriguing. I will have you, Rebecca." He saw something flicker in her eyes.... Excitement? Panic? A combination of the two, perhaps. "Because I'm sure of it, because I know you're sure of it, I'll do my best to give you a little more time."

Her natural humor worked through the sliver of unease she felt. "I'm not sure whether I should thank you politely or run like hell."

He grinned, surprising himself, then flicked a finger down her cheek. "I wouldn't advise running, *matia mou*. I'd only catch you."

She was sure of that, too. One look at his face, even with the smile that softened it, and she knew. Kind, yes, but with a steely underlying ruthlessness. "Then I'll go with the thank-you."

"You're welcome." Patience, he realized, would have to be developed. And quickly. "Would you like to swim? There's a bay. We're nearly there."

The water might, just might, cool her off. "I'd love it."

Chapter Five

The water was cool and mirror-clear. Rebecca lowered herself into it with a sigh of pure pleasure. Back in Philadelphia she would have been at her desk, calculator clicking, the jacket of her neat business suit carefully smoothed over the back of her chair. Her figures would always tally, her forms would always be properly filed.

The dependable, efficient Miss Malone.

Instead, she was swimming in a crystal-clear bay, letting the water cool and the sun heat. Ledgers and accounts were worlds away. Here, as close as a handspan, was a man who was teaching her everything she would ever want to know about needs, desires, and the fragility of the heart.

He couldn't know it, she thought. She doubted she'd ever have the courage to tell him that he was the only one who had ever made her tremble and burn. A man as physically aware as he would only be uncomfortable knowing he held an inexperienced woman in his arms.

The water lapped around her with a sound as quiet as her own sigh. But he didn't know, because when she was in his arms she didn't feel awkward and inexperienced. She felt beautiful, desirable and reckless.

With a laugh, Rebecca dipped under the surface to let the water, and the freedom, surround her. Who would have believed it?

"Does it always take so little to make you laugh?"

Rebecca ran a hand over her slicked-back hair. Stephen was treading water beside her, smoothly, hardly making a ripple. His skin was dark gold, glistening-wet. His hair was streaked by the sun and dampened by the water, which was almost exactly the color of his eyes. She had to suppress an urge to just reach out and touch.

"A secluded inlet, a beautiful sky, an interesting man." With another sigh, she kicked her legs up so that she could float. "It doesn't seem like so little to me." She studied the vague outline of the mountains, far out of reach. "I promised myself that no matter where I went, what I did, I'd never take anything for granted again."

There was something in the way she said it, some hint of sadness, that pulled at him. The urge to comfort wasn't completely foreign in him, but he hadn't had much practice at it. "Was there a man who hurt you?"

Her lips curved at that, but he couldn't know that she was laughing at herself. Naturally, she'd dated. They had been polite, cautious evenings, usually with little interest on either side. She'd been dull, or at least she had never worked up the nerve to spread her wings. Once or twice, when she'd felt a tug, she'd been too shy, too much the efficient Rebecca Malone, to do anything about it.

With him, everything was different. Because she loved him. She didn't know how, she didn't know why, but she loved him as much as any woman could love any man.

"No. There's no one." She closed her eyes, trusting the water to carry her. "When my parents died, it hurt. It hurt so badly that I suppose I pulled back from life. I thought it was important that I be a responsible adult, even though I wasn't nearly an adult yet."

Strange that she hadn't thought of it quite that way until she'd stopped being obsessively responsible. Stranger still was how easy it was to tell him what she'd never even acknowledged herself.

"My aunt Jeannie was kind and considerate and loving, but she'd forgotten what it was like to be a young girl. Suddenly I realized I'd missed being young, lazy, foolish, all the things everyone's entitled to be at least once. I decided to make up for it."

Her hair was spread out and drifting on the water. Her eyes were closed, and her face was sheened with water. Not beautiful, Stephen told himself. She was too angular for real beauty. But she was fascinating...in looks, in philosophy...more, in the open-armed way she embraced whatever crossed her path.

He found himself looking around the inlet as he hadn't bothered to look at anything in years. He could see the sun dancing on the surface, could see the rip-

ples spreading and growing from the quiet motion of
their bodies. Farther away was the narrow curving
strip of white beach, deserted now, but for a few birds
fluttering over the sand. It was quiet, almost unnaturally quiet, the only sound the soft, monotonous slap
of water against sand. And he was relaxed, totally,
mind and body. Perhaps he, too, had forgotten what
it was like to be young and foolish.

On impulse he put a hand on her shoulder and
pushed her under.

She came up sputtering, dragging wet hair out of her
eyes. He grinned at her and calmly continued to tread
water. "It was too easy."

She tilted her head, considering him and the distance between them. Challenge leaped into her eyes,
sparked with amusement. "It won't be the next time."

His grin only widened. When he moved, he moved
fast, streaking under and across the water like an eel.
Rebecca had time for a quick squeal. Dragging in a
deep breath, she kicked out. He caught her ankle, but
she was ready. Unresisting, she let him pull her under.
Then, instead of fighting her way back to the surface,
she wrapped her arms around him and sent them both
rolling in an underwater wrestling match. They were
still tangled, her arms around him, her hands hooked
over his shoulders, when they surfaced.

"We're even." She gasped for air and shook the
water out of her eyes.

"How do you figure?"

"If we'd had a mat I'd have pinned you. Want to go for two out of three?"

"I might." He felt her legs tangle with his as she kicked out lazily. "But for now I prefer this."

He was going to kiss her again. She saw it in his eyes, felt it in the slight tensing of the arm that locked them torso to torso. She wasn't sure she was ready. More, she was afraid she was much too ready.

"Stephen?"

"Hmm?" His lips were a breath away from hers. Then he found himself underwater again, his arms empty. He should have been furious. He nearly was when he pushed to surface. She was shoulder-deep in the water, a few feet away. Her laughter rolled over him, young, delighted, unapologetic.

"It was too easy." She managed a startled "whoops" when he struck out after her. She might have made it—she had enough of a lead—but he swam as though he'd been born in the water. Still, she was agile, and she almost managed to dodge him, but her laughter betrayed her. She gulped in water, choked, then found herself hauled up into his arms in thigh-deep water.

"I like to win." Deciding it was useless to struggle, she pressed a hand to her heart and gasped for air. "It's a personality flaw. Sometimes I cheat at canasta."

"Canasta?" The last thing he could picture the slim, sexy bundle in his arms doing was spending a quiet evening playing cards.

"I can't help myself." Still breathless, she laid her head on his shoulder. "No willpower."

"I find myself having the same problem." With a careless toss, he sent her flying through the air. She hit the water bottom first.

"I guess I deserved that." She struggled to her feet, water raining off her. "I have to sit." Wading through the water, she headed for the gentle slope of beach. She lay, half in and half out of the water, not caring that the sand would cling to her hair and skin. When he dropped down beside her, she reached out a hand for his. "I don't know when I've had a nicer day."

He looked down to where her fingers linked with his. The gesture had been so easy, so natural. He wondered how it could both comfort and arouse. "It's hardly over."

"It seems like it could last forever." She wanted it to go on and on. Blue skies and easy laughter. Cool water and endless hours. There had been a time, not so long before, when the days had dragged into nights and the nights into days. "Did you ever want to run away?"

With her hand still in his, he lay back to watch a few scattered rags of clouds drift. How long had it been, he wondered, since he'd really watched the sky? "To where?"

"Anywhere. Away from the way things are, away from what you're afraid they'll always be." She closed her eyes and could see herself brewing that first cup of coffee at exactly 7:15, opening the first file at precisely 9:01. "To drop out of sight," she murmured, "and pop up somewhere else, anywhere else, as someone completely different."

"You can't change who you are."

"Oh, but you can." Her tone suddenly urgent, she rose on her elbow. "Sometimes you have to."

He reached up to touch the ends of her hair. "What are you running from?"

"Everything. I'm a coward."

He looked into her eyes. They were so clear, so full of enthusiasm. "I don't think so."

"But you don't know me." A flicker of regret, then uncertainty, ran across her face. "I'm not sure I want you to."

"Don't I?" His fingers tightened on her hair, keeping her still. "There are people and circumstances that don't take months or years before they're understood. I look at you and something fits into place, Rebecca. I don't know why, but it is. I know you." He tugged her down for the lightest, the briefest, of kisses. "And I like what I see."

"Do you?" She smiled. "Really?"

"Do you imagine I spend the day with a woman only because I want to sleep with her?" She shrugged, and though her blush was very faint, he noticed it and was amused by it. How many women, he wondered, could kiss a man into oblivion, then blush? "Being with you, Rebecca, is a difficult pleasure."

She chuckled and began to draw circles in the wet sand. What would he say, what would he think, if he knew what she was? Or, more accurately, what she wasn't? It didn't matter, she told herself. She couldn't let it spoil what there was between them.

"I think that's the most wonderful compliment I've ever had."

"Where have you been?" he murmured.

When she moved restlessly, he held her still. "Don't. I'm not going to touch you. Not yet."

"That's not the problem." With her eyes closed, she tilted her chin up and let the sun beat down on her face. "The problem is, I want you to touch me, so much it frightens me." Taking her time, she sat up, gathering her courage. She wanted to be honest, and she hoped she wouldn't sound like a fool. "Stephen, I don't sleep around. I need you to understand, because this is all happening so quickly. But it's not casual."

He lifted a hand to her chin and turned her to face him. His eyes were as blue as the water, and, to her, as unfathomable. "No, it's not." He made the decision quickly, though he had been turning the idea over in his mind all day. "I have to go to Athens tomorrow. Come with me, Rebecca."

"Athens?" she managed, staring at him.

"Business. A day, two at the most. I'd like you with me." And he was afraid, more than he cared to admit, that when he returned she might be gone.

"I..." What should she say? What was right?

"You told me you'd planned to go." He'd push if necessary. Now that the idea had taken root, Stephen had no intention of going anywhere without her.

"Yes, but I wouldn't want to be in the way while you're working."

"You'll be in my way whether you're here or there."

Her head came up at that, and the look she gave him was both shy and stunning. He stifled the need to take her again, to roll until she was beneath him on the sand. He'd said he'd give her time. Perhaps what he'd really meant was that he needed time himself.

"You'll have your own suite. No strings, Rebecca. Just your company."

"A day or two," she murmured.

"It's a simple matter to have your room held for you here for your return."

Her return. Not his. If he left Corfu tomorrow she would probably never see him again. He was offering her another day, perhaps two. Never take anything for granted, she remembered. Never again.

Athens, she thought. It was true that she had planned to see it before she left Greece. But she would have gone alone. A few days before, that had been what she thought she wanted. The adventure of seeing new places, new people, on her own. Now the thought of going with him, of having him beside her when she first caught sight of the Acropolis, of having him want her with him, changed everything.

"I'd love to go with you." She rose quickly and dived into the water. She was in over her head.

Chapter Six

Athens was neither East nor West. It was spitted meat and spices roasting. It was tall buildings and modern shops. It was narrow, unpaved streets and clamorous bazaars. It had been the scene of revolution and brutality. It was ancient and civilized and passionate.

Rebecca quite simply fell in love at first sight.

She'd been seduced by Paris and charmed by London, but in Athens she lost her heart. She wanted to see everything at once, from sunrise to moonlight, and the heat-drenched afternoon between.

All that first morning, while Stephen was immersed in business meetings, she wandered. The hotel he'd chosen was lovely, but she was drawn to the streets and the people. Somehow she didn't feel like a visitor here. She felt like someone who had returned home after a long, long journey. Athens was waiting for her, ready to welcome her back.

Incredible. All her life she had accepted the parameters set for her. Now she was touring Old Athens, with its clicking worry beads and its open-fronted shops, where she could buy cheap plaster copies of monuments or elegant antiques.

She passed tavernas, but she was too excited to be tempted by the rich smells of coffee and baking. She heard the clear notes of a flute as she looked up and saw the Acropolis.

There was only one approach. Though it was still early, other tourists were making their way toward the ruins in twos and in groups. Rebecca let her camera hang by its strap. Despite the chattering around her, she felt alone, but beautifully so.

She would never be able to explain what it felt like to stand in the morning sun and look at something that had been built for the gods—something that had endured war and weather and time. It had been a place of worship. Even now, after centuries had passed, Rebecca felt the spiritual pull. Perhaps the goddess Athena, with her gleaming helmet and spear, still visited there.

Rebecca had been disappointed that Stephen couldn't join her on her first morning in Athens. Now she was glad to be alone—to sit and absorb and imagine without having to explain her thoughts.

How could she, after having seen so much, go back to so little? Sighing, she wandered through the temples. It wasn't just the awe she felt here, or the excitement she had felt in London and Paris, that had changed her. It was Stephen and everything she'd felt, everything she'd wanted, since she'd met him.

Perhaps she would go back to Philadelphia, but she would never be the same person. Once you fell in love, completely, totally in love, nothing was ever the same.

She wished it could be simple, the way she imagined it was simple for so many other women. An attractive man, a physical tug. But with Stephen, as with Athens, she'd lost her heart. However implausible it seemed, she had recognized the man, as well as the city, as being part of her, as being for her. Desire, when tangled up with love, could never be simple.

But how could you be sure you were in love when it had never happened to you before? If she were home, at least she would have a friend to talk to. With a little laugh, Rebecca walked out into the sunlight. How many times had she been on the receiving end of a long, scattered conversation from a friend who had fallen in love—or thought she had. The excitement, the unhappiness, the thrills. Sometimes she'd been envious, and sometimes she'd been grateful not to have the complication in her own life. But always, always, she'd offered calm, practical, even soothing advice.

Oddly enough, she didn't seem to be able to do the same for herself.

All she could think of was the way her heart pounded when he touched her, how excitement, panic and anticipation fluttered through her every time he looked at her. When she was with him, her feelings and fantasies seemed reasonable. When she was with him, she could believe in fate, in the matching of soul to soul.

It wasn't enough. At least that was what she would have told another woman. Attraction and passion weren't enough. Yet there was no explaining, even to herself, the sense of rightness she experienced whenever she was with him. If she were a fanciful person she would say it was as though she'd been waiting for him, waiting for the time and the place for him to come to her.

It sounded simple—if fate could be considered simple. Yet beneath all the pleasure and that sense of reunion was guilt. She couldn't shake it, and she knew she wouldn't be able to ignore it much longer. She wasn't the woman she had let him believe her to be. She wasn't the well-traveled at-loose-ends free spirit she pretended to be. No matter how many ties she'd cut, she was still Rebecca Malone. How would he feel about her once he knew how limited and dull her life had been?

How and when was she going to tell him?

A few more days, she promised herself as she began the walk back. It was selfish, perhaps it was even dangerous, but she wanted just a few more days.

It was midafternoon before she returned to the hotel. Ignoring the fact that she might be considered overeager, she went straight to Stephen's suite. She couldn't wait to see him, to tell him everything she'd seen, to show him everything she'd bought. Her easy smile faded a bit when his secretary Elana opened the door.

"Miss Malone." Gracious and self-confident, Elana waved her in. "Please sit down. I'll let Stephen know you're here."

"I don't want to interrupt." Rebecca shifted her bags, feeling gauche and foolish.

"Not at all. Have you just come in?"

"Yes, I..." For the first time, Rebecca noticed that her skin was damp and her hair tousled. In contrast, Elana was cool and perfectly groomed. "I really should go."

"Please." Elana urged Rebecca to a chair. "Let me get you a drink." With a half smile, Elana began to pour a tall glass of iced juice. She had expected Stephen's mystery lady to be smooth, controlled and stunning. It pleased her a great deal to find Rebecca wide-eyed, a little unsure, and clearly a great deal in love.

"Did you enjoy your morning?"

"Yes, very much." She accepted the glass and tried to relax. Jealousy, she realized, feeling herself flush at the realization. She couldn't remember ever having experienced the sensation before. Who wouldn't be jealous? she asked herself as she watched Elana walk to the phone. The Greek woman was gorgeous, self-contained, coolly efficient. Above all, she had a relationship with Stephen that Rebecca knew nothing about. How long has she known him? Rebecca wondered. And how well?

"Stephen's just finishing up some business," Elana said as she hung up the phone. With easy, economical moves, she poured herself a drink, then walked to the chair facing Rebecca. "What do you think of Athens?"

"I love it." Rebecca wished she'd taken the time to brush her hair and freshen her makeup. Lecturing herself, she sipped at her juice. "I'm not sure what I expected, but it's everything and more."

"Europeans see it as the East, Orientals see it as the West." Elana crossed her legs and settled back. It surprised her to realize that she was prepared to like Rebecca Malone. "What Athens is is Greek—and, more particularly, Athenian." She paused, studying Rebecca over the rim of her glass. "People often view Stephen in much the same way, and what he is is Stephen."

"How long have you worked for him?"

"Five years."

"You must know him well."

"Better than some. He's a demanding and generous employer and an interesting man. Fortunately, I like to travel and I enjoy my work."

Rebecca rubbed at a spot of dust on her slacks. "It never occurred to me that farming required so much traveling. I never realized how much was involved in growing olives."

Elana's brows rose in obvious surprise, but she continued smoothly when Rebecca glanced back at her. "Whatever Stephen does, he does thoroughly." She smiled to herself, satisfied. She hadn't been certain until now whether the American woman was attracted to Stephen or to his position. "Has Stephen explained to you about the dinner party this evening?"

"He said something about a small party here at the hotel. A business dinner."

"Men take these things more lightly than women." Feeling friendlier, Elena offered her first genuine smile. "It will be small, but quite extravagant." She watched as Rebecca automatically lifted a hand to her hair. "If you need anything—a dress, a salon—the hotel can accommodate you."

Rebecca thought of the casual sportswear she'd tossed into her bag before the impulsive trip to Athens. "I need everything."

With a quick, understanding laugh, Elana rose. "I'll make some calls for you."

"Thank you, but I don't want to interfere with your work."

"Seeing that you're comfortable is part of my work." They both glanced over when the door opened. "Stephen. You see, she hasn't run away." Taking her glass and her pad, she left them alone.

"You were gone a long time." He hated the fact that he'd begun to watch the clock and worry. He'd imagined her hurt or abducted. He'd begun to wonder if she would disappear from his life as quickly as she'd appeared in it. Now she was here, her eyes alive with pleasure, her clothes rumpled and her hair windblown.

"I guess I got caught up exploring." She started to rise, but before she could gain her feet he was pulling her out of the chair, seeking, finding her mouth with his.

His desperation whipped through her. His hunger incited her own. Without thought, without hesitation, she clung to him, answering, accepting. Already seduced, she murmured something, an incoherent sound that caught in her throat.

Good God, he thought, it wasn't possible, it wasn't sane, to want like this. Throughout the morning while all the facts and figures and demands of business had been hammering at him, he'd thought of her, of holding her, of tasting her, of being with her. When she had stayed away for so long he'd begun to imagine, then to fear, what his life would be like without her.

It wasn't going to happen. He scraped his teeth over her bottom lip, and she gasped and opened for him. He wouldn't let it happen. Where she came from, where she intended to go, no longer mattered. She belonged to him now. And, though he'd only begun to deal with it, he belonged to her.

But he needed some sanity, some logic. Fighting himself, Stephen drew her away from him. Her eyes remained closed, and her lips remained parted. A soft, sultry sound escaped them as her lashes fluttered upward.

"I . . ." She took a deep breath and let it out slowly. "I should go sightseeing more often."

Gradually he realized how hard his fingers were pressing into her arms. As if he were afraid she would slip away. Cursing himself, he relaxed. "I would have preferred to go with you."

"I understand you're busy. I'd have bored you silly, poking into every shop and staring at every column."

"No." If there was one thing he was certain of, it was that she would never bore him. "I'd like to have seen your first impression of Athens."

"It was like coming home," she told him, then hurried on because it sounded foolish. "I couldn't get enough." Laughing at herself, she gestured toward her bags. "Obviously. It's so different from anywhere I've ever been. At the Acropolis I couldn't even take any pictures, because I knew they couldn't capture the feeling. Then I walked along the streets and saw old men with *kom—konbou—*" She fumbled over the Greek and finally made a helpless gesture.

"Kombouloi," he murmured. "Worry beads."

"Yes, and I imagined how they might sit in those shadowy doorways watching the tourists go by, day after day, year after year." She sat, pleased to share her impressions with him. "I saw a shop with all these costumes, lots of tinsel, and some really dreadful plaster copies of the monuments."

He grinned and sat beside her. "How many did you buy?"

"Three or four." She bent down to rattle through her bags. "I bought you a present."

"A plaster statue of Athena?"

She glanced up, eyes laughing. "Almost. Then I found this tiny antique shop in the old section. It was all dim and dusty and irresistible. The owner had a handful of English phrases, and I had my phrase book. After we'd confused each other completely, I bought this."

She drew out an S-shaped porcelain pipe decorated with paintings of the wild mountain goats of Greece. Attached to it was a long wooden stem, as smooth as glass, tipped by a tarnished brass mouthpiece.

"I remembered the goats we'd seen on Corfu," she explained as Stephen examined it. "I thought you might like it, though I've never seen you smoke a pipe."

With a quiet laugh, he looked back at her, balancing the gift in both hands. "No, I don't—at least not of this nature."

"Well, it's more ornamental than functional, I suppose. The man couldn't tell me much about it—at least not that I could understand." She reached out to run a finger along the edge of the bowl. "I've never seen anything like it."

"I'm relieved to hear it." When she sent him a puzzled look, he leaned over to brush her lips with his. "*Matia mou,* this is a hashish pipe."

"A hashish pipe?" She stared, first in shock, then in fascination. "Really? I mean, did people actually use it?"

"Undoubtedly. Quite a number, I'd say, since it's at least a hundred and fifty years old."

"Imagine that." She pouted, imagining dark, smoky dens. "I guess it's not a very appropriate souvenir."

"On the contrary, whenever I see it I'll think of you."

She glanced up quickly, unsure, but the amusement in his eyes had her smiling again. "I should have bought you the plaster statue of Athena."

Taking her hands, he drew her to her feet. "I'm flattered that you bought me anything." She felt the subtle change as his fingers tightened on hers. "I want time with you, Rebecca. Hours of it. Days. There's too much I need to know." When she lowered her gaze, he caught her chin. "What are those secrets of yours?"

"Nothing that would interest you."

"You're wrong. Tomorrow I intend to find out all there is to know." He saw the quick flicker of unease in her eyes. Other men, he thought with an uncomfortable surge of jealousy. The hell with them. "No more evasions. I want you, all of you. Do you understand?"

"Yes, but—"

"Tomorrow." He cut her off, suddenly, completely, frustratingly Greek. "I have business that can't be avoided now. I'll come for you at seven."

"All right."

Tomorrow was years away, she told herself. She had time to decide what she would say, how she would say it. Before tomorrow came tonight. She would be everything she'd ever wanted to be, everything he wanted her to be.

"I'd better go." Before he could touch her again, she bent to gather her bags. "Stephen..." She paused at the door and turned to look at him as he stood in the middle of the room, comfortable with the wealth that surrounded him, confident with who and what he was. "You might be disappointed when you find out."

She left quickly, leaving him frowning after her.

Chapter Seven

She was as nervous as a cat. Every time she looked in the mirror Rebecca wondered who the woman was who was staring back at her. It wasn't a stranger, but it was a very, very different Rebecca Malone.

Was it just the different hairstyle, poufed and frizzed and swept around her face? Could it be the dress, the glittery spill of aquamarine that left her arms and shoulders bare? No, it was more than that. More than makeup and clever stylists and glamorous clothes. It was in her eyes. How could she help but see it? How could anyone? The woman who looked back from the mirror was a woman in love.

What was she going to do about it? What could she do? she asked herself. She was still practical enough to accept that some things could never be changed. But was she bold enough, or strong enough, to take what she wanted and live with the consequences?

When she heard the knock on the door, Rebecca took a deep breath and picked up the useless compact-size evening bag she'd bought just that afternoon. It was all happening so fast. When she'd come back from Stephen's suite there had been a detailed message from Elana listing appointments—for a massage, a facial, hairstyling—along with the name of the manager of the hotel's most exclusive boutique. She hadn't had time to think, even for a minute, about her evening with Stephen. Or about any tomorrows.

Perhaps that was best, she decided as she pulled open the door. It was best not to think, not to analyze. It was best to accept and to act.

She looked like a siren, some disciple of Circe, with her windswept hair and a dress the color of seductive seas. Had he told himself she wasn't beautiful? Had he believed it? At that moment he was certain he'd never seen, never would see, a more exciting woman.

"You're amazing, Rebecca." He took her hand and drew her to him so that they stood in the doorway together. On the threshold.

"Why? Because I'm on time?"

"Because you're never what I expect." He brought her hand to his lips. "And always what I want."

Because she was speechless, she was glad when he closed the door at her back and led her to the elevators. He looked different from the man she had first met, the one who dressed with such casual elegance. Tonight there was a formality about him, and the sophistication she had sensed earlier was abundantly apparent in the ease with which he wore the black dinner jacket.

"The way you look," he told her, "it seems a shame to waste the evening on a business dinner."

"I'm looking forward to meeting some of your friends."

"Associates," he said with an odd smile. "When you've been poor—and don't intend to be poor again—you rarely make friends in business."

She frowned. This was a side of him, the business side, that she didn't know. Would he be ruthless? She looked at him, saw it, and accepted it. Yes, a man like Stephen would always be ruthless with what belonged to him. "But enemies?"

"The same rule, in business, applies to friends and enemies. My father taught me more than fishing, Rebecca. He also taught me that to succeed, to attain, you must learn not only how to trust, but how far."

"I've never been poor, but I imagine it's frightening."

"Strengthening." He took her hand again when the elevator doors opened. "We have different backgrounds, Rebecca, but, fortunately, we've come to the same place."

He had no idea *how* different. Trust. He had spoken of trust. She discovered she wanted to tell him, tell him everything. Tell him that she knew nothing of elegant parties and glamorous life-styles. She was a fraud, and when he found out he might laugh at her and brush her aside. But she wanted him to know.

"Stephen, I want to—"

"Stephen. Once more you outdo us all in your choice of women."

"Dimitri."

Rebecca stopped, caught on the brink of confession. The man who faced her was classically handsome. His silver mane contrasted with bronzed skin lined by a half century of sun. He wore a mustache that swept majestically over gleaming teeth.

"It was kind of you to invite us here this evening, but it would be kinder still to introduce me to your lovely companion."

"Rebecca Malone, Dimitri Petropolis."

A diamond glittered on the hand he lifted to clasp Rebecca's. The hand itself was hard as rock. "A pleasure. Athens is already abuzz with talk of the woman who arrived with Stephen."

Certain he was joking, she smiled. "Then Athens must be in desperate need of news."

His eyes widened for a moment, then creased at the corners when he laughed. "I have no doubt you will provide an abundance of it."

Stephen slipped a hand under Rebecca's elbow. The look he sent Dimitri was very quick and very clear. They had competed over land, but there would be no competition over Rebecca.

"If you'll excuse us a moment, Dimitri, I'd like to get Rebecca some champagne."

"Of course." Amused—and challenged—Dimitri brushed at his mustache as he watched them walk away.

Rebecca had no way of knowing that to Stephen a small dinner party meant a hundred people. She sipped her first glass of wine, hoping she wouldn't embarrass them both by being foolishly shy and tongue-tied. In the past, whenever she had found herself in a crowd, she had always looked for the nearest corner to fade into. Not tonight, she promised herself, straightening her shoulders.

There were dozens of names to remember, but she filed them away as easily as she had always filed numbers. In the hour before dinner, while the guests mixed and mingled, she found herself at ease. The stomach flutters and hot blushes she'd often experienced at parties and functions simply didn't happen.

Perhaps she was the new Rebecca Malone after all.

She heard business discussed here and there. Most of it seemed to be hotel and resort business—talk of remodeling and expansions, mergers and takeovers. She found it odd that so many of the guests were in that trade, rather than prosperous farmers or olive growers.

Stephen came up behind her and murmured in her ear, "You look pleased with yourself."

"I am." He couldn't know that she was pleased to find herself at ease and comfortable in a party of strangers. "So many interesting people."

"Interesting." He brushed a finger over her wispy bangs. "I thought you might find it dull."

"Not at all." She took a last sip of champagne, then set the glass aside. Instantly a waiter was at her side, offering another. Stephen watched her smile her thanks.

"So you enjoy parties?"

"Sometimes. I'm enjoying this one, and having a chance to meet your associates."

Stephen glanced over her shoulder, summing up the looks and quiet murmurs. "They'll be talking about you for weeks to come."

She only laughed, turning in a slow circle. Around her was the flash of jewels and the gleam of gold. The sleek and the prosperous, the rich and the successful. It pleased her that she'd found more to talk about than tax shelters.

"I can't imagine they have so little on their minds. This is such a gorgeous room."

She looked around the huge ballroom, with its cream-and-rose walls, its glittering chandeliers and its gleaming floors. There were alcoves for cozy love seats and tall, thriving ornamental trees in huge copper pots. The tables, arranged to give a sense of intimacy, were already set with ivory cloths and slender tapers.

"It's really a beautiful hotel," she continued. "Everything about it runs so smoothly." She smiled up at him. "I'm torn between the resort in Corfu and this."

"Thank you." When she gave him a blank look, he tipped up her chin with his finger. "They're mine."

"Your what?"

"My hotels," he said simply, then led her to a table.

She spoke all through dinner, though for the first fifteen minutes she had no idea what she said. There were eight at Stephen's table, including Dimitri, who had shifted name cards so that he could sit beside her. She toyed with her seafood appetizer, chatted and wondered if she could have made a bigger fool out of herself.

He wasn't simply prosperous. He wasn't simply well-off. There was enough accountant left in Rebecca to understand that when a man owned what Stephen owned he was far, far more than comfortable.

What would he think of her when he found out what she was? Trust? How could she ever expect him to trust her now? She swallowed without tasting and managed to smile. Would he think she was a gold digger, that she had set herself up to run into him?

No, that was ridiculous.

She forced herself to look over and saw that Stephen was watching her steadily. She picked up her fork with one hand and balled up the napkin in her lap with the other.

Why couldn't he be ordinary? she wondered. Someone vacationing, someone working at the resort? Why had she fallen in love with someone so far out of her reach?

"Have you left us?"

Rebecca jerked herself back to see Dimitri smiling at her. Flushing, she noticed that the next course had been served while she'd been daydreaming. "I'm sorry." With an effort she began to toy with the *salata Athenas*.

"A beautiful woman need never apologize for being lost in her own thoughts." He patted her hand, then let his fingers linger. He caught Stephen's dark look and smiled. If he didn't like the boy so much, he thought, he wouldn't get nearly so much pleasure from irritating him. "Tell me, how did you meet Stephen?"

"We met in Corfu." She thought of that first meal they had shared . . . quiet, relaxed, alone.

"Ah, soft nights and sunny days. You are vacationing?"

"Yes." Rebecca put more effort into her smile. If she stared into her salad she would only embarrass herself, and Stephen. "He was kind enough to show me some of the island."

"He knows it well, and many of the other islands of our country. There's something of the gypsy in him."

She had sensed that. Hadn't that been part of the attraction? Hadn't Rebecca just discovered the gypsy in herself? "Have you know him long?"

"We have a long-standing business relationship. Friendly rivals, you might say. When Stephen was hardly more than a boy he accumulated an impressive amount of land." He gestured expansively. "As you can see, he used it wisely. I believe he has two hotels in your country."

"Two? More?" Rebecca picked up her glass and took a long swallow of wine.

"So you see, I had wondered if you had met in America and were old friends."

"No." Rebecca nodded weakly as the waiter removed the salad and replaced it with moussaka. "We only just met a few days ago."

"As always, Stephen moves quickly and stylishly." Dimitri took her hand again, more than a little amused by the frown he saw deepening in Stephen's eyes. "Where is it in America you are from?"

"Philadelphia." Relax, she ordered herself. Relax and enjoy. "That's in the Northeast."

It infuriated Stephen to watch her flirting so easily, so effectively, with another man. She sat through course after course, barely eating, all the while gifting Dimitri with her shy smiles. Not once did she draw away when the older man touched her hand or leaned close. From where he sat, Stephen could catch a trace of her scent, soft, subtle, maddening. He could hear her quiet laugh when Dimitri murmured something in her ear.

Then she was standing with him, her hand caught in his, as he led her to the dance floor.

Stephen sat there, battling back a jealousy he despised, and watched them move together to music made for lovers. Under the lights her dress clung, then swayed, then shifted. Her face was close, too damn close, to Dimitri's. He knew what it was like to hold her like that, to breathe in the scent of her skin and her hair. He knew what it was to feel her body brush against his, to feel the life, the passion, bubbling. He knew what it was to see her eyes blur, her lips part, to hear that quiet sigh.

He had often put his stamp on land, but never on a woman. He didn't believe in it. But only a fool sat idly by and allow another man to enjoy what was his. With a muttered oath, Stephen rose, strode out onto the dance floor and laid a hand on Dimitri's shoulder.

"Ah, well." The older man gave a regretful sigh and stepped aside. "Until later."

Before she could respond, Rebecca was caught against Stephen. With a sigh of her own, she relaxed and matched her steps to his. Maybe it was like a dream, she told herself as she closed her eyes and let the music fill her head. But she was going to enjoy every moment until it was time to wake up.

She seemed to melt against him. Her fingers moved lightly through his hair as she rested her cheek against his. Was this the way she'd danced with Dimitri? Stephen wondered, then cursed himself. He was being a fool, but he couldn't seem to stop himself. Then again, he'd had to fight for everything else in his life. Why should his woman be any different?

He wanted to drag her off then and there, away from everyone, and find some dark, quiet place to love her.

"You're enjoying yourself?"

"Yes." She wouldn't think about what he was, not now. Soon enough the night would be over and tomorrow would have to be faced. While the music played and he held her, she would only think of what he meant to her. "Very much."

The dreamy tone of her voice almost undid him. "Apparently Dimitri entertained you well."

"Mmm. He's a very nice man."

"You moved easily from his arms to mine."

Something in his tone pried through the pleasure she felt. Carefully she drew back so that she could see his face. "I don't think I know what you mean."

"I believe you do."

She was tempted to laugh, but there was no humor in Stephen's eyes. Rebecca felt her stomach knot as it always did when she was faced with a confrontation. "If I do, then I'd have to think you ridiculous. Maybe we'd better go back to the table."

"So you can be with him?" Even as the words came out he realized the unfairness, even the foolishness, of them.

She stiffened, retreating as far as she could from anger. "I don't think this is the place for this kind of discussion."

"You're quite right." As furious with himself as he was with her, he pulled her from the dance floor.

Chapter Eight

Stop it." By the time he'd dragged her to the elevators, Rebecca had gotten over her first shock. "What's gotten into you?"

"I'm simply taking you to a more suitable place for our discussion." He pulled her into the elevator, then punched the button for their floor.

"You have guests," she began, but he sent her a look than made her feel like a fool. Falling back on dignity, she straightened her shoulders. "I prefer to be asked if I want to leave, not dragged around as though I were a pack mule."

Though her heart was pounding, she sailed past him when the doors opened, intending to breeze into her own rooms and slam the door in his face. In two steps he had her arm again. Rebecca found herself guided, none too gently, into Stephen's suite.

"I don't want to talk to you," she said, because she was certain her teeth would begin to chatter at any moment. She didn't argue well in the best of circumstances. Faced with Stephen's anger, she was certain she would lose.

He said nothing as he loosened his tie and the first two buttons of his shirt. He went to the bar and poured two brandies. He was being irrational and he knew it, but he seemed unable to control it. That was new, he decided. But there had been many new emotions in him since Rebecca.

Walking back to Rebecca, he set one snifter by her elbow. When he looked at her . . . he wanted to shout, to beg, to demand, to plead. As a result, his voice was clipped and hard.

"You came to Athens with me, not with Dimitri or any other man."

She didn't touch the snifter. She was certain her hands would shake so hard that it would slip out of her grip. "Is that a Greek custom?" It amazed her—and bolstered her confidence—to hear how calm her voice was. "Forbidding a woman to speak to another man?"

"Speak?" He could still see the way Dimitri had bent his head close to hers. Dimitri, who was smooth and practiced. Dimitri, whose background would very likely mirror Rebecca's. Old money, privileged childhoods, quiet society. "Do you allow every man who speaks to you to hold you, to touch you?"

She didn't blush. Instead, the color faded from her cheeks. She shook, not with fear but with fury. "What I do, and with whom I do it, is my business. Mine."

Very deliberately he lifted his snifter and drank. "No."

"If you think that because I came here with you you have the right to dictate to me you're wrong. I'm my own person, Stephen." It struck her even as she said it that it was true. She was her own person. Each decision she made was her own. Filled with a new sense of power, she stepped forward. "No one owns me, not you, not anyone. I won't be ordered, I won't be forced, I won't be pressured." With a flick of her skirts, she turned. He had her again quickly, his hands on both of her arms, his face close.

"You won't go back to him."

"You couldn't stop me if that was what I wanted." She tossed her head back challengingly. "But I have no intention of going back downstairs to Dimitri, or anyone else." She jerked her arms free. "You idiot. Why should I want to be with him when I'm in love with you?"

She stopped, her eyes wide with shock, her lips parted in surprise. Overwhelmed by a combination of humiliation and fury, she spun around. Then she was struggling against him. "Leave me alone! Oh, God, just leave me alone!"

"Do you think I could let you go now?" He caught her hair in his hand, dragging it back until her eyes met his. In them she saw triumph and desire. "I feel as though I've waited all my life to hear you say those words." He rained kisses over her face until her struggles ceased. "You drive me mad," he murmured. "Being with you, being without you."

"Please." Colors, shapes, lights were whirling in her head. "I need to think."

"No. Ask me for anything else, but not more time." Gathering her close, he buried his face in her hair.

"Do you think I make a fool of myself over every woman?"

"I don't know." She moaned when his lips trailed down her throat. Something wild and terrifying was happening inside her body. "I don't know you. You don't know me."

"Yes, I do." He pulled away just far enough to look down at her. "From the first moment I saw you, I knew you. Needed you. Wanted you."

It was true. She knew it, felt it, but she shook her head in denial. "It's not possible."

"I've loved you before, Rebecca, almost as much as I do now." He felt her go still. The color fled from her face again, but her eyes stayed steady on his.

"I don't want you to say what isn't real, what you're not sure of."

"Didn't you feel it, the first time I kissed you?" When he saw the acknowledgment in her eyes, his grip tightened. He could feel her heart thundering, racing to match the rhythm of his own. "Somehow you've come back to me, and I to you. No more questions," he said, before she could speak. "I need you tonight."

It was real. She felt the truth and the knowledge when his mouth found hers. If it was wrong to go blindly into need, then she would pay whatever price was asked. She could no longer deny him . . . or herself.

There was no gentleness in the embrace. It was as it had been the first time, lovers reunited, a hunger finally quenched. All heat and light. She gave more than she'd known she had. Her mouth was as avid as his, as seeking. Her murmurs were as desperate. Her hands didn't shake as they moved over him. They pressed, gripped, demanded. Greedy, she tugged the jacket from his shoulders.

Yes, he'd come back to her. If it was madness to believe it, then for tonight she'd be mad.

The taste of her, just the taste of her, was making his head swim and his blood boil. He nipped at her lip, then sucked until he heard her helpless whimper. He wanted her helpless. Something fierce and uncivilized inside him wanted her weak and pliant and defenseless. When she went limp in his arms he dived into her mouth and plundered. Her response tore at him, so sweet, so vulnerable, then suddenly so ardent.

Her hands, which had fluttered helplessly to her side, rose up again to pull at his shirt, to race under it to warmed flesh. She could only think of how right it felt to touch him, to press against him and wait for him to light new fires inside her.

With an oath, he swept her up into his arms and carried her to the bedroom.

The moon was waning and offered only the most delicate light. It fell in slants and shadows on the bed, dreamlike. But the vibrating of Rebecca's pulse told her this was no dream. There was the scent of jasmine from the sprigs in the vase beside the bed. It was a scent she would always remember, just as she would remember how dark and deep were the color of his eyes.

Needful, desperate, they tumbled onto the bed.

He wanted to take care with her. She seemed so small, so fragile. He wanted to show her how completely she filled his heart. But his body was on fire, and she was already moving like a whirlwind beneath him.

His mouth was everywhere, making her shudder and arch and ache. Desires she'd never known sprang to life inside her and took control. Delirious, she obeyed them, reveled in them, then searched for more.

They rolled across the bed in a passionate war that would have two victors, touching, taking, discovering. Impatient, he peeled the dress from her, moaning as he found her breasts with his hands, his lips, his teeth. Unreasoning desire catapulted through him when he felt her soar.

Her body felt like a furnace, impossibly hot, impossibly strong. Sensations rammed into her, stealing her breath. Mindless and moaning, she writhed under him, open for any demand he might make, pulsing for any new knowledge he might offer.

Finally, finally, she knew what it was to love, to be loved, to be wanted beyond reason. Naked, she clung to him, awash in the power and the weakness, the glory and the terror.

He raced over her as if he already knew what would make her tremble, what would make her yearn. Never before had she been so aware, so in tune with another.

She made him feel like a god. He touched, and her skin vibrated under his hand. He tasted, and her flavor was like no other. She was moist, heated, and utterly willing. She seemed to explode beneath him, lost in pleasure, drugged by passion. No other woman had ever driven him so close to madness. Her head was thrown back, and one hand was flung out as her fingers dug into the sheets. Wanton, waiting, wild.

With her name on his lips, he drove into her. His breath caught. His mind spun. Her cry of pain and release echoed in his head, bringing him both triumph and guilt. His body went rigid as he fought to claw his way back. Then she seemed to close around him, body, heart, soul. As helpless as she, he crossed the line into madness and took her with him.

Chapter Nine

Aftershocks of passion wracked her. Stunned and confused, she lay in the shadowed light. Nothing had prepared her for this. No one had ever warned her that pleasure could be so huge or that need could be so jagged. If she had known... Rebecca closed her eyes and nearly laughed out loud. If she had known, she would have left everything behind years ago and searched the world for him.

Only him. She let out a quiet, calming sigh. Only him.

He was cursing himself, slowly, steadily, viciously. Innocent. Dear God. She'd been innocent, as fresh and untouched as spring, and he'd used her, hurt her, taken her.

Disgusted with himself, he sat up and reached for a cigar. He needed more than tobacco. He needed a drink, but he didn't trust his legs to carry him.

The flick of his lighter sounded like a gunshot. For an instant his face, hardened by anger and self-loathing, was illuminated.

"Why didn't you tell me?"

Still floating on an ocean of pleasure, she blinked her eyes open. "What?"

"Damn it, Rebecca, why didn't you tell me you hadn't been with a man before? That this—that I was your first?"

There was an edge of accusation in his voice. For the first time, she realized she was naked. Her cheeks grew hot as she fumbled for the sheet. One moment there was glory; the next, shame. "I didn't think of it."

"Didn't think of it?" His head whipped around. "Don't you think I had a right to know? Do you think this would have happened if I had known?"

She shook her head. It was true that she hadn't thought of it. It hadn't mattered. He was the first, the last, the only. But now it occurred to her that a man like him might not want to make love with an inexperienced woman. "I'm sorry." Her heart seemed to shrivel in her breast. "You said that you loved me, that you wanted me. The rest didn't seem to matter."

She'd cried out. He'd heard the shock and pain in her voice. And he hadn't been able to stop himself. Yes, he needed a drink. "It mattered," he tossed back as he rose and strode into the other room.

Alone, she let out a shuddering breath. Of course it mattered. Only a fool would have thought otherwise. He'd thought he was dealing with an experienced, emotionally mature woman who knew how to play the game. Words like *love* and *need* and *want* were interchangeable. Yes, he'd said he loved her, but to many love was physical and physical only.

She'd made a fool of herself and she'd infuriated him, and all because she'd begun a relationship built on illusions.

She'd knowingly taken the risk, Rebecca reminded herself as she climbed out of bed. Now she'd pay the price.

He was calmer when he started back to the bedroom. Calmer, though anger still bubbled inside him. First he would show her how it should have been, how it could be. Then they had to talk, rationally, coherently.

"Rebecca…" But when he looked at the bed it was empty.

She was wrapped in a robe and was hurling clothing into her suitcase when she heard him knock. With a shake of her head, she rubbed the tears from her cheeks and continued her frenzied packing. She wouldn't answer.… She wouldn't answer and be humiliated again.

"Rebecca." The moment of calm he'd achieved had vanished. Swearing through gritted teeth, he pounded on the door. "Rebecca, this is ridiculous. Open this door."

Ignoring him, she swept bottles and tubes of toiletries off the bureau and into her bag. He'd go away, she told herself, hardly aware that she'd begun to sob. He'd go away and then she'd leave, take a cab to the airport and catch the first plane to anywhere.

The sound of splintering wood had her rushing into the parlor in time to see the door give way.

She'd thought she'd seen fury before, but she'd been wrong. She saw it now as she stared into Stephen's face. Speechless, she looked from him to the broken door and back again.

Elana, tying the belt of her robe, rushed down the hall. "Stephen, what's happened? Is there a—"

He turned on her, hurling one short sentence in clipped Greek at her. Her eyes widened and she backed away, sending Rebecca a look that combined sympathy and envy.

"Do you think you have only to walk away from me?" He pushed the door back until it scraped against the battered jamb.

"I want—" Rebecca lifted a hand to her throat as if to push the words out. "I want to be alone."

"The hell with what you want." He started toward her, only to stop dead when she cringed and turned away. He'd forgotten what it was like to hurt, truly hurt, until that moment. "I asked you once if you were afraid of me. Now I see that you are." Searching for control, he dipped his hands into the pockets of the slacks he'd thrown on. She looked defenseless, terrified, and tears still streaked her cheeks. "I won't hurt you again. Will you sit?" When she shook her head, he bit off an oath. "I will."

"I know you're angry with me," she began when he'd settled into a chair. "I'll apologize if it'll do any good, but I do want to be alone."

His eyes had narrowed and focused. "You'll apologize? For what?"

"For..." What did he expect her to say? Humiliated, she crossed her arms and hugged her elbows.
"For what happened.., for not...explaining," she
finished lamely. "For whatever you like," she continued as the tears started again. "Just leave me alone."

"Sweet God." He rubbed a weary hand over his
face. "I can think of nothing in my life I've handled
as badly as this." He rose, but stopped again when she
automatically retreated. "You don't want me to touch
you." His voice had roughened. He had to swallow to
clear his throat. "I won't, but I hope you'll listen."

"There's nothing more to say. I understand how
you feel and why you feel it. I'd rather we just left it
at that."

"I treated you inexcusably."

"I don't want an apology."

"Rebecca—"

"I don't." Her voice rose, stopping his words,
stopping her tears. "It's my fault. It's been my fault
all along. No, no, no!" she shouted when he took another step. "I don't want you to touch me. I couldn't
bear it."

He sucked in his breath, then let it out slowly. "You
twist the knife well."

But she was shaking her head and pacing the room
now. "It didn't matter at first—at least I didn't think
it would matter. I didn't know who you were or that I
would fall in love with you. Now I've waited too long
and ruined everything."

"What are you talking about?"

Perhaps it was best, best for both of them, to lay out the truth. "You said you knew me, but you don't, because I've done nothing but lie to you, right from the first moment."

Slowly, carefully, he lowered himself to the arm of a chair. "What have you lied to me about?"

"Everything." Her eyes were drenched with regret when she looked at him. "Then, tonight... First I found out that you own hotels. *Own* them."

"It was hardly a secret. Why should it matter?"

"It wouldn't." She dropped her hands to her sides. "If I was what I'd pretended to be. After we'd made love and you—I realized that by pretending I'd let you have feelings for someone who didn't even exist."

"You're standing in front of me, Rebecca. You exist."

"No. Not the way you think, not the way I've let you think."

He prepared himself for the worst. "What have you done? Were you running away from America?"

"No. Yes." She had to laugh at that. "Yes, I was running." She gathered what composure she had left and folded her hands. "I did come from Philadelphia, as I told you. I've lived there all my life. Lived there, went to school there, worked there." She found a tissue in the pocket of her robe. "I'm an accountant."

He stared at her, one brow lifting, as she blew her nose. "I beg your pardon?"

"I said, I'm an accountant." She hurled the words at him, then whirled away to face the window. Stephen started to rise, then thought better of it.

"I find it difficult to imagine you tallying ledgers, Rebecca. If you'd sit down, maybe we could talk this through."

"Damn it, I said I'm an accountant. A CPA, specializing in corporate taxes. Up until a few weeks ago I worked for McDowell, Jableki and Kline in Philadelphia."

He spread his hands, taking it all in. "All right. What did you do? Embezzle?"

She tossed back her head and nearly exploded with laughter. If she said yes he'd probably be intrigued. But the time for intrigue was over. The time for the truth was now. "No. I've never done anything illegal in my life. I've never even had a parking ticket. I've never done anything at all out of the ordinary until a few weeks ago."

She began to pace again, too agitated to keep still. "I'd never traveled, never had a man send a bottle of champagne to my table, never walked along the beach in the moonlight, never had a lover."

He said nothing, not because he was angry or bored but because he was fascinated.

"I had a good job, my car was paid for, I had good, conservative investments that would have ensured me a comfortable retirement. In my circle of friends I'm known as dependable. If someone needs a sitter they know they can call Rebecca. If they need advice or someone to feed their fish while they're on vacation they don't have to worry. I was never late for work, never took five minutes extra for lunch."

"Commendable," he said, and earned a glare.

"Just the type of employee I imagine you'd like to hire."

He swallowed a chuckle. He'd been prepared for her to confess she had a husband, five husbands, a prison record. Instead she was telling him she was an accountant with an excellent work record. "I have no desire to hire you, Rebecca."

"Just as well." She turned away and started to prowl the room again. "You'd undoubtedly change your mind after I tell you the rest."

Stephen crossed his ankles and settled back. God, what a woman she was. "I'm anxious to hear it."

"My aunt died about three months ago, suddenly."

"I'm sorry." He would have gone to her then, but he could see she was far from ready. "I know how difficult it is to lose family."

"She was all I had left." Because she needed something to do, she pushed open the balcony doors. Warm, fragrant night air rushed in. "I couldn't believe she was gone. Just like that. No warning. Of course, I handled the funeral arrangements. No fuss, no frills. Just the way Aunt Jeannie would have wanted. She was a very economical woman, not only in finances but in dress, in speech, in manner. As long as I can remember, people compared me to her."

Stephen's brow lifted again as he studied the woman being buffeted by the breeze—the short red silk robe, the tousled hair.

"Soon after her death—I don't know if it was days or a week—something just snapped. I looked at myself, at my life, and I hated it." She dragged her hair back, only to have the wind catch it again. "I was a good employee, just like my aunt, a good credit risk, a dependable friend. Law-abiding, conservative and boring. Suddenly I could see myself ten, twenty, thirty years down the road, with nothing more than I had at that moment. I couldn't stand it."

She turned around. The breeze caught at the hem of her robe and sent it dancing around her legs. "I quit my job, and I sold everything."

"Sold?"

"Everything I owned—car, apartment, furniture, books, absolutely everything. I turned all the cash into traveler's checks, even the small inheritance from my aunt. Thousands of dollars. I know it might not sound like a lot to you, but it was more than I'd ever imagined having at once."

"Wait." He held up a hand, wanting to be certain he understood everything. "You're telling me that you sold your possessions, *all* your possessions?"

She couldn't remember ever having felt more foolish, and she straightened her shoulders defensively. "Right down to my coffeepot."

"Amazing," he murmured.

"I bought new clothes, new luggage, and flew to London. First-class. I'd never been on a plane before in my life."

"You'd never flown, but took your first trip across the Atlantic."

She didn't hear the admiration in his voice, only the amusement. "I wanted to see something different. To *be* something different. I stayed at the Ritz and took pictures of the changing of the guard. I flew to Paris and had my hair cut." Self-consciously she lifted a hand to it.

Because he could see that she was overwrought, he was careful not to smile. "You flew to Paris for a haircut."

"I'd heard some women discussing this stylist, and I— Never mind." It was no use trying to explain that she'd gone to the same hairdresser, to the same shops, for years. The same everything. "Right after Paris, I came here," she went on. "I met you. Things happened. I let them happen." Tears threatened. She could only pray he didn't see them. "You were exciting, and attracted to me. Or attracted to who you thought I was. I'd never had a romance. No one had ever looked at me the way you did."

Once more he chose his words carefully. "Are you saying that being with me was different? An adventure, like flying to a Paris salon?"

She would never be able to explain what being with him had meant to her. "Apologies and explanations really don't make any difference now. But I am sorry, Stephen. I'm sorry for everything.''

He didn't see the tears, but he heard the regret in her voice. His eyes narrowed. His muscles tensed. "Are you apologizing for making love with me, Rebecca?"

"I'm apologizing for whatever you like. I'd make it up to you if I could, but I don't know how, unless I jump out the window.''

He paused, as if he were considering it. "I don't think this requires anything quite that drastic. Perhaps if you'd sit down calmly?''

She shook her head and stayed where she was. "I can't handle any more of this tonight, Stephen. I'm sorry. You've every right to be angry.''

He rose, the familiar impatience building. But she was so pale, looked so fragile, sounded so weary. He hadn't treated her gently before. At least he could do so now.

"All right. Tomorrow, then, after you've rested.'' He started to go to her, then checked himself. It would take time to show her that there were other ways to love. Time to convince her that love was more, much more than an adventure. "I want you to know that I regret what happened tonight. But that, too, will wait until tomorrow.'' Though he wanted to touch a hand to her cheek, he kept it fisted in his pocket. "Get some rest.''

She had thought her heart was already broken. Now it shattered. Not trusting her voice, she nodded.

He left her alone. The door scraped against the splintered jamb as he secured it. She supposed there might have been a woman somewhere who'd made a bigger fool of herself. At the moment, it didn't seem to matter.

At least there was something she could do for both of them. Disappear.

Chapter Ten

It was her own fault, she supposed. There were at least half a dozen promising accounting positions in the want ads. Not one of them interested her. Rebecca circled them moodily. How could she be interested in dental plans and profit sharing? All she could think about, all she'd been able to think about for two weeks, was Stephen.

What had he thought when he'd found her gone? Relief? Perhaps a vague annoyance at business left unfinished? Pen in hand, Rebecca stared out of the window of the garden apartment she'd rented. In her fantasies she imagined him searching furiously for her, determined to find her, whatever the cost. Reality, she thought with a sigh, wasn't quite so romantic. He would have been relieved. Perhaps she wasn't sophisticated, but at least she'd stepped out of his life with no fuss.

Now it was time to get her own life in order.

First things first. She had an apartment, and the little square of lawn outside the glass doors was going to make her happy. That in itself was a challenge. Her old condo had been centrally located on the fifth floor of a fully maintained modern building.

This charming and older development was a good thirty miles from downtown, but she could hear the birds in the morning. She would be able to look out at old oaks and sweeping maples and flowers she would plant herself. Perhaps it wasn't as big a change as a flight to Paris, but for Rebecca it was a statement.

She'd bought some furniture. *Some* was the operative word. Thus far she'd picked out a bed, one antique table and a single chair.

Not logical, Rebecca thought with a faint smile. No proper and economical living room suite, no tidy curtains. Even the single set of towels she'd bought was frivolous. And exactly what she'd wanted. She would do what she'd secretly wanted to do for years—buy a piece here, a piece there. Not because it was a good buy or durable, but because she wanted it.

She wondered how many people would really understand the satisfaction of making decisions not because they were sensible but because they were desirable. She'd done it with her home, her wardrobe. Even with her hair, she thought, running a hand through it. Outward changes had led to inner changes. Or vice versa. Either way, she would never again be the woman she'd been before.

Or perhaps she would be the woman she'd always been but had refused to acknowledge.

Then why was she circling ads in the classifieds? Rebecca asked herself. Why was she sitting here on a beautiful morning planning a future she had no interest in? Perhaps it was true that she would never have the one thing, the one person, she really wanted. There would be no more picnics or walks in the moonlight or frantic nights in bed. Still, she had the memories, she had the moments, she had the dreams. There would be no regrets where Stephen was concerned. Not now, and not ever. And if she was now more the woman she had been with him, it had taken more than a change in hairstyle.

She was stronger. She was surer. She was freer. And she'd done it herself.

She could think of nothing she wanted less than to go back into someone else's firm, tallying figures, calculating profit and loss. So she wouldn't. Rebecca sank into the chair as the thought struck home.

She wouldn't. She wouldn't go job hunting, carrying her résumé, rinsing sweaty palms in the rest room, putting her career and life in someone else's hands again. She'd open her own firm. A small one, certainly. Personalized. Exclusive, she decided, savoring the word. Why not? She had the skill, the experience, and—finally—she had the courage.

It wouldn't be easy. In fact, it would be risky. The money she had left would have to go toward renting office space, equipment, a phone system, advertising. With a bubbling laugh, she sprang up and searched for a legal pad and a pencil. She had to make lists—not only of things to do but of people to call. She had enough contacts from her McDowell, Jableki and Kline days. Maybe, just maybe, she could persuade some of her former clients to give her a try.

"Just a minute," she called out when she heard the knock on the door. She scribbled a reminder to look for file cabinets as she went to answer. She'd much rather have some good solid oak file cabinets than a living room sofa.

She knew better than to open the door without checking the security peephole, but she was much too involved with her plans to think about such things. When she opened the door, she found herself face-to-face with Stephen.

Even if she could have spoken, he wasn't in the mood to let her. "What in the hell do you think you're doing?" he demanded as he slammed the door behind him. "Do you deliberately try to drive me mad, or does it come naturally to you?"

"I—I don't—" But he was already yanking her against him. Whatever words she might have spoken dissolved into a moan against his lips. Her pad fell to the floor with a slap. Even as her arms came up around him he was thrusting her away.

"What kind of game are you playing, Rebecca?" When she just shook her head, he dug his hands into his pockets and paced the wide, nearly empty room. He was unshaven, disheveled and absolutely gorgeous. "It's taken me two weeks and a great deal of trouble to find you. I believe we'd agreed to talk again. I was surprised to discover you'd not only left Athens, but Europe." He swung back and pinned her with a look. "Why?"

Still reeling from his entrance, she struggled not to babble. "I thought it best that I leave."

"You thought?" He took a step toward her, his fury so palatable that she braced herself. "You thought it best," he repeated. "For whom?"

"For you. For both of us." She caught herself fiddling with the lapels of her robe and dropped her hands. "I knew you were angry with me for lying to you and that you regretted what had happened between us. I felt it would be better for both of us if I—"

"Ran away?"

Her chin came up fractionally. "Went away."

"You said you loved me."

She swallowed. "I know."

"Was that another lie?"

"Please don't." She turned away, but there was nowhere to go. "Stephen, I never expected to see you again. I'm trying to make some sense out of my life, to do things in a way that's not only right but makes me happy. In Greece, I guess, I did what made me happy, but I didn't think about what was right. The time with you was..."

"Was what?"

Dragging both hands through her hair, she turned to him again. It was as if the two weeks had never been. She was facing him again, trying to explain what she feared she could never explain. "It was the best thing that ever happened to me, the most important, the most unforgettable, the most precious. I'll always be grateful for those few days."

"Grateful." He wasn't sure whether to laugh or murder her. Stepping forward, he surprised them both by slipping his hands lightly around her throat. "For what? For my giving you your first fling? A fast, anonymous romance with no consequences?"

"No." She lifted a hand to his wrist but made no attempt to struggle. "Did you come all this way to make me feel more guilty?"

"I came all this way because I finish what I begin. We'd far from finished, Rebecca."

"All right." Be calm, she told herself. When a man was this close to the edge, a woman's best defense was serenity. "If you'll let me go, we'll talk. Would you like some coffee?"

His fingers tightened reflexively, then slowly relaxed. "You've bought a new pot."

"Yes." Was that humor in his eyes? she wondered. "There's only one chair. Why don't you use it while I go into the kitchen?"

He took her arm. "I don't want coffee, or a chair, or a pleasant conversation."

It seemed serenity wouldn't work. "All right, Stephen. What do you want?"

"You. I'd thought I'd made that fairly obvious." When she frowned, he glanced around the apartment. "Now tell me, Rebecca, is this what you want? A handful of rooms to be alone in?"

"I want to make the best of the rest of my life. I've already apologized for deceiving you. I realize that—"

"Deceiving me." He held up a finger to stop her. "I've wanted to clear that point up myself. How did you deceive me?"

"By letting you think that I was something I'm not."

"You're not a beautiful, interesting woman? A passionate woman?" He lifted a brow as he studied her. "Rebecca, I have too much pride to ever believe you could deceive me that completely."

He was confusing her—deliberately, she was sure. "I told you what I'd done."

"What you'd done," he agreed. "And how you'd done it." He brought his hand to her throat again, this time in a caress. His anger hadn't made her knees weak. She felt them tremble now at his tenderness. "Selling your possessions and flying to Paris for a new hairstyle. Quitting your job and grabbing life with both hands. You fascinate me." Her eyes stayed open wide when he brushed his lips over hers. "I think the time is nearly over when you'll be so easily flattered. It's almost a pity." He drew her closer, slowly, while his mouth touched hers. Relief coursed through him as he felt her melt and give. "Do you think it was your background that attracted me?"

"You were angry," she managed.

"Yes, angry at the idea that I had been part of your experiment. Furious," he added before he deepened the kiss. "Furious that I had been of only passing interest." She was heating in his arms, just as he remembered, just as he needed, softening, strengthening. "Shall I tell you how angry? Shall I tell you that for two weeks I couldn't work, couldn't think, couldn't function, because you were everywhere I looked and nowhere to be found?"

"I had to go." She was already tugging at his shirt to find the flesh beneath. To touch him again, just for a moment. To be touched by him. "When you said you regretted making love..." Her own words brought her back. Quickly she dropped her hands and stepped away.

He stared at her for a moment, then abruptly swore and began to pace. "I've never thought myself this big a fool. I hurt you that night in a much different way than I'd believed. Then I handled it with less finesse than I might the most unimportant business transaction." He paused, sighing. For the first time she saw clearly how incredibly weary he was.

"You're tired. Please, sit down. Let me fix you something."

He took a moment to press his fingers to his eyes. Again he wanted to laugh—while he strangled her. She was exactly what he needed, what he understood. Yet at the same time she baffled him.

"You weaken me, Rebecca, and bring out the fool I'd forgotten I could be. I'm surprised you allowed me to set foot into your home. You should have—" As quickly as the anger had come, it faded. As quickly as the tension had formed, it eased. Everything he'd needed to see was in her eyes. Carefully now, he drew a deep breath. A man wasn't always handed so many chances at happiness.

"Rebecca, I never regretted making love with you." He stopped her from turning with the lightest of touches on her shoulder. "I regretted only the way it happened. Too much need and too little care. I regret, I'll always regret, that for your first time there was fire but no warmth." He took her hands in his and brought them to his lips.

"It was beautiful."

"In its way." His fingers tightened on hers. Still so innocent, he thought. Still so generous. "It was not kind or patient or tender, as love should be the first time."

She felt hope rise in her heart again. "None of that mattered."

"It mattered, more than I can ever tell you. After, when you told me everything, it only mattered more. If I had done what my instincts told me to do that night you would never have left me. But I thought you needed time before you could bear to have me touch you again." Slowly, gently, he drew the tip of her finger into his mouth and watched her eyes cloud over. "Let me show you what I should have shown you then." With her hands locked in his, he looked into her eyes. "Do you want me?"

It was time for the truth. "Yes."

He lifted her into his arms and heard her breath catch. "Do you trust me?"

"Yes."

When he smiled, her heart turned over. "Rebecca, I must ask you one more thing."

"What is it?"

"Do you have a bed?"

She felt her cheeks heat even as she laughed. "In there."

She was trembling. It reminded him how careful he had to be, how precious this moment was to both of them. The sun washed over the bed, over them, as he lay beside her. And kissed her—only kissed her, softly, deeply, thoroughly, until her arms slipped from around him to fall bonelessly to her sides. She trembled still as he murmured to her, as his lips brushed over her cheeks, her throat.

He had shown her the desperation love could cause, the sharp-edged pleasure, the speed and the fury. Now he showed her that love could mean serenity and sweetness.

And she showed him.

He had thought to teach her, not to learn, to reassure her but not to be comforted. But he learned, and he was comforted. The need was there, as strong as it had been the first time. But strength was tempered with patience. As he slipped his hands down her robe to part it, to slide it away from her skin, he felt no need to hurry. He could delight in the way the sun slanted across her body, in the way her flesh warmed to his touch.

Her breath was as unsteady as her hands as she undressed him. But not from nerves. She understood that now. She felt strong and capable and certain. Anticipation made her tremble. Pleasure made her shudder. She gave a sigh that purred out of her lips as she arched against his seeking hands. Then he nipped lightly at her breast and she bounded from serenity to passion in one breathless leap.

Still he moved slowly, guiding her into a kind of heated torment she'd never experienced. Desire boiled in her, and his name sprang to her lips and her body coiled like a spring. Chaining down his own need, he set hers free and watched as she flew over the first peak.

"Only for me," he murmured as she went limp in his arms. "Only for me, Rebecca." With his own passions strapped, he slipped into her, determined to watch her build again. "Tell me you love me. Look at me and tell me."

She opened her eyes. She could barely breathe. Somehow the strength was pouring back into her, but so fast, so powerfully. Sensation rolled over sensation, impossibly. She moved with him, pressed center to center, heart to heart, but all she could see were his eyes, so dark, so blue, so intense. Perhaps she was drowning in them.

"I love you, Stephen."

Then she was falling, fathoms deep, into his eyes, into the sea. With her arms locked around him, she dragged him under with her.

He pulled her against him so that he could stroke her hair and wait for his pulse to level. She'd been innocent. But the surprise, the one he'd been dealing with for weeks, was that until Rebecca he'd been just as innocent. He'd known passion, but he'd never known intimacy, not the kind that reached the heart as fully as the body. And yet . . .

"We've been here before," he murmured. "Do you feel it, too?"

She linked her fingers with his. "I never believed in things like that until you. When I'm with you it's like remembering." She lifted her head to look at him. "I can't explain it."

"I love you, Rebecca, only more knowing who you are, why you are."

She touched a hand to his cheek. "I don't want you to say anything you don't really feel."

"How can a woman be so intelligent and still so stupid?" With a shake of his head, Stephen rolled on top of her. "A man doesn't travel thousands of miles for this, however delightful it may be. I love you, and though it annoyed me for quite some time I'm accustomed to it now."

"Annoyed you."

"Infuriated." He kissed her to cut off whatever retort she might make. "I'd seen myself remaining free for years to come. Then I met a woman who sold her coffeepot so she could take pictures of goats.''

''I certainly have no intention of interfering with your plans.''

''You already have.'' He smiled, holding her still when she tried to struggle away. ''Marriage blocks off certain freedoms and opens others.''

''Marriage?'' She stopped struggling but turned her head to avoid another kiss.

''Soon.'' He nuzzled her neck. ''Immediately.''

''I never said I'd marry you.''

''No, but you will.'' With his fingertips only, he began to arouse her. ''I'm a very persuasive man.''

''I need to think.'' But she was trembling again. ''Stephen, marriage is very serious.''

''Deadly. And I should warn you that I've already decided to murder any man you look at for more than twenty seconds.''

''Really?'' She turned her head back, prepared to be angry. But he was smiling. No one else had ever smiled at her in quite that way. ''Really?''

''I can't let you go, Rebecca. Can't and won't. Come back with me. Marry me. Have children with me.''

''Stephen—''

He laid a finger to her lips. ''I know what I'm asking you. You've already started a new life, made new plans. We've had only days together, but I can make you happy. I can promise to love you for a lifetime, or however many lifetimes we have. You once dived into the sea on impulse. Dive with me now, Rebecca. I swear you won't regret it.''

Gently she pressed her lips to his fingertip, then drew his hand away. ''All my life I've wondered what I might find if I had the courage to look. I found you, Stephen.'' With a laugh she threw her arms around him. ''When do you want to leave?''

* * * * *

Nora Roberts

There's something I've discovered over the last ten years. I love writing romances. I love writing long ones and short ones, sexy ones and funny ones. Some of the best times of my life have been spent trying to think of new ways to make the old boy-meets-girl theme work one more time. Some of the most frustrating times of my life have been spent doing exactly the same thing.

When Silhouette published my first book in 1981, it was a tremendous thrill for me. This *Silhouette Summer Sizzler*, "Impulse," is number 63—I think. Whatever the number, the thrill is exactly the same. No matter how many books, no matter how much things change, nothing quite tops the kick of seeing one of my stories on the shelf. Unless it's getting a letter from a reader who has enjoyed it.

But what has changed? Certainly something must have in all this time and after all these books. It might be nice for me to tell you that I lead a glamorous, glitzy, jet-setting life, that I shoot off to all these fabulous places with my characters while my staff keeps my country estate in perfect order. After over sixty books I should be pretty good at telling a story.

The truth is, as I'm writing this I'm sitting in my cramped, messy office, wearing sweats and fighting off a cold. I live in fear that when my sons come home from school they'll have questions about long division or molecules. There's a basket of laundry no one has bothered to fold and breakfast dishes in the sink.

I guess the staff took the day off.

These are the little reasons why we need romance in our lives. It's certainly why I need it in mine. Children grow up eventually, bless them, and dishes have a way of getting washed sooner or later. Most of us face baskets of laundry with alarming regularity. But without that special person in our lives the days would be very dull and nights much too long.

Every time I write a romance I like to think of it as a celebration. Every couple who comes together in a novel is a symbol of what each of us hopes for—love, happiness, companionship.

I sincerely hope that each of you who reads my books finds something in them that makes you smile.

Nora Roberts

RAVISHED!

Parris Afton Bonds

For Betty Domitrovich and Etta Henry
Your love of people shines through.

A special thanks to my sister,
Nancy Kaptain, R.N.,
for her technical advice.

My Most Memorable Vacation

My most memorable vacation comes easily to mind. In 1985 I made plans with a special person and special writer, Rita Clay Estrada, to take a two-week tour of Europe. Each of us hoped to get a novel out of the trip.

Since we live in different cities, she came to my house so we could plan our self-guided vacation. Just poring over the books and maps spread out on the living room floor filled us with excitement. Even if the trip hadn't gone off as planned, I can honestly say that the anticipation was a joy in itself.

During this time, my grandmother died at the age of ninety-eight. I had been watching my mother, who had cared for Grandmother for twelve years, deteriorate in health. Her skin had taken on a gray tinge, her shoulders were bowed, her back was stooped. I decided then to take my mother with me to Europe, even though she had always refused to board an airplane.

Rita, wonderful Rita, encouraged me to bring her, even though both of us realized that the trip wouldn't be quite the exuberant one we had anticipated. Traveling with a grieving mother back and forth across the face of Europe could certainly put a damper on a vacation.

Well, I didn't know my mother very well. She kept Rita and me laughing the entire trip. Tears streamed down our faces, and our stomachs ached from the laughter. In Italy, men fell in love with Mother, with her wrinkled Madonna's face, her shining brown eyes and her lovely, smiling mouth. The Italian males tripped all over each other trying to help her with her luggage, assist her in and out of taxis and explain the sights to her—while Rita and I stood by, our mouths agape.

After a whirlwind two weeks of sight-seeing I returned home, physically exhausted but inwardly relaxed. I had enough ideas for *four* books, which I eventually did write and publish. But what made the trip my most memorable vacation was seeing my father's astonished face when he met Mother and me at the airport. He stared at her, and I did, too, seeing through his eyes the metamorphosis in her. Her back was as straight as a nun's, her shoulders were squared, her face was radiant.

The joy of that vacation carries over even today. One of us has only to remark, "Remember the bells of St. Abbott?" or mention some other absurd memory and we break up laughing. And aren't laughter and love the best medicine?

Chapter One

Dear Mary: I'm having a wonderful time here in Bahia Escondida. Your time-share condo is fabulous. You won't believe it—I had poolside margaritas with a French actor! Love, Nelli.

Dear Lana: I'm having a marvelous time here in Bahia Escondida. Posada Tangolunda, its newly developed resort, is dreamy. You won't believe it—a Texas congressman took me dancing! Love, Nelli.

Dear Carol: I'm having an enchanting time here on Mexico's Yucatan Peninsula. Bahia Escondida is soooo romantic. You'll never believe it—I had brunch with a Broadway producer! Love, Nelli

In the same way that your life flashes before your eyes in the single instant before disaster, all the foolishly fabricated postcards Nelli Walzchak had written to the other nurses back at Kansas General returned to haunt her. They'd never believe the truth now. She wasn't certain *she* did. Surely she was still dreaming.

But, no. The moon-drenched apparition that leaned over her bed suddenly clamped a hardened hand over her mouth. Dreams didn't *feel* like this.

Real panic, the kind that strains your heart muscles and sends the EKG needle off the graph paper, stole her breath—that and the large hand of the beard-shadowed man who was hunkered over her.

"Scream," he muttered, "and I'll do a tracheotomy on you." Cold metal pressed against her throat. "Understand?"

She mumbled something unintelligible beneath his hand.

"I want your word," he said, easing the pressure of the knife against her skin.

Her head bobbed. She would promise anything—to vote Republican, to contribute to the next PBS fundraiser, to alphabetize her spice rack—if only he wouldn't hurt her.

Nelli could feel the heat of his damp palm and smell his edgy desperation. In her nostrils, it mingled with her own fear. Over the ridge of his hand she stared wide-eyed up at him. Slitted dark eyes bored into hers. She knew he was making up his mind about her. Then, ever so slowly, he removed his hand.

It was her one chance—and she knew enough to seize it. She whipped away, rolled aside and scrambled on her knees across the bed. A king-size bed whose terrain was too wide to allow her to evade the hand that snatched at her calf. She jerked hard, but he held fast. In his grip, her pajama bottoms began slipping over her hips.

"Please," she gasped. "Let me go." Her slip-sliding knees were taking her nowhere. "I won't tell anyone! I swear! Only don't—"

With a mere twist of his wrist, he flipped her over onto her back and fell across her. The breath whooshed out of her lungs as, with one hand, he locked her wrists above her head. "Don't what?" he muttered against her cheekbone. "Don't . . . shall we say, 'ravish' you?"

Her eyes snapped open. "Are you crazy?" Sheer rage bubbled up inside her. "What woman in her right mind wants to be terrified in the middle of the night by a strange man wielding a knife?"

His lips moved down the slope of her cheek to hover near her mouth. "But that's not what came to mind first, is it? Not terror."

His voice. It was as smooth as brandy-laced eggnog. Strangely reassuring, considering the circumstances. "You're crazy. *I'm* crazy! Lying here talking about being ravished with a man who's holding a knife to my throat."

"Have you ever been? Ravished that is?" His mouth was practically brushing hers. Tingling sensations rippled through her, and heat suddenly pooled in her stomach.

"No, but I don't need to be electrocuted to realize that I don't want that particular experience, either." He had to weigh a ton. His massive chest—quite bare, she realized—was flattening her breasts.

His fingers snarled in her unbound tresses, his teeth glinting in a slightly skeptical but amused grin. "Any woman who wears her hair drawn back in a spinster's bun has to be repressed."

She gasped. "How do you know how I wear my hair?"

He raised himself on one elbow, but took the precaution of restraining her with a heavy-muscled thigh angled across her body. "In a one-burro pueblo like Bahia Escondida, everybody knows everything."

That was true. Bahia Escondida had once been a nearly inaccessible fishing village of dusty streets and a handful of small, inexpensive hotels. Nelli had been appalled by the raw sewage that still trickled down those streets. Since mainly Europeans and a few adventurous North Americans, drawn to Bahia Escondida's surf and solitude, frequented the hideaway, naturally everyone knew everyone else's business. But recently the off-the-beaten-path coastline had been enhanced by an exclusive time-sharing condominium that was the forerunner of a planned resort community of hotels, villas and houses.

"After all," the stranger continued, "you're among the first of the tourists to arrive at the new resort. Men, especially Latin men, are bound to talk about a champagne blonde." His free hand slid along her rib cage, curved in to follow the indentation of her waist and flared out with her hip. "Particularly one with such a luscious hourglass figure."

An unfamiliar ache budded deep in her belly, just beneath his leg. "I don't believe you."

"Why should I lie?" The moonlight gilded his mouth, which was curved like a scythe. "The fact that you wear glasses certainly doesn't detract from their appreciation of you as a woman." His hand returned to her rib cage, just below her breast. "Nor the fact that you're a career woman. A nurse."

Her mouth fell open. "How did you know that?"

"Why, the taxi driver who brought you here from the airport last week spread the word that you wore them."

"Not the glasses. That I'm a nurse."

He shifted, and his hand brushed the underside of her breast. So lightly that she wasn't sure she wasn't imagining it. Or dreaming it. Maybe this whole, absurd conversation was just a nightmare. "Your flight bag. Father Hidalgo, the parish priest, mentioned that it has the logo of the American Nursing Association. And your nursing license. It was next to the credit card you presented to the clerk at the registration desk."

"Nosey little pueblo," she murmured, but her irritation was distracted by the grazing motion of his lips gliding gently along the line of her jaw. "What are you doing?" She could hardly breathe. Her voice sounded like the ocean breeze soughing through the palms.

"I don't know," he muttered. "Must be the tropical heat. I came here because of something urgent. Not to hurt you, believe me. You were right. I *am* crazy."

Still, he bent his head and kissed her. She knew then she had never really been kissed. Not like this. Despite the reluctance that underscored his kiss, she felt as if he were filling her with pure liquid pleasure. Its path left a radiating, golden heat, and her blood carried that glow, burnishing her throughout. Her fingertips, her toes, even her hair, came to life. Eddies of yearning grew into waves of desire.

He slid atop her, and his tongue gently nudged at her lips. They treacherously complied and parted for him. Glorious! she marveled. This feeling of a man, heavy on her, dominating her, taking over for her. It was wonderful, losing herself so completely! Like a cat, she arched her body and rubbed against him. Ahhh, yes, glorious! She began making strange, mindless little purring noises that finally reached through to her numbed brain.

What in God's name was she doing?

She stiffened, then began to fight him. Her fists broke free from his relaxed grasp to pummel his chest. Her leg jerked up, catching him painfully.

With a smothered oath and a groan, he recaptured her hands. In the moonlight, his eyes glittered feverishly, as if he, too, were coming to his senses. "Get something on. Jeans or something."

"What?"

"You're coming with me." He rose and tossed her the sundress she had draped over a chair before she went to bed. "Here, this will do."

He must have been used to being obeyed without question, because he wasn't even looking her way, apparently assuming she would dress and tag along quietly. She took advantage of this lapse on his part and screamed. In the space of a heartbeat, he lunged at Nelli and silenced her with a hand clamped over her mouth again—not that anyone would have heard her. The roar of the surf just beyond the condos would have drowned out her scream.

"Damn it! I should have known better than to trust an uptight virgin!"

He released her mouth just long enough for her to retort, "I'm not a—"

This time she was more effectively gagged with the satiny case he ripped off her pillow. After he finished knotting the fabric behind her head, he said, "Save your explanations for later. We've got a boat ride to take."

Her hands clawed in fear at his arms, and he grabbed her wrists. At the same time, he ripped away the cord of braided rayon belting from her pajama top. "I had hoped to persuade you to accompany me willingly, but I see that stronger measures are called for."

As he lashed Nelli's hands behind her, her gaze darted around the shadowy bedroom for a source of help. The terrace doors, opening onto the balcony, told her how he had gained entry. Abruptly her eyes were drawn back to him as he bent over her bed and retrieved the shiny, steel object lying on it. Why, the knife he had threatened her with was a common screwdriver!

He hustled her across the bedroom and into the living room. In the tiled vestibule, he unlocked and opened the front door, then stood listening and searching the dark in the cobblestoned compound beyond. As if satisfied, he turned back for her. But the salt-tinged breeze had revived her. She shoved past him and sprinted down the stairs. There was a guardhouse at the condominium entry gate! If she could only make it there, she would be safe.

Behind her, she heard his sprinting footfall on the flagstone steps. She got no further than the lush jungle-landscaped path before her captor tackled her and she went sprawling. All hope went out of her. Almost passively, she let him roll her over to straddle her. Tears spilled out of the corners of her eyes. Expecting pain—or worse, death—she flinched when he raised his hand.

But his fingers only brushed away her tears. "I have to give you high marks for determination, lady."

Mutely, her heart thudding, she gazed up at him. In the leaf-dappled moonlight, she could see that he was in his late thirties and rather handsome in a roguish sort of way. Shaggy golden brown hair grew past his nape. Dark blue eyes were flanked by weather lines. Strong angles marked his high forehead, cheekbones and square jaw. His beard-stubbled face emphasized the mobile mouth that seemed ready to smile at the slightest provocation.

"Let me go," she begged, her words indecipherable behind the gag.

"*¿Quién es?*" a man's voice called out—the voice of the night guard who patrolled the low, rambling wall fronting the beach.

Her renewed attempts at screaming produced only muffled grunts. The satin pillow case gagging her tasted wretched, and she began choking instead. With a curse, her captor swooped her bodily over his shoulder. With every loping step he took, her head banged against his back.

"Lady, it's no wonder...you're unmarried," he grunted. "What man...in his right mind...damn!" he mumbled. "My toe!"

From her peculiar viewpoint, she could make out the mangrove root on which he had stubbed his foot. Good! she thought.

Her head bobbled as he took off running again, past a gurgling fountain and deeper into the garden. Behind them, the guard thrashed through the artistically planted undergrowth. She heard her abductor chuckle and wanted to echo his earlier curse. Her stomach jolted with each bounce. Then, all at once, she could feel the sultry breeze off the Pacific. He had circled back to the gate of the condominium wall that fronted the sloping beach. With her added weight, his feet sank in the sand, but that didn't slow him. Nevertheless, she could hear his labored breathing.

She was being kidnapped! Really kidnapped!

No one would ever believe it. Not Mary or Carol or Lana or any of the other floor nurses who worked under her. Would she even live to return and tell about it? Fear sapped the last of her strength. She could only watch the single trail of footprints that her kidnapper left on the wet beach. All at once, he halted.

"Don't struggle," he growled, "or you'll only hurt yourself."

Nelli understood his warning when she realized he was putting her into a rowboat. The bench smacked hard against her fanny and she let out a grunted "Umph!"

As he pushed the rowboat out into the surf, she watched the play of the muscles in his arms and shoulders with unwilling admiration. After he swung aboard, he paused to strip off her gag and unknot her wrists. She tensed to spring, and he said, "I wouldn't try it, Nelli Walzchak. I'm stronger than you."

At the sound of her name, she froze, her hands gripping the splintery slat of the bench seat. What else did he know about her?

He began rowing rapidly, his arms strained against the building waves. The moonlight gave the flickering illusion of an Atlas come to life. Suddenly the bow of the boat tilted precariously, and she was flung ignominiously face forward into his lap.

"Don't move!" he barked and rowed even more furiously.

For interminable moments the little boat rode the crest of a wave; its roar filled her ears. Seawater poured into the skiff, drenching her, and she knew their fate depended on her abductor's nautical skill. On her knees in half a foot of water, she wrapped her arms around his waist and buried her face against his stomach. With each lurch of the rowboat, she gasped. Those deep inhalations filled her with the odor of his wet skin—salt and sweat and an unnerving, wholly male smell.

She was accustomed to the sight of the male body, from strapping campus jocks in for physicals to bedridden old men nearing the end of their days, and she was used to viewing all of them with detachment. In earning her reputation as a highly professional nurse, she'd had to teach herself to deal clinically with people, to avoid emotional attachments. She supposed that was the reason she had so little in the way of a personal life: she never even dated.

But she was *not* repressed the way this...this pirate claimed!

Was she?

What was it Mary had said when urging her to use the two-week time share she herself couldn't. *You never set foot outside your door at home, but you'd damn well better down in Bahia Escondida!*

Well, she had certainly set foot outside the condominium. But she appeared to be going much farther than any of the other nurses could have envisioned. Straight to Davy Jones's locker if the violent pitching of the rowboat was any indication. She could feel the muscles in her abductor's back knotting and swelling and shifting with his efforts.

Suddenly the bow of the skiff reared like a horse pawing the air, then plunged. She screamed and clutched her kidnapper. At the bottom of the trough, it was as if a deafening silence reigned. Like the eye of the hurricane, she thought. Then the water came crashing down over them. Miraculously the little boat shot free, as though squirted from a water gun. After a long moment, she lifted her head and peered around cautiously. Incredibly, moonlight silvered a peaceful, placid sea. Beyond, white-foamed waves lapped the beach.

"You were concerned?" the man asked, grinning cheerfully down at her.

Embarrassed at her worshipful position, she scrambled back to the bench. "And you weren't?" she gritted.

He resumed rowing. "Ocean's always like that with a full moon. Then again, having a woman's head buried in my lap detracted somewhat from my usual skills."

"Oh, I had imagined that someone who knew all about a woman's fantasies would be accustomed to that sort of thing."

"There. You brought it up again." His wide mouth beckoned her to an odd restlessness, just as the moonlight was doing. "I think you have a latent obsession with the subject of ravishment."

"Me?" She realized he was baiting her. So, hiding behind a facade of bravado, she demanded, "Where are you taking me?"

He nodded off to his left. "There. To the *Seasiren*."

Nelli peered in that direction. Without her glasses, she was hopelessly nearsighted, but by squinting she could make out a cabin cruiser anchored in the bay. At that moment all she could think was that it looked like a ghost ship.

When she looked back at her companion, he was staring at her with fascination. She glanced down and at once understood why. Her wet pajamas were clinging suggestively to her breasts and hips, the thin cotton material revealing the dusky rings at the tips of her breasts.

Immediately she crossed her arms defensively in front of herself. "What do you want from me?" she breathed.

He looked at her with fierce, burning eyes. "*Dios mio*, are you not woman enough to guess?"

Chapter Two

Nelli's shivering had a rippling effect. It began in her feet, which were bare on the cabin planking, and continued up her legs, then spread through her chilled torso to her fingertips. She felt as if even her hair had goose bumps.

She wrapped her arms around herself, all the while studying her "cell" by lamplight. The cabin was in a state of predilapidation. The stove was crusted with built-up soot, the small refrigerator dented, the table scarred and its leather-cushioned seats cracked.

In racks behind the leather seats were charts, reference guides and what looked to her uneducated guess like a sextant.

Only when she realized that her drenched pajamas had dripped a puddle at her feet did she leave the companionway and venture further inside. Dry. She had to get dry. And she had to find something that covered her better. Quickly—before her abductor, who was busy above deck at the moment, setting course, came below.

The overhead cabinets produced no towels. A portal off to her left caught her attention, and she peeked through at a wall-to-wall bed. Immediately she backed away—right into her captor. With a gasp, she whirled around. He caught her shoulders.

"You had better get out of those wet pajamas."

"I'm—I'm all right."

That scythe of a grin curved his lips. "You're trembling."

"They'll miss me."

The cabin lamps were brighter than the moonlight, and revealed her abductor for the first time. Sun-and-salt-bleached jeans had been cut off in ragged slashes at midthigh, exposing long legs roped with muscles. His skin was deeply tanned to the color of teak—his face, his arms, his legs, his chest. Against that tanned skin, his eyes seemed an even deeper blue. They mocked her. "Who'll miss you, Nurse Walzchak? No one. At least, not for another week."

"A week?" She ignored the fear her croaking voice betrayed. She wasn't sure if she was horrified that he knew the exact length of time she had remaining at Bahia Escondida or pleased that her abduction might last no longer than a week. After all, she had heard of women held captive for years.

"After that, it'll be too late for anyone to do anything."

"Oh, God!" she gasped. She swayed on her feet, telling herself that no doubt the rocking boat had contributed to her sudden imbalance. She braced her hand on the wall, waiting to find her sea legs. They didn't come. Surely she wasn't going to collapse. She had never been the sort to faint.

But then, neither had she ever been kidnapped in the middle of the night by a man who lacked only a gold earring in order to pass for a pirate.

He reached past her, grabbed the top sheet from the bed and thrust it into her arms. "Take your pajamas off. In there." He pointed behind her to a narrow door that she had missed in her reconnoitering.

The cubicle she entered was a narrow bathroom, barely large enough for a sink and a head that did double duty as a shower stool. When she glimpsed her face in the mirror, she gasped. Her normally pale complexion was chalk white, and her hair was plastered to her face and neck. What man would find her appealing enough to kidnap?

A pervert.

Or an idiot.

But her abductor didn't seem to be either—yet.

She stayed in the bathroom as long as she could, but fear of him coming in after her, trapping her in the confining space, finally drove her out. With the sheet wrapped around her sarong-style, she crept outside. She almost sagged in relief on finding that he was still up top.

"Bring me a beer from the refrigerator, would you?" he called from above.

She spun around and, with a thudding heart, stared up through the darkened companionway. She didn't want to go up there, but if she didn't take him the beer, he'd come down. And that would be worse. The bed was here. Waiting.

The refrigerator was crammed with cans of Mexican beer. She grabbed one and, drawing a steadying breath, climbed the stairs to emerge on deck. The sea breeze warmed her skin and teased her hair. In the night-shrouded darkness, her eyes adjusted. Stars studded the sky, and the moon rolled out a silver carpet across the water. Her gaze found him, sitting at the helm.

Silently, resentfully, she passed him the chilled can. His dark eyes glanced at her questioningly. "You don't want one?"

She summoned anger to fuel her courage. "Your refrigerator could stand to be stocked with some *real* food, you realize."

He shrugged. "So could my wallet." He nodded at the cushioned bench across from him. "Have a seat."

She sat tensely on the edge of the worn cushion and tried vainly to comb her snarled hair with her fingers. He popped the tab and took a deep draught. She waited, but he said nothing. There was only the gentle swirl of water against the hull and the low purr of the engine. Occasionally he sipped from the can as he kept the boat on course.

What course?

She shifted uneasily. "Where are you taking me?"

He finished off the can before answering. "Twenty-five miles up the coast. To a little cove where my partner and I have our base."

She smothered a groan. *Two* men! "I think I'll have that beer," she squeaked.

His grin was utterly charming. "Careful, it'll take some of the starch out of your uniform."

"What?"

"Bring me another one while you're at it, would you?"

Down below, Nelli popped a beer tab and chugalugged its contents. Her tongue practically rolled up like a window shade. "What a god-awful taste!" she wheezed. But a pleasant sensation followed. She collected another can of beer and started back up the companionway.

The manner in which he eyed her as she walked toward him made her wish she did have her uniform on. Uniforms always put distance between people. Uniforms bestowed authority. Wrapped in the sheet, she felt like Dorothy Lamour.

And he looked like Errol Flynn in *Captain Blood*.

He took the can from her, and she nearly flinched when their fingers touched. Electricity. How could static electricity arc like that when the very air was heavy with water vapor?

When his fist abruptly smashed his empty beer can, she did flinch. "Believe me," she managed to say frostily, "a show of strength isn't necessary."

His grin thinned to a razor slash. "Not a show of strength. Just a habit leftover from Nam. All beer or soft drink cans had to be crushed—or else the Cong would buy them from the local kids and use them as casings for hand grenades."

Now she knew she was in trouble, dealing with a derelict of the Vietnam war. Many such vets had come and gone in the emergency room. Warrior kings without a kingdom.

"Put your analysis at rest," he drawled, as if reading her mind. "I'm not planning on running amok."

She looked away from his jewel-blue eyes to take a fortifying swallow of her beer, then bravely pointed out, "You just did. Kidnapping me."

"Last resort. I tried regular channels. Appealing to the guard at the front gate. Telephoning the manager at the registration desk. No way they'd consider letting a 'vagrant' through to you."

Her gaze ricocheted back to him. "You can't really believe they'd give you permission to walk right in and commandeer a woman for seduction?" Her dismay was underlaid with relief, however; his words implied that his intentions might not be so bad.

His grin actually nicked a dimple below each of his broad cheekbones. "There you go, Nelli. What a ridiculous thought. Especially coming from a shrinking old maid. I think I—"

"I am not a shrinking old maid!"

His gaze raked over her, moving from her feet—her toes bare of polish—up along her sheet-molded torso, to settle on the upper curves of her breasts, just where the sheet's knotted ends dipped dangerously low. She fought an urge to yank the sheet up to her chin.

"Well, maybe not an old maid exactly," he conceded and took another swallow, never taking his eyes off her.

His half-lowered lids clearly suggested that he was inventorying her assets. And she knew from experience that she would come up on the debit side. She had never been one of those long-stemmed American beauties. Oh, she was tall, all right, but thin and gangly, especially as a child. A champagne blonde, this man had called her. But the mirror said she was more dishwater than champagne.

"I think," he continued, his head canted as he perused her, "that I will investigate this hang-up you have with passion—"

"That *I* have—"

"—after you take care of Mario."

She blinked. "Mario?"

"My partner."

"How am I suppose to, er, take care of this Mario?"

"Why, cure him, of course. That's why I came after you." He squashed the second beer can in one hand with a grinding sound. "Mario hit his head the day before yesterday on one of the deck cleats. Later that day he said he had a headache. Then he began complaining of chills and fever. When he became semiconscious—you know, going in and out of it—I was afraid to move him and instead high-tailed it down the coast to Bahia Escondida for help."

She couldn't help it. She felt like crying. She couldn't remember ever feeling so deflated. Not that being snatched from her condo and forced to board this derelict of a boat was anywhere close to a romantic interlude. It was just that for once there had been the will-o'-the-wisp of a promise. Unsummoned, the idle hopes and secret, burning tears of times past flooded her memories.

Junior high had been bad enough. No boy had given her a second glance until the ninth grade, when the quarterback with the heartbreaking looks paused to talk to her outside geometry class one morning. For a week he had done that, and for a week her dreams had been ecstasy. Then, by Friday, he had apparently worked up enough nerve to ask her if he could cheat off her paper in the upcoming mid-year exam. Despite her qualms, she had acceded. After that exam, he never talked to her again.

High school had been even more lonely. The ringing telephone never signaled a male voice asking for her. Her college years had at last yielded a boyfriend. A steady one who wanted to stay steady, to see her on a steady basis and his own terms, when there wasn't anything going on with the guys. When she finally realized that there would never be anything permanent with Tim—and that she was just prolonging her pain—she gathered her courage and ended the relationship.

Her first years in nursing had been the worse. Her world had consisted mostly of either doctors or pa-

tients. Too often the interns had wanted nothing more
than quick gratification from the nurses, and the male
patients had never seen her as a woman but had been
infatuated only with her profession—the healing, be-
nevolent nurse.

Her frustration overrode her relief that she had been
abducted for nothing more than her professional
skills. She hurled her half-full can at the man and
missed by a yard. "Why you skid-row beachcomber!
You castaway surf bum. You panhandling expatriate.
You—"

"Now just a minute, Nelli," he said, springing from
his seat to grab her flailing fist. "What happened to
your Hippocratic oath? Aren't you supposed to swear
to help—"

Tears clouded her already dim vision. "I didn't take
any damned oath!" She swung at his chest with her
other fist, and he coughed out an *oooff* sound.

"I'm not a life-support system you just roll into a
room and plug in!" she cried. "I'm a human being. A
person with feelings. A woman with needs. A—"

She broke off, aghast at herself. How had that last
part ever slipped out?

His mouth curved. "Ahh, she does live and breath
and talk—and desire." He captured her other wrist
and drew her body flush against his length. "Your
mouth is puckered in the most delectable O," he
murmured softly against her lips. "As if you're beg-
ging to be kissed. Come on, Nelli. I told you I won't
hurt you. I just need you to help Mario. Relax." He

brushed his lips back and forth over hers. "I'm not asking you to surrender your precious virginity. Just trade kisses. Why resist something so pleasurable—and harmless, at that?"

"Who are you?" she breathed.

He nuzzled her ear. "Daniel O'Shay. Late of the U.S. Special Warfare School, Military Assistance Command, Team 84, Ninth Infantry Division. A good man and true. Well, that last part may be a little tarnished, but what the hell."

With that decisive statement, he captured her mouth. It was a raiding kiss—hard and firm and thorough. It swept over her lips as if he were searching for land mines. Those land mines went off inside her instead, jarring her to the core, exploding behind her eyes in glorious colors, like fireworks. His teeth nipped her lips until they parted for his plundering tongue. It filled her and she felt as if she were overflowing, swollen to ripeness. Felt as if honey and warmed rum were mingling in her veins. Felt hot and weak and dizzy.

"Don't just be a taker, Nelli," he muttered in a feverish voice. "Kiss me back."

"Yes . . . yes," she sighed. She stood on tiptoe, her arms sliding up over his massive shoulders and around his neck. Her mouth parted over his, and daringly she slipped her tongue between his lips, then hesitantly touched the tip of his tongue. Such a small act to work such riotous emotions. She felt . . . rapturous. She was certain her brain's pleasure center was going haywire.

Such joy! She wanted to sing; she wanted to laugh; she wanted to faint; she wanted . . . she wanted more! She didn't want it to end. Ever!

Her fingers dug into his shoulders as his tongue took over. It played with hers, flicked and teased and conquered. His hands left her back to slide slowly downward, as if reveling in every inch of her—past her waist, over her hips, and at last cupping her buttocks to guide that feminine part of her to its male counterpart. The honey and heated rum swirled and settled low, heavy, needing release.

"Am I being . . . ravished?" she whispered breathlessly against his throat. He smelled as fresh as the sea.

He laughed, a pleasant, husky male sound that made her sharply realize how absent it had been in her life. His roughened hand snagged in her now-dry hair as he stroked its length, which cascaded well past her shoulder blades. "Not yet, Nelli. Not completely. And if I don't tend to the wheel," he said, setting her from him, "we may well end up as shark bait."

With a pang, she watched him turn his attention back to navigating. She felt flustered and embarrassed. And totally unsure of herself—a condition she had never experienced as head floor nurse. *Knowledgeable Miss Walzchak. Competent Miss Walzchak. Efficient Miss Walzchak.*

Poor Miss Walzchak.

Vainly she tried to get control of her ragged breathing. All this was just the magic of a full moon, a shimmering sea, a tropical night. By daylight, she would revert back to her decorous Dr. Jeckyll.

"Tell me more about your partner. Mario." She was relieved that her voice held its usual, professional tone—except she'd never noted its stringent quality before. "Where did he hit his head? Any bleeding?"

"Of course. The deck cleat left a nasty gash that—"

"No. I mean bleeding from the mouth or ears. Did you check to see if his eyes were dilated?"

"No, nothing like that. And yes, I checked his eyes." Dan shoved his hand through his thick, tousled hair. "I've seen men shell-shocked in Nam, punctured like a sieve by bullets, but Mario is just a kid. Only eleven."

"Eleven?" she echoed. "I thought you said he was your partner."

He flicked her a glance. "He is. For over two years now. Mario is a street kid. No one wants him. Nevertheless, he always sports a cheerful grin. Whenever I'd put into Bahia Escondida for refueling, he'd be there ahead of the other urchins, offering to watch the rowboat, volunteering information about the best buy on beer...local gossip...world events that had transpired between my visits. The kid's bright, I tell you. And no slouch when it comes to work."

Her eyes narrowed. "What kind of work?"

He slid her a roguish look. "Diving for sunken treasure."

"You're kidding." She saw his mouth flatten. "No, I don't suppose you are."

He said nothing.

"Why, the chances of finding sunken treasure are—"

"A man by the name of Mel Fisher did it a few years ago." Dan gave the wheel a spin. "Located a three-hundred-year-old Spanish galleon, off the coast of Key West."

"—one in a thousand. One in a million, even."

He shrugged. "Doesn't matter. I'm not going anywhere, so I might as well opt for that—" his voice mimicked hers "—'one in a million' chance."

"An adventurer. A dropout." Her withering tone said everything.

His enthusiastic tone said everything back. "Got my eye on a spot no more than fifty or sixty feet deep. I did a lot of research at the Benjamin Franklin Library in Mexico City. Went through archives. Read bills of lading. The galleon I'm looking for carried silver bullion. Think of it, Nelli! Chests full!"

Curiosity got the best of her. "How do you support yourself meanwhile?"

"There's an offshore coral reef brimming with Technicolor marine life. I gather the coral, and Mario strings necklaces that we sell in Bahia Escondida."

"Why me? Surely Bahia Escondida has a doctor!"

"Only the *farmacia* common to every *pueblecita*. The kind of place that also carries chips and colas and lipstick. Oh, when the resort was being built last year, the construction company brought in its doctor for the workmen. And I understand Posada Tangolunda is supposed to supply a house doctor, but Father Hidalgo informed me that the man has been delayed.''

"And that's when Father Hidalgo suggested abducting me as a substitute?''

"Hell, no. If Father Hidalgo had been available, he could have summoned you for me. His word holds weight in Bahia Escondida. But he's off somewhere in the mountains giving the last rites to someone. The locals told me about your arrival, and since I didn't know when Father Hidalgo would be back, I was desperate.''

"And resorted to kidnapping.''

He flashed her a sheepish look. "Mario's sick. I didn't know what else to do.''

"Well, your description's given me a clue to his condition,'' she said crisply. "But I'll need to see him, of course.''

"We should be there in another thirty minutes or so. You know, Nelli, you're really being a good sport about all this, everything considered.''

She gave him a jaundiced look. "Do I have a choice?''

"Sure. We all have choices. You chose to come to Bahia Escondida, didn't you?''

"Not exactly.'' She pursed her lips. "You might say I was coerced.''

He raised a brow with the suggestive look of a demon.

"All right, maybe not coerced. But I was tired of being chided by my friends about not getting out more. One of my nurses had a two-week time-share down here, but she was going to have to forfeit at the last moment because of a family wedding. She and the other nurses practically challenged me to come."

Dan surprised her by leaning over and dropping a kiss on her lips. "See what you would have missed if you had refused? The adventure of a lifetime!"

The moonlight gilded his angular face, and Nelli had to remind herself that gilt was nothing more than an illusion. And he was nothing more than an adventurer.

And this was her adventure.

She groaned inwardly.

Chapter Three

As Nelli's plane had banked on its final approach to the tiny Bahia Escondida airport, she had glimpsed spoon-shaped bays, strung like emeralds and sapphires along Yucatan's eastern coastline.

The cove Dan put into at dawn was much like those she had spotted from the air. See-through water tumbled against a crescent of sparkling sandy beach that was surrounded by jet-black and hunter green jagged rock and thick jungle. The turquoise waves washed her image of an idyllic tropical setting, the Caribbean flowing eternally over shifting sandbars into palm-ringed lagoons.

Dan navigated between the rock outcroppings, which were jutting through the surface of the crystal water, and tied up at a rickety dock that tested Nelli's trust in do-it-yourself carpentry. So did the palm-and-corrugated-tin house she glimpsed among the coconut palms. The word "seedy" came to mind. Yes, this would certainly be an interesting topic for the Nurses' Lounge.

"Not quite your San Diego Yacht Club," he commented jauntily, taking her elbow as she hung back. He propelled more than assisted her along the dock's rotten planking. "But then, the dues here are relatively low."

"And the waiting list is short, I'd imagine." She maintained her poise by avoiding eye contact with him.

When they reached the beach, she jerked her elbow from his grasp and trod across the wet sand on her own. Her pride was still lacerated. She had made a fool of herself in the past hour. And Dignity, with a capital *D*, was all she had left right now.

Actually the hut was more substantial—and larger—than it had initially appeared, much like the *palapa* restaurants dotting the condominium's beach. Bamboo blinds draped the hut's front porch, which was overrun with purple bougainvillea and frangipani.

Inside, the shade was a pleasant relief from the already-hot morning sun. Once her eyes focused, she was mildly surprised by the quality of the furniture in the main room. Admittedly the pieces appeared to have seen better days, but she had expected a Gauguinish South Seas tableau—hammock, reed floor matting and a brightly plumaged parrot. Instead well-built mahogany and rattan furniture, along with a lovely hand-woven rug, graced the main room.

Dan caught her assessing gaze and said, "I raided the furniture from an abandoned banana plantation back in the hills. Mario's in the rear bedroom."

She followed him past one bedroom and into another where a boy, thin and drawn, lay rigid on a narrow bed. The sheet covering him, she observed with encouragement, appeared clean though wash worn. An adhesive bandage was neatly wrapped around his dark-thatched little head. His skin, which was coppery like an Indian's rather than Dan's bronzed tan, had a yellowish undertone.

The boy didn't awaken at their approach so Nelli bent over him, calling softly, "Mario?" She didn't expect him to answer, but she wanted to test his reflexes. His lids didn't flutter, nor did the little knotted hand she touched move in response. She noted that his skin was slightly feverish.

She folded back the sheet and took one of Mario's brown legs, which was poking like a broomstick out from his oversized khaki shorts.

"What are you doing?" Dan asked.

"Something I saw a doctor do at Kansas General Hospital," she said as she flexed the boy's thigh at a right angle to his abdomen, keeping the knee bent.

"Don't you want to see his wound?"

She shook her head. "This may give us the answer to his illness, if it's what I suspect. I'm looking for what's called Kernig's sign." When she extended the leg fully, the boy winced, and she could feel the slight spasm of the hamstring muscles.

Maintaining a neutral expression, she straightened. "Of course, pathology reports would be a great assistance, but if I were to hazard a guess, I'd say that tubercle bacilli entered the meninges through a compound skull fracture—"

"In simple language, doc," he snapped. A muscle ticked in his jaw, and his eyes held grim shadows.

She sighed. "That's just the trouble. I'm no doctor. But from the signs, it looks like bacterial meningitis. Fortunately, the degree of inflammatory reaction isn't too severe—subacute, I'd say."

She saw his brows level over glowering eyes and quickly added, "That means fewer complications, although the illness is more prolonged and relapses are apt to occur. That is, assuming Mario gets immediate treatment."

"What kind of treatment?"

"Well, penicillin, mainly. But without a doctor's prescrip—"

"You don't need one here in Mexico."

"That *farmacia* at Bahia Escondida that you mentioned, could you get—"

"Whatever you need, I'll get it."

With unhesitating precision she rattled off what she would require: penicillin, syringes and hypodermic needles.

"I'll be back in three hours, tops," he promised.

As he strode from the room, her gaze followed his lean, superbly conditioned body. He moved with the assurance of a man bred for wide open spaces, a man in touch with both the earth and the sea.

Wistfully she turned her full attention back to the boy and deftly caught her tangled hair up into a severe knot at her nape. Such grooming was a given that made her feel professional and businesslike, though she honestly couldn't say she would perform her job any less well if she did not wear her hair in that practical style.

Aspirin, alcohol, cool compresses—with those she could begin to work immediately. She found them where Dan had indicated, in a cheap aluminum hutch in a make-do kitchen that wasn't in much better condition than the cabin cruiser's deteriorating galley.

Taking a mismatched chair from a rickety kitchen table, she positioned it next to Mario's bed and began bathing his skin with an alcohol-soaked washcloth. Periodically she checked his pulse, watching for any change in his responses.

For years, ever since becoming head floor nurse, she had been tied up in the bureaucratic paperwork that came with an administrative desk. And while she was almost sinfully proud of her performance as an administrator, and enjoyed making the requisite—and vital—daily decisions, she missed the close patient contact. In fact she had forgotten just how much she missed it.

Since her stay looked as if it would be a prolonged one, she took advantage of a lull in her vigil and wandered into Dan's bedroom to search for something more adequate to wear than a bed sheet. Immediately the double bed snagged her gaze. It was mussed, exhibiting the signs of a man who had sprawled in sleep across its width, a man who had slept restlessly and risen anxiously.

The room had no closets, but a battered chest of drawers that in a strange way matched his battered double bed contained a cache of T-shirts. The first one she found was faded black and looked long enough to fall well below her hips, hitting at midthigh.

She was wearing it when he returned shortly before noon with the medical supplies. Feeling shy in her abbreviated outfit, she forced herself to lift her eyes to his. Under the impact of his dark, passionate gaze, hot blood surged painfully into her cheeks. Scandalizing images of his bed and what it would be like to share it with him tantalized her prim and proper thoughts, which heretofore had been held in obedient restraint.

His tanned, handsome face, with its flashing eyes, strong chin and mocking mouth, did strange things to her; made her weak, made her giddy. His gaze traveled the length of her bare legs. "In that garb," he said, his voice husky, "you could revolutionize the nurses' uniform industry."

She swallowed hard. Was this what she had missed out on in high school and college—the thrilling byplay, the flirting, the seductive exchange of glances that made you feel very much a woman? "You were able to get everything?"

"I like your hair better down around your shoulders."

She ignored his charming smile. "The penicillin, the syringes, the—"

He produced a brown paper-wrapped package. "Everything." His eyes, glinting with amusement, roamed to her bound hair. "Including a tooth-brush—and a hairbrush."

She felt foolishly pleased. "My first gift from a man," she murmured, taking the package.

"Hey, don't go getting ideas." His mouth creased into an inverted sickle. "My mistress is the sea and all that."

Instantly she regretted her revealing statement. "Who said anything about being your mistress? I merely said—"

"I know what you said." His eyes lowered to that familiar half-mast that focused his gaze solely on her, and his lips curled into a cocky smile. "And I know what you're thinking."

"I am not!" She whirled away, with his low, silky laughter following her.

She stalked toward Mario's bedroom, highly aware of the big man trailing close on her heels. "How long before we'll see results?" he asked as she mechanically prepared the injection.

"Within twenty-four hours, hopefully." Nelli turned the small vial upside down. She was all business now, so totally dedicated to the task at hand that she was unaware of Dan leaving the room.

A short time later the smell of coffee reached her and lured her into the kitchen. The table had been set with two plates filled with slices of papaya, avocado, mango and bananas.

"Thought you might be hungry," he said with a negligent glance at her as he passed her a coffee cup.

She seated herself at one of the wobbly chairs. "I'm famished. It's been hours since I last ate." She made the mistake of swallowing the coffee before taking a tasting sip. She coughed and rolled her eyes.

"Strong enough to straighten your hair, isn't it?" he said cheerfully.

"Yes, indeed," she rasped. She cleared her throat and asked, "The army teach you to make coffee?"

He settled into eating with a gusto that fascinated her. "The army taught me a lot of things, but that wasn't one of them."

"How long were you in Vietnam?"

He paused and fixed her with a hard look. "Long enough that I began to ask myself what I was doing over there. I asked myself how many more times could I kill before I reached the point where I couldn't stop."

Unable to say anything, she touched the back of his hand, then quickly removed her fingers. The crisp hair matting his skin reminded her of how potent his masculinity was.

He took a swallow of his coffee, but it didn't ease the raw tone in his voice. "The week before my tour of duty was up, I somehow passed into the outer limits of human anguish. With no sweat, I put down my M-16 and walked away. I never found out if I was listed as AWOL or MIA. I didn't care. Still don't."

She kept her voice neutral. "You've never had the desire to rejoin society?"

That saber curve returned to his lips. "The rat race? A job and wife that require an accounting of my time? No, thank you."

His offhandedness annoyed her. "I'd say you were irresponsible."

"I'd say you were uptight."

"I think I'd better go back and sit with Mario."

"Fine. I've got repairs to make on the boat."

But they both sat glaring at each other until the hollow squawk of a heron broke the deadlock. She returned to Mario, where she administered the penicillin every three hours. In between she dozed, unable to keep her eyes open after having had only a few hours sleep. Occasionally she walked out onto the veranda, just to keep alert, she told herself. But her gaze always strayed to the turquoise waters and the cabin cruiser floating at the dock. Sometimes the clang of a hammer from the boat broke the peace of the late afternoon.

Dusk thinned the pencils of sunlight that were shafting through Mario's window. Her lids grew heavy. Dan found her asleep, her head cradled in her folded arms on Mario's bedside. She stirred as Dan scooped her up against his chest and strode out of the room.

Slowly her eyes drifted open, and she stared up at the strong, angular face above hers. "What are you doing?" she whispered.

"Taking you to bed."

Her heart caught in her throat. She couldn't let him discover how uptight she really was. A fiasco of monumental proportions loomed in her mind. She shook her head. "No."

"Yes. I'm tired, too."

Why should she feel disappointment? Why didn't she feel sheer relief?

Gently, as though he held an infant, he lowered her onto his double bed. He stood over her for a moment, watching her with sleepy blue eyes, tall, tanned, raffish-looking without his shirt and only his cutoffs to remind her that he wasn't some Adam returned to Eden. Then, as if exhausted, he collapsed beside her. The mattress sagged with his weight, and she rolled against him. She stiffened, afraid to move. For several seconds she thought he had instantly gone to sleep.

But then he gathered her in one arm, saying drowsily, almost as if in regret, "Nelli, you're way too vulnerable."

She searched for the truth in her mind, thought about asking him what else he saw in her, then realized he was already asleep and snoring softly.

A hand was violently shaking her awake. She stirred, squinted one eye, focused on the man sitting beside her and, with a groan, remembered her abduction.

"Squall coming!" he shouted.

She put her hand to her temple, rubbing it. The curdled gray light of predawn filled the room. She couldn't have gotten more than a couple of hours' sleep at the most. "You don't have to shout."

Then she realized that he did. The window shutters were banging back and forth in a frenzy. Instantly she snapped alert, prepared for whatever emergency was looming. Her gaze sought his, which was anything but sleepy. She imagined him leading a jungle patrol in Vietnam—tense, vigilant, resourceful. "Are we in danger?"

"Not unless it's in the forefront of a hurricane."

"December is a little late in the year, isn't it?"

His hand clamped on her wrist, dragging her bodily from the bed. "Lady, this is the Yucatan Peninsula. Anything can happen."

She tugged her hand away and grabbed the clapping shutters in a fruitless attempt to latch them.

"Later," he told her, recapturing her wrist. "The *Sea-siren* first!"

"Mario's room!" she said.

"Already secured. Let's go."

Outside, black swirling clouds boiled almost low enough to touch. The wind roared in her ears and unraveled the knot of hair at her nape. Palm leaves whipped like windmill blades, and breakers licked at the rickety pier with greedy tongues.

As they started across the shifting, swaying wharf, she clutched at Dan's arm and choked back an outcry of fear. They could easily be swept away by one of the waves. Water sprayed them as the cabin cruiser bucked and tossed on the smashing breakers.

Only a frayed rope secured the boat to the wharf piling—and even that snapped as they watched.

"Wait!" he yelled at her against the wind.

He moved a slight distance away, and she staggered with the sudden buffeting of the wind. She leaned forward against its onslaught, while keeping her worried gaze clamped on him. After backing up, he took several running steps and leaped across the widening strip of water that separated the boat from dock. An impossible feat. She squinched her eyes. When next she looked, he was hanging over the side, clinging to the foredeck safety rail as the boat backed away even further. It reared and dipped, and at one point his thighs were all but submerged by the sea.

Her lungs suspended operation while, muscles straining, he hauled himself aboard. When he reached the helm he revved up the engine, and the cabin cruiser, its bilge pump heaving, chugged back toward the dock. For a split second she thought he was going to plow through the wharf right over her, but she held her ground. At the last second he shut the engine down. He vanished below deck and reappeared with a coil of rope that he quickly knotted around a deck cleat.

"Catch!" he called.

Without taking time to think, she lunged to grab the rope's tail end and almost toppled into the sea. Somehow, despite the unexpectedly heavy weight of the rope, she kept her precarious balance. Water was already spilling over the dock and swishing around her instep. The cabin cruiser yanked away rebelliously, but she held fast, feeling every muscle in her arms and shoulders protest at the sudden exertion.

"The piling," he shouted, his hands positioned megaphone style, but it was all she could do to hold on.

With another leap, he bridged the distance from boat to dock and set about quickly mooring the cabin cruiser. Without having to be told, she swung aboard and hurried below to batten down all the hatches. Dan found her down there and hauled her topside. "Let's get the hell out of here!" he yelled.

Rain began to pelt them like little needles. Her water-drenched hair whipped across her face so she was running blindly, with only his hand at her arm to guide her. The wind fought them all the way. Finally Dan pulled her up under the veranda. The thatched roofing sounded as if it were going to be ripped away, and the screen door slammed crazily in distress.

He backed her against the side of the hut, his body protecting hers from the raging elements. Cold and afraid, she was shivering violently. Her hair skimmed the edge of his jaw, and he caught the plastered strands and pushed them behind her ear. An exhilaration that came from shared danger and possible death triggered raw emotions in both of them. His mouth dragged over her lips brutally, back and forth. She felt an unbearable excitement. Pressed hard by his body, she could feel the detail of him, the warm skin, the solid motif of muscle and bone. She could easily get drunk on his kisses and caressing hands.

"You're incredible," he told her, his voice thick with arousal.

"Incredible?" She was dazed by the wrath of the elements and his virile power.

"Yeah. You know, courageous. You don't panic. Dependable."

Nelli sobered instantly. Dan watched her retreat inside the hut. She fascinated him. Everything about her, from the puritanical simplicity of her hairstyle to the enchanting upcurve of her rare, elusive smile.

With a little mental exercise, his mind's practiced eye conjured up her creamy flesh, her brown satin brows and lashes, her delicious jasmine-colored lips, the smears of deep rose rimming her cheekbones. Like a taproot, a new emotion reached down to his dormant soul—an emotion that was incomprehensible and strangely disturbing.

He knew he wanted this woman, but beyond that thought he would not let himself venture. Introspection might reveal an undercurrent of his character that he would rather ignore.

Chapter Four

All day the wind blustered, and the storm's eerie light ionized the inside of the hut. For the most part, Nelli hovered at Mario's bedside. The boy was regaining consciousness for longer periods of time, but he was weak, barely even cognizant of her presence.

Wearing a preoccupied scowl, Dan wandered in and out of the bedroom. Once, when Mario was awake, Dan placed his large, weather-tanned hand on the boy's forehead and asked in a low, soothing voice, "How are you, partner?"

Mario managed to make an okay sign with his thumb and forefinger.

Dan prowled the room some more; then, after Mario's long-lashed lids drifted closed again, he padded off into the other room. It was obvious that Mario's illness had upset him to the soul, and the confining storm made him restless. She had the impression that he'd rather be out battling the wind and waves.

She was accustomed to waiting, but she wasn't accustomed to the intense presence of a man. Hospitals and illness tended to dilute masculinity's essence, alter the male sex into an androgynous strain. But Dan wouldn't—and couldn't—be ignored. He simply pervaded the hut.

It was ridiculous, but she felt tiny sparks all over her skin. Even with him in the other room—or out on the veranda, monitoring his boat and the storm—she was captivated by his image. The wide mouth with its pagan smile...his deep blue eyes that harbored secret fires...his unexpected bursts of laughter...but most of all, his lean, hard body with every cell meant for the purpose of being a man.

For a while she toyed with Mario's cigar boxes of beads, coral and shells with which he made necklaces. Then, toward late afternoon, she glanced up to find Dan leaning indolently against the doorjamb, arms folded, watching her.

"Hungry?"

She shook her head. "Not really."

"Coffee?"

She raised her eyes to the ceiling.

His bright, humorous eyes drew her gaze. "That bad, huh?"

She laughed. "Allow me to fix the coffee this time, all right?"

He stood aside and, with a sweeping hand, ushered the way for her. He showed her how to operate the gas burners on the recalcitrant portable stove, then settled back in one of the mismatched chairs and, legs stretched out and arms locked behind his head, observed her as she scooped out the coffee grounds. His smile was faintly amused.

The storm howled outside, but within, the serene light of the kerosene lantern cradled them in its golden glow, inviting confidences. "Back in Kansas," she said softly, "it's probably snowing right now."

"Where I'm from the snowbirds are just settling in—Tucson."

She smiled. "Do you miss it? Not Tucson, I mean the States. The American way of life? Its culture?"

He shook his head. "Not all that much. I've been in exile too long. I guess I picked up enough culture along the way to get me by." He rose and crossed over to the hutch. Pulling out a cassette player, he plunked in a tape. "Puccini," he said.

"Let me guess. *La Bohème*."

His eyes flared with astonishment. "You're an opera afficionado?"

She chuckled and passed him a cup of coffee. "No. A Puccini fan."

"*Manon Lescaut* is his best."

"I'm here to say that it's *Tosca*. And, maybe, *Madame Butterfly*." Which was a rather stupid statement, she realized, since she was there solely because she had been kidnapped.

"You picked all that up in Kansas?"

She shrugged modestly. "Why not? *South Pacific*'s Kansas-born Nelly Forbush discovered music and another culture. Why can't I?"

She watched him wince as he tasted her coffee. His brows dipped at the ends. "I've tasted water stronger than this."

"I imagine you've tasted a lot of things stronger than that," she retorted.

"Which reminds me." He rose and went to the hutch. Hauling out a bottle of rum, he commented, "A gift from her majesty, Dedee Something or other. I think she was Mobile's homecoming queen back in '58."

A twinge of—surely not jealousy? maybe indignation—made Nelli sit up straighter. She had the disagreeable thought that perhaps she wasn't the first woman to be kidnapped by this adventurer.

He held out the bottle to her. "Want some?"

She shook her head, her mouth pursed in disapproval. "My stomach is not made of cast iron, thank you."

He took a walloping gulp straight from the bottle and wiped his mouth with the back of his hand. "Is that why you became a nurse—your namesake, Nelly Forbush?"

She sipped at the coffee. "No. I hadn't heard of *South Pacific* when I made up my mind at six to become a nurse. It was just something I always wanted to do."

"Because it was safe."

Hearing the taunting in his voice, she glanced over at him. "I beg your pardon?"

"*Safe*, Nelli." He directed a scorching gaze at her hair and its tight little knot at her nape. "Any woman who keeps her crowning glory hidden is most certainly afraid to take chances."

Her hand went to the knot, fingering it self-consciously. "I wear it like this to keep it out of my way. And I take chances every day. As a nurse, I—"

"Professionally," he said, taking another swig from the bottle. "But not personally."

"—do take chances. Why, the week before I left for this vacation, the director of nursing offered me the position of supervisor for the oncology unit."

He leaned across the table and poured rum into her coffee cup. "Did you take it?"

Nelli frowned at the golden liquid, mumbling, "I told her I'd think about it." She should have remonstrated with Dan over the way he had added liquor to her coffee even though she'd told him not to, but instead she took a sip. It was warm and smooth and soothing.

"See," he said, his dark-lashed eyes dancing. "You were afraid to take a chance. You had to *think* first. Do you ever *feel*? Just react to your feelings?"

Heat suffused her cheeks, and she ducked her head, taking another swallow from her cup. "Feelings can be misleading."

She watched as one end of his mouth curled like the barb of a fishing hook. "So can facts."

His nearness, his maleness, was distracting: his strong jaw, stubbled with a week's growth of beard; his broad chest, bare and bronzed; his biceps, rippling almost indecently with muscles.

Strange, how she had given up noticing the distinctions of sex, unless they related to someone's medical condition. What other major forces of nature had she factored out of her life?

Why had she never noticed how *La Bohème* soared so wondrously? Why hadn't she detected the bewitching scent of the veranda's flowers that crept in under the door?

He finished off the bottle, then set it down to reach across the table and take her hand. She almost jumped at the touch. "For instance," he said, holding her palm against his, fingertip to fingertip, "take the fact of our hands. As a nurse, you observe the blood, bone, veins, skin. But as a woman, do you notice how soft your hand is compared to mine?"

As he talked, she stared at their mated hands, almost mesmerized by his low, coaxing voice. She felt the unfamiliar response of her body as it welcomed his touch.

"Do you notice how my fingers are almost as long as your entire hand? How porcelainlike your skin is? How tanned mine is? If you do, then you're moving past observations into feelings."

Feelings! At that moment, she felt as if her body had gone to sleep on her, then suddenly regained sensation, so that little darting needles of feeling made it tingle all over.

At what point had the numbness of her life become unbearable?

She caught herself just before she swayed toward him. As it was, he swayed—not from the sensuality of the moment but from too much rum. Rising unsteadily, he gazed down at her from beneath lashes that curled diabolically. "I think we've both gone too long without enough sheep—sleep."

He was right, of course. They'd had only snatches of rest. But though she might have imbibed somewhat imprudently of the demon rum, she was still enough in possession of her faculties to reason that another night in Dan's bed could lead to a disaster that would shame her whenever she recalled it once she was back in Kansas. Moonlight and magic were fine as a fantasy, but they meant nothing in the everyday world of practicality.

"I'll sleep aboard the boat," she said primly.

He cocked his head. "Listen—outside."

She heard the howling of the wind.

"It wouldn't be shafe—safe," he said, almost cheerfully.

Reluctantly she rose and followed him toward his bedroom. "The couch!" she said, her voice brightening with relief.

He tugged her into his bedroom, his grasp on her wrist unbreakable. "You wouldn't be shafe there, either, if I wanted you. But I don't. I just want to sheep."

She stiffened indignantly but was yanked forward as he fell across the bed, pulling her onto it with him. She was anchored by one of his solid thighs. She lay rigidly, afraid to move, afraid to attract his attention. Despite his assertions of fatigue, she didn't trust his type—the plunder-and-pillage type.

Then she heard his soft snore. She sprawled there, nestled against him as the night deepened, listening to this distinctly male sound, feeling the hardness of his body supporting hers, smelling what was purely male essence. There was a scarcely veiled danger about him, even in sleep, and a sensuality that wasn't blunted by his flaming strength.

She thought about the Nurses' Lounge and the talk that went on inside. Bragging by the single nurses about their latest boyfriends and the night before. Complaining by the married ones about their spouses and the night before. But Nelli had noticed that those wives nevertheless exchanged sly, conspiratorial smiles, as if they shared some amusing secret of happiness.

She wanted someone of her own to come home to. Someone of her own! The revelation was so astounding that tears sprang to her eyes. She blinked them back, smothering little gasping breaths. At her side, her hand knotted the bed sheet. What in heaven's name was wrong with her?

She hadn't worried before about her lack of desire, since her work endlessly fascinated her and consumed every moment. But now she was fascinated by Daniel O'Shay and his wild, broken life.

Several times she shifted onto her elbow and leaned over to gaze with wild curiosity—and with a ridiculous fear that made her heartbeat accelerate—at this giant in repose. Each time she was struck dumb with primal longing. She was left helpless, quivering, from his overpowering maleness. It hit her like a blow, and it made her angry. Angry at him.

He had aroused her latent sensuality. Now she was poignantly aware of all the arid, passionless nights that made up the thirty years of her hollow life.

Around midnight, welcoming the opportunity to escape the sweet torture of Dan's powerful body juxtaposed with hers, she rose to check on Mario and give him his next dosage of penicillin. The fever seemed to be gone. As she smoothed back his rumpled hair he smiled in unconscious contentment. How could such a lovely child have no parents, no one to love him? Well, he did have Daniel O'Shay, didn't he?

Daniel O'Shay.

Somehow the man had slipped into her life and taken hold of it. She was full of him—there in his house, his bed, his ship. He was a buccaneer like the pirates who had sailed this Spanish Main, except that instead of stealing silver bullion he had stolen her senses. He had dulled the quick incisive mind, which she had always relied on.

The delicious night murmured outside. Restlessness drove her out onto the veranda, where flaming vines ran rampant with the frangipani. The heavy scent of lush flowers made her dizzy, and in the moonlight, their hot colors singed her senses. The wind had died down to a breeze that licked at her blush-warmed face. Silhouetted against the heavens, tall palms jutted suggestively, erotically.

Embarrassed—and bewildered—by the focus of her sensuous fantasies, she hurriedly turned her steps toward the starlit beach. She was practically running. Running from the romantic lull of the tropical night. Running from the primitive felicity of the enchanted surroundings. Running from sentiments she couldn't cope with. Running away from herself.

Her bare feet slapped against the hard-packed sand, and the thunderous sound of smashing breakers drowned out the little sobs that escaped her parted lips. Riding in the dark blue bay, Dan's cabin cruiser looked like a shadowy phantom, seeming to follow her, but she knew it was only her nearsightedness that created the illusion.

A hand closed on her upper arm and spun her around. A scream burst from inside her but was drowned out by the booming crash of the waves. Dan, barely panting from his sprint, stared down at her with smoldering eyes. "You were running away?"

"No," she gasped. "Yes." She shook her head violently. Her hair flew around them, flicked her shoulders and his face. "Yes! Yes!"

"Why? What have I done?"

"Nothing. I want—I want...oh, God!"

Shamed, she pulled away and turned to run again. Clumsily she almost stumbled on a lone starfish that had been washed up on the deserted beach. She regained her balance, then sank to her knees, her face buried in her hands. It was too much. She was overwhelmed. Confused. Disoriented.

He crouched behind her and his hands cupped her shoulders, pressing her back into him. "I know," he whispered into her ear. "Me too. I want, too. I want *you*."

His hands slid over her shoulders and down her heaving chest to cover her breasts. Softly he squeezed and kneaded them as his teeth nipped at her nape. She was on fire. Her head was pounding like the surf. Her blood was rushing through her body. She thought she would faint with the force of the sensations ravishing her.

And that was her answer. She shifted slightly, turning her face up to his. Her lips moved, although she wasn't sure she actually spoke. It was more like a sigh of quiet ecstasy. "I want to be ravished."

Chapter Five

I want to ravish you." Dan's voice sounded raw, as if, like her, he was being assaulted by the sweet pain of newly discovered sensations. "I woke up thinking about you, so hard that it hurt."

Against her back, she felt him throbbing with passion. "I know that kind of hurt." She drew his hand further down so that it cupped her belly. "I hurt... here."

With his hand bracing her hip, he turned her to face him and pressed her down onto the sand. Crouched over her on one knee, he pushed up the T-shirt she wore and tore down her panties. Her breasts, bared to the soft, damp breeze, puckered. Nelli watched while he shucked off his cutoffs. The sight of him, totally naked and with all-over tan, set off an explosion of desire inside her. She felt alive with her need, light-headed and breathless, as if she had been running for miles along the beach. And reckless. Insanely reckless.

He straddled her thighs and began to rub his lips over her shoulder, over her face, softly, gently, inching down toward the curve of her breasts. Her eyes rolled closed, and he dipped his head to suckle one breast. She gasped as his tongue swirled and his lips tugged at her suddenly hard nipple; her body arched violently.

"I didn't know anything could feel so wonderful," she breathed.

"It can feel wonderful in other places." His hand slid between her legs. "Here, too." His palm cupped her and pressed hard.

How had she gone so long without knowing these exquisite sensations? Her hands caught his head, tunneled through his hair and probed his muscular neck. "Please!" she begged. "Please, now!"

"Wait." He bent over and swiftly plundered her soft and secret place.

It took her breath away. Her fingers ground into his shoulders. Her heels dug into the sand as he sought and probed and teased. Goose bumps erupted on her skin; the tiny hairs on her arms sprang erect. Breathing shallowly, she focused solely on his touch.

At last, when she thought she could endure no more of this painful pleasure—and as the tide lapped at their legs—he moved up with it, over her, inside her. When he pushed into her, it was as if he were pushing through her soul, searching for nourishment, the life force that only she, the eternal woman, could give.

A rhythm that matched the ebb and flow of the waves took over then, the rich tempo of life was in his thrust and pull. She discovered her own rhythm, glorying in her soft, ripe womanliness. Her breasts were full and erect, her nipples swollen with arousal. The water swirled her hair and anointed their thighs.

While they made love, Dan raised himself on both elbows and clutched her sand-dusted fingers with his passion-clumsy ones. His eyes, as deep blue as the Caribbean, gazed down into hers.

"I could grow addicted to this," she murmured with an embarrassed laugh.

His laughter, mingling with hers, was a wave of elaborate delight.

Then her smile faded into a rictus of sweet pain, and she cried out, "Yes, yes, yes!"

As if he, too, were consumed by her private ecstasy, he lowered his head to kiss her fiercely, to share that joy. All the while his body pummeled hers, driving her into a delirium of passion. He loved her wildly. It was as if she had been waiting for this preordained moment when she would burst forth in dazzling perfection like a jungle flower drenched in midnight dew.

From afar she heard Dan's wrenched groan. "Oh, Nelli," he rasped. "Keep still!"

But she couldn't. The feeling that had been inexorably building within her was too strong to overcome. Explosion after sweet explosion ripped through her and she was unable to stop sobbing. Tears of terrible joy washed from her eyes, and she made little sounds, like those of a newborn.

He lay inside her, his face only inches from hers, his fingertips gently stroking her cheeks. Dazed, she stared back at him. Her flesh radiated the heat of satisfaction, and her wet cherry lips curled into an uncontrollable smile. "I feel wonderful."

He grinned. "I didn't know that behind that prim-and-proper facade there was such a lovely sea siren."

"Neither did I," she said wonderingly. "I thought I didn't need the lovemaking most women seem to live for." The mention of love made her want to ask, "Do you love me?" But she knew better. Thank God for her common sense; it gave her strength.

Nelli also knew that there could be nothing beyond this week. They had nothing—absolutely nothing—in common. The constraints of civilization would be like a death knell for a man like this. And he didn't want a woman getting in the way of his dream of sunken galleons and silver booty.

So she returned his smile with what was undoubtedly, for the first time in her life, a coquettish one. "I feel you inside me."

Dan laughed in sheer joy, and she discovered that she craved him again. They lay there, bound by their euphoria, until he raised himself on one elbow, and she cried out, "Don't go away!"

His long mouth crooked in a self-mocking smile. He ran a finger from the tip of her earlobe down her throat in a line that ended in a lingering stroke between her breasts. "Nothing in the world could make me leave you right now."

Later, as they rose to return to the hut, hand in hand, she paused and stooped to pick up the lone starfish they had passed earlier. She would take that and her memories back with her to Kansas.

"*¿Quien es?*" From sleepy brown eyes, Mario stared first at Nelli, who sat on the bed beside him, then at Dan.

The kid still didn't look in top form, Dan thought, but at least he was fully conscious. "Nelli Walzchak—*una enfermera, compadre.*"

Nelli smiled at Mario and handed him the cup of coffee Dan had prepared earlier. That warm, direct yet personal smile really got hold of you, he decided.

If you let it.

Without glancing at him, she asked, "Does Mario understand English?"

"Enough. When he's got his sea legs under him." Dan noticed that she had avoided eye contact with him since awakening this morning. He supposed that in the bright sunlight of midmorning she was already regretting her unrestrained responses of the night before; her cool replies would have chilled a jalapeño, and her hair was knotted in that no-nonsense style that defied a man to show interest.

Not that he was interested.

Oh, hell. Yes he was.

He couldn't remember wanting a woman as badly as he did this one. He thought of all the women who had come and gone in his life. All had held only passing interest for him. Not that his interest in Nurse Nelli was a permanent condition.

All in all, there hadn't been that many women who'd shared his address, and he liked it that way.

Still, he certainly wasn't going to be put out if Nelli Walzchak elected to stay a few extra days. Gazing at the thrust of her sweet, dusky breasts beneath his T-shirt, he mumbled something about Mario's condition. "...think the kid should stay in bed for a while, don't you? You know, relapses and all that stuff you warned me about."

"Of course he should," she said crisply, but the smile she aimed at Mario was serene and reassuring. "Mario's going to teach me Spanish, and I'm going to teach him to give injections."

"Injections?" Mario said and glanced at Dan for an explanation of the unfamiliar word.

"Injections?" Dan echoed.

"Sure." With a tender look at the boy, Nelli said, "Mario might want to be a nurse one day. Or a doctor, even. You said he was bright. Besides, if he's going to live on a deserted quarter-mile spit of sand, he should know how to handle medical emergencies."

Finally she looked at him with that completely-in-control gaze. "You should, too, for that matter. Then you wouldn't have to kidnap your medical help."

What could he say? His mouth flattened. "A once-in-a-lifetime mistake, I hope." He turned to leave, muttering, "I've got things to do."

"How about shaving, for one?"

With exaggerated slowness, he looked back over his shoulder at her.

"Also," she said matter-of-factly, "there's the slight problem of all that beer and rum. Don't you think milk would be better for Mario and you than—"

"Lady, I may be poverty-stricken and prone to lunatic things like hauling an old maid out of her bed at midnight, but by damn, I'll drink beer and rum and anything else when I damn well want to. And shave when I damn well want to. Which I don't."

On board his boat, Dan puttered around, asking himself where in the world he was supposed to get fresh milk for Mario. Didn't fruit provide all the necessary vitamins? Besides, when he'd met Mario, the kid had been drinking straight *sotol*. Throughout the afternoon, Dan busied himself making adjustments and repairs that he had been putting off because they hadn't been pressing. They still weren't; he just didn't know what else to do with himself.

No, that wasn't true. He knew, all right. He should have his head examined, because all he could think about was Nelli Walzchak. The way she squirmed sensuously under him. The feverish way her eyes glowed, and the funny little kitten sounds she made when they made love.

He knew that he should haul her back on a fast boat to Bahia Escondida. But, in truth, Mario was too ill for him to take the time away. And too ill to accompany him. That meant another day's postponement of his dream of treasure, since he couldn't safely make the dives without Mario's assistance on deck.

With sweat streaming down his rib cage, Dan tossed the needle-nose pliers into the tool chest and headed below for a beer. The chilly can made him think of the chilly woman ashore. She had been so hot last night.

The cabin was steamy and stifling, and he went back up on deck. When he sighted Nelli walking briskly along the dock toward him, he frowned and rubbed his stubbled jaw. As she neared, he could see the determined set of her delicious mouth. Trouble in paradise.

He remained where he was, sitting on the bulwark, his ankle propped on the opposite knee. He cocked an affable grin, but all the while his eyes were on the shapely length of her legs, spread apart to counterbalance the slight shifting of the dock. Her legs were satiny to the touch, he recalled vividly. "Want a beer, Nelli?"

She braced her hands on her hips. "I want a bath."

He waved a hand toward sea. "Plenty of water."

"Salt water. You hauled this 'old maid' away from the luxuries of civilization, so you are certainly obligated to see that I at least have some basic amenities."

He could tell he had hurt her feelings, and he was sorry about that. Inspiration, though, distracted him from true regret. He uncoiled, saying, "Surprisingly our little paradise does offer bath water for milady."

She took a nervous backward step, although half a foot of water separated him from the dock and her. "Good. Mario's asleep," she rattled on, not looking at him directly, "so I'd like to bathe now. I'm all stinky from—from—" Her words faltered, and a flush painted her cheeks a becoming rose.

He bounded over the bulwark and landed lightly beside her, causing the planking to shift precariously. She grabbed at his forearm, and then just as quickly jerked her hand away.

"I hate to see you wash away our lovemaking." His voice was as husky as a wino's after a three-day binge, but its rasping quality had nothing to do with drinking. "I watched you move around the hut this morning, wet from my release, wet with your own wanting."

Her gaze flew up to his. "That's not true!"

"Isn't it?" He rubbed his knuckles along the graceful column of her neck then rested a fingertip in the hollow formed by the juncture of her collarbone. "Your pulse is dancing."

Nelli's eyes closed, her lashes looking like arcs of black fringe. She made a little mewling sound before her eyes snapped open. "Don't," she whispered. "I—I'm not good at this sort of thing."

He brushed her lips with his. "I didn't ask for your degree."

Her eyes—warm brown orbs that should never be hidden by glasses—entreated him. "Dan, I have to go back to Kansas. Don't make it harder for me."

He lifted his head and stared at the shoreline while he regained his self-control—but not his scruples.

Squinting at the sunlight reflecting off the water, he frowned and said, "All right. Let's go get that bath."

"If you'll just direct me to—"

"You'd never find it. The lagoon is several hundred yards back up in the hills."

She eyed him with open suspicion. "I can manage on my own, thank you, so just—"

"—and what with the snakes, I had better go with—"

"Snakes?"

His eyes clamped on her sweet, responsive mouth, which rounded to form a tremulous O. "The common garden variety. Nothing poisonous, usually."

She swallowed. "Usually?"

"Well, sometimes a water moccasin, maybe a coral. Still, I'd feel better if we stopped off and got my machete. I make a habit of carrying it along when I go for a bath."

She moved nearer to him as they returned to the hut. It was all he could do to keep from grinning; instead he whistled. Armed with soap and a towel, she stuck close to him as he led the way along a trail that was banked with overgrowth. For effect, he hacked away every so often at the grapevines draping from the mahogany and sapodilla trees.

Each time, Nelli cringed and gasped, "That's not a snake is it?"

The air shivered with bird song, and the plumelike grass smelled of morning's dew. You could almost inhale the green and the boughs above them sagged with it. He wondered if she could detect the new life amid the wizard's cauldron of scents—bud-bursting orchids and overripe fruit and sweet grass.

The lagoon was the size of an Olympic pool, and had a natural rock decking around three-fourths of its perimeter. The other fourth was fringed with wall-high cane and water hyacinth that hid the burbling streams feeding the pool. Nearby the jungle was filled with wading birds—wood ibis, white heron, snakebird.

"Oh, Dan, it's lovely!"

The winsome look on her face threw him off balance. He strode past her and, dropping the machete, proceeded to shuck his cutoffs. "This is one to tell the nurses back home about."

"What are you doing?"

He glanced at her over his shoulder. "Preparing to bathe. Don't look so shocked. I know nurses have to bathe male patients."

"But they don't bathe *with* them."

He turned around and planted his hands on his hips. "After last night, Nelli, isn't this—"

"Turn back around! It was dark then."

"Suit yourself, but I thought you wanted to bathe."

"Not with you, thank you! I'm returning to the—" She spun around to leave, but the view of the dense trees was formidable; she glanced back at him with an anxious expression.

At that moment he dived in, then quickly surfaced to sputter, "The water is great!" The longing in her eyes would have melted the heart of any man. "Come on in and try it."

Nelli edged toward the bank. Her tongue stole out to lick her lips, and he almost came out of the water then and there. "You'll stay on the far side?"

"Hey, I want a bath just as badly as you do."

"Well..." She took several cautious steps toward the turquoise water. Her mind apparently made up, she turned her back to him and tugged off his T-shirt and her panties—peach-colored panties. He got a glimpse of lusciously curved hips and a tiny waist before she grabbed her towel. Holding it modestly in front of her, she eased first one foot, then the other, into the water. Then, casting aside the towel, she swiftly submerged herself up to her neck. Bliss glistened in her eyes and parted her lips, and her head tilted back in the ecstatic gesture he had observed in women who were caught in the throes of passion. The temperature of the water around him immediately went up ten degrees.

"I knew you'd like it," he said and took a few strokes that carried him around a curve of the lagoon and measurably closer to her. She was loosening the knot in her hair and combing her fingers through the tangled strands. She looked like a model in some Madison Avenue shampoo commercial, with her hair fanned out in the water.

"Like it? I love it!"

"Tell me this isn't better than a hot tub." He swam closer. Dollops of creamy-white water lilies separated them.

She flicked him an annoyed glance. "Daniel O'Shay, you're not abiding by your promise to stay on the far side."

"I made no such promise."

"Aha! Just as I thought—you're not to be trusted!" She ducked under the water and came up moments later on the opposite side from him. The joyous sound of her laughter rang through the glade.

He laughed, too, for the sheer pleasure of it. Her breathless laughter was as contagious as her smile. "You'd be disappointed if I were trustworthy. Admit it. It'd spoil your image of me as a rapacious buccaneer. And spoil your 'What I did on my winter vacation' stories."

As he talked, he rolled over onto his back and swam toward her with casual strokes, as if he were just getting in a couple of relaxing laps at the country-club pool. But she was on to him and splashed a wave of water at him with a slicing karate chop of her hand. "Oh, no, you don't, my hearty buccaneer. Back away!"

Dan rolled back over and swam steadily toward her, saying nothing. Sometimes silence is the best form of aggression, he thought. When he saw the panic tense her face, he jackknifed deep under the water. In the clear, green depths, her legs swayed back and forth. He could imagine her frantically searching the surface for him. Pushing upward, he emerged inches away from her, and she screamed and started thrashing at him.

"Hey, stop, Nelli! You'll drown us both!"

He caught her hands, and she went suddenly still, droplets clinging to her eyelashes. She stared at him as if in fearful anticipation. Some remnant of sensitivity flinched inside him. "I thought you'd like this, Nelli."

"I do," she said in a voice that held little breath. "But I just wanted a bath and—"

"Next time, Nelli, we'll use the cabin cruiser's shower."

Her eyes widened. "It has fresh water?" Her words were a choked whisper.

"Why, sure. You don't think this—" He suddenly realized he had betrayed himself.

She jerked away from him and hauled herself onto the bank, and her softly rounded buttocks captured his gaze. As she scrambled to her feet, she glared down at him, eyes blazing. "Daniel O'Shay, you are indeed the dregs of humanity."

Chapter Six

Dan followed her as, with hands clenched, she picked her way along the trail leading back to the hut. She closed her ears to his charming importuning. As furious as she was with him—and with herself—she was also terribly apprehensive about what slimy thing she might step on next. Her gaze darted from one side of the path to the other, and her ears strained for any slithering noise.

All she heard was the crunch of grass beneath her feet—and then the shouted, "Snake!"

"Dan!" she screamed in a voice that ran up and down the scale. She whirled back toward him and threw her arms around his neck in a viselike grip. Automatically he caught her to him. In his embrace, she shuddered violently and her heart beat against her rib cage.

He stroked her shoulders, calming her. "You're all right, Nelli. I won't let you get hurt."

She couldn't remember feeling such pulse-stopping panic in all her life. She never panicked in emergency situations that required her professional attention.

She also couldn't remember ever feeling breathless excitement from standing next to a man, much less being held by one. Beneath her palms, she could feel the play of his muscles. Still clutching his shoulders, she peered up at him; his eyes glittered with amusement. "I swear, O'Shay," she threatened, "if you fabricated that snake, I'll use that machete on *you*!"

He nodded off to their right, and she peeked in that direction. A coral-banded serpent was gliding through the grass. Revulsion shimmied up her spine, and renewed trembling palsied her hands and chin. Her blood chilled to the temperature of a Yukon winter.

Dan set her to one side and raised his arm in a wide arc. The machete cleaved the snake in one mighty whack. Paralyzed, she watched as he bent over to study his kill and rubbed his beard-shadowed chin thoughtfully. "Hmm. First viper I've seen in these parts in years."

"Viper? That does it. I'm sleeping aboard the boat. It has no snakes—and it has *fresh* water!"

He trailed after her. "What about Mario? You can't desert him now. He's ill. He's—"

She kept walking. "He's not so ill that the two minutes it would take me to get from the boat to the hut would make a difference."

"At least have dinner first."

Nelli paused and sighed. He was truly irresistible. It was difficult to think straight these days, she was so light-headed from always wanting him.

Later, as she lingered over dinner, she was almost sorry she had insisted on sleeping aboard the boat. The fresh whole snapper Dan had grilled outside had been savory, the conversation stimulating, and for the first time Mario had eaten at the table. She learned that his people were the last of the pure Mayas. Though friendly, the Indians of Yucatan were wary, Dan explained. "Probably a throwback to the days when their pueblo was frequently sacked by ocean-going freebooters."

She had to remind herself that Daniel O'Shay was just such a freebooter.

Although Mario had obviously been weakened by his illness, he was full of improbable questions. "You ever held a brain? You think a person could really sew this Frankenstein? How deep is the Rio Grande? Draw me a map where to cross the best."

His narrow face with its wide brown eyes was so intense, so hungry for information. She glanced across at Dan. He shrugged. "The kid's a movie buff. He wants to hit Hollywood and make his own one day."

"And the discovery of your Spanish galleon is going to make his dream come true?" She didn't even bother to hide the cynicism in her voice. "Don't you think that's a little unfair, to delude the child into believing in such a farfetched scheme?"

His can of beer paused midway to his lips. A hard look deepened his blue eyes to almost pure black. "Why not? It keeps him off the streets."

She thought about that discussion later, as she lay aboard the cabin cruiser in its queen-size bed. What did Dan want beyond the mere discovery of such monumental treasure? What was his dream?

And that triggered other thoughts. What was he doing right now? The hut was dark; was he already asleep? She thought of the way he softly snored. The women in the Nurses' Lounge complained about the way their husbands' snoring kept them awake.

She smiled in the darkness. She liked the sound of a man's snoring, she decided. It was reassuring. Silly, but the sound made her feel safe, secure.

The gentle rocking of the boat soon lulled her to sleep. When she awoke, sunlight was streaming through the porthole—and Dan was bending over her. His grin was positively rakish. What a lovely dream.

"Want to go on a treasure hunt this morning?"

She smiled sleepily. "Treasure hunt?"

"Yeah. You know, silver bullion and sunken ships. Mario usually helps me, but I thought it would be better if he recuperated for a few more days. How about it?"

"Umm hmm." She nodded and stretched.

He lowered his head and dropped little kisses all over her face. She hadn't been kissed that much since she was a child. His half beard rasped her lips, but she loved the texture. Purely male. His roughness. Her smoothness. His hardness. Her softness. How perfectly the two sexes complemented one another.

"Maybe we should postpone that treasure hunt," he mumbled against her lips.

"Not on your life," she said and scrambled out of his reach, suddenly aware that this was reality, not a dream. "I've never been on a treasure hunt," she improvised. "This may be my one and only chance."

While Dan got the boat and diving gear ready for the outing, Nelli gave Mario his medicine and changed his head bandage. "Make sure Dan doesn't dive *mucho*," the boy told her as she finished wrapping the last adhesive strip around his forehead.

His almond eyes looked so serious—too serious about life for a boy of eleven—and his illness had underlaid his coppery skin with a pallid tinge. "How much is too much, Mario?"

"Three, four times. Give him a beer. *Mucho* beers. He gets *mucho* relaxed. Won't dive."

"We're only going for half a day, he said. Don't worry, all right? I'll watch him for you."

At that, Mario smiled and gave her the okay sign with his forefinger and thumb meeting in a circle. "A-1, okay!"

Before joining Dan, she requisitioned another of his T-shirts because the black one was getting rather rank. The one she pulled on had two small holes—one near her navel and one just above her right breast—but it seemed to be in better shape than anything else that was available.

The day was gorgeous, just like the travel magazine ads always promised. Overhead, gulls and pelicans flashed against a perfect sky. Dolphins and sailfish played in water that was as clear as a mountain spring. Its salty tang titillated her nostrils, which had become desensitized by the strong odor of hospital antiseptics. While Dan steered the cruiser farther out to sea, Nelli sat languidly with her eyes closed and her face turned up to the soul-warming sunlight.

"Beats Kansas in January, doesn't it?" he drawled and took a sip from his can of beer. "Down here you can make like a lizard on the sand or sightsee underwater for the rest of your days and never miss suburban society."

She regarded him from beneath her lashes. If he shaved and quit drinking and became responsible... She must be losing her mind to entertain such thoughts. "Dan, I don't believe you really want to find that treasure."

He gave her a fish-eye glare. "I think the sun must be getting to you, lady."

She sat up straighter. "I'm serious. If you discovered this sunken galleon, your entire life would change, wouldn't it? I'm not just talking about dealing with the notoriety and the subsequent sycophants out to wrest some of your doubloons from you. But you'd have all that money and you'd have to do something with your life. There'd be no more room for excuses."

"My, my, Nurse Nelli really is into psychoanalysis." He automatically smashed his beer can, and she flinched. "Well, how about some self-analysis while you're at it, Nurse Nelli? I'll help you out. After all, I did get in almost three years at Stanford before Uncle Sam called on me to fulfill my patriotic responsibility."

"Stanford?" she almost stuttered. Why she should be astonished that he was college educated was beyond her, when so many things had hinted at it. His speech, for one. His knowledge, for another. It wasn't the kind that came from drifting from one port to another.

"Let's see," he said, eyes half closed, as if in concentration. "Nurse Nelli doesn't have enough confidence in her own femininity, so—"

"I do so!"

"—therefore, she can only respond when cornered—"

"Maneuvered," she shot back.

"Ravished." The scythe of his smile was cutting.

"Plundered," she countered, her smile arch sweet.

Abruptly he shut down the engine. With his handsome face full of menace, he rose from behind the wheel, and she gasped, "What are you doing?"

"Not what you're hoping."

"You don't know what I'm hoping!"

"Oh, yes I do." His hand curled around the back of her neck, his fingers tugging at the wispy tendrils escaping her knot of hair. "You're hoping I'll take you in my arms and kiss you until you're breathless, and then lay bare your old maid's love-starved body and fill you with—"

"Shut up!" She pushed him away. Her throat was parched, and her breasts rose and fell in treacherous agitation.

He planted his fists on his hips. "You know, lady, I bet you haven't panted so hard since the last time I 'forced' you to—"

"You're—you're disgusting."

He laughed, his teeth gleaming white against his sun-toasted skin. "And you're a mouse."

"A mouse!" she fairly shrieked.

"You'd give anything to trade places with me, but you don't have the courage to live life boldly, to meet it on its own terms, do you?"

Watching his slim-hipped figure stride away, triumphantly male, she steamed and fumed. She'd go back to Bahia Escondida at once. Back to Kansas. She didn't have to listen to this sort of thing from anyone.

But, of course, she did. She was his captive until he decided to return her to Bahia Escondida. Tears stung her eyes. How unjust. She had been perfectly content with her life, and then this had to happen: he had exposed her life for the sham it was, for its emptiness.

After a while he returned from below lugging scuba diving gear—two metal tanks roped with rubber hoses, a face mask, fins and a weight belt. He set them down on the deck and crossed back to the control console. "Mario already knew how to skin-dive and could go down as much as thirty feet with me. I don't suppose you're familiar with scuba diving, are you?"

The whining sound of the anchor being lowered drowned out her, "No," and she shook her head. She didn't want to talk to him, anyway.

"Well, you can still make yourself useful by keeping watch. You know, for a change of weather, other boats that might be snooping, sharks. That kind of thing." He began to strap on a weight belt. "If you notice anything unusual, just crank up the engine. I'll hear it below."

"Sharks?" Her voice was a croak.

He slid on the two tanks. "Most likely I'll spot any before you do. I shouldn't be down for more than an hour to an hour and a half, tops."

She anxiously bit on her lower lip. "If something should happen..."

"It won't."

"But if it does?" she persisted. She didn't like situations where she was unfamiliar with the ground rules, where she didn't have enough information to make solid decisions.

"Then you'll really be marooned."

She gasped a little, and he said, "If something should happen to me, all you can do is return to the cove, pick up Mario and get yourselves back to Bahia Escondida. Now come over here. I'll show you how to start the engine and give you a quick course in boat handling."

He explained the panel controls to her with a simplicity that should have put her a little more at ease but didn't. Starboard throttle, port-engine clutch, trim tabs, voltmeter, bilge alarm, tachometers and compass—it boggled her mind.

When he crossed over to sit on the side of the boat, she said impulsively, "Dan—be careful."

His gaze raked over her. A week ago she might have been offended, but now this totally male assessment made pleasurable chills ripple through her. "There's a set of drawers below the bed. There are some long-sleeve shirts and pullovers. Put one on or you'll blister."

"All this time, I could have been wearing—"

But he had already gone over the side with a tremendous splash.

"—something that covered me better," she continued in a small voice, finishing with a rueful smile.

She found a white dress shirt—with a Brooks Brothers label, no less—that had admittedly seen better days. Her mouth pursed in contemplation. Dan must have held some intermittent white-collar jobs in the interim since Vietnam. Obviously her ravisher hadn't been a full-time buccaneer.

A pity. The truth would ruin the impact of her story in the Nurses' Lounge.

She knew full well, though, that this was an adventure that she'd never reveal, a tale of ecstasy in an untamed world. The adventure belonged solely to her and didn't deserve to be tossed about for the entertainment of female voyeurs.

She paced the deck and glanced periodically at her wristwatch. Her time had always been so measured—in tense minutes and sometimes even vital seconds—that it was difficult to relax. She had been a slave to watches and clocks, whereas here time was of only marginal value, its passage vaguely noted in weeks or years.

Soon she would have to leave, before she learned how to let time pass, to enjoy it. It wasn't an important ingredient in the banquet of life, just a side dish enhancing the entree—love.

Love.

So it really did exist.

Amazing!

You think there's no one out there for you, then suddenly you recognize the person. The fact that they may be entirely wrong for you has nothing to do with it.

Having gotten her sea legs by now, she resumed pacing, navigating around the coils of rope, the ring buoys and hoisting tackle. She was worried about Dan. If something went wrong below, there was absolutely nothing she could do to help him. It was out of her hands. And she was used to being in charge.

As far as warning him about approaching ships or a change of weather on the horizon—well, without her glasses, she could barely see past the bow. She was useless to him, out of her element. And he was so damned self-sufficient, anyway.

The steamy air intensified the briny smell of the sea as the sauna-hot sun beat down on her. Its rays were more intense than a tanning bed's ultraviolet light, but she didn't seek out the shade below. She held her post—paced, listened, watched. When an hour crept by, then another agonizing thirty minutes, she could feel unfamiliar stirrings of panic—and other emotions, too. Mainly self-disgust. Why hadn't she taken the exquisite gift of passion Dan had given her and enjoyed it for what it was? Why had she let pride dampen the pleasure?

Plopping sounds, like a large fish breaking the surface, grabbed her attention. Dan had come up and was removing his mask. Sunlight glinted off his tanned, water-beaded face. He grinned up at her, his smile as dazzling as the sunlight. "Skin diver's paradise below."

No, paradise was right here. Right at this moment.

At the sight of that grin, all sorts of funny things happened inside her. She felt dizzy—surely too much sun. Blood beat in her eardrums—a change in air pressure, undoubtedly. She was breathless—most certainly the heavy humidity.

"Did you find anything?"

"Not even a doubloon." He heaved his half-naked body up the ladder and began stripping off his gear, water pooling on the deck at his feet. He was so tall, so muscular, so damned good-looking, even with that raspy half beard.

A certain shy nervousness made her step back from him. "I'll get you a towel," she said—and, remembering Mario's admonishment, added, "—and a beer."

He lifted a roguish brow. "A beer? My, my, Nurse Nelli, the torrid tropics are beginning to corrupt your strong moral fiber."

She hurried below, where she leaned against the cabinet and took several deep, restorative breaths, then grabbed a towel and a chilled can of beer—then another for herself. At the moment, she figured she needed it more than Dan did.

She found him sitting on the deck, his head tilted back against a cushioned seat, his eyes closed. His gear lay beside him in a puddle of water. At the sound of her approach, he opened his eyes and smiled wryly. "I'm getting too old for this sort of thing."

"Oh, I don't know," she said, squatting beside him to pass him the towel. "Jacques Cousteau still manages quite well, and he's no spring chicken."

Dan's eyes narrowed to slits against the harsh sunlight. "Yeah, well, *frére* Jacques is amply endowed with funds."

Nelli popped the tab off one of the beers and handed the can to him. "Tell me," she said, choosing her words carefully, "how have you earned *your* funds since the, uh, Vietnam days in order to finance this, er, expedition?"

He flung aside the damp towel and took the can. "That ugly word—work, sweetheart. In a Japanese brokerage house. For a Taiwanese computer manufacturer. At the University of Manila."

"What happens if you don't find the ship, Dan?"

He shrugged. "Nothing, really. I die a beach bum, but a contented one. After all, Nurse Nelli, I don't have ulcers or gastritis, and I'm not paying a fortune to enrich some psychoanalyst."

She wrinkled her nose. "Stop calling me that—Nurse Nelli." She popped her can's tab and lifted her beer against his in a toast. "Here's to *your* fame and fortune, Daniel O'Shay. May it come soon."

He clicked his can against hers but didn't drink. Instead he cocked his head, studying her. "You know, I really like you, Nelli. You really are dependable."

She smiled. "That's the second time you've told me that. I do believe, coming from you, that has to be the ultimate in compliments."

"I meant it seriously." His twinkling blue eyes grew solemn. "Of all the women—"

Nelli pressed her fingertips against his lips. "No. I don't want to be compared. I want..." She set her beer can down. "I want to make love to you, Daniel O'Shay."

He stilled, his eyes searching her face. A suspicious expression tugged at his mouth. "Why?"

"It may be the only chance I'll ever get in life," she answered honestly, although it wasn't the complete truth.

"Now, *that's* certainly not the ultimate in compliments, but I admire your spunk."

"I don't want your admiration," she cried. "I feel so—so frustrated! Since arriving in Bahia Escondida,

I feel weepy all the time. I'm not that way. I don't understand. I only know—"

With a burning look, he set his can alongside hers and said softly, "Shut up, Nelli. And come over here and make love to me."

Chapter Seven

Decorous Nurse Nelli. Prosaic Nelli Walzchak with her narrow mind-set. Insanely romantic Nelli, who had extinguished her emotions—only to have them flare into a bonfire under Dan's hot, rapacious mouth.

Desire swept through her body with the force of a typhoon. Stripped of her clothes, naked to the sunlight, she sighed languorously as his exploring hands rescued her from years of dry, empty existence and brought her latent sensuality to life. How had she endured so long without this sweet, erotic singing in her blood?

She was the original Eve, devoid of shame. Inexorably female. Her limbs were sprawled in ecstatic abandon. Where Dan's hands and mouth did not touch, the sea breeze teased until she tingled with rapture. Her breasts were full and erect, thrusting forward, aching with the force of Dan's passion. The cabin cruiser, swaying on the roll of the waves, seemed to lend its rhythm to their coupling.

She gloried in the sensation of being held by this man, of having his sea-roughened hands subdue her, of feeling his chest and arms and thighs hard against her. She knew now that an empty bed was the coldest, most miserable place in the world.

Her lips grazed the muscled ridge of his bronzed shoulder. She wanted to savor the feeling of him lying heavily on her. Would she ever get enough of this? Could she ever escape this madness?

She would have to.

"I thought I was...was going to make love...to you," she gasped against the proud curve of his cheekbone. He was so arrogantly male, so sensual. Behind her lids, golden bursts of dazzling light merged one into another.

Dan clamped his hand on her wrist and drew her palm up to his lips, where he laved it with his tongue. She looked up at him with a passion-dazed face. "There's time, Nelli. We have all the time in the world."

But they didn't. Time was running out for her. Too quickly. She was surprised to find that she was weeping softly. He raised himself on one elbow and pushed her hair back from her face. "What is it?" His eyes darkened with concern. "What is it, Nelli?"

She rolled away from him and sat up. He cast her a quizzical look, but before he could say anything else, she clasped his shoulders and pressed him onto his back. His seafarer's wind-crinkled eyes watched her intently, quietly, as she leaned over him. His pupils were dilated and dark with blatant desire. With this beautiful man, she felt wild and reckless. He was as passionate and alluring as a turbulent sea storm bursting with bolts of lightning. And for these few days, he was hers.

She twined her fingers in his thick, sun-streaked hair. "You're beautiful, Dan. Beautiful!"

His smile was more a grimace, and his sculpted mouth was bracketed by little weathered lines at the corners. "I've never had a woman tell me that. They always wanted to hear it, instead."

"You're beautiful here." She traced the line of his sensual lips. "And here." Under her hands, with their heightened sensitivity, she discovered the erotic tension in the muscles of his shoulders. "Here, too." Her fingertips grazed his taut nipples. She delighted in learning the supple firmness of his skin, underlaid with steel. "And here." Her palm planed over his flat stomach. "And here." She cupped his silky manhood, and as he groaned, she felt the rippling contraction of his body.

Coquettishly she teased, "Repressed, am I?"

His broad-shouldered, gorgeously naked body trembled in a purely sensual reaction, and his virile heat soaked into her. His mouth curved into a half smile, and a challenging light seeped into those strange blue eyes. "I'm still not quite convinced."

"I'll take care of that," she murmured. She found herself having trouble breathing properly. She moved up over him and lowered her head, and then her mouth took possession of his. The entire boat seemed to quiver as she clutched him tightly with a hunger and yearning that stunned her. His strength strained against her, and exquisite sensations zephyred along her nerve endings.

"I'm convinced," he gasped against her lips, and his hands slid down her back to capture and knead her buttocks, pressing her belly against the hardened ridge of his arousal as his long legs locked over hers.

She drew a shuddering breath. "I'm so glad this happened to me. And so grateful!"

He stared up at her with eyes that were hooded by thick, dark lashes. The wide curve of his mouth was still wet with her kiss. "I'm the one who's grateful, Nelli." His voice was thick with the desire she had aroused. "I never meant to cause you problems, I swear. I was just so damn desperate. I must have been out of my head crazy."

Nelli turned her head away so that he wouldn't see the sudden glistening in her eyes. Her body flowed against his; she felt him shudder and nipped his earlobe. "I know, Dan. I know."

His lips were in her hair. "I've spent the last seventeen years satisfying women, playing the stud, but I think this is the first time time a woman truly wanted to satisfy me."

She dragged her mouth away from his ear to search his golden face. It blazed with a searing sensuousness. Raw desire consumed her. She wriggled away and thrust her face against his damp skin, craving the taste and the smell of him. She needed this intimacy to carry with her always, to console her on the lonely nights that stretched ahead into infinity. Her tongue explored him, testing the goose-pimpled skin, the saltiness, as she inhaled his musky odor. The air was heavy with their arousal.

Dan's arms tightened around her, and he pulled her under him. For a long moment he gazed into her eyes—a moment so fiercely, unbelievably erotic that she felt as if she were melting. "Say you don't regret it. Say you don't regret being kidnapped by me."

"I want you," she whimpered.

"Say it, sweetheart!"

She cried out as he stroked deeply into her. "Never—not for one heartbeat will I ever regret being kidnapped by you!"

Caressing words tumbled into her mouth. Then his lips deserted hers to strew kisses over her love-ready flesh—on the delicate plane of her collarbone, the underside of her wrist, the vale between her breasts, then her aching nipples. His kiss brought an even sharper ache low in her belly, an ache that carried with it anguished delight.

She felt the stammer of her heartbeat, and her head arched back. He dipped his face to kiss the milky softness of her throat, then lifted his head and watched her with eyes gleaming from beneath half-open lids. She could feel the strong thudding of his heart. Or was it hers?

His hand stroked her face softly—infinitely tender—and then her hair. This man who held her, who made love to her, was gentle yet tough, commanding yet giving.

With caressing hands, he spread her legs apart and helped her wrap them around his hips. He filled every inch of her, lifting her hips with his hands, and filling her time after time. Her soft cries as he moved within her goaded him to wildness.

Passion made a rich, rushing sound in her head, like the whistle of the sea wind through the palm trees. It was more than she could bear. She hardly knew what she was doing, what she was saying. "Please.. yes...love..." Had she cried out that she loved this— or *him?*

Then she forgot to worry as her thought became a restless blur. She saw him as a vision above her, with the brilliant sunlight making a halo around him. "You're so delicious. So enchanting," he said raggedly, the words like honey poured on her skin.

A pure joy filled her heart. "No man has ever said anything like that to me."

"They should have. They're fools." He kissed her hungrily, rocking his mouth over hers.

Her veins became channels of flame. Her breath poured over her lips as she sobbed, and then it was as if a great dam burst inside her. She clung to him fiercely, so she wouldn't be swept away. A wondrous feeling—that of being replete and complete—settled over her like golden lace. At that same moment, he filled her with his own goodness; she couldn't tell his dampness from her own.

Later she lay enclosed in his arms, drifting, cherishing the moment. He lifted one of her hands, running his thumb over its contours. She tingled all over at his touch. "You have strong, capable hands, Nelli."

She wanted to pull away because she had always considered her fingers too blunt, her hands too wide. Her nails were cut short for practical reasons. "Thank you," she murmured awkwardly.

"You're flushed," he said with a frown. "Is the sunlight too—"

"No, it's not that. I'm just not accustomed to compliments."

He looked as though it were difficult for him to speak. Instead he leaned over and kissed her, just above her heart. "I haven't done much to make you like me," he said, his voice a caress of regret, "but I hope you'll eventually get over this episode."

Mario met them on the veranda. "No galleon?"

"Not a doubloon," Nelli said, mimicking Dan's statement earlier, though she doubted her smile held his confident charm.

Mario shrugged. "*Mañana*, maybe."

"Maybe," Dan tossed off the word. "Anyone for grilled lobster? I'm starving."

"Count me in," she said, trying to join in the light-hearted mood. But a complex web of frustration and anger and—always, now—desire wrapped her. For Dan, this was merely—what had he called it?—an episode. He couldn't comprehend that it had irrevocably altered the course of her life.

While he went out to check the pots he used to trap lobsters, she examined a restless Mario for signs that the meningitis was abating. His fever was certainly gone, and when she positioned his leg in the telltale position of the Kernig's sign, the hamstring muscles gave no indication of spasms.

"I think you're definitely on your way to recovery," she told him.

His dark eyes danced. "No more injections, no?"

"Yes, more injections, yes."

He wrinkled his nose.

She reached out a hand to tousle his thick, straight hair. "And after I leave, you'll have to give them to yourself as I taught you."

"But you don't leave soon, no?"

Nelli paused, bit her lip, then lowered his leg to his mattress. "Soon."

"But we need a woman here."

She eyed him askance. His face held an artlessness she didn't quite trust. "You've gotten along just fine until now without a woman." Then, unable to help herself, she added, "At least, without having one around permanently. I suppose there have been other women here from time to time?"

The boy's grin was one of pure understanding. His perception unnerved her. "Never. Dan says women, they are bad luck on a boat."

She felt a wave of pleasure at the knowledge. "Well, men like you and Dan would never make it corralled in a house, either."

Over dinner, Mario reported to Dan her plan to leave soon. Dan peered at her with a scowl. "Do you think that's wise? After all, Mario's not out of the woods yet. You told me you were concerned about relapses."

"Nothing you can't handle," she said, trying for an offhand tone. "If he should take a turn for the worse—" she gave Mario an affectionate glance "—then you can sail *up* the coast this time. Kidnap some other nurse."

She could see that her change of attitude—from feminine softness to a distant, professional briskness—puzzled him. "What is it, Nelli?"

If she broke out in tears just one more time, she swore, she'd . . . she'd curse a blue streak. If she kept up this crying, she'd get so dehydrated she'd need an IV.

She blinked away embarrassed moisture and strove for calm and logic. "Look, O'Shay, you've got your life plan, and I've got mine. I've simply got to get on with things."

"What is your life plan?"

She looked from his handsome face to the ever-serious Mario. The diffused light of dusk streamed through the high, dust-streaked windows, its honeyed softness painting the tableau of man and child in sepia tones that made them look as if they were tapped in on old tintype, a tintype she would carry in her memory forever.

She fixed her gaze on Dan and answered bluntly. "To be the best nurse I can be. Ultimately to run Kansas General Hospital."

Their gazes held. He reached for his beer, tossed down a deep draught and asked, "When do you want to go back?"

She took a steadying breath. Her eyes were as bright as sequins. "Tomorrow morning."

"I see."

With troubled velvet-brown eyes, Mario looked from Dan to Nelli.

She curved her lips but didn't quite work up to a polite, social smile and wiped her hands. "That lobster was the best I've ever tasted." Not that she was an authority on seafood. "Well, if you two don't mind, I'm going out to the boat. I'd like to get to bed soon in order to get an early start tomorrow for Bahia Escondida."

Moonlight gilded the night with romance. Nelli sat in a deck chair, one knee folded up under her chin, watching the eternal journey of the waves toward the beach, smelling the seductive scent of tropical flowers wafting from shore.

Her thoughts were poor, storm-tossed things. Dan's kind didn't marry. To him, "wife" was a four-letter word. While he thrived, she would wither in this undemanding—but also unproductive—life-style.

She accepted the realization that the pain and longing and yearning that would now be a constant part of her days and nights were better than her former sterile, empty life.

As she watched the stars, Dan came to her, a pagan half smile on his lips. She said nothing, but let him draw her from the chair and drag her back against the scorching hunger of his body. His hands lifted the hem of her shirt, desperately seeking and then discovering her quick-rising, aching breasts. He filled his palms with them.

She leaned her head back against his shoulder and closed her eyes. "Touch me everywhere. Hurry. There is only this night."

"A farewell, then." With unhurried grace, his fingers loosened the knot of her hair and winnowed through it, as if delighting in the soft blond cloud. He buried his mouth in her unbound tresses. "No trace of artifice. No perfume. Yet the scent of you, Nelli, is so sweet it calls to me. I wish that I could be like you...innocent again."

She gasped and sagged against him as he covered her belly with slow erotic strokes while his lips ruffled soft kisses along her hairline, below her ear and at her nape. His thumbs returned to make long, sensitive forays around her tight nipples.

She turned around then, in the shelter of his arms, and whispered, "God knows what it will be like during the years of lonely nights to come."

"They won't be lonely for either of us." He bent and scooped her into his arms. "Not with this to remember." He cradled her as he descended the companionway, then carried her into the alcove and laid her on the bed. Her tresses cascaded over the mattress.

He knelt on one knee beside her, the water brightness of his eyes holding hers with a jeweled quality. His lips hovered over hers without touching. Heat spread through her, pooling painfully in her stomach. She closed her eyes shutting out the dark, romantic look on his face and focused on the gentle, knowing movements of his hands.

"If I had to be introduced to passion," she murmured, "I'm glad it was at the hands of a master."

His chuckle opened her eyes. The chimera of a beguiling smile had replaced his usual grim scythe of a grin. "Technique has nothing to do with it, sweetheart. It's all here." His fingers disturbed the scattered curls at her temple. "All in the mind. If you want it to be pleasurable, memorable, sensual...your mind will make it so."

"And I wanted it, didn't I? Subconsciously this was what I wanted all along. I wanted to be ravished."

"Yes."

The monosyllable spoke volumes.

"I understand," she mumbled.

His expression softened briefly. "I reluctantly admit," he said with dark irony, "that a happily married woman would have found my, er, advances distasteful."

"And I welcomed them, for all that I demurred."

"Don't regret it, Nelli." His whisper was thick, fervent.

She felt the coaxing pressure of his thighs against her legs and the now-familiar hardness of unrelenting muscle against her stomach and breasts. "I don't."

She could tell by his bleak expression that he didn't fully believe her. She knew he felt as if he had done her some terrible damage. "If you think that later, when I reflect back on this, I'm going to hurt, you're wrong. I'm going to view all this as a wonderful dream."

In her heart of hearts, though, she realized that the episode had been more than a dream; it had been a miracle. She had been liberated from the strictures of her cold, empty life.

Nelli passed her finger over the fullness of his lips. "Do you think you can make a true sea siren out of me?"

He shook his head. His eyes, as though lit by the night's galaxies, shone brightly. "No. You already are. Don't ever forget that. Ever." Then he kissed her with a sort of desperate, thirsty kiss, as if to make himself drunk on her.

Chapter Eight

Snow fell over the parking lot of Kansas General Hospital like confetti on a military parade. And that made Nurse Nelli Walzchak think of war and Vietnam and soldiers and, lastly, Daniel O'Shay.

She turned up the collar of her coat and carefully picked her way along the icy sidewalk. Inside the warm, brightly lit rooms were bustling with activity. At six in the morning hospital corridors were busier than the streets. She had missed this, the feeling that something was always happening. She was glad to be back in her element.

Even though her shift didn't start for another thirty minutes, she made the rounds, looking in on the seven patients on the floor who were on IVs, checking to see if any of the bottles needed to go piggyback, so they wouldn't run out of fluids.

Finally she went to the Nurses' Lounge, a small room behind the kitchen, for Report. The narrow room had no windows, and second-hand couches were positioned on either side of a cigarette-burned table.

Mary Luther, the charge nurse on the night shift and the one who had forfeited her two-week time-share at the Bahia Escondida condominium, sat with the patient-care files. She delivered a brief history on each patient and went over what had happened in the past eight hours.

Seven other people were in the lounge that morning—two more registered nurses, three licensed practical nurses and two nursing assistants. Everyone was sipping freshly made coffee. While Mary gave her rundown, Nelli took notes. As head floor nurse, she was responsible for how the floor was organized, how it functioned and how the staff felt about working on it.

"Patient 735, bed B, Darryl Thomas, appendectomy. We medicated him for pain once. His incision looks okay."

"Patient 736, bed A, Lydia MacElroy, cystoscopy. We've had trouble with her and her cat. Her husband keeps sneaking it into the room, Nelli, so you might want to have her monitored whenever her husband's visiting."

With an efficient smile, Mary finished giving the morning's report. And then the chatter came at Nelli like a barrage of machine-gun fire.

"So, tell us," Lana said pointedly. "How was Bahia Escondida?"

Mary prodded with an expectant grin. "Well?"

"What a gorgeous tan," Linda said slyly. "I've never seen you looking . . . healthier."

Carol peered at Nelli over the rim of her coffee cup. "Come on, Nelli. We've all been dying to hear the *intimate* details!"

Nelli looked at each avid face. Surprisingly what came to mind had nothing to do with the buccaneer Daniel O'Shay. "As much as I liked the village, I never got used to the sight of sewage trickling down the streets and into the middle of the bay—or to the poor, underfed children and—"

"What?" The word was a chorus.

"Surely you can remember more than sewage!" Mary said. "How about that French actor and—"

"Nelli," Carol interrupted, "you can't leave us drooling, not after all those postcards."

Nelli looked at the cluster of women. "I get no respect on this floor." Then she smiled. The truth was she *did* get it—and gave it. But nursing was more than just getting the job done and being respected for doing it right. Anyone could do physical care. To her, a good nurse was someone who put *caring* behind the *care*.

"My friends," she told them, "the postcards were all fabrications—to appease you. I'm sorry, okay?"

She left her nurses with their mouths open, their eyes wide.

After she made sure that her staff had the morning care under control, she sought out one of the surgical residents to discuss a patient. She had dozens of things to do and often wondered where in the world she was going to find the time to do them all.

As she conversed with the resident, something in the back of her mind began to nag her. It went back to patient care.

seafood, she would listen to the soft sounds of Puccini from her cassette player and fortify herself with a fifty-cent beer.

All the while, she would watch the boats bobbing on the waves, hoping to catch sight of one weathered cabin cruiser in particular.

Of course, she never did. Occasionally trawlers sailed into the bay, but they didn't bear the name *Seasiren*. Occasionally she heard that it had put in for supplies. The natives were always full of gossip, and though her command of Spanish was abysmal, she understood enough from her patients to know that the American adventurer hadn't yet found his fortune.

She searched the face of every kid walking the beach, peddling tarnished jewelry, turtle-shell bottle openers and hemp hammocks made at the nearby henequen-crushing plant. But none of the boys was Mario.

Then one day she glanced up from tending a patient and saw Mario standing just inside the open doorway. The July afternoon was sweltering and, without air conditioning, perspiration beaded her face. For a moment she thought it was sweat that stung her eyes. Then she knew it was tears. "Mario," she whispered.

He looked down at his dusty bare feet, then back at her. He was smiling now. "We heard an American nurse, she was living and working in Bahia Escondida."

We!

She swallowed. "How are you and . . . Dan?"

"A-1, okay," the boy said, making a circle with his thumb and forefinger.

"No doubloons?"

His mouth flattened disconsolately, and he shook his shaggy head. "No doubloons."

"Would you stay for a lemonade?"

"I can't. The boat, she is waiting."

After that, Mario occasionally came to visit. Sometimes he would sit fascinated and watch her while she worked. But he never mentioned Dan directly, and she never asked.

But at night, when the moonlight silvered the tiled floor of the room behind the clinic where she lived, and tropical flowers perfumed the air with their intoxicating scent, she would lie in her bed and fantasize—about a buccaneer and a ravished maiden.

Fortunately her work consumed most of her time, so she had little left in which to yearn. Her position as village nurse was more rewarding than that of hospital floor nurse. The people trusted and liked her. They were simple and direct and fun loving, despite their impoverished lives. Their primitive, superstitious nature often hampered her modern medical treatments, but in no way interfered with her relationship with them.

Months passed into a full year. On the anniversary of her move to Mexico, she donned heels and her one cocktail dress—a rather plain black affair. Instinct had long ago told her that she just wasn't the dazzling type and never would be. She celebrated alone that evening at the resort's best restaurant with a five-course dinner in which seafood played no part—and she had one glass of wine too many. After she left, she was greeted along the way by the villagers. She had the suspicion that the natives, concerned for her tipsy state, were solicitously accompanying her home.

Her euphoria lasted past disrobing and well after she collapsed onto the bed, humming a silly romantic serenade. "I'm so glad I came here," she murmured sleepily.

The abrupt shifting of her mattress, and the feathery brush of a kiss, convinced her that she was beyond mere tipsiness. When she opened her eyes, a man's shadowy face hovered over hers, and brilliant blue eyes burned into her. The deep, rhythmic rush of the sea filled her ears.

The natives' superstitions had to be rubbing off on her. With a soft sigh and a drowsy smile, she closed her lids, mumbling, "I'm bewitched."

"No, you're kidnapped. Or about to be."

At the rough rasp of a distinctly male voice, her eyes snapped open again. "Daniel O'Shay," she breathed.

"The one and only." He dropped kisses all over her face and throat and chest.

"Oh, no," she murmured. "This can't be happening."

"I swear you'll enjoy it this time, Nelli." He was still kissing her.

"What?" she mumbled against his beard-stubbled cheek.

"A honeymoon to Fiji. Or maybe Paris. Yeah, Paris. Bahia Escondida is already just about as South Seas as you can get. Hell, we'll go wherever you want."

"Honeymoon?"

He lay half atop her. She almost purred at the weight of his heavy body. "Then we'll return and build a modern house overlooking the bay. Air conditioning, hot and cold running water, the works."

"Honeymoon?"

He nuzzled her ear. "Of course, we'll update your clinic. The village is going to need a secondary school. I'm putting in a yacht club, too. It'll keep Mario busy for a while until he completes his education."

She pressed her fingers against his lips. "Dan—you found the sunken galleon?"

"Yeah." His teeth sparkled in the dark. "This afternoon. As soon as I located the cache of silver bullion, I headed straight for Bahia Escondida and you."

Her throat became peppery. "Why didn't you come sooner? You knew I was here, waiting."

The smile faded from his mouth. "I couldn't, Nelli. Not until I had something to offer you."

Her face flushed hot with love, and she stared up at him from under half-closed lids. Her fingers winnowed through his sun-streaked hair. "Oh, Dan, I just wanted you. Only you."

His hand slipped beneath her pajama top to caress her breast. Eagerly his pleasure-giving fingers stroked its fullness, caressed her nipple. "Nelli, you don't know how much I wanted you. All those damned miserable, lonely nights. I tried to deny that it was love. I told myself I was just wanting a woman. But putting into port for one just didn't interest me enough to rev up the *Sea-siren*'s engines."

His firm, hot mouth took hers with all the hunger and yearning of their long separation. She felt him tremble against her with the sudden force of it.

"I love you, Nelli. Hell, I've been fighting it since that first time I crawled into your bed. At that moment, in the moonlight, seeing your face with those begging-to-be-kissed lips...feeling your lush body beneath those decently prim pajamas...well, I almost concurred and gratified you then and there."

She made a moue. "Gratified yourself, you mean."

His hand curved under her breast to explore the galloping pace of her heartbeat. "Both of us."

"I concede," she said, smiling happily. "I'm as sex starved as you once accused me."

His grin leveled into a solemn line. "Honestly, Nelli, that night in your bedroom, it wasn't sex that came to my mind. It was your naive expression that hit me. All I could think was, 'oh, to be that innocent again.'"

Nelli rubbed her lips back and forth across his beard-stubbled jaw. "I don't want you to be that innocent. I want you as you are. You're everything I ever wanted in this life, and the next."

His hand slipped down to stroke her through her pajama bottoms. "Everything you ever wanted?"

She laughed softly. "Well, that, too."

Laughing, he dragged her against him. "I've been to handling school. I can handle that."

She would have kissed him then, but he rose up on one elbow. His face was darker than the night shadows. "You never answered my question."

"What?"

He cleared his throat. "Will you marry me?"

"You never asked me."

"Well, will you?"

Her fingers traced the hard angle of his jaw. "Only if you swear to shave every day of your life. Or almost every day," she qualified. "After all, Bahia Escondida's most prominent citizen has to set an example."

He groaned. "I swear."

"And swear to reduce your beer intake."

He rolled his eyes. "I swear."

"And swear to ravish me at least once a day for the rest of our lives."

An expression of enormous delight swept over his face and curved his mouth, but he said solemnly, "I swear."

Then he began to laugh with her in shared pleasure. They lay entwined in each other's limbs, drowning in laughter and pure joy and wild desire.

* * * * *

Family Summers

As a mother of five sons, I've always found summer vacations to be cheerful chaos. But keeping the children corralled and their hands off priceless antiques or ancient cave rocks often seemed to require so much effort that my husband and I would return home wondering what had happened to our anticipated relaxation.

Now our oldest two have left home and my husband and I realize how much we miss their presence on those trips—and how special those trips were. Those memories are a bank that I can draw on during the times when, on business trips, I am traveling alone.

True, our family argued, but we also laughed and shared. And, oh, the wonder I would sometimes glimpse in my sons' bright eyes at the sight of the Grand Canyon and Old Faithful, the White House and the battleship *Alabama*, the Eiffel Tower and the Mona Lisa.

Those summer vacations were more than mere sightseeing. They were lessons in learning to be flexible, in learning appreciation of people and things, in learning that we are all essentially alike, though our exteriors vary.

Those vacations were also lessons in the wonders to be found on the printed page. My husband and I invariably took with us books to read—and purchased still more books, dealing with the areas through which we were traveling. As a result, our sons have acquired the invaluable habit of reading.

These summers my husband and I often take our three sons who remain at home to Lake Amistad on the Rio Grande. We enjoy water sports and love the peaceful sound of water slapping against our cabin cruiser during the night.

Even more, we love the colors and scents of old Mexico, just across the Texas border from Lake Amistad and nearby Del Rio. Since two of our sons were born in Mexico City, we have a deep appreciation for Mexico's people and culture. And we have discovered that there is nothing like a border town for excitement.

When I count my blessings, one of them is simple sunlight. I can't imagine living farther north, where the summers are shorter. I live for those months when the days are long and lazy, the sun bright and warm, and my family gathers together for those wonderful days of summer vacation.

Parris Afton Bonds

THE ROAD
TO MANDALAY

Kathleen Korbel

Caribbean Adventure

What could possibly be more romantic, more breathtakingly beautiful, than the sight of a tall ship racing before the wind, the Caribbean sky arcing overhead and the island of Nevis falling behind? Nothing.

"The Road to Mandalay" was born on such a ship. My husband and I had both been lured by the romance of sail for years. When we got a chance to see the Caribbean from the deck of a tall ship, we jumped at it. Windjammer Cruises was our host, the S/V *Polynesia* our ship, and fantasies couldn't have been made of better stuff.

We helped haul sails up to the notes of "Amazing Grace" lifting from bagpipes. We gathered for our daily rum swizzle on the foredeck with all our new friends and stretched out on the wooden decks to watch the islands go past. The only sound we'd hear was the wind and the flapping of the sails. We traveled slowly, gracefully, the ship as much a source of delight as the surrounding scenery.

At night we slept up on deck, watching the brilliant Caribbean sky arc over the tilting masts, listening to the trades flap through the sails, sharing the magic of a full moon and the shimmering sea. And in the morning we'd wake to watch the flying fish skitter through the water as we docked at a new island.

We walked the back roads of islands the big ships couldn't reach, where life ambled at a stroll unchanged for generations, where Alexander Hamilton and Josephine Bonaparte were born. We snorkeled through water so clear that the seabed seemed to skim our fingers.

I also broke my foot jumping from a rock, and my ankle swelled so badly I couldn't get my shoe back on the whole way home. Try feeling good about going barefoot through Miami International. I learned that sailors walk the way they do to keep the ground down—it tilts after a few days at sea—and a friend who went with us swam to and from the ship rather than risk seasickness on the johnboat.

But none of that mattered. And every time I look at ''Mandalay'' I'll remember the romance, the grace, of that time, and I'll know I'm going to return.

Chapter One

The island of St. Maarten huddled beneath sodden gray skies. Sheets of rain sliced across vague, pastel-shaded mountains and pockmarked a gunmetal ocean. A hundred small sailboats bobbed and swayed in the harbor like winter trees in the wind. Not exactly Kate Manion's idea of the perfect day in paradise.

Kate considered the dismal scene from her vantage point in a launch located halfway across the bay and wondered, not for the first time, what she was doing here. No more than forty-eight hours earlier she'd still been a sane person, sitting in her little cubicle at work, trying to coax some sense out of her computer, and wondering what delicacy she was going to pull out of the freezer for dinner. Now she sat with twenty other bedraggled souls on their way to a week of sun and fun on the ocean. She never should have let Betty Williams sit down at her desk.

"Get ready, we're comin' alongside!"

At the command, Kate turned to consider the ship that would be her home for the next week.

Ship? She was crazy. She'd never been out on the water in her life. Skiing was done in the snow and swimming in the heated pool at the Y. This was madness.

Then she caught sight of the four masts that soared up over her head—immense black poles that speared a leaden sky. No, she amended, *this* was the madness. Not only had she let herself be talked into her first vacation in six years, or her first trip outside the States, but she'd stood perfectly still and let Betty Williams convince her to trust herself for a week on an honest-to-God relic from the *Mutiny on the Bounty*. It was a tall ship, complete with sails, wooden decks, Union Jack fluttering in the wind—and, she realized, hearing the slightly plummy tones floating down from the deck above her, Englishmen.

"All right now, everyone, the launch is bobbing a bit, so you'd do best to take hold of a hand as you climb out."

"Toto," she said to herself with an eye to the alien sight above her. "I don't think we're in Kansas anymore."

"All right, now, miss. You're next."

Kate swung her overnighter to her shoulder and gingerly got to her feet. Even in the quiet bay the launch seemed to dance precariously beneath her. The first of the steel rungs up to the ship was at least waist high. After considering the prospects for a minute, she turned to offer a wry grin to the black man who stood by to steady her departure.

"This is all very nice. I don't even have to wait to make a fool of myself."

All the same, Kate took hold of the little man's hand and stepped onto the side of the launch. The minute she put one foot up onto the rung, the launch suddenly dropped away. Her right foot flailed somewhere in the air, and her hand began to slip. The heavy overnighter began to pull her toward the water.

Just as Kate was beginning to entertain visions of following her underwear to the bottom of the bay, another hand caught her free arm. For a long moment, only the strength of those steely fingers kept her upright. Regaining her perilous balance, she looked up.

It almost cost her her footing again, but Kate got a good look at the Englishman. It figured that she'd perform for him. He was just about the best-looking man she'd seen since puberty. For the moment, though, all she could focus on was a set of very amused gray eyes. Eyes the color of snow clouds and dove wings. Eyes that drew her close and warmed the chill of the rain.

"I'll mention you in my first letter home," she promised shakily when she managed to get her foot back to safety.

He smiled and Kate was hooked. "My pleasure," he assured her, handing her up to the deck. "If you went swimming now, you'd miss your rum swizzle." Then he let go of her hand and turned to the next passenger.

Another crew member was already guiding Kate away, rattling off registration instructions as he thrust the aforementioned drink into her hand. Kate accepted both without bothering to look away from where her benefactor helped the other passengers on board.

It was incredible. She felt as if she'd just stood up in an old open biplane, with the rushing wind catching her breath somewhere in her chest. If she'd been a heroine in a soap opera, she was sure her cheeks would be rosy with a sweet glow. The guy wasn't all that great looking that he should take her breath away. But he did.

He was almost six feet tall, she figured as she sipped the fruity rum in her glass, and thin. No, not really thin. There were any number of powerfully developed muscles in those arms. Her own arm was still tingling from the grip of his callused hand. He just didn't have the broad, triangular frame of a football player. It was more the build of a runner or swimmer: long, sleek lines.

He was good-looking in that classic outdoors way that exuded health and energy. He'd spent a lot of time in the sun, letting it burnish his skin and bleach what had once probably been brown hair. Wet now, that hair clung to his forehead and neck in disarray, and was about four weeks past its last decent cut. Instead of the crisp white uniform he wore now, Kate could easily imagine him in stripes and thigh boots, boarding a merchantman with a cutlass between his teeth.

The idea made her grin as she settled herself into line. Kate could just imagine what Granda Sean would think of her pining over an Englishman. The old man was probably spinning in his grave just with her considering it. Don't worry, Granda, she thought, casting a jaundiced eye at the much more generously endowed young lady who stood ahead of her in line. I don't think I have to worry about suffering at that Englishman's hands this trip. Besides, she decided, taking another sip of her drink, this was all just a quick escape from reality. Work still waits back in Detroit next Monday. Breathless or no, an Englishman from the eighteenth century doesn't fit into that scenario.

She'd just ignore him. Considering that there were at least a hundred people on his boat, it shouldn't be all that difficult to do.

"Elizabeth Williams?"

Kate looked up from her reverie with a start. The eyes across from hers were the same ones that had watched her mishap with such amusement. The same cool gray eyes that had given her weak knees, and they were doing it again.

"Are you the only crew member on this boat?" she demanded instinctively, wondering how he'd gotten around behind that table so quickly.

He grinned, and the planes of his face collected into weathered lines, his cheeks furrowed like washed-out gullies. Kate thought they weren't called character lines for nothing.

"There are one or two others who help out," he assured her.

Kate found herself unconsciously pushing her tangled mass of dark hair back off her forehead, as if straightening up for a date. "Kate Manion."

"Pardon?"

"Elizabeth Williams couldn't make it, so she gave me her reservation." And I'm never going to forgive her for it, Kate thought dourly. This isn't what I'd consider relaxing. "She should have contacted your offices."

Nodding, he scanned the printout in his hand. "She may have, I'm not sure. The purser's usually the one to do this, and the computer—"

Kate couldn't help a frustrated sigh. "I know all about computers."

He looked up, chuckling. "You don't get along?"

Kate's answering smile was dry. "About as well as Faust and the devil." It was her tragic flaw, Betty had told her, that she absolutely hated the things. Word around the office was that if it were up to Kate, everybody would still be using quill and ink. They weren't that far wrong.

"Well," she said now, wishing she could stop staring at him, "if you're going to throw me off, at least let me have another rum swizzle. It might numb the ride back in that little roller coaster you call a boat."

"I'll let you stay," he assured her with a conspiratorial grin as he scribbled something on the sheet. Left-handed, Kate noticed. Of course, that made it perfect. "Just don't let anybody know."

"And if the captain comes up and asks who I am?"

He smiled. "I already know who you are."

Kate scowled. "Thank you. It's been a long time since I've embarrassed myself twice within a single hour. Is there anything else I need to do before throwing myself overboard?"

He chuckled. "Sign this. If you want to take your luggage with you, it'll be in cabin fourteen, port deck."

Kate looked up from where she was signing her name. "Port?"

His grin was dry as he motioned to the hand holding her pen. "Left."

She smiled back in kind. "Of course."

Jack Whelan looked down at the strong, spiked handwriting and then back up at the petite woman who was walking out the door. Face and voice didn't match on that one at all. He'd noticed it when he'd first seen her fighting to stay upright on the slick ladder. She had the face and figure of a tree nymph—slim and gently rounded—and the height of an almost-grown boy. Her hair was so dark that the pale light failed to catch any highlights, making its tumbled length look all the wilder.

The only way to describe her features was fresh. She had a milky complexion with a smattering of freckles and a slight lilt to her nose, soft lips and deep-set blue eyes. She had a face arrested of aging, like a female Peter Pan.

Her manner was a different matter altogether. She spoke with assurance, stood easily as if asking no one's leave or pardon, and measured the deck with rapid, precise steps. She's no gentle fairy or flighty nymph, he thought. That woman is a lioness in a lamb's stature.

By the time the rain passed, Kate had paced every inch of the ship. They still sat at anchor, the lights of Phillipsburgh twinkling off to the right. The clouds had begun to clear, leaving tattered black rags to chase among the brilliant stars and mantle the moon. An intricate spider's web of lines danced along huge white masts as the ship dipped with the waves.

Kate wondered at the people who ambled along the decks or sat talking so quietly in the dining room. Hadn't they also come from work? Didn't they need to unwind? In comparison with her pace, they seemed to have already unwound before even embarking on the trip.

She guessed Betty had been right after all. She really did need the chance to get away from all the pressures her job and her family had been piling up on her. Kate couldn't remember the last time she'd taken any kind of trip. There hadn't seemed to have been a chance the past few years as she'd put herself through school toward her goal of being a securities broker. Then there was her job as controller for the firm that sponsored her schooling. To call that stressful would be a gross understatement. The last four controllers before her had left restrained and medicated. When Betty had caught Kate picking fights with the brokers and snapping at the secretaries, she must have been worried about a fifth.

Maybe Betty knew what she was doing after all.

"I can't use the ticket," she'd said, her brown eyes just shy of deadly serious. "So, you go. There's nothing you can't put off for a week or so. Tell the company you're taking that four weeks they owe you. Lay in the sun, fall in love, and if you have any sense at all, you won't come back."

"I can't take four weeks," had been Kate's typical reply.

Betty had tried to look very patient. "Just go on the cruise. Look up a friend of mine named Samantha

Blake and let her look after you for a few days. After that you can improvise.''

When she'd found herself yelling at her own father, Kate had surrendered. The very next morning, she'd stepped into the vice president's office to announce that she was taking a vacation, collected her paycheck and spent the rest of the day cruising stores for the perfect suntan lotion. Now she had embarked on, as Winnie the Pooh was want to say, an Adventure.

The first notes from a guitar floated up from the dining room. Someone had mentioned entertainment at nine o'clock. Instinctively Kate checked her watch only to realize it wasn't there; Betty had stolen it at the airport. At home her watch ruled her life, its quick consultation as familiar to her as breathing. After measuring so much of her life by the thing, Kate wondered how long it would take her to realize it wasn't there anymore.

Another chord floated up, a minor one, and Kate forgot her watch. She followed the notes in out of the wind.

The dining room was filling with passengers. At one end a local player had set up. A shaggy, ethereal looking escapee from the sixties, he focused on the music of his era. Kate decided she liked him. Grabbing a cup of coffee and the economics book she'd been about to read, she curled into one of the booths.

Somehow the single voice accompanied by only the acoustic guitar kept the cover of that book closed. Joni Mitchell, Elton John, Crosby, Stills and Nash, Harry Chapin; the poets of her youth, sentiments she understood.

The music was simple, hopeful, a reflection of other times and feelings that Kate wished had never died. It resurrected memories as bittersweet as the music, childhood moments everyone regrets giving away. The place where this music lived, anything was still possible. The world was still hers for the taking, and reality hadn't yet invaded to fulfill parental prophecies.

So enraptured was she by the dreams that still echoed in the songs, Kate didn't notice the tall, blond captain stroll in and take a seat along the other wall. Nor did she see the amazement flare in his eyes when he happened to look towards her. Kate was fifteen years away, and there were tears in her eyes.

Jack had watch at midnight, so he kept himself to one beer. He'd been nursing it out at the bar when, just like every other time Mark played, he'd been drawn inside by the music. There was such a sweet melancholy feeling to it. The thrumming of guitar strings was a pleasant change from the driving percussion of the more popular steel bands.

The dining room was pretty full of first nighters, some couples, some singles, their eyes already on the move for anything interesting. There was also a pretty hardy party atmosphere brewing, which wasn't fair to Mark. Jack took another swig of his beer, thinking that he'd give it about another half hour before the drinkers began to ruin the music.

He'd been casting a casual eye over the assembled group, assessing them for the voyage ahead, when he spotted her. Betty. No, not Betty, Kate. The Peter Pan with teeth.

Her hair caught his attention first. He'd been about to take another swig of beer when she turned a little. His hand came down, the beer forgotten. The light had just glinted off the dark mass of her hair, startling him. He'd thought it was black, but it wasn't. It was auburn. An incredible color, so dark that the red in it was a surprise—a shaft of ruby as she turned her head, a flash of burnished copper, a midnight bay that bewitched. Jack had never seen anything like it before. His fingers itched to touch it.

But then his eyes fell to her face, and all else was forgotten. When he'd met her before, he'd thought her unusual, an attractive woman with eyes that flashed a unique intelligence, but nothing that particularly stood out in a pretty good-looking crowd.

Suddenly he saw that he'd been wrong. With her attention on the music, she more than stood out; she shone. Jack had never seen such brilliant eyes, the blue of a hot sky. It was as if instead of listening to the music she were devouring it whole.

That was what set her apart, what made her mesmerizing—that bright hunger, a sheer delight in the world around her that sharpened her features and animated her movements.

Jack had been on the *Caribbe* for four years. In that time he'd met a lot of women, many beautiful, most intelligent. He'd dated poets and painters and at least one lawyer. But as he sat alone in the crowded cabin, he was assailed by a premonition he'd never had before. He felt as if he were on a collision course with a comet.

He watched her for half an hour as the rowdies gained strength and Mark fought to hold out against them. When she finally stalked out of the room, he followed.

The lights had been turned off on top, leaving only a few anchor lights shining up along the masts. The wind still had control, keeping all but the hardy or foolish below decks. Kate walked back to the rail and leaned against it, coffee still in hand. It had been all she'd been able to do to keep from screaming at those children. Alcohol had such a tendency to make perfectly reasonable people act like spoiled brats. The ones in that dining room had all but ruined the music for her.

She had grown used to listening alone, internalizing the savage pleasure music gave her. She wasn't used to having to share it with the unwashed masses. She also wasn't used to the wave of melancholy those songs were stirring in her. It had been so long since she'd let them bother her. Why now?

The chords still drifted up to her, then the piercing, bittersweet tenor. Kate leaned farther into the railing, her head down and eyes closed to better hear the song, the tang of salt water tickling her nostrils, the wind teasing her hair.

The singer had moved on to Gordon Lightfoot now, swelling the ache within her. She had wanted so much when she'd first heard his music. She was going to be the next Mary Cassatt, a new Georgia O'Keefe. Kate Manion would set the art world on its ear and spend the rest of her life channeling the sweet madness of life back into canvas. She was good at her present work, but she was alive at her easel.

But that was just the way of life, wasn't it? You made do with what was dealt you. There wasn't much to do when the money ran out and your parents became ill but get a job and try your best to survive. It's what she'd done, and she'd done it well. The problem with getting the chance to take time off for a cruise into fantasy was that it gave you the time you didn't want to resurrect the regrets you so carefully swept beneath a blanket of work and ambition.

"Are you all right?"

Kate hadn't heard the soft pad of footsteps behind her. When she heard his voice, she brought her head up with a snap. He stood just a few feet away, hands in pockets, feet apart to take up the ship's sway. His hair glowed just slightly under the frail light, and his eyes had disappeared into the shadow. Kate's mouth went dry.

"Uh, yes," she allowed with a hesitant nod. "I'm fine."

He nodded back and stepped up to lean alongside her at the rail. "Just wanted to make sure you weren't serious about throwing yourself over."

Kate couldn't help a smile as she, too, looked out over the water to where the island's lights did a slow dance above the black sea. "Oh, I couldn't do that. I'd never hear the end of it from Betty."

"She always do this kind of thing for you?"

They didn't change positions, as if watching the night were their true business, not talking to each other.

Kate smiled out to the stars. "Only when she thinks I'm about to commit mayhem up in the executive suites at work. And this is the first time that's happened." She could feel him next to her, the warmth of his body shielding the wind, the tang of his after-shave weaving among the salt.

"She's very generous."

Kate had to shake her head. "Practical, actually. Betty was just made an executive."

The singer had finished his song downstairs, and the English captain considered the sea. He wasn't going anywhere.

"What kind of work do you do?" he asked.

"We work for an investment firm." The words sounded like a sigh. Kate really hadn't meant them to. She was good at what she did and took pride in it. But it had all been getting a bit claustrophobic lately. "We work in the currency market. Buying and selling. I'm the controller."

"Who does what?" He'd turned now, and there was more than a passing curiosity in his eyes.

Kate obliged. "Makes sure that all the transactions the brokers want made are made. The correct amount to the correct bank, correct country, all that."

"Do you want to be an executive, too?"

She shook her head a little. "A broker. I begin my apprenticeship in January."

His eyebrows went up. "Sounds impressive."

Impressive, challenging, demanding. All that and more. "Good work if you can get it."

He nodded toward the book still in her hands. "I assume this is part of the price?"

Kate considered the text, which was heavy and full of small print and deadly boring. "You assume correctly. Finals in three weeks."

"But you're on vacation."

"From work, maybe. There is no escape from postgrad Economics."

He just shook his head. "We're going to have to see about that."

Kate looked over at him, then. He was her age and more. It showed not in the openness of his eyes, but in the crow's feet that crowded their edges.

"What about you?" Kate asked deliberately. "Have you always done this?"

He never hesitated, nodding with another grin. "Always. I was going to be a banker when I grew up, but gypsies stole me away as a child."

Kate chuckled. "Gypsies deal in horses, not sailboats."

"Ah well, yes," he allowed, his grin broadening. "There you are. Marauding Vikings kidnapped me from the gypsies."

Kate hadn't seen the shadow until it detached itself from the surrounding darkness. "Jack? That you?"

His expression briefly betraying irritation, Jack straightened and turned. "Yes, Brian. What is it?"

"Problems with the sonar."

Jack nodded. "Be right there." The man faded away again.

Kate prepared to make understanding noises as he made his excuses. Jack surprised her,

"You going to sleep on deck?"

Kate looked around her at the windswept deck. "Why? I've stowed away in a perfectly good cabin. Besides, it's not going to rain in there."

He threw his head back a moment to consider the conditions of the sky, and Kate saw the fragile light slide down the line of his throat in sharp relief. "Oh, the weather'll clear tonight. We'll have fine sailing tomorrow."

Kate managed to drag her sight from the powerful tendons in his throat just in time to meet his eyes.

"I usually take the twelve-to-four watch," he said. "It's a good time to get to know the ship. A lot of people come up and sleep on deck. You might try it."

Kate wanted to say something intelligent. She would have settled for something funny. The trouble was, she was stunned. It sounded as if he were asking for more time with her, and to her very pragmatic mind, it didn't make any sense. There were still too many eminently more beautiful women on board and his duties to consider. Kate finally settled for the obvious.

"I'll, uh, have to think about it."

Jack nodded. "Good. In the meantime, promise you won't do anything drastic."

"No more drastic than studying economics."

His parting smile was prophetic. "We'll cure you of that, you know."

Kate watched him go with mixed feelings. A handsome, intelligent, all-too-pleasant man with a great set of arms. Another left-hander in a right-handed world. Why was it that she couldn't attract men like that in Detroit? She always got the engineers, the office men who couldn't decide if they wanted to make a commitment or go to a football game. Never the kind with the easy self-assurance of a man who doesn't have to rely on his good looks to succeed. She turned back to her music, wishing that just one of the men she'd dated had had character lines.

Jack reached the steps at the far end of the deck and turned once more to consider Kate Manion. She was a faint shadow against the gray sea; her head bowed once more. He realized that she had bent back down to take in the music from below. He could see the burnished highlights of her nymph's hair, could almost imagine the unique life that shone from those china blue eyes. With a small shake of his head, he thought how special that small lioness was for the way she ingested the world around her. Now all he had to do was find a way to get her to share it with him.

Chapter Two

Kate fell in love with the *Caribbe* the minute the big ship's sails went up.

The day had dawned as beautifully as Jack had predicted, a postcard Caribbean morning with its gem-quality blues and lush greens. The sea lay still and translucent beneath them, and the ship reflected off the water like an apparition. Kate spent the morning testing the feel of warm wood against her bare feet and measuring the scenery for her paint box.

At noon the first shout went up. The anchor was already clattering out of the water as the *Caribbe*, dancing fettishly like a racehorse in the starting gate, began to turn into the wind. There was another shout and everyone began to haul on ropes.

The sails filled, full bellied and graceful, their lines stretching into the brilliant blue of the sky. When one sail caught, the ship began to move. When all four did, she flew. Kate stood at the rail, holding on as if she were on a carnival ride, her eyes a brighter hue than the sky.

"Something, isn't it?"

Kate turned to see Jack smiling at her on his way by. She grinned like a school kid at the world's fair. "Not bad at all. This sailing stuff might just catch on."

"Try it tonight," he suggested.

Even knowing he was already out of earshot, Kate nodded to herself. "I just might." Then she turned her eyes back to the sails rather than tempt herself unnecessarily with the pleasing sight of Jack in his white shorts.

It took Kate a while to settle into one place. She wasn't sure if it was the quiet or the inactivity that preyed on her so much, but something was still proving a shock to her nervous system. She couldn't remember a time in her life when she hadn't had a strict regimen governing her time so that she could accomplish all she had to. School, work, housework, family responsibilities, hobbies, all took a portion of time that never seemed ample enough. She'd simply always been on the move, so that to have nothing to do left her with the feeling she'd forgotten something important. And after spending the last twelve years in the offices of currency brokers, she was lost without the heart-pounding noise and frenetic pace of the place.

A week without anything to do but get a suntan, sketch and ogle handsome men. She wasn't sure she was up to it.

When Kate finally did manage to light, it was to sit on the deck with a pile of textbooks. She was reaching for her marketing textbook, intent on making good on the work she'd missed the night before, when she spotted her sketchbook peeking out underneath. It was like seeing a chocolate bar in a cupboard of wheat germ and vegetables. It called to her.

There was so much here that begged to be put down on paper. The wonderful symmetry and line of the ship, the varied faces who inhabited her, the play of light and dark on her geometric planes. Plagued by the suspicion that she was going to be punished for it, Kate gave into temptation.

The sun was straight up and hot on her bare shoulders, the wind a cool balm that pleasantly ruffled her hair. St. Maarten was dropping away to the stern and another island was rising like a low cloud to port. Singing with the wind, the *Caribbe* danced through the waves like a young girl. A perfect day in paradise.

"Well, of course you're Kate Manion."

Kate squinted up at the assertion. She found a very long pair of legs topped by one of those beautiful California girls with soft blond hair and a figure that would have put a swimsuit manufacturer in a swoon.

"I am?" Kate countered, her hand shielding her eyes from the sun.

The blonde immediately crouched down on her haunches, and Kate was forced to face features that matched the body.

"Of course," the woman enthused with a huge smile and an outstretched hand. "I couldn't have missed you. I'm Samantha Blake. Betty's friend. People call me Sam."

Kate took hold of the offered hand with a certain fatalism. Of course. The friend she was supposed to look up. The one who was going to look after her.

"You have the whole ship buzzing, you know," Sam continued without much pause as she resettled her frame onto the deck.

"Me?"

She nodded brightly. "Jack remembered your name."

Kate waited a moment for the rest of the revelation. Sam was smiling expectantly enough.

"And?" Kate prompted gently.

"Well, he remembered your name," she persisted as if Kate had missed the obvious. Still getting no comprehension, the woman allowed herself a sigh. "I asked Jack if he knew who Kate Manion was. Well, let me tell you. His description would have held up in court. He even told me about your hair. But then, I've never seen a color like that, either. At first I thought it was black, then maybe brown. It's not either, though."

"No," Kate demurred, eyes up as if considering the tumble of curls that framed her face like a mane. Cropped off at her shoulders, it was usually worn in a sleek blow-dried style that offset the youth of her features. The heat and humidity had taken care of that, though. "I think if I were a horse I'd be a bay," she said, instinctively picking at her hair. "I guess it's an off brand of auburn."

"It's beautiful," Sam said. "I'd love hair that color."

Kate couldn't help her surprise as she looked at the other woman's pale gold hair that no magic box could reproduce. She'd been thinking the same thing.

"So, Betty told me I was supposed to make sure you slowed down long enough to relax," Sam went on brightly. "She said your office was a madhouse. She could never hold still."

"Easier to dodge flying missiles that way," Kate allowed with a grin, thinking how much she liked this bright, bubbly young woman who looked as though she didn't know what fast forward meant. "Betty said you ran a bookstore?"

Sam nodded. "On St. Thomas. I left my partner there for a couple of weeks. She spent the first half of this year chasing the perfect wave. Now it's my turn." She hardly took a breath as she reached over to pick up one of Kate's heavier texts. "This isn't vacation reading. Come on down to my cabin later. I have a huge stack of romances. Perfect for the beach... Hello, what's this?"

Instinctively Kate reached out to snatch the sketchbook back. She'd been finishing a sketch of one of the crewmen. He crouched on her page, bare chested in the afternoon sun, dark muscles bunched in exertion, skin glistening with sweat. Kate had used charcoal on it.

Sam drew a long finger along his lines, nodding her head in delight. "Betty never told me you were an artist. This is great."

"It's just a hobby," Kate protested, furiously embarrassed by the attention. No matter how long she drew, she still always felt that it was her mother who'd just caught her sketching instead of doing homework, painting instead of doing housework. After her mother had finally told Kate just what she'd thought about the time Kate was wasting on "just a hobby," Kate had relegated her painting to the furtive hours she'd managed to steal late at night. It had remained her private passion.

"A hobby?" Sam echoed with a quick shake of her head as she riffled through the crowded pages, completely unaware of Kate's discomfort. "Don't be silly. This is wonderful. Stuff half as good as this sells all the time."

Kate shrugged, feeling increasingly uncomfortable. A schoolgirl's talent, her parents had called it. Enough to give her pleasure, but never enough to consider seriously. She would have to find real work to support her avocation. And she had.

"Will you do one for me?" Sam asked, holding the book out as if in example.

"For you?" Kate couldn't quite comprehend a request like that. "Of what?"

Sam looked around, absently tapping the pages with her fingers. "Oh, I don't know." Then she grinned. "Oh, yes I do. Draw me a picture of Jack, right now, with his shirt off."

Kate started rather badly, her head shooting up with an almost audible snap. It was a totally sophomoric reaction. Her reaction to seeing him was even worse.

She'd been right. He did have the long lines of a swimmer; there wasn't an ounce of fat on him. His torso was lean and so tightly muscled that she could have seen him breathe half a block away. Sweat glistened on the sun-tipped hair that fanned across his chest and tapered toward his belly. There went Kate's breath again.

"Yes," Samantha decided with a nod. "I'll hang it up over my desk in homage to this moment."

"He does have nice arms, doesn't he?" Kate couldn't help but respond. She wished there weren't a veritable swarm of long-legged beauties vying for his attention while he worked. It only served to remind her why she shouldn't waste her time on him.

She didn't see the way Sam looked at her with a question that turned to secret anticipation. "Well, he knows who *you* are, Kate. And he's unbelievably single. Why don't you try your hand at him?"

Kate had to laugh, a sharp, wry sound. "We're not talking about macramé here, Sam. Besides, I don't want to be trampled to death in the crowd." Retrieving her sketchbook, she folded it away and picked up the more necessary one on economics.

Sam apparently wasn't in the mood to call retreat. "Oh, why not? What do they have that you don't?"

Kate never bothered to look up. "Long legs, legendary figures and a killer instinct. I don't travel in packs."

Sam laughed at Kate's dry assessment, then shook her head. "Kate, I think you're selling yourself short. You're just as pretty as they are. Prettier, in fact. You have such an—"

Kate immediately raised a warning finger. "If the word 'elfin' so much as crosses your lips, you'll find your luggage bobbing in the wake of the ship."

"What's so bad about looking...like that?" Sam demanded with highly amused eyes.

"Nothing," Kate answered matter-of-factly. "If you're auditioning for a part in *The Wizard of Oz*."

"And you don't find him attractive in the least."

"What would I possibly find enticing about a man who has a chest fit for sculpting?"

"Not to mention a tush that begs to be pinched."

Kate had to grin. "You noticed that, too, huh?"

Sam's answering grin held a measure of triumph. "I'll make a wager with you, Tinker Bell."

"What's that?"

"By the end of this cruise, you'll be the one Jack wants to take home to mother."

Kate did laugh at that, delighted by Sam's boundless optimism. "You've been reading too many of those romances you sell, Sam. Jack would no more take me home to his mother than I would apply for a job as cook on this ship."

Sam offered a nod. "We'll see." Without another word, she turned to the thick book she'd brought on deck.

Kate bet there weren't any statistics in that book. Just the painting of two very well-built people in a rather athletic grasp. From the look of the costumes, they'd taken time out from the Civil War to tumble about on Sam's book cover. For a moment Kate almost asked to borrow it. Then she shook off the temptation and dived back into her text.

By bedtime Kate had to admit to herself that she had failed again. The economics text was safely tucked into her berth downstairs while the sketchpad was still in her hands up on deck, where she'd spread out her blankets and pillow to sleep. There seemed to be some magic at work in these glittering, moonlit waters that prevented her from doing anything constructive as she sailed over them.

Kate took a quick look through the completely filled pages. Characters, ships, geometric designs suggested by sails and rigging crowded the paper. And one other thing. Flipping through again, Kate realized that she'd taken an uncommon interest in one subject in particular.

Filling at least four of the pages were varied studies of hands. Hands working, hauling rope, tinkering with engines, accenting a point in conversation or just resting along the rail. Long, lean hands with bone and muscle that looked sculpted from marble rather than flesh. Hands with a few scars tracing the skin to save them from perfection.

Kate looked down at the hasty strokes that suggested tendon and vein in sharp relief, long, agile fingers that seemed to never remain still, and recognized her fascination with them. They were not only a portrait of strength and grace, but fitting tools of their owner. They were Jack's hands.

Wonderful, she thought as she started off into the milky darkness of a moonlit night. Instead of gaining distance, she was pacing her way closer. There were enough views of Jack on these pages to do a full-size statue. This had all the earmarks of pining from afar, and she couldn't think of anything she found more distasteful.

Even as she dismissed her attraction, Kate conjured up Sam's words. Jack had remembered her name. She wondered why that should be so significant. She wondered why she wanted it to be so very much to be.

"I see you've taken my advice."

Kate started at the sound of Jack's voice. Damn. She wished he'd stop sneaking up on her like that. She looked up to see him framed by the fragile light of the moon and thought she'd love to be able to catch that silver of his hair on paper—or in her hands. His shirt was back on, but it was open so Kate could see the hair that curled into the damp hollow of his throat, and the perspiration that still glistened there. She wanted to taste it.

Dragging her eyes away, she saw that he was smiling with that same easy-going grin that he offered to everyone.

"I'll try anything once," she countered a bit limply. No, I won't, she thought immediately. I'm not a risk taker. It's this damn moonlight. It makes me want to give in to temptation.

Jack raised his eyebrows as he dropped to his haunches beside her. "That kind of talk could get you some interesting invitations."

Kate couldn't help a slow smile as she wrapped her arms around her knees, slipping the sketchbook neatly out of Jack's sight. "Isn't that what vacations are for?"

Had she really said that? Nobody back in Detroit would have believed it. *She* didn't believe it. But there was something so fatally attractive about this man on this soft, moon-washed night when all the predatory females were still downstairs swinging and swaying to the steel band, and the dreams seemed to be saved just for her.

"Then why aren't you downstairs partying?" Jack asked softly.

His words were more than a challenge, Kate understood. They held a real question.

She shrugged, succumbing to the gentle humor she found in his expression, wanting to drift in that cloud-soft gray of his eyes. "Maybe later. I actually only give in to impulse after a fight."

He nodded. "That's what I thought. Not very typical of the single ladies we tend to get around here."

"Most of the single ladies you get don't have to be coerced into taking the cruise," Kate admitted.

"Most of the single ladies aren't shee," he smiled, his gaze drifting up toward her hair.

He lost her. "Pardon?"

Before she knew what was happening, he'd lifted a hand to her hair, weaving his fingers through it. "Your hair gave you away."

Kate sat very still, her eyes wide. She hadn't realized what he'd intended to do until he'd done it. Just the feather-light whisper of his fingers against her hair sent her pulse racing. She felt her own fingertips go cold as the sudden dread of anticipation paralyzed her.

Then, still watching the ruby light in her hair, Jack uttered the fatal words.

"Dryads have hair this color. A darker red than the deepest leaves of autumn." He smiled, his eyes drifting down to hers. "Has anyone ever told you you look like a wood nymph?"

Only half the population of Detroit, Kate thought wryly. Well, at least she'd have the satisfaction of telling Sam I told you so.

"Sure," she assured him with a dry nod. "Walt Disney wanted to cast me in *Fantasia*."

Jack grinned even more broadly, oblivious to the challenge in Kate's expression. "Not *Fantasia*," he disagreed. "*Midsummer Night's Dream*. Tell me, do wood nymphs accommodate themselves to water?"

Kate made it a point to look around her. "I think that's what I'm doing now."

"Not on it," he laughed. "In it. Have you ever been snorkeling?"

She shook her head. "Not much call for it in Detroit."

"Then you'll have to take my beginner's class when we reach Nevis. It's something you don't want to miss."

She couldn't help it, her eyes lighting with dry humor. "The class?"

Jack's gray eyes danced cheerfully. "The snorkeling."

"When do we get to Nevis?"

Jack took a moment to scan the horizon, his eyes squinted in concentration. Kate could see him as one of the crew on an original man-of-war, an officer in silk shirt and breeches, rain-colored eyes quartering the horizon for signs of ships. The image tested her courage, provoking the urge to run from something too enticing. She wasn't sure she wanted to be there when this attraction died, when Jack strolled off to entertain someone else and she withered alone on the windy deck.

"We might get to Nevis tomorrow," he finally said. "I'm not sure. We're headed that way."

Kate grimaced and turned to follow the direction of his gaze to cover her discomfort. "Nothing like exact navigation."

Jack chuckled, a quiet sound of private amusement. "Well, we tend to go whichever way the wind takes us. It's all so much more romantic that way. Besides," he smiled just as Kate let her gaze stray back to him, "isn't it much more fun sometimes to not know exactly where you're headed?"

Kate wrapped her arms more tightly around her knees, aware of the band of yearning that tightened in her chest. "Not according to my mother, it isn't."

Jack held her gaze again, his expression more intense than his words. "Every mother's wrong once in a while," he said. "I'll expect you in class."

Kate nodded, her chest beginning to hurt. "I'll be there, professor."

Jack was about to get back to his feet when he reached over to tap on the exposed edge of Kate's sketchbook, his gaze trapping her with calm consideration. "And bring that with you. I love to look at a girl's etchings." With another chuckle from her blank look of surprise, he straightened. "Night, Kate."

He remembered her name. Kate hoped more and more that it really did mean something.

Tucking her sketchbook back out of the way, Kate pulled her blanket up and turned over to get some sleep. She ended up facing a too-nonchalant Sam as she staked out her own space alongside.

"Just thought you'd like to know," the blonde said with severely repressed delight, gauging Jack's distance before continuing. "I was just strolling the party downstairs, and the talk down there is all about Jack and 'that little redhead.'"

Kate reached over to pat her arm in conciliatory fashion. "Then you'll be happy to know that my reputation is safe. Your bet's already been settled."

"He asked you to marry him?"

"He called me an elf."

Sam assumed a position of outrage. "I don't believe it."

"Believe it," Kate suggested with a dry grin. "Actually he called me a dryad, but it's only a variation on a theme." He also made my heart do triple time with a simple invitation, she silently added.

"But he remembered your name."

Kate saw the real disappointment in Sam's expression and had to smile. "The last I heard, that wasn't a reason to hear the patter of little feet, Sam."

Sam shook her head. "Do you know how many single women come on these cruises?"

"If this trip is any indication," Kate answered. "The entire eligible population with a B-cup or bigger."

"He never remembers a name. I've been on three times and he still calls me Sue. The ship joke is that if Queen Elizabeth wanted Jack to recognize her, she'd have to board with the crown on." Frustrated, Sam turned on Kate. "He remembered *your* name."

Kate shrugged as she snuggled into the covers, her answer much more offhand than her thoughts. "Probably his old mum's name."

Even so, by the time she finally fell asleep, she had worked herself up to believing it meant something, too.

It was close to four in the morning when Jack made his last circuit of the deck, checking the sails to make sure they were taking full advantage of the wind, scouting for problems. The ship was quiet, the passengers long since asleep, and only Ronnie behind the great wheel to keep him company.

Jack was glad to be back on the twelve-to-four rotation. He loved the nights down here, crystal clear and crisp, the big ship pushed smoothly through the blackness. It was as if the *Caribbe* were his alone—her power and grace, the strong curve of her decks and the great gray ghosts that were her sails. She sang to him in the night, this ship did. Songs of far-off ports and vast, bottomless oceans, the music heard by generations of Englishmen before him.

He was just finishing his far lap of the jibs and mizzen, stepping carefully to avoid the occasional bundle of a sleeping passenger, when the beam from his torch glinted briefly from the tantalizingly familiar red of Kate's hair. He stopped there at her feet, unable to resist a bit of innocent voyeurism.

She lay on her side, curled toward him in fetal position, one arm thrown out before her as if reaching for something. She'd gotten some sun that day, and it had pinked her nose and cheeks, making her look, if possible, even younger. Vulnerable. A child lost in sleep, her covers haphazard from restlessness. Jack actually had to stop himself from pulling them back up.

Maybe it was the timing. It had been getting harder to go back down to that cabin alone the past few months. He hadn't even gotten the same pleasure from the spare, clean lines of his home on St. Maarten. Jack had spent seven years on the windjammers, years he wouldn't trade for anything, years that had won him back his health and sanity. But he had the sneaking suspicion that it was getting to be time to move on again.

Was his sudden attraction to a passenger just another symptom of the same problem? Had she walked aboard his ship just as he was looking for something more in his life?

Jack had to smile as he watched her. The wash of light irritated her enough to wrinkle her nose against it and resettle. It amazed him how he wanted to protect her now. Awake, she was an entirely different person—no frail wildflower in need of a guardian, that one. When he touched her she gave off sparks that crawled in his belly. And yet, now she looked for all the world the epitome of childhood innocence, waiting to discover the world. And he realized that he wanted to be the one to show it to her.

Watch out, Jack my lad, he could hear his father say. Sounds as if this bit of a wench has you on the lead.

She does at that, he thought with a sudden smile of surprise. She does at that, Father. The problem is, I don't think I want to get free.

Chapter Three

The ship didn't reach Nevis the next day. It seemed that Antigua had somehow gotten in the way, so they docked there instead. Kate found herself whisked off for a tour that involved marathon shopping with Sam and lunch with the Brenners, an older couple Sam had adopted from a previous cruise.

By the time Kate made it back to the ship, she had gained a gold rope bracelet from the duty-free shops and a lifelong friend in Dick Brenner, the earnest little retired mailman from Cleveland who shared her passion for art. He and Kate had sat out in the sunlight while his wife, Martha and Samantha decimated some of the boutiques on the island. All in all she'd passed a pleasant day on a beautiful island with nice people. It didn't keep Kate from feeling a little guilty about enjoying herself when work still waited back on the ship.

After dinner another party began to take shape. As the ship sailed for its next port beneath the molten silver sky, music tapes were fed into the sound system and the passengers began to gather down by the bar. Back in the empty dining room, Kate was setting up for her own siege.

"You're not going to the party?" Sam asked, hands on hips.

"Not tonight," Kate answered, pulling the rest of her things from her bag and piling them on a table. "Tonight I study."

Sam grimaced with a certain amount of disbelief. "Study?"

"Study," Kate answered with a definite nod of the head. "As in school, which is still in session while I'm off on this little jaunt. I just consider my time tonight a down payment for one of those pesky pipers back home."

"Come on, Kate," her friend objected. "Lighten up. You're on vacation. You can't be expected to do homework."

"I can if I want to keep my grade point average up until I graduate in January." She tried to scoot by the blonde to get a cup of coffee from the great urns by the kitchen. Sam followed right on her heels.

"Good God, Kate. It's only a week."

Kate stopped and sighed. This was such a different world. Didn't people here have goals to attain? Ambitions that carried with them certain costs? "I've been working my way up this particular ladder for about twelve years now, Sam. I can't let anything stand in its way."

Positioned much as a mother would be to prevent a child from running into a busy street, Sam fired off her best shot. "I bet if Jack were the one asking you to close that book, you'd let him get in the way."

"Not," Kate retorted, pushing by, "if he did it naked."

Two hours later Kate sat alone in the dining area, books and notebooks spread out before her, pen in hand, still trying to drag her attention back from the music that drifted in.

They were doing it again. Someone had found an old sixties tape, and it was distracting her.

No, she thought, looking down at the suddenly unappetizing statistics that crowded the page before her. It wasn't the music. It was something else. The music was only making it worse.

It was Sam and the ship and the islands. It was Jack.

Kate was on her feet before she realized it, propelled by a sudden emptiness she refused to name, a yearning that carried a specific name on it.

She was glad Sam had challenged her. It made her remember just what her life was about. Kate didn't live in the timeless moment of a Caribbean cruise. She lived in the stainless-and-cement world of a city, surrounded by family obligations, work demands, ambitions. She'd been such an idiot that night before, wanting to be something special to Jack. What difference would it make? She was going back to her reality, and he was remaining in his.

Skirting the party for the purpose of avoiding Sam and an "I told you so," Kate climbed the steps to the top deck where the wind matched her restless mood. She measured the deck with even steps and watched her frail shadow glide ahead of her. At the stern, one of the native seamen stood at the giant wheel. Kate gave in to a sudden impulse and approached.

"Can I steer?"

"Of course." He flashed a lazy grin and stood aside so that she could take hold of the great wooden spokes. "Just keep it on the same course," he instructed. "West-southwest. See?"

Kate nodded, already mesmerized. The feel of the wheel was incredible, like the reins of a racehorse. There was something so hypnotic about standing here, the deck stretching away from her, the dance of the ship rhythmic in the dark brilliance of the night.

Kate hadn't noticed anyone in the chart house until the door opened beside her.

"Should I get on my life vest now?"

A chill shot up her spine as she turned to greet the newcomer.

"I'm very disappointed," she admitted with a grin. "This doesn't even have power steering."

Jack came alongside her, close enough that Kate could catch the scent of his after-shave and see the moonlight in his eyes.

"You're veering off a little," the crewman warned her gently.

With an almost palpable start, Kate returned her attention to the wheel. Just what she needed, she thought grimly. Another distraction. Especially one that smells and looks like that.

"I guess this means I can't be captain," she apologized with a rueful grin.

"Not unless you're planning a mutiny," Jack grinned back. "If you are, let me know. I bet you'd look great with a cutlass in your teeth."

Kate grimaced. "I don't do steel."

Damn, she thought, dragging in a deep breath. What was it about standing here next to him that filled her with such heady exhilaration? Was it the wind that fingered her hair, or the wash of moonlight, the snap of the sails in the wind? Or was it the ghostly gray of Jack's eyes when he watched her? She could feel her determination to maintain her distance dissolve before Jack's bright gaze. What was that life she was supposed to get back to?

"So," he asked, standing very close to her as she clutched the wheel. "How did you like Antigua?"

"Antigua?" Suddenly Kate couldn't conjure up any memory of the island. She'd just been there. What was wrong with her? "I think I liked it almost as much as it liked me."

Jack nodded, never taking his eyes from her. "Succumbed to the duty-free disease, did you?"

As her answer, Kate lifted her arm with the bracelet. The gold slid down her smooth arm, gleaming softly in the moonlight. She didn't see Jack's eyes widen a little.

"Very nice," he nodded. "You have good taste in excess."

Kate was having trouble breathing again. "Thanks. It's amazing what madness comes over a person in a tropical climate."

"Yes," he agreed, his eyes saying so much more. "Isn't it?"

For a long moment Kate couldn't take her eyes from his. They were magnetic, hot. The once-cool gray drew her close and held her with the intimation of promise. Out on that windswept deck where the night was chilled, Kate felt suddenly stifled.

A small cough interrupted her thoughts. "You're—"

Kate snapped to attention. "Veering again. I'm sorry." She turned back to the stretch of deck before her. "So, tell me. How do you steer this thing?"

"I told you," Jack answered with a soft smile. "We go with the wind."

"Virtually impossible all the time," she retorted with a steadying breath she hoped he didn't see. Why wasn't she already back downstairs? Why wasn't she back in Detroit? "At least that's the way it seemed in *Two Years before the Mast*."

"You're looking for sailing lessons?"

"Basics. I have no aspirations to take one of these things home with me." The wind had returned once she'd turned away from Jack. The night was chilly again. She wasn't sure whether that was relief she felt or not. "How do you know where you're going? Do you still use the sextant and all that?"

"When I'm in the mood."

Jack got a glare for his humor, which he returned with a bigger smile. "We have all the advances of modern science," he said. "Radio, VHF, SSB, radar, echofinder for depth. Want to see?"

"I'd love to."

Kate didn't realize what a mistake she'd made until she handed the wheel back over to the broadly grinning mate and followed Jack into the cramped cabin that housed the equipment. The stifling feeling in her chest returned, getting worse with each minute that she spent crowded next to Jack, bathed in the soft red light that illuminated the various screens and maps cluttering the little room.

"What's that?" Kate asked, pointing to a clump of shadows that materialized on the edge of the radar.

"Well," Jack answered, peering at the screen with a show of concentration that somehow entailed moving nearer to Kate. "It's either some small islands or very large sea serpents."

Most of Kate's concentration was centered on managing her next breath. She didn't have claustrophobia, but she couldn't stay this close to Jack without his crowding her air. She made it a point to edge back out the door as she spoke. "I do like a man who knows his business."

Just as Kate was stepping out the door, the ship took an odd dip that pulled her off balance. Jack instinctively reached out to steady her.

Kate flashed him a rueful grin. "You always manage to see me at my most graceful. I can usually keep my balance in Detroit. Then again," she amended, righting herself and doing her best to ignore the sparks shooting up her arm, "the ground doesn't bounce there."

Jack didn't seem to see the necessity in letting go of Kate's arm once they'd reached the deck. "Don't feel badly," he smiled as they headed along together. "I'd been sailing for ten years when I fell overboard in a storm." His shrug was deprecating. "Suddenly the deck was four feet down and angled straight for the ocean. I slid right off."

Kate looked up at him, instinctively following his story as well as his footsteps. "You're kidding."

"Oh, no," he answered with an earnest shake of his head. "I was dumped into twenty-foot swells in my clothes and shoes, no life jacket. And my mates didn't even know I'd gone over. They sailed right on past." Steering her toward the stairs and back to the dining area, Jack shook his head with some wonder. "I remember thinking that this was it for old Jack. I was going down for the third time and there wasn't any help in sight."

Kate stopped, forcing him to pull up a step lower. "What happened?"

Jack had been waiting for that. His sudden grin was rakish. "I drowned." He was all set to walk on when Kate, without missing a beat, responded with a like grin.

"Oh, thank God. I thought something awful might have happened."

Jack's laughter rolled out over the water as he led her back to the dining room. Kate didn't think to question his actions—or maybe she refused to question them. It had been a long time since she'd felt such a giddy bubble of anticipation, and she didn't really want it to die. They ended up in the empty room with her books still on the table, waiting like ghosts of her commitments.

"What's your verdict on the *Caribbe*?" Jack asked as they each poured themselves a cup of coffee from the big, gleaming urns.

"Shangri-la," Kate said with an amazed shake of her head. "I didn't think there was anyplace in the world with this much solitude."

Jack made it a point to consider the noise level from the party with a rather skeptical grin. "Solitude?"

"You have to understand," Kate explained, walking back toward her booth. "Our office has been blacklisted by the EPA for noise pollution. A Def Leopard concert is quieter."

He nodded. "Sounds interesting." He didn't sound as if he were all that sure. Following Kate to the booth, he picked up one of the books. "Oh, no. This isn't what I think it is."

"If you think it's homework, it is."

He lifted stern eyes at her. "In Shangri-la? Unheard of."

Kate relieved him of the book and set it back down. "Some of us have to head back down the mountain," she reminded him.

When she slid back into the booth to continue her work, Jack considered her. Then he slid in across from her.

"You know, a captain could ban that kind of antisocial activity."

Kate just smiled. "But he wouldn't."

Taking a sip of his coffee, Jack smiled back. "I guess not. Especially when it's going to be so much more fun to teach you how to give it up on your own."

Kate wasn't quite sure what she saw in his eyes just then, but it made her shiver. The anticipation skimmed her like a sudden current. With just his words Jack threatened to make even the dining room too small to share.

It didn't dawn on her until too late that he'd started rummaging through her books even as he kept that amused half smile on her. Suddenly, though, his gaze turned and with it his attention. That was when Kate's heart really lurched.

"Ah hah!" he accused with a smile. "Here it is. I knew I'd find it underneath all this responsibility."

Before Kate could even gather the control to draw breath, Jack was flipping through the pages, his eyebrows up, his amusement fading into honest respect.

"I was wondering," Jack admitted, almost to himself. There was such life on each page, such vibrant energy. The teeming, pulsing life behind those delicious blue eyes that never quite came to life when talking about work fairly vibrated from these pages. The real secret to Kate Manion.

"My alter ego," she explained, her voice almost an apology. "I drink one rum swizzle and think I'm Pablo Picasso."

Jack looked up, a new understanding in his eyes. "A closet artist."

Kate made the attempt to shrug offhandedly. "I'm left-handed. The myth is that all left-handers feel more of an urge to be creative."

"Is it?" He nodded in amusement. "I thought the myth was that we were all a little mad."

Without looking at him she admitted the truth. "That's the same thing sometimes, isn't it?"

Jack saw the mist rise in Kate's eyes—the self-conscious pain of a need that had been locked away so long that it had become a quiet kind of obsession. In those crystal eyes he saw a twin torment to the one he had carried for so long back in the gently wooded hills of Kent. He came very close then to sharing it with her, and he hadn't done that since Nathaniel had come and saved him.

"Jack, there you are."

They both looked up with a start to see a tall, well-built blonde considering them from the doorway. Her very cool look of amusement led Kate to immediately dub her the Ice Queen. Strolling just a little closer, the woman seemed quite capable of banishing Kate from her attention.

"We've been partying for three hours," she pouted, "and you haven't been there yet." She wasn't talking to Kate, either.

"I'm on watch," Jack said, lifting his cup. "I can't drink."

One flawless eyebrow arched. "You can dance."

He smiled and nodded. "Sure thing."

The blonde's answering smile was flavored with subtle triumph. At least it was until Jack turned back to Kate.

"Tomorrow, then?"

"We'll be there?"

"Hard not to be. We're next door to it right now."

Kate nodded with more assurance than she felt. "I'll be there."

When he smiled this time, it was Jack who excluded one of the people in the room, and it wasn't Kate. Getting to his feet, he handed Kate back her book. "You have a talent there, my little nymph. Don't waste it."

For a few long moments Kate sat watching the empty door, listening to the laughter and heady percussion of the party outside, thinking of the special smile in Jack's eyes when he'd left her. The exhilaration still hummed inside her. The hours until the morning stretched too long.

How long had it been since she'd looked forward to the start of a new day? When was the last time she'd actually felt flushed from a man's attentions?

Kate found herself fingering the gold-chain bracelet and thinking of the tiny island where she'd bought it: lush vegetation and a centuries-old village where history slept; bright sun and intoxicating colors, the world walking at a slow pace and smiling. She'd never been out of Michigan before nor even seen an ocean until the plane had circled Miami. And now she'd stepped right onto Peter Pan's ship where you never had to grow up or deal with reality—where, with just a little help, you could fly.

She could, she thought to herself. This was a place where reality didn't exist, so why force it? Why not, just for a little while, recapture the excitement of discovery? She had plenty of time to recover her place on the careful path that parents, necessity and success had carved out for her. Why not fly just for now?

It was a harmless sin, airing out still rooms, rearranging furniture just a little to make it new. Just as long as she didn't come away from the cruise with the desire to leave the room altogether. She didn't want the furniture of her life to seem suddenly unattractive, because that was the furniture she had to live with.

What could it hurt, though, to enjoy the attentions of a handsome man, or trade her books in for her paint box for a week, to resurrect the delight she'd so carefully folded away beneath her work suits? Maybe everyone was right. A week in fantasyland couldn't hurt anything.

When Kate slammed her book shut and walked out on deck to join the party, she did it with a determination dimmed only by the trepidation she couldn't quite quell. It had been a long time since she'd thrown caution to the wind.

"Where is everybody?"

Kate took one last look around the empty quay before facing Jack again. She'd shown up for her lesson to find only Jack there to greet her.

He shrugged with an offhand grin as he waved for a waiting taxi. "No one else signed up."

When Kate didn't follow him to the taxi, he turned to see why.

"Did you *ask* anyone else?" Kate demanded, perilously close to grinning. She'd spent the entire night before worrying about making a fool of herself in front of the Ice Queen, only to realize that that wasn't what she should have been worrying about at all.

Jack's answering grin lit his gray eyes with delighted mischief. Striking a studious pose, he sought to remember. "Matter of fact," he admitted. "I didn't. Let's get a taxi."

Before Kate could protest, he had her by the hand and deposited her into the vintage taxi driven by a large, smiling black woman who seemed to know Jack quite well.

"Isn't this kidnapping or something?" Kate asked, the impulse to grin finally getting the better of her as the driver, one Philomena, turned toward the town.

Jack shook his head, his eyes still bright. "Simple misrepresentation. I am going to teach you to snorkel. I simply decided not to do it in a crowd."

Unconsciously Kate pulled her fingers through her hair, her habit of settling down. The locks immediately fell back into their now-customary disarray. "You couldn't have just asked me?"

With an air of stern surprise, he shook his head. "For a fairy child, you certainly don't know much about the fairy ways," he scoffed. "You have to be tricked into doing what I want or you'll turn me into a donkey."

"If you don't stop calling me a fairy child," Kate warned, though her attempt to control her delight failed, "I'll turn you into a toad."

Philomena slowed and turned into the Island Road. Jack didn't bother with directions. He kept his eyes on Kate. She could feel their sudden heat like sunlight striking through the trees.

"But you are a fairy child," he protested, his voice suddenly soft. He reached over to touch Kate's hair as if his hand had been drawn to it of its own accord. "I've seen your pictures in my book of fairy tales, and you had gossamer wings and danced on bluebells. Or did you wander the deep lakes where Excalibur lays?"

Kate sat very still before his eyes and touch wondering what had happened to the bantering in his voice, unsure how to answer. She should smile and make some dry retort, putting the subject safely back within the comfortable realm of humor. But somewhere with the touch of his fingers she lost her humor. His gaze held hers like a disturbingly familiar caress and made her tremble.

Kate suddenly ached for more, every nerve ending anticipating the heat of his touch. She didn't notice that she was breathing a little faster, or that she clasped her hands as if afraid of letting go. She didn't know that in the space of that few seconds she'd memorized the texture of his eyes—the gray shot through with tiny shards of blue, the rims the color of snow shadows, the lashes soft, sable brown. Eyes that beckoned and comforted—that threatened to steal her heart.

The town was giving way to palm plantations, the trees marching in parallel columns along the road. Light filtered in past the high leaves to dapple the brightly colored houses and nourishing the brilliantly colored flowers that tumbled over fences and walls like waterfalls. Kate turned toward the scenery to regather her composure.

"This is a beautiful place," she murmured, thinking that time stood still on this island, just like the ship. No seasons, no media, no mass transportation. Just lazy roads that wound around verdant, eternal mountains and ever-blooming flowers. The real world slipped even farther away, and the day she had with Jack stretched endlessly ahead. That idea sent an unaccustomed flush of both anticipation and dread through her.

"Nevis is kind of a home away from home," Jack allowed, following Kate's gaze. "Isn't that right, Philomena?"

The cabbie grinned back in the mirror. "When you need to get away from the rat race on St. Maarten," she sang out with delight, "you come to Nevis. We treat my friend Jack right, you know."

Kate couldn't help but laugh. "The rat race on St. Maarten?"

Philomena shook her head. "Too busy over there. They hurry all the time."

Jack gave Kate's shoulder a squeeze. "You have to reset your clock down here, Kate. It's a different world."

Kate finally gave in and turned to him with a rueful smile of surrender. "It is that."

It was a world of miracles, too, Kate discovered the minute she slipped into the water. Jack had spent time teaching her the basics of snorkeling, and she'd listened, nodding, intent on his words. Then he'd led her by the hand into the waves, and the learning became instinct. Sheer delight took over.

It was like flying, sailing weightlessly above an entirely new world. As the waves sped along beneath her, Kate drifted gently back and forth, buoyed by the salt water, eyes on the alien landscape which was almost within her reach.

She discovered the ghostly pastels of shifting water and coral reaching out to her with stubby fingers or crouching in bouquets like cauliflower heads. Sea fans like multicolored lace swayed to the rhythm of the sea, and a carpet of shimmering grass waved in an invisible wind. Then Kate spotted the fish, suddenly darting out toward her and away. First one, then a few, then a school of hundreds, wheeling and skimming past her in a bright shower.

The electric colors of the fish made her laugh when she realized that their blue was brighter than the stripe on her suit. When they disappeared into the coral, Kate followed and ended up with a snorkel full of water.

Jack had been snorkeling for ten years. He still enjoyed it as a quick fix on the underwater world if he couldn't use his scuba gear. When he saw Kate's reaction to it, though, it all changed. Suddenly something he enjoyed became cherished again.

It was like watching children open presents on Christmas; you fed on the wonder in their eyes to rediscover your own. Even through the mask, Kate's eyes were mesmerizing. Wide open and electric, each new experience was telegraphed in them like heat lightning on a summer night. Her joy grabbed him in the gut, wrenching him back to the summer days of his youth when he had first tasted the Caribbean waters.

When she surfaced, he followed, coming up scant feet away from her. She pulled out the mouthpiece and lifted her goggles, while bobbing gently in the waves. The seawater beaded on her cheeks and lips, molding that spectacular auburn hair into a soft, wavy cap that curled along her throat. Jack half expected to see her wreathed in mother of pearl or the gold of long-sunken treasure ships.

"How do you like it?" he asked. Bloody silly question, actually. She looked as though she'd been the first to witness heaven.

When Jack first spoke Kate started, and he could tell she'd forgotten about him. He saw the initial surprise, the shy hesitation, as if she had caught him intruding in her private world. It couldn't be kept in, though. She ended up laughing with the abandon of a child.

"Has this always been here?" she demanded, instinctively pushing wet hair from her forehead.

Jack found himself smiling back at her. "If you'd like, I'll tell you I had it put together just for you."

She grinned. "You have a wonderful eye for fish."

"If you think this is something, follow along and I'll show you what I can do with coral."

He reached out to take her hand. Again there was hesitance, a flicker of disquiet. That quicksilver motion of bright hesitation, as if caught between worlds and longing to escape, made him wonder if maybe there wasn't something of the fairy in her after all.

You're getting fanciful, old son, Jack thought to himself. You're a practical man who's always dealt with life like the sea. But suddenly you're thinking of poetry and fairy tales.

Jack saw the uncertainty die in Kate's eyes. A determination took hold, gleaming in her eyes like sunlight. Then she took hold of his hand, and he followed her back into the waves. It was there that he surrendered to her magic.

Chapter Four

Kate took a sip of her gin and tonic and gazed around Jack's favorite restaurant on the island. No more than four whitewashed walls and a hardwood floor polished to a flawless gloss, the room contained six tables and a couple of straggly plants that hung in deep, cool windows. The small, cluttered bar in the next room also seemed to be the local gathering place for English expatriates.

Deeper and deeper, Granda, Kate thought with a wry smile. And here I promised you wouldn't have to worry about my attracting any Englishmen. Every rebel ancestor in the Manion clan must be spinning in his grave right along with you.

It's all a lark, Granda, she thought, taking another sip as she waited for Jack to return from the rest room. A fantasy. Surely a good Irish girl can't be condemned for that.

The problem was that the knot in her chest belied her assertions. If it were only fantasy, she wouldn't already ache with melancholy just knowing that she could never have another day like this.

Again she thought of the wonders she'd seen that day and felt the familiar excitement crowd her chest. She had never known such breathtaking beauty. It didn't take much for her to begin transferring the magic of that underwater world into her painting.

But that wasn't what ached in her so badly. The coral reef would wait for her to return. She could squeeze in another vacation some year, sating herself on it for a week and then going home. She couldn't do the same with Jack.

Kate was still amazed at the instant, unspoken camaraderie they'd shared today. They had glided along side by side, pointing and gesturing at the strange wonders they found, eyes instinctively meeting with delight in the fragile splendor of this new world. Suspended like flyers over a dreamlike panorama that only they shared, they had discovered a communication that transcended language, a bond that defied explanation.

"You look like you swallowed a squid."

Startled, Kate looked up to see Jack approach. He was back in chinos and a knit shirt, which didn't do anything to slow her pulse rate. He'd looked so good in his trunks, so sleek in the water, his powerful legs scissoring effortlessly as he led her through his wonderland. She'd stolen her share of looks his way and thought of how watercolors would do him justice, the shadows flickering over his skin and his eyes laughing behind the goggles.

"I was just thinking how you'd look on paper," she admitted.

Pulling out his chair, he sat down. "That bad, huh?"

Kate couldn't help but grin. "You mistake concentration for displeasure. I figure I could probably fudge a little and make you come out okay."

"Thanks," he scowled. "I'll always come to you for my compliments."

"Anytime."

"So, where is it, then?"

Intent on tasting the lobster sandwich on her plate, Kate looked up to see Jack lift his beer for a swig, his eyes never leaving hers.

"Where is what?"

He set the bottle down. "The sketchbook. I thought I was going to get to look at your etchings. After all, I showed you my fish."

Kate didn't even realize that she had retreated. "And your fish were lovely," she murmured, taking a bite of the lobster, the garlic butter dribbling out over her fingers. "But I didn't bring the sketchbook. Besides, you already saw it."

Jack shrugged comfortably. "Just a glance. I want to see more. I'd like to understand how Picasso becomes an office worker."

Kate almost flinched, suddenly uncomfortable with his assurance. "Oh, that's easy. I was kidnapped by a marauding band of accountants."

Jack chuckled and Kate thought how intimate it sounded.

"Why didn't you pursue your painting?"

She shrugged. "Painting's a hobby. Work's work. I paint when I don't have anything else to do."

This time Jack shook his head, the humor in his eyes suddenly fading. "Kate Manion," he accused, his consternation surprising her. "You're lying through your teeth."

Kate grew very still. Quicksand, she thought with sudden, unaccustomed panic. I've fallen into it, sudden and lethal and too unbelievably inviting. She was at once uncertain and excited, afraid of what he offered and yet drawn by it.

"I told you," she said with a timorous smile. "It's my alter ego. My creative side."

He didn't smile back. Instead his eyes flashed. Kate couldn't know that he was angry at her family for tying back her wings to keep her from flying. "So, why should you hide it all away?"

In Detroit it would be so easy to explain. In the Caribbean, the idea of responsibility seemed faintly alien. "I am not Picasso," she said. "Or Cassatt or Gauguin. I paint because I enjoy it." Because she needed to. Because the world gathered itself into such breathtaking colors, such seductive shapes that it had to be collected. Why should it frustrate her so much? Why should it frighten her that Jack saw that frustration even when she hadn't mentioned it?

She saw his gray eyes go dark, like a stormy sky, and their intensity seared her. She felt cornered by them, by Jack. She wanted to back away. She wanted more. She came very close to running.

Because the two of them fenced on the edge of silence, they didn't see the little man barreling toward them.

"Well, Jack me lad, so you've drug yourself back, 'ave you?"

Jack turned to greet his friend. Kate all but gasped, so intent was she on Jack's silent accusation. It wouldn't have been so bad if he weren't so right.

"Is this the young lady of the hour?"

Kate finally had to turn to greet the newcomer. A swarthy, solid little man, he had a pirate's smile and enough tattoos to qualify him for a sideshow tent. It didn't take Jack's introduction for Kate to know that Nathaniel had been career Navy. He and his wife were the owners of the restaurant and, from the sound of it, the nucleus of the British colony here.

"Watch 'im then, lass," he advised, sending a wink Kate's way. "'E does love the ladies. And most of the ladies 'ave loved him back."

Jack didn't seem to mind the accusation at all. "Thanks for the character reference, Nathaniel."

"Anytime, lad, anytime. Just trying to keep the female population safe, aren't I?"

By the time Nathaniel wandered back to the bar, Kate was left with the feeling that she'd been caught in an explosion. The little man's opinions were just as salty as his language, and he shared both liberally. No one was safe from his tongue, and no one seemed to mind. Kate laughed more in that fifteen minutes than she had in six months.

"Where did you find him?" she asked Jack, quietly, wiping at her eyes with the terry cloth and thinking how grateful she was to the older man for breaking up the unbearable tension.

"Nathaniel found me," Jack admitted with a wry smile. "He got me my job on the *Caribbe*."

Kate's eyebrow rose. "Does that mean he's a gypsy or a Viking?"

Jack chuckled. "Neither. I met him one day when I was a kid wandering the Naval Yards. Nathaniel was a chief mate. He taught me a lot about ships." Reminiscing, he grinned. "Taught me a lot about other things, as well. I got the bootstrap once when I complained at dinner that we were having bloody lamb again. Father did not appreciate that kind of language from a seven-year-old."

Kate could just imagine. "What were you doing when he found you this job?"

Jack's expression became enigmatic. "Nothing nearly as much fun."

Kate scowled. After what Jack had said about her, she felt she deserved an answer. He'd seemed so sure, as if he'd once been where she was.

"I could just ask Nathaniel, you know," she warned leaning over a little. "I'm sure his version of the story would be much more ... colorful."

"Eat your lunch. Nathaniel made it just for you."

Kate shook her head, eyes suddenly alive with challenge. "After you tell me. I figure it must be very mysterious if you don't want to talk about it. Spy? Criminal escaping the long arm of the law? What did you do, embezzle all the funds from your local bank? Blackmail a local don?"

It was Jack's turn to scowl. "Hardly. I was in the family business. Manufacturing."

"What's wrong with manufacturing?" Kate asked, finally finishing off her sandwich, the sherry and garlic laced lobster momentarily taking her attention.

"I'm sure there's nothing wrong with manufacturing," Jack assured her. "I just found out after a few years that it wasn't for me."

Kate nodded to herself. "Not romantic enough."

Kate's words brought Jack up short. He snorted with dry amusement. "I'm hardly a romantic."

Kate saw Nathaniel lean back in his chair and almost found herself laughing again. He had obviously been listening, and just as obviously had his own opinion on the matter.

Jack wasn't nearly as delighted, although there was some dry humor to be found in the impatience that clouded his eyes.

"You're right," Kate retorted with delight. "Come to think of it, I can't think of anything less romantic than signing on as captain of a sailing vessel that's been obsolete for a hundred years. That ranks right up there with accounting and . . . manufacturing as practical careers."

This time Nathaniel failed to keep his opinion to himself. His hooting laughter ricocheted off the cool walls like crossfire. "Mind this one, Jack me lad!" he shouted from his precarious perch on the bar stool. "Spend much more time with her and she'll have you pinned to the board like a bleedin' butterfly!"

Bearing Nathaniel's delight with amused restraint, Jack scowled at Kate. "You know, of course, that I'll never hear the end of this."

Kate refused to offer commiseration. "Lunch was your idea."

He sighed, tilting his bottle for another swig and setting it back down. "If I have any sense, it'll be my last."

Kate grinned at him as she licked at fingers still oily with garlic sauce. Jack saw in her face a playful gamin. But in her eyes, the deepest sky blue of innocence, he discovered the unconscious sensuality of a woman who knew her strengths and capitalized on them. She was just like a jewel, flashing different colors from each facet as she turned.

"Don't worry," she assured him with a pat to his hand. "If you'd like, I'll tell everyone that we spent the day discussing Wall Street and kicking sand in the faces of skinny tourists."

Jack grimaced. "And I suppose brokers are immune to romance."

"Absolutely," Kate nodded, the light in her eyes dancing like sunlight on water. "The most romantic thing I get to do is quote the price of French francs."

Jack leaned toward Kate, triumph in his eyes, his hand reaching over to capture hers. He liked the moist feel of the fingertips she'd just licked, the glisten of oil on her full lips. "In that case," he challenged, his thumb beginning to instinctively trace patterns over her smooth, soft palm. "A broker wouldn't be caught dead crying over old music or laughing at fish."

Kate's eyes filled with sudden anticipation. Jack could see that he had surprised her. He wondered whether anyone else had ever spoken to this softer, sensual side of her. Had anyone ever really taken the time to discover it?

There was such delicious wonder in her eyes now, just like when she'd opened them for the first time to a coral reef. The sun glowed in her, sparkling with delight and tremulous excitement at his attention. A fairy caught at the edge of the glade. Jack wanted to capture that fairy, follow her into the depths of her forest and lose himself in her.

"I bet she wouldn't even spend all her free time and money painting."

Kate couldn't believe it. A bright elation took wing in her chest and tried to escape its confines. How had he known that? Why would he ever have taken the trouble to understand things that had until now only been hers?

She didn't know how to deal with this. In only a few days this man had discovered more about her than people who'd known her for years.

"She would sooner be flogged," she managed a bit breathlessly. There was something terribly hypnotic about the way his thumb rasped against her sensitive skin.

"What were you doing when *you* found out about the ship?" he asked, somehow closer without moving.

Kate couldn't quite catch her breath. "I told you." She was afraid. She was hungry. There was too much promise here to accept, too much enticement to back away.

Jack shook his head. "That doesn't tell me anything. What's waiting for you in Detroit?"

Nothing, she wanted to say. Nothing but a job I do too well and a father and sisters who need me too much, a little apartment I've grown accustomed to and a stack of paintings I've never let anyone see.

"Reality," she said instead.

His eyebrows went up. "This isn't reality?"

Kate shook her head again and the sunlight tumbled among the loose curls. "No. It's a place you can go to escape the pressures of life. Temporary shelter. The real world begins at the Miami Airport."

"That categorizes an awful lot of hard-working people," Jack accused with an amused smile. His thumb reached the sensitive skin on the inside of Kate's wrist where faint blue veins converged like rivers beneath the quickening pressure of his touch. He found the artery there and tested it. Kate started as if he'd lit a nerve ending.

"Stop that," she ordered, jerking her tingling arm away. She had goose bumps all the way to her shoulder.

"Why?"

Even with the hammering of her heart, she refused to flinch before the calm regard of Jack's eyes. "Because you're not real, either."

"That's going to be bad news for my parents," he said. "They spent an awful lot of money and attention on me."

Kate grinned, giving measure for measure as she sought to quell the storm Jack had deliberately stirred in her chest. "It won't be as much of a surprise as you think," she assured him. "Manufacturers don't consider tall ship captains as real people, either."

"Why don't you?"

Kate never turned away or sought to cover her churning emotions by studying her glass. Instead she kept Jack's eyes trapped so they couldn't get away from her. "How many days have I been on this cruise?" she finally asked.

Her question threw him off. Straightening in his chair, he took a moment to study her. "Three. Why?"

Kate nodded, as if giving benefit for a correct answer. "And how many are left?"

"Two."

She nodded again. "My mother said never to consider letting a man have his way with me unless I'd known him six months. She actually said not to do it at all, but we came to a compromise."

Kate thought Jack would be surprised by the direct approach. He wasn't. "You're considering that, are you?"

Kate smiled and leaned back in her chair. "Hard not to when I'm having my wrist explored like a wall with a secret panel."

"I prefer to think of it as a work of art," he obliged with a delighted smile. "You certainly don't mince words, do you, Kate?"

Her eyes lit up like an afternoon sky. "I only have three more days in paradise," she said quietly. "I can't afford to waste them."

Jack allowed himself a slow, amazed shake of the head. "This conversation certainly hasn't taken the tack I thought it would. I'd envisioned something more along the lines of trading childhood stories, that kind of thing." Lifting his bottle, he finished his beer in a gulp. "Which means we should take this conversation outside. Nathaniel prides himself on the ability to eavesdrop. Don't you, Nathaniel?''

Nathaniel, still on his bar stool in the other room, merely nodded. "Indeed I do, lad.''

Kate accepted Jack's proffered hand and got to her feet.

Outside, the trade winds sliced along between the buildings and sent the trees shuddering. Kate couldn't help but smile at the beauty of the little island. She loved the wind, loved the colors, loved the heady, fecund aromas; it buoyed her like a balloon in a breeze. The fact that Jack was holding her hand had nothing to do with it.

"Don't go home.''

Kate started at the sound of Jack's voice. It was as if he had given voice to the very temptation that had just wormed its way into her mind.

"What?''

He smiled and stopped so that she had to face him, her hand still tight in his. They were alongside the little town square—a patch of grass and blooming flowers and old stone. Like anywhere in the world, old men lined the benches and watched the world go by.

"Stay here with me a while longer. I begin holiday next week and don't have anything planned.'' Nothing he couldn't cancel, anyway.

"Jack,'' she retorted, her voice small and strained. "Listen to yourself. This isn't something you say after four days.''

An eyebrow went up. "You were the one who said she didn't have any time to waste.''

"But you don't know anything about me.''

He shrugged, his thumb once again stroking her palm, his eyes intense. "I know that I haven't seen the world with such fresh eyes since I was a boy. I know there's a well of wonder in you that tastes like champagne. And I know that more than anything in the world right now, I want to do this."

Before Kate could react, Jack took her by the arms and dragged her to him, and her bag thumped to the ground. His arms enfolded her to him. His hands kept her there. His mouth slanted down on hers. His fingers, those strong, sensual tools that she'd drawn several times, rasped lightning through her.

Kate raised her face instinctively, meeting his hungry mouth with her own. She drank in the heady elixir of the scent and the smoky taste of his tongue. She even discovered the tang of garlic and sherry, and thought the flavors were delicious on him.

Just the touch of his hand made her breathless. Now enclosed within the iron grip of his arms, she felt as if she'd lost contact with the ground. Her skin shrieked where it met his, thigh against steely thigh, arms blindly seeking the corded muscles of his back. Her breasts were crushed against his chest, the sensitive flesh catching fire.

Suddenly Kate needed that embrace. A fire erupted in her belly where there had been none before. Frissons of delight slithered up and down her back. Within the space of a single kiss, Kate forgot her responsibilities and remembered what it was like to dream.

Slowly Jack straightened, feathering kisses on her swollen, soft lips as if it made them easier to part. Kate understood. For the first time in her life, she savored the taste of danger—because Jack was dangerous. There was no mistaking that. With only that kiss Kate knew he had the potential to turn her away from sanity.

"I have a story for you," he said, lifting a finger to trace her lips. "It's about a man I knew who was very much like you."

Kate didn't see the town around them anymore. She didn't notice that at the other side of the square the old men watched them with passive faces. She didn't smell the moist grass under her feet. She didn't even realize that they might as well have stayed under Nathaniel's protective eye for all the privacy they'd gained. Her world dissolved into the gray of Jack's eyes, was bounded by his smile and the gentle lesson in his words. She listened because of the spell Jack wove, and stayed to float in the cadence of his soft voice.

"When he was a boy," Jack began, "he wanted to go to sea. He didn't care how. When you're that age you think that anything's possible, that you'd be willing to give up anything to get it. The boy's mother told him he was daft. His father had built up a business just to hand it over to the boy, and that should be enough for anyone. Sailing's for weekends, she'd say. For getting away from what you had to do."

"Well, that boy's father died when he was very young, and the boy did take the business over. He did his duty, kept the company, pulled his family through and exchanged what he wanted to do for what he should do, just like his old mum had said. But all that time, he had a poem tacked on his wall. *Mandalay* by Kipling. Know it?"

Her eyes widening, Kate nodded.

Jack nodded back. " 'On the road to Mandalay/ Where the flyin' fishies play/an' the dawn comes up like thunder/outer China 'crost the bay.' "

Kate saw the dream crystallize in his eyes all over again, the bittersweet light of childhood dreams coveted in attic rooms and private hiding places. It finally made her realize why he knew her so well.

"To the boy, that poem had been the words of his dream. To see those places, to ply those oceans. The man kept the poem hung in his office and named his weekend boats after it."

"And what happened to him?" Kate asked, oblivious to everything but the remembered pain and longing in Jack's eyes.

When he looked down at her, though, he smiled, and the promises were fulfilled. "He landed in the hospital with a bleeding ulcer. It made him realize that he was thirty-three and losing his last chance at that dream. So when he got out, the only thing he took with him was his poem. He sailed his *Mandalay* to the islands, got a job as an engineer on a windjammer and hasn't ever looked back."

"And what about his family?"

The smile grew wider. "His sister took over the business with smashing results, and they all come to visit on holidays."

"And they lived happily ever after."

Jack shrugged. "Except for the odd attacks of influenza and such."

Kate knew he could see the skepticism that warred with the hunger in her eyes. She envied his courage—

envied him the family that had let him go. But Kate had read enough fairy tales to recognize one. Maybe Jack could wander the Caribbean, but she couldn't. Her reality still waited to be reckoned with in Detroit.

"Stay a while, Kate. Dust off that artwork and see what it's like away from the pressure."

Kate could see that his invitation was serious. She just couldn't manage a sane answer while she was still surrounded by the scent and sensation of him. She shouldn't have to make a rational decision anywhere on this trip. But Kate had been trained well. She knew where home was and how to get there. All she could hope was that the pain would fade once it was caged back in her apartment.

She gently disentangled herself from Jack's arms, not even allowing herself the pleasure of holding his beautiful hands as she gave her answer.

"No, Jack. I have one week off and then I go back to Detroit."

"To the real world."

She nodded, tears glittering at the edge of her eyes. "Yes. I'm just not the kind of person who can play life by ear."

"Not even for me?" He asked wistfully, looking as if he were already watching her walk away.

Kate reached up to touch his cheek. "Not even for you. Although, if anybody could sorely tempt me, you could."

Jack took her hand in his and turned it, dropping a kiss on the palm. "Well then, all is not lost."

Kate pulled away. "Jack—"

Reaching down he retrieved her bag, and then her hand. "You know how we romantics are. I'll still expect you on deck every night."

And finally, crumbling beneath the bright assurance in his eyes, Kate nodded. "I think that can be arranged."

She followed quietly then, the residue of their day roiling in her chest. A chance. A door suddenly open, if just a little. Kate couldn't bear the possibility that she could really throw her life away and start over. Things like that just didn't happen. No one really got second chances.

She'd wake up in the morning to realize that Jack had done nothing more than weave a new fairy tale to entertain her. She would leave the cruise and go back to school and shut herself back up in a life that had already begun to feel too small just within the time it had taken to share a coral reef with a handsome man.

And knowing that that was how this fairy tale had to end was the cruelest reality of all.

Chapter Five

When the passengers were set ashore on the little island of Monterrat the next day, the passengers were promised that the walk up to the Great Alps Falls would take no more than twenty minutes. When Kate and Sam reached the end of that twenty minutes with no end in sight, they realized that the crew must have been talking about Olympic sprinters.

The expedition had seemed a great idea at the time, especially for Kate who was doing her best to stay away from Jack. A walk on a tropical island to the mysterious canyon falls was romantic. Breathtaking. Foolhardy.

By the time they reached the small meadow on the edge of the canyon—and the bugs were biting and their feet hurt from stumbling over roots and rocks and probably the remains of other unlucky hikers—they were beginning to reassess their situation. Then Kate spotted the Brenners.

Grabbing Sam's arm, Kate sprinted across the field.

"Mr. Brenner, are you all right?" she asked, crouching down to where the two of them sat beneath an ancient, gnarled old tree.

Mr. Brenner was leaning against the trunk, white and shiny with perspiration, his breathing labored. Kate was afraid he was having a heart attack.

"Old fool," Mrs. Brenner snapped from where she sat next to him, fanning his face with her handkerchief. "He forgets he's not twenty anymore. He was just determined to get up there this time."

"We've been on...the trip...three times," the little man gasped, his eyes filled with apology. "Everyone says the...falls are...great..."

"And you have emphysema and a heart condition, Dick Brenner," his wife informed him archly. "The last thing you need is a walk in this jungle humidity. We're too old to do this. I keep telling you."

"Do you want us to get help?" Sam asked.

Both shook their heads.

"Just walk with us on the way back," Mrs. Brenner suggested, eyes glinting with her husband's disappointment. "By then we'll get our breath back."

Kate couldn't miss the yearning on the little man's face as he gazed into the deep green of the dense foliage ahead. The look spoke of more disappointments than this one, more experiences forfeited to compromised lungs. It didn't seem at all fair.

"Tell you what," she offered, making it a point to sit down. "Why don't I just sit here? I think I'd rather enjoy your company than the rest of that hike." Sam sat right alongside.

Mr. Brenner shook a reprimanding finger at her. "Don't you...dare!" he argued. "You got better...things...to do than...baby-sit me."

"I've seen the falls already," Sam offered quietly. "Besides, it's hot up there."

"I'd probably get bitten by a snake or something," Kate added with a grin.

"No!" he insisted, actually taking her arm with a cold hand. "You . . . see it. Get a picture . . . for me."

Kate considered his conviction a moment and realized that it would be a greater insult to him if she stayed. He pressed a little camera he'd said his children had bought for the trip into her hands and then patted her like a favorite daughter.

"You've got the . . . chance . . . now. Don't . . . waste it."

"All right," she acquiesced with a smile. "I'll get a picture of Sam standing under the falls in her bikini. Just for you."

"That . . . will be . . . worth the . . . wait."

Mr. Brenner was right. The falls were worth the walk after all. Tumbling over a hundred feet into the corner of the canyon, the water thundered past curtains of exotic foliage and shattered against a tumble of boulders. It was a secret place, a surprise deep in the jungle; a place Kate could imagine being used for pagan rites of cleansing and passage—cold and clean and dark.

By the time Kate and Sam made it back to hand Mr. Brenner his camera, he looked much more his old self. Kate realized that he'd been able to cope well with his ailment on board ship because there wasn't that much space to cover or activity that would tax him. If she hadn't seen him under that tree, she might never have known he was sick. But the memory of his white face and disappointed eyes haunted her.

That night Kate was dreaming of the falls, of the yearning in Mr. Brenner's eyes, when she woke to find Jack sitting next to her. It was completely dark, and the ship creaked and hummed with the night wind. Jack hadn't spoken or reached out to touch her. She'd just known that he was there. He sat in the dying moonlight with his back to the mast, looking out over the night sky and the ocean below. In that moment Kate recognized a man at peace.

His eyes were bright and open, his face crinkled with an inward smile that didn't have to touch his lips. His face was calm, unafraid, uncluttered by doubts and pressures and hesitations—untouched by dreams unmet.

"Are you still on watch?"

Jack looked down at her without surprise, and her heart lurched in a way that was totally inappropriate for a man she'd known less than a week.

"I'm asleep," he said.

"Oh, is this your slot?" Kate asked with the stirrings of a grin. "I didn't see your name painted on the deck."

His teeth flashed abruptly. "Pretty sassy for four in the morning."

"I try to be my best at all times. Now, go to bed."

"Scoot over."

Kate shook her head, shooing him as if he were a fly. "*Your* bed. You have to work in the morning."

"I also have to talk to you."

Kate couldn't help a scowl. "Now?"

Jack made it a point to look around. "Can you think of a better time? I'm not going to get another day off to squire you around, and there aren't any witnesses except Ronnie over there. And he likes his job."

Kate took the trouble to sit up before answering. "Is this something you do all the time?"

Jack smiled, reaching over to finger the curls that danced along Kate's shoulder. "Matter of fact, I didn't even think of it till I saw you sleeping so peacefully over here."

"And you couldn't bear to leave me alone." When his fingers fell to her shoulders, Kate shuddered. They penetrated like a night breeze sending chills skittering down her spine. Kate felt her nipples tighten beneath her T-shirt and pulled the covers up over her bent knees. This was neither the time nor place to consider the havoc his hands could wreak against her skin.

"What are the Tigers?"

Kate started. "Huh?"

"The Tigers." Jack motioned to the black-and-white striped oversize shirt Kate wore. "What are they?"

"Uh...baseball." She couldn't seem to concentrate. The moon, straddling the horizon, threw Jack into a soft relief so that his hand looked etched. Kate could feel it wander down her arm, unleashing a host of goose bumps and further interfering with her thinking circuits.

"Baseball, is it? Detroit, I suppose."

"Jack..." His fingers brushed against the sensitive skin of her breast. Kate was so taken back by the exquisite shock of it, the sudden yearning that leaped all the way to her toes, that she didn't notice him bend closer.

Suddenly his head was down to hers, his mouth seeking plunder. His fingers had taken hold of her arm, steadying them both as the ship danced its slow waltz beneath them. The wind tugged at Kate's hair, pulling it across Jack's cheek and then sending it tumbling behind her. She could smell salt, the heady musk of male, the sharp tang of soap. She tasted sweet agony.

"Jack, please..."

He took another kiss. Slowly his tongue teased her and the tips of his fingers traced hot chills along her throat. It was all she could do to keep from moaning from the harsh pleasure his touch ignited in her.

Finally he returned to her breast, and Kate instinctively arched into his hand. She felt heavy against him, full and aching. He played her like an instrument, kneading and stroking, taunting her with his approach to the nipple that waited in hard anticipation for his attention. Kate shuddered, then sighed. But when she finally felt the rasp of his palm against the tight bud, she jerked away.

"I thought," she accused breathlessly, her eyes bright with the sweet pain that was sweeping her, "that you wanted to... talk."

Jack's eyes were liquid with arousal, his body taut. "I thought I was communicating pretty well."

"You were coercing. That's different." She should feel betrayed. Outraged. Incensed that he would so quickly plumb the depths of her unspoken needs. All Kate could think of was that she could still see the moist residue from her kisses on his lips.

When he chuckled, the soft sound of it rolled through her with a delicious intimacy. "That was merely an impromptu expression of attraction. But if it helps me make my point, I'd be happy to continue.''

"What point?" What a stupid question. Just the flare in his eyes answered her with a promise she was too afraid to hear. "Forget that," she amended quickly, a restraining hand against his chest. "If you want to talk, talk. Otherwise, I'd suggest a cold shower. Better yet, a cold swim."

"Stay."

He never moved, never lifted a hand to bridge the windswept gap between them. All the same, Kate felt him reach for her as acutely as if he held her in his arms.

"I told you . . ."

"An Englishman never takes no for an answer. How else do you think we built the Empire?"

Kate actually flashed him a dry grin. "By raping Ireland?"

Jack chuckled again, leaning closer. Kate could feel his heart beating against her hand, and it didn't seem to be any slower than hers. "Time to heal old wounds, don't you think?"

"Not according to my Granda Sean," she smiled sweetly.

"Give me a real reason."

"For not staying?" Kate tried to meet his eyes and faltered. "I already did."

Jack lifted her chin with a finger to take away that choice. "Sam says you're due four more weeks accumulated vacation."

Kate moved away just enough to cast a withering look at the bundle asleep a few feet away. "So much for passenger confidentiality. Jack, I can't—"

"Can't," he countered with a scowl, his hold tightening. "Can't. Do you spend your whole life saying that?"

"No," she retorted. "I do not. I just have—"

"Responsibilities."

"Yes."

"Commitments."

"Yes, dammit!"

"And what about you?" he demanded, dropping his hand to her shoulder, his eyes hot and angry all of a sudden. "What is there left for you in all this?"

She wanted to say a lot. She wanted to say that she was happy, satisfied, fulfilled. All she could see, though, were those haunted eyes, the little old man who had postponed his pleasures until he'd had the time only to realize that it was too late. Kate remembered Mr. Brenner sitting by the tree, gazing into the slash of forest, wanting so much to go farther.

"I'll think about it."

She saw Jack's eyes immediately brighten and realized how surprised she was herself.

"I said I'd think about it," she repeated with an upraised hand.

"Think quick," he advised, trapping her hand and kissing it. "Day after tomorrow we anchor at St. Maarten."

"And that's when I'll tell you."

Making a face, he kissed her upturned lips. "You sure know how to torture a man."

"Take it or leave it," Kate retorted, struggling to match his light tone even as her ears pounded with the chance she was taking. "It's the best I can do."

Lifting a finger to outline her lips, Jack bestowed a bright, knowing smile on her. "Bring your paints," he said. "I love to see a woman at her easel."

Kate sat up that night, and she sat up the next, strolling the deck, sitting back by the wheel, coffee cup in hand, listening to the rhythmic music of ship and ocean. Jack would wind his arm around her shoulder and she'd pull her blanket over both of them as they shared an easy intimacy, sketching lives and dreams and trepidations. She let Jack peruse her painting and he let her draw his past and future for him. And slowly Kate opened up about what it had been like to be the child of older parents, the only one who was always responsible, always accountable. She watched the moon die and starlight take over with its even frailer magic, and found herself bewitched by the sea and the night and the man who shared the darkness with her as the ship sailed on to morning.

By the last night on board, Kate realized she had begun to fall in love. Jack was like a book with a remarkable first page, a symphony that opened with a haunting first line. Kate was driven to dig deeper, to delve into him like an enticing maze. Here was a man sailing along in the Caribbean who quoted Yeats and Kierkegaard, who had been educated at Eton and yet walked comfortably among people of any social station.

Kate found that she admitted more to him during their late-night visits than she had to anyone since she'd been a teen and believed dreams were made to be shared. She didn't know whether it was due to him or the late hour, but she found herself amazed at the ease with which she offered bits of herself to him.

She was also beginning to deliberately turn from the picture of what her life would look like once she got home. The rooms she'd aired out had, indeed, grown smaller. By the time the ship dropped anchor for the final time, she was truly torn over what she was going to do.

Goodbyes were heartfelt. Addresses were exchanged and Sam did her best to spirit Kate away for some time on the Virgins. When Kate stepped back onto the pier at Phillipsburgh, it was Jack who waited for her.

"The captain is officially on holiday," he smiled softly, reaching over to pick up her bag for her. "And at your pleasure. What shall it be?" Before Kate had the chance to answer, he let his smile droop just a little with the weight of his jest. "Just don't say the airport."

Kate's smile was tremulous and shy. "A phone," she answered instead, a mix of terror and anticipation chasing across her eyes. "I have to check with work to see if I can afford another week off."

"Two."

Now her smile widened and Jack saw the allure of adventure begin to take her. "One. I'm feeling guilty enough. I'm missing my father's birthday on Wednesday.''

"He celebrated them without you before you came along,'' Jack assured her, sweeping her along to where his four-wheel-drive vehicle waited. The excitement was catching up with him, too. God, he wanted her to stay. He hadn't realized just how much until he'd seen the timorous courage in her. "Far from the madding crowd, my nymph,'' he promised, tucking her in. "I have cool drinks, soft tropical breezes, and a phone.''

Twenty minutes later Jack pulled up in front of his home. A stark whitewashed affair high above Guana Bay with more windows than walls, its interior a slash of color. Varnished hardwood floors and white walls held Caribbean weavings in brilliant hues, simple hand-hewn furniture and a balcony that overlooked the bay. It was a bewitching place, full of the lush music of wind and ocean and rich with the heady aromas of the island. It was Jack's respite from a claustrophobic ship, the earthbound side of his dream.

"Like it?'' he asked, handing Kate a drink. He'd popped himself a beer and took the first pull from it.

Kate took a sip of rum and fruit juice and nodded, her eyes staring out to where the breakers glittered in the morning sun. "It's wonderful. No wonder you never went back to England.''

"Oh,'' he sighed contentedly, "there are times I miss the odd foggy day and heathered moor.'' With a grin, he followed her gaze. "But not often.''

"You're lucky,'' she said. "Not very many people can live out their dreams in such style.''

Jack looked over to discover a wistful light in Kate's eyes. The wind pulled her light cotton shirt across firm breasts and teased her hair, scattering rubies through it. He surprised himself by reacting to her statement with anger—anger at what she let herself settle for, at those who loved her yet let her settle for it. That bewitching glow of discovery should never be allowed to die, but she was fully intent on snuffing it out completely.

"Make your call," he suggested with a nod to the phone. "I'll go whip up some quaint local fare for lunch."

Kate got through to the office as she stood barefoot on Jack's hardwood floor, iced drink in hand and the doors open to the sea breeze. The full cotton skirt she wore swirled gently around her bare legs.

The first thing that struck her was the noise. It was an assault, a shock to her system now that she was away from it. The machines, teletypes, computers, typewriters, phones. The yelling for orders and screaming over petty mistakes that weren't petty when considered in terms of millions of dollars.

As she waited to be put through to Harry, her boss, Kate unconsciously rolled the cool glass across her forehead, not realizing that a familiar dull ache had materialized behind her eyes that made her squint a little.

"*Kate?* Kate, where the hell are you?" The decibel level of Harry's voice pushed the phone from Kate's ear. This is long distance, she thought absently. It should at least sound more...distant.

"I'm in St. Maarten, Harry," she said.

"What? Dammit, you know better, Kate! I can't hear you!"

"St. Maarten!" she shouted, the sound echoing from the fresh white walls startled her. "Harry, my vacation..."

"No, you idiot, I did not say sell! I said they'd let us know! Listen for a change, dammit! What, Kate? C'mon, I don't have the time!"

The throbbing built with the volume of his voice, the familiar rasp of his unconscious abuse. Across from Kate the ocean glistened like polished metal beneath the high, endless sun of the Caribbean. Not yet, she thought. Not yet.

"I can't get back, Harry!" she yelled.

"What! What do you mean?"

Across the room Jack stepped out of the kitchen to watch, a towel thrown over his shoulder, a beer in his hand.

"There's a...hurricane!" Kate lied, not seeing him. "A hurricane threatening. They closed the airport! I'm stranded."

"Closed the airport?"

"It's very small! Tiny! I don't know when I'll get out! Maybe a week! Maybe longer, if there's damage to the runway." Inside her chest, her heart hammered with the lie. Her stomach roiled with Harry's anticipated reaction.

"Another week! We'll be down the tubes by then! You can't!"

"I have the time coming. Mark me down for more vacation. Can't be helped, Harry! I'll call when I can."

When Kate hung up the phone, she looked up to see Jack smiling at her with satisfied eyes.

"There's no hurricane," he said quietly. "They'll know."

Kate smiled giddily at him. "You're talking about Detroit. Harry doesn't even take the time to listen to heat indexes. He won't pay attention to a hurricane unless it hits the Great Lakes."

Jack's smile grew wider at her audacity, a new light of appreciation warming his eyes.

"For a week," Kate cautioned, the headache already forgotten. "Only a week."

Jack smiled with certain eyes. "It'll be enough."

Chapter Six

The call to her family was a lot more difficult to make. It wasn't the noise that bothered Kate as much as the silence.

"But Kate," her sister, Margaret, was saying with sincere distress. "Daddy's birthday—"

"I know, Mag," Kate interrupted. "But it can't be helped. We'll celebrate it again when I get back."

Now the voice grew slightly, unconsciously accusing. "And what am I supposed to tell Daddy? He's going to be eighty, you know."

Kate didn't realize that her eyes had closed against the high, bright light. "I'll call him and explain. It's just this once, and there's nothing I can do about it." She thought about the plane she could still catch and her father waiting in that sterile, impersonal retirement apartment, and she almost wavered.

"Well, can you at least give us a number so we can call you when we're together?"

"Number?" Kate's eyes opened, for a moment looking a bit lost.

"Mine," Jack said simply from beside her.

She looked over at him, and then down at the phone. "Uh . . . five-seven-six-one," she said.

"That's it?"

"It's a small island."

"What room number, Kate?"

Kate looked up at Jack, her heart lurching a little with the weight of old taboos. "No number," she admitted. "I'm staying with a friend."

The silence that crackled across the line grew even more profound. "Oh."

Her father wouldn't understand, either; she knew that. Kate had never missed a holiday or a birthday with him. Since her mother had died, it had always been Kate who had been his companion. She'd always made it a point to be. And, inevitably, her father had come to rely on that tradition as much as any other.

"This is stupid," she said with a shake of her head as she stalked out to the balcony. "I should go home."

Jack followed right on her heels. "Too late. You'd never make the plane."

She looked up to see that he really did understand her turmoil. There was a softness in his eyes that stole away her fear, cushioned her doubts. There was a wealth of memories of birthdays missed and guilt overcome.

Finally Kate placed her tentative trust in his hands. "You really wouldn't mind if I painted here?"

Jack shot her a smile of pure joy. "I've been saving my balcony for just such an occasion."

"And we could see the island?"

"Every rock and restaurant."

"And have a sail on the *Mandalay*?"

She could see that she had touched him. "You want to?"

Kate offered her best grimace. "Kipling," she mourned. "I don't suppose you could have named the damned thing after a Yeats poem."

"Think of it this way," he countered with a sly smile. "I could have named her The English Flag."

Kate giggled, suddenly flushed with exhilaration. "Or the Gunga Din."

She'd done it. She'd called the world and made her escape. Even if she only had the courage to do it for a week, it would be a week more than she'd even managed in the past.

And it wasn't just the escape. It was the man who had helped her engineer it, who had goaded and chided and cast his spell so that she couldn't think about school or traffic or birthday obligations anymore. He'd called her a fairy child, but it had been Jack who had woven the magic spell with his understanding and laughter. An Englishman with a penchant for madness. Kate found herself smiling at the idea, and knew she wouldn't soon stop.

Jack was as good as his word. After lunch he loaded Kate and her swimming gear into the car and proceeded to show off his island. They walked and climbed and swam, exploring salt ponds and nude beaches and steep mountains. Jack shared a sunset picnic of pâté and wine with Kate on one of the French beaches and sat in the grass outside a native church to hear reggae gospel music. Then, as the moon topped the glistening Caribbean, he brought Kate back to share his home.

The problem was that he'd already promised to share it with somebody else. They saw the lights when they topped the last rise to the house. Jack bit back a curse. The decibel level was already impressive, and a good baker's dozen vehicles were scattered over his sparse lawn. In the aftermath of Kate's decision to stay, he'd completely forgotten.

"Company?" Kate asked with an arched eyebrow.

"End of cruise party," he snarled, suddenly impatient with every one of his crew. "I forgot. It's my turn."

Doing her best to quell the sudden disappointment that she and Jack were not going to be alone with the moonlight in that bright little house after all, Kate offered a grin. "Not such a bad argument for getting locks installed."

"Wouldn't make any difference," he answered, his hands up on the steering wheel, his shoulders slumping a little even as he smiled. "Ronnie's a locksmith. Tradition is very important to this bunch."

"Would they mind very much if you just didn't show up?"

Casting a jaundiced eye toward the crowd that was visible through his windows, Jack shook his head. "Evidently not."

Kate shrugged her shoulders. "Then let's not go."

For a moment Jack sat next to her, tapping his fingers against the steering wheel and watching the party. Then suddenly, he straightened. "Come on," he instructed, opening his door.

Kate followed, not exactly sure what Jack was up to. She hoped he didn't really want to go to that party. After having him all to herself all day, she suddenly didn't want to have to share him again.

Kate tailed Jack around to the back of the car where he dug into the trunk for a blanket they had used for their beach picnic and the bottle of wine they'd bought in Phillipsburgh for their quiet evening together. Without a word, Jack balanced his booty in one hand, took Kate's in his other and led her away from the house.

The night was the most intoxicating the tropics had to offer, warm with soft breezes that bore the aromas of a thousand flowers. The sky arced far away in black and crystal starlight. A huge, yellow moon hugged the horizon and cast light over the restless sea. Behind Kate the mountains rose, blacker than the sky. Before her the water filled the horseshoe bay with rhythmic thunder. The night was magic, and that magic infused her like heady wine.

Kate watched the moonlight reflect in Jack's hair and gild his clothes. The cotton of his shirt strained across the smooth, broad muscles of his back as he walked. If Kate kept just a little way behind him on the path she could watch it. She could also enjoy the shadows that contoured his backside.

If Kate hadn't been thinking of how her hands would feel against him, she would have realized Jack had stopped. She almost ran right into him.

"Much more to my liking," Jack murmured, his voice a gentle counterpoint to the rush of the ocean.

They were down next to the beach, only a field of thick ground foliage separating them from the sand and surf. Kate looked up to see the soft attraction in Jack's eyes. Her heart faltered and picked up speed. She had reached the last point where she could turn back, shrink into her shell and still go home without palpable regrets. On this beach waited a destiny she'd chosen when she'd made that phone call, and surprisingly enough, she wasn't afraid.

"You have excellent taste in romantic settings," she said, the breathlessness of her voice surprising her.

Arms still full, Jack bent to deliver a long, sweet kiss that robbed Kate of the rest of her breath. "I have excellent taste, period."

Kate's eyes found his in the darkness. "I'll take honesty over humility any day."

The beach, when they found it moments later, was even more bewitching than the cove. Waves broke into ghostly phosphorescence, and the arms of the bay rose to erase part of the sky. The wind, warm and alive, pulled brisk fingers through Kate's hair and swirled in her skirt.

"Yes," she decided with a definite nod. "It's the perfect place for an assignation." It was, too—woven in the spell of endless summers and a mystical sea.

Kate caught a flash of Jack's teeth as he turned back to her with a rakish grin. "You're going to start that again, are you?"

She nodded, taking the blanket from his arms and spreading it out over the sand. It was a good thing Jack couldn't see the trembling of her hands or hear the trip-hammer of her heart. It would give away the uncertainty of her courage.

"I didn't stay on this island just to paint sunsets," she said, straightening back up to face him with that breathless smile of discovery. "Unless that's why you asked me to stay."

For a long moment Jack didn't answer. Kate waited. She tried to remember how to breathe, tried to decide whether to escape or succumb to the maelstrom of feelings his nearness incited. Jack didn't take his gaze from her. Gray met blue, and Kate felt the heat rise between them like the morning sun, infusing her like a potent liquor. Then he lifted the bottle he carried for her to see.

"Wine?"

Kate sighed. Her smile broadened lazily as her heart hammered at her ribs. "Love some."

They eased down to sit side by side on the blanket, their bodies a hair's breadth apart. Kate could feel the tension crackle across that space like electricity. She was sure she was going to need some wine just to prime her vocal chords. Jack's nearness combined with the hypnotic spell of the night was beginning to overtake her. She couldn't think of anything to say except how much she wanted to feel the weight of him against her, to dine on his smoky taste and feast on the sensation of his hands against her skin. Suddenly Kate knew that she couldn't leave him without making love to him, and that was too important to say.

Jack handed her a glass of wine, his fingers lingering over hers a moment before retreating. Kate found herself looking stupidly at her tingling fingertips as if expecting to see physical evidence of the lightning she felt crackle when he touched her. She took a drink of wine, trying to counter the fire leaping through her. The wine didn't help. It only sapped more of her control.

"This is a far better place for a party," Jack was saying.

Kate nodded, wondering if she could ask for more. "A little hard to hear the music...."

Jack looked over to see her hair in a slow dance with the wind. Again, instinctively, he reached out to let its silken banners slip through his fingers.

"No more beautiful music than that of the ocean," he murmured, his voice hushed.

It was all Jack could do to keep from pulling Kate into his arms and ravaging her. There was no patience in him tonight, only hunger. He'd tasted her and found that it hadn't been enough. So sweet and pliant and soft in his arms, and yet demanding just as much as he. She was a woman who played no games with her desires, assumed no roles to please herself or capture him, and it made the allure of her all the more intoxicating.

She would end up draining him, consuming him as she did the rest of the world. And Jack, who had made it a point for so long to avoid losing himself in any woman, suddenly realized that he needed that now.

Kate sought his eyes again, and lost her teasing grin to the dark passion that sparked even in that shadowy gray. "I like the exclusive guest list, too." She couldn't even feel the wind anymore.

Jack nodded slowly as if he couldn't quite pull any more words together, his eyes never leaving hers, his hand still trapped in the web of her hair. Kate saw the turmoil in him that must have been mirrored in her own eyes. She didn't want to leave, didn't want to go back to the hard, hot streets of Detroit.

God, she thought, her breathing ragged for the effort it suddenly took to remain still. I want him to make love to me. Would it be so very wrong to let impulse take over, just this once? She was going home soon, away from the soft magic of these islands and the sweet freedom in Jack's eyes. Would it be so selfish to want to take some of him away with her?

As if in answer to her unspoken plea, Jack brought his hand up to the line of her jaw, his fingers gentle against her skin. With his other hand he took her glass and set it aside with his, his eyes never breaking contact with hers. She was drowning in his touch, just his fingertips stealing her breath. The world was closing in, the only music the shallow rush of Jack's breathing and the throbbing in Kate as she waited.

"Want to see my etchings?" she whispered above the wind.

Jack smiled, his eyes savoring every part of her face. "Only if you let me show you mine."

Kate drew a finger along the soft line of his lips. "This wasn't quite the compromise my mother had in mind."

Taking her hand in his, Jack raised it to kiss her palm, his eyes still on hers, the heat in that gray finding her belly and flaring. Kate knew her lips had parted. It seemed easier to breathe that way as the taste of his lips against her skin sent sharp little aches through her. She looked down at her hand, then back up at Jack.

"It's still better than three days," he smiled lazily, nibbling at her wrist and sending shock waves to her toes.

Kate ran a tongue over her dry lips and saw Jack's eyes follow her action with hunger. Her leg was touching Jack's. It felt so hot, so enticing... The tension his touch generated was beginning to coil in her sharper than any desire she had ever known.

She hadn't realized that he'd moved his other hand. He slid it along her neck, his fingers cooler than the breeze, and excited more hot chills along her spine. What would they feel like against her breasts, she wondered? His mouth, so warm and soft, devouring her button-hard nipples. She began to tremble and knew that he felt it.

Jack nodded with that same slow smile that brought his face to life and drew her close for a quick kiss. "Besides fairies must be captured by the dark of the moon."

Kate demanded the next kiss, catching his lips with her teeth and tasting it with her tongue. So soft. So tangy with the hint of salt. "Jack," she said. "It's not the dark of the moon."

Grinning down at her like a pirate, Jack eased Kate down on the blanket. "Close enough."

For just a moment Kate held back, knowing that this would be her last chance. "I'll still get on that plane next week."

She'd half expected Jack to pull away. He didn't. Instead he let his gaze wander to where his fingers still sifted through the silk of her dark curls. When he lifted his eyes to hers, she saw acceptance flavor his desire. "Then we have to keep this week for ourselves," he said. "No outside world, no work, no families. Just us. Promise?"

Kate smiled into his gray eyes. "I was hoping you'd say that."

Jack drew a thumb along her jaw, the rasp like slow lightning. When he let his finger stray to her lips, Kate opened them and took the fingertip into her mouth, stroking the strong callused tip with her tongue. She didn't take her eyes from his as his pupils grew large.

"Come here, nymph," he whispered.

Kate chuckled deep in her throat, for once reveling in the name. Jack's nymphs were different creatures than the ones she'd always been compared to, and she thought she liked them better. They were more mysterious, more dangerous. And tonight, for the first time in her life, that was how she felt.

Jack tried his best to maintain some kind of control. He wanted Kate to have her full share of their lovemaking. But the minute he heard that chuckle, so ripe with sensuality, he knew it would be futile. That hot ache that had been building inside him seared through to bubble in his blood.

Her skin was so soft, so milky and delicate beneath the dark leather of his hands. Her eyes were laughing, inviting, demanding, that blue like sapphires and the sky at his back. It wasn't just that she was aroused, it was that she allowed her desire to meet his. Her eyes would never close when he made love to her. Tonight, she was a lioness again.

Jack never remembered stripping away Kate's blouse. Suddenly her shoulders were bare, her high breasts cupped in lace and satin. His hands trembled as they sought her creamy skin. He swept up and claimed one breast, testing the full heavy weight of it and circling the nipple to even stiffer attention with his thumb. Kate writhed with his touch, her hair fanning like a dark sunset on the blanket, her lips opening. Her dance was like an invitation, and Jack accepted, dipping to taste her.

Kate shuddered. She heard her own breath escape in a surprised hiss as Jack took her nipple in his mouth. She felt him tangle his hand in her hair, holding her against him, pulling her closer. She arched against him, seeking the hot pleasure of his mouth.

The night shimmered with moonlight, trembled with the wind. The scent was earthy and close. All Kate could see or feel or hear was Jack. She brought her hands to his chest to feel the fresh perspiration on a cool night, to let her own fingers relish the delicious texture of hair that curled damply at his throat. She found his heart, bounding against the light cotton of his shirt, and tested the taut muscles of his chest with skimming fingertips. She thought that they tingled, but she wasn't quite sure. She couldn't keep her mind on her hands when she realized what havoc Jack's hands were letting loose.

Shivers chased up and down her spine like overlapping waves breaking against that growing ache deep in her belly. Still plundering the soft delights of her breast with his mouth, Jack let his fingers dip to the back of Kate's knees.

Kate gasped again. No one had ever thought to find that place, and suddenly she realized what she'd been missing. Then Jack loosened her bra, and Kate forgot her knees.

She writhed beneath him, the tension unbearable. There was a storm building in her, and only he could release it. His mouth trapping hers, Jack eased away the rest of her clothes until she lay under him, the wind teasing the moist trail of Jack's kisses. Then his clothes were gone, too.

His bare skin gleamed in the moonlight like marble—like a beautiful, flawless statue. Kate wanted to laugh, the unaccustomed intensity of their matched passion surprising her. She shivered with impatience, wanting the weight of him on her, the throbbing life of him sheathed safely inside her. Unable to bear his hesitation any longer, Kate lifted her arms to him.

Jack's eyes grew dark with the wonder of the woman beneath him. "Am I to capture you then, nymph?" he whispered with a private smile, returning to her.

Kate reached out to take hold of him. "I think you're about to have my buried treasure."

For just a moment she marveled at the feel of him, the power, the soft steel. Then his fingers dipped into the curling hair above her thighs and ignited that storm.

Dipping and wheeling into the hot, moist recesses of her, Jack stirred the fire, gathered the lightning. Kate clutched at him, rocking against the shuddering sweep of torment. She tangled her fingers in his hair and arched against him. He teased her, lifting above her and letting her only taste his fullness before backing away, tormenting her with the promise of more.

Kate gasped, groaned. The storm was breaking over her, and she had to share it. Taking him back in her hand, she showed him the way home.

From that moment, Jack was lost. The feel of her surrounding him, of her swollen, bruised mouth against his and her slender body dancing with his, sent him over the edge. Instead of giving, he took. He dragged her to him, his hands harsh against her soft skin, his mouth grinding onto hers as she matched his tempo and rocked with him. Her gasps grew to little cries as he thrust into her. Her nails raked his back and her eyes glittered in the moonlight. Jack buried his head into her shoulder and buried himself into the depths of her and met her storm as it broke over them both and shattered the night.

For a few disjointed moments Kate thought it was early morning in Detroit, and the first sun was sneaking up over the dormer window. She knew she would hear the alarm at any minute, but for now she just wanted to bask in the stillness of daybreak.

Resettling herself a little, she punched at the pillow that always ended up wound around her, trying to soften it a little. When the pillow let out a surprised curse, Kate's eyes flew open.

It was dawn, all right, but she sure wasn't in Detroit. She was curled into the planes of Jack's body, the blanket under and around them. The fresh translucent light of morning was coming up fast, and Jack was rubbing his ribs.

"Is that a good morning custom unique to Detroit?" he demanded.

Kate bestowed an apologetic grin. "I'm sorry. I thought you were a pillow."

"A likely excuse. I'm not at all sure at this point I want to give you a good morning kiss. I might not recover."

Kate raised herself to tease his chest with the fall of her hair and challenge his eyes with the smoke in her own. What was it about him that ignited such an insatiable appetite? "That is a point to consider," she admitted with a lazy smile.

Jack groaned in mock exasperation. "You keep this up and I'll be too exhausted to enjoy my holiday."

"That's not what you said last night," she goaded as his physical reaction immediately belied his protests.

His eyes grew dark, his smile the same one Kate had discovered under moonlight. "No," he answered, his hands coming up to pull her against him. "It's not, is it?"

This time when they made love, it was not so much an act of discovery as one of celebration. Jack found the places he'd made special the night before. Kate arched to meet his touch, her moans of delight speeding his hands. Their lips touched, fled, then met, the taste they shared musky and full. The wind carried their murmurs and the growing light bathed their communion. And when their shuddering cries lifted to the morning, they fell into each other's embrace, spent and trembling.

Kate fed on the feel of Jack in her arms, the glistening line of perspiration along his forehead and the staccato of his racing heart. It was as if he'd always been there, belonged there with her to share that bittersweet glow that now suffused and united them just as his entering her had.

His handsome, bright face rested against her breast, and she stroked a hand through the damp gold of his hair. For just that moment as the sun first kissed the rolling waters and the world sighed quietly around them, Kate knew what it felt like to be free. She lay in paradise, protected from the rest of the world by the arms of the bay, the arms of her lover.

"Damn you, witch," Jack whispered in a voice at once full of wonder and pain, "but I think I'm falling in love with you."

Kate lay quietly, her fingers still running absently through his hair, her eyes watching the frail robin's egg sky of morning where thin streamers of clouds stretched like rose banners before the sun.

"Oh, Jack, I wish I were a witch," Kate sighed, sating herself on the peace of this moment to take away with her. "If I were, I could keep the rest of the world away from us. I could have the magic to keep us together."

Jack lifted his head and raised himself to consider her, his eyes striving for humor and finding none. "Does that mean you're in the same woeful condition?"

Kate tried to smile. "Silly, isn't it? A week together on a boat and one night making love in the sand."

"Repeatedly."

Her smile broadened a little, the pain clearer. "And quite wonderfully. No one has ever made me feel so... desirable. So beautiful."

"Then they've been idiots. And you shouldn't go back."

"I thought we weren't going to talk about that."

Reaching down, Jack traced the tears that sparkled in Kate's eyes and edged her cheeks. "If you go, you'll never come back."

Kate couldn't manage an answer. She knew he was right; knew that once she regained her footing in the everyday world of home with its realities and emotional chains, that the world Jack inhabited would begin to fade. The startling colors would evaporate along with her belief that a man could really offer her as much as Jack did. She had lived in this skin less than a week. It had taken more than thirty years to mold the other.

"Do you know?" He asked with a tender smile. "That you have the most eloquent eyes when you're sad? They're like the last blue of an autumn sky." Bending, he kissed her, his lips searching hers as if memorizing their taste, as if taking some of her away with him. "Maybe you have to go back," he finally said. "Maybe you have to face your responsibilities. But I've just realized something."

"What?"

"Wherever you go, I'm coming to get you. You've made me unhappy with what I have, nymph. I want more now. I want you."

Kate couldn't believe the soaring joy his words ignited in her. Her heart battered against her chest like a bird trying to beat its way free of a cage. "Really?"

Jack lifted a hand to her. "Come away with me, Kate. Paint in my house. Be my partner. We can charter the *Mandalay*. I've been thinking of quitting the windjammers for a while now anyway. It's time I went into business for myself."

Kate sat up, dragging the blanket with her. Suddenly she was cold, and it was from more than just the air. He was moving too fast—too fast even for him, she was sure, weaving dreams from air.

"Jack," she cautioned, a hand to his chest. She felt the delicious warmth of his skin and dropped it away again. "Slow down."

Pulled up as if on a short lead, Jack looked at her. Kate could see by the wonder in his eyes that he was as surprised by his words as she. She could also see the commitment settle in right before her eyes. Now that he had said it, he meant it. All that did was make her hurt even more. She wanted it, too. She wanted him. But she hadn't yet learned to live on dreams.

"All right," he nodded. "What do you want to do?"

"Go home," she said immediately. "I have to talk to my family, try to ease them into the idea that I might move away. I have to put some money away, and train a replacement. And school…there's school. I could move at end of term and see how we do. If I got a leave of absence from work, I'd still have my job if it didn't work out."

Kate saw her words steal some of the light in his eyes. "If I let you settle up, do you promise you'll try to come back?"

"Will you really come for me?"

A gull wheeled over them, its cry sharp and sad. The wind whistled through the sand. Jack lifted a hand and captured Kate's cheek. "If I have to do it at the dark of the moon and risk my soul."

In the end, all Kate had to offer was hope. She didn't have the experience to give more. "I'll try," she promised, her tears tempering her sudden, flashing smile. "I'll try."

Chapter Seven

Kate sat on the balcony laying down a wash for a study of the bay. It was almost sunset, and the light was like poured honey across the hills. Two days after she'd made her decision, the excitement was still rising. She felt so reckless, so bold.

She'd awakened that morning to find Jack watching her with the most wonderfully possessive smile, and it had surprised her again. She could wake every morning to that smile. She could fall asleep every night nestled next to him, and be able to reach out to him in the night if she felt lonely or afraid. He told her anything was possible, and she was just starting to believe it.

"Company, Kate!"

Startled by Jack's voice, Kate turned toward the apartment. She hadn't even heard him come in. He'd only been gone an hour or so, into town to restock the larder. Kate couldn't believe how intently she'd been listening for his voice.

"Out here!" she called, rinsing her brushes. Beyond her the sun caught the edges of a thundercloud, setting it on fire and streaking the sky. Kate didn't even notice. She'd turned to look for Jack.

He peeked around the corner, smiling. "I didn't expect you to be anyplace else. Come see what I brought you.'' Before Kate could answer, he'd backed away again. ''Take a look at those,'' he was saying. ''She painted all four in two days.''

Now who could that be? she wondered. And why was Jack showing off her paintings? He knew how she felt about that. She'd shown the completed ones to him, shyly excited by the pleasure and pride in his eyes. But she wasn't exactly ready to have him hand them out as door prizes yet.

When Kate stepped inside, it was to see that Jack had not one, but two people with him. And one of them was Sam.

''I knew it!'' Sam greeted her with a bear hug and a huge, self-satisfied grin. ''I just knew it! So, tell me all about it.''

''Knew what?'' Jack asked from where he was handing a beer to the other guest, a middle-aged man with that nut-brown Caribbean tan and the timeless eyes of a refugee from the real world.

''Nothing,'' Kate answered with a pointed look at Sam. ''Sam, I haven't even figured it out myself, yet.''

''What's to figure?'' the blonde demanded in a stage whisper. ''He loves you, he asked you to come live with him. 'And they lived happily ever after.'''

Kate just glared. ''I thought you had to get back to the bookstore.''

Accepting a drink from Jack, Sam shook her head, her smile mysterious and very smug. ''I had some hobnobbing to do before I headed back.''

For some reason Kate looked over at the other guest when Sam said that. He was standing over her four watercolors of the island, beer in hand, his eyes and lips pursed in concentration. Kate looked over to Jack and then to Sam for introductions, but none seemed to be forthcoming. The man shifted his weight and took a drink. Everyone watched him. Kate watched everyone else.

"Yes," he finally said, bringing the other three heads up with attention. "Yes, you're right, Sam. These might do very well."

"Might?" Sam retorted indignantly.

"These might do very well for what?" Kate asked, doing her best to keep her voice even. There was a current in the air that made her very nervous. Jack was smiling. Sam was smiling. The man was nodding.

With Kate's words, a feigned look of surprise bloomed in Jack's eyes. "Oh, Kate, didn't I introduce you? This is Paul Stanford of the Stanford Galleries in Phillipsburgh. He's a friend of Sue's, and he wanted to get a look at your work."

"Sam's." The blonde scowled, but Kate didn't notice.

Mr. Stanford had already turned to Kate with a considered smile and an outstretched hand, both of which she accepted with mute trepidation.

"I'm always looking for good local artists," he admitted. "Not this starving artists stuff. Real work. There's quite a market in the islands, you know. I can't promise you fame and fortune. I can't even promise that the tourists would buy you. I never know what they'll favor, but you have a definite style. I'd be happy to try if you would."

Kate couldn't quite pull off an intelligent thought. "Try what?"

Mr. Stanford smiled, the genie granting a wish. "To sell your work, if you'd like."

Kate knew that all eyes were on her. She saw the pride in Jack's—the anticipation, the accomplishment—and she felt Sam's bright gaze on her from the other side of the room. Absurdly Kate remembered the day when at age fourteen she'd snuck out of the house to enter an art show. She had been dizzy all the way there, and received her mother's harsh reprimand with a yellow ribbon in hand when she'd gotten back home. Terror tasted the same at any age.

"Thank you," she said, struggling with the fearsome prospect of hope. "I'd like that very much."

"Just like that?" she asked a while later after Mr. Stanford left.

"Sometimes it happens that way," Sam assured her, all innocence and enthusiasm.

Kate's answer was understandably curt.

"Don't you want to paint?" Jack asked from where he lounged on one of the chairs, legs thrown over the side and a beer in hand. Kate wished that he didn't look so good, that she didn't feed on the pride in his eyes. Her knees were still weak, and she had that dizzy feeling again.

"You and Sam just happened to run into each other in Phillipsburgh," she retorted, her voice dry. "And who did you bump into but Mr. Stanford, who just happened to mention that he's looking for some new talent, had you seen any?"

Jack's smile remained absolutely unrepentant. "Something like that."

Kate found herself battling her own smile. "I should be mad."

Sam giggled. "You should be outside on the balcony painting."

"You're welcome," Jack said to Kate, correctly reading the ambivalence.

"I haven't said I was grateful," she countered, giving in and letting him share her excitement.

"I was hoping you'd show me instead."

For a minute Kate lost herself in the slow heat of Jack's smile. "Sam—"

"Yeah, I know," the blonde answered with a grin and a wave of the hand as she grabbed her purse. "Nice seein' you. Stop by sometime, and call before you come by. Well, I'll be home day after tomorrow. Come see me."

Jack unwound himself from the chair, but it was Kate he approached.

Kate never saw Sam leave. "I thought we were going to sail the *Mandalay* tonight."

Reaching her, Jack lifted his hands to cup her face and drew it near him. "I don't think we'll make it tonight."

They didn't.

The *Mandalay* was everything a dream demanded. Sleek, fast and silent, she had a midnight blue hull and teak deck. When Kate stepped aboard the first time, she was assailed by the feeling of familiarity. It was as if she'd been there before, almost as if she could find her way around in the dark.

And it was definitely Jack's. He strolled the deck as if it were an extension of himself, running loving hands over rigging and gleaming rails. He introduced Kate to the forty-nine-foot racer as if the two were rivals for his affections, which, Kate imagined, was at least partly true.

It was not the boat that kept her attention as they walked her length, but rather the fierce delight in Jack's eyes.

"Elizabeth Taylor looked at her horse that way in *National Velvet*," Kate finally said with a grin.

Jack looked up from the wheel he was testing, a meticulously miniaturized version of the *Caribbe*'s. "What?"

She motioned around her. "As if the horse would talk back. You have that same attitude of listening."

"Oh, but she does talk to me," he admitted with a smile, one foot up on a block. "All the time."

Kate nodded, thinking that she'd never seen a happier person. "When the wind finds the sails. I know. I heard it on the *Caribbe*."

Jack's smile widened as he considered the untapped romance in Kate's soul. "There's nothing like it in the world."

It didn't take Kate long to fall for the *Mandalay*. Bright and quick on the water, the vessel responded to Jack's touch like a woman and met the waves like a dancer. Kate found a peace aboard that she'd never known before.

She and Jack were alone in the world, their boat the only sign of life above the teaming sea. There was the vast cobalt sky, met only by distant islands like mossy clouds along the horizon that bracketed all the water the world seemed to hold.

Kate absorbed the shifting colors, the race of cloud and the slice of sail, and immediately set them in her mind to paint. Then she remembered and flushed.

"Was he serious?" she asked for the first time from where she sat alongside Jack in the stern, her face up to the sun and a drink in hand. She wondered if Jack heard the fear that still raced through her. He was offering such a big world, when hers had been so rigidly restricted.

He must have heard. Without a word, he dropped a kiss on her upturned lips, and it was a gesture of support. "He was serious. When you know Mr. Stanford better, you'll know that we might have been able to get him up to see the paintings, but he can't be coerced into selling any."

Kate sighed. It sounded more like a shudder. "Too good to be true is still too good to be true."

"In that case," Jack assured her, slipping an arm around her and bringing her close. "I'm really sitting in an office in Bayswater and you're in front of a computer in Detroit." Bending to take another kiss, he smiled. "Does it feel like that?"

Kate knew he could feel the tumble of her heart. She wanted so much to grab the tail of his kite and fly. "No," she admitted, savoring the most delicious pillow of gray she'd ever laid herself down on. "It doesn't. Do you love me?"

He smiled and her fingers edged closer to the bright rags that danced through the air. "Madly. Do you love me?"

"Yes." The admission was as much a relief as a surprise for her. Whatever else happened, she had that to hold on to. Even if the kite slipped away. Even if the book closed, and the fairy tale was put back on the shelf and allowed to grow dusty, she at least had fourteen impossible days in the sun when she loved a man.

"Then come here, nymph," he commanded, drawing her back to him. "And show me."

Jack took a look at the compass, then at the swelling sails and the island growing on the horizon, and pulled the wheel a little to port. Kate was up in the bow again, sunning. He took a drink of beer and thought how delicious her hot, slippery body would feel against his. It had been too long since they'd made love. Hours, at least. He was getting impatient for her again.

It seemed the more he enjoyed her, the more he wanted her. And she still hadn't reached her potential. Her enthusiasm faltered sometimes, like a child taking new steps. Occasionally he saw a mood catch her, a hot fire that lit her eyes with wonder or hunger. More often than not, she stifled it. Her lack of confidence in herself made her unsure of him. But then there were moments that were pure magic.

"Jack, hurry! Come here and see this!"

Just the sound of her voice made Jack tie off the wheel. Heading forward, he found her leaning over the side, the wind fanning her hair out behind her in heavy silken banners, her face alight and laughing.

They'd picked up dolphins, a whole school of them, darting and wheeling alongside the ship, their backs polished silver in the sunlight. Jack took one look at one of God's most graceful creatures gamboling about in the waves, and then found his eyes drawn back to Kate.

She was mesmerizing, brilliant, like a ray of sunshine through a cloud bank. Just as on the day they'd snorkeled, she let the amazement of her discovery fill her like a physical radiance. But this time when she turned to Jack, she didn't instinctively seek to quell it, afraid to bare it to him. She sought to share it with him, and it affected him like a fever. When he finally tore his eyes away from her and looked back at the dolphins, it was as if he'd never seen them before.

He didn't wait any longer to make love to her. They lay together out beneath the vault of blinding blue, surrounded by the happy chatter of the dolphins, where the wind burnished them and the sun warmed them, and they shared their delight in each other.

"Do you realize you're naked?" Jack asked sometime later, his hand across her hip. Kate lay curled against him, her head at his shoulder, her leg across his. Above them the rigging hummed with the wind and the sails strained, full bellied with the wind.

"No more naked than you," she retorted evenly, winnowing her fingers through the hair on his chest.

Jack smiled and lifted a hand to her hair, a favorite pastime of his lately. "Yes," he answered, "but I'm not the one with my bum facing that freighter over there."

Kate didn't move. "I don't see any freighter. What's more, I don't hear any freighter."

He made a lazy shrugging motion. "They're there nonetheless." Neither his hand nor voice changed pace. "The decks are fairly bristling with binoculars."

Kate resumed her foray. "Shall I wave?"

Jack dropped a kiss into the wild curls that tumbled over his shoulder. "I'm sure they'd appreciate it."

Kate waved lazily over her head and was promptly met with two blasts from an air horn.

"Oh, my God!"

She came bolt upright before she realized that that was probably as much a mistake as ignoring Jack. The ship repeated its salute with much more enthusiasm.

"They have good taste," Jack offered with mischievous glee, settling his hands behind his head for his own perusal. Ten days ago, Kate would have shrunk away like a wilted flower. He actually saw her smile at the situation, and it made him want to laugh.

Kate leveled a barely serious glare at him. "You set me up."

His grin widened. "I'm just as naked as you are."

"Well," she decided, a smile of revenge in her eyes. "My mother always told me a person should be able to rise to any occasion."

Without waiting for his reaction, she slowly got to her feet and turned toward the freighter. Jack hadn't exaggerated. The entire crew looked to be on the decks, less than two hundred feet away. They were waving and whistling, and more than one was in danger of falling overboard.

Kate took it all in calmly. Jack didn't even see a blush on her face as she pulled herself up straight with a great amount of dignity. Then, with a slow, controlled smile, she bowed.

"She what?"

"Bowed. Like she was the Queen at Ascot."

Nathaniel took the news with awed silence, and then slapped Jack on the back. Jack laughed along with his friend, shaking his own head with wonder.

"Then," Jack finished, taking another swig of beer, "she turned and strolled below decks like she was on her way to a bloody ball."

"I'll tell you, lad," the older man crowed. "I like 'er. She's got class, has that little snip. Class." He nodded sagely and punctuated his opinion with a long pull from his own beer.

They'd gotten in about noon and headed straight up to Nathaniel's place. For a while Jack had been afraid they were going to have a freighter escort all the way in, but when Kate had refused to reappear for a second curtain call, the old ship had finally gone on its way.

"She's the best thing that's ever happened to me, Nathaniel," Jack admitted. "I think I've been waiting all this time for her to set foot aboard ship."

Nathaniel looked over with an appraising eye. "Ya haven't known her very long, lad."

"Long enough, Nathaniel. Long enough."

They considered each other in silence a minute before Nathaniel took another drink from his bottle. "I've never heard you like this before. Sounds serious."

"Serious enough," Jack answered evenly. "I'm going to ask her to marry me."

Nathaniel almost dropped the bottle. "And the *Caribbe*?"

"Gets my notice the minute she tells me yes."

Again Nathaniel kept his silence a moment before answering. "What does she say now?"

Jack was forced to smile. "Something about having a real job and responsibilities to shoulder."

"Oh, aye," the older man retorted with a knowing grin. "I've heard that tune a time or two. Seems to me, there was a time you was the loudest singer of all."

"I can save her, Nathaniel."

Nathaniel snorted. "Gotta do somethin' about that low opinion ya have of yerself, laddie."

Jack smiled. "She can save me, too."

Before Nathaniel could comment on that, the door opened behind them and Kate ushered her new friend, Nathaniel's wife, Lovey, in before her.

"Fun place to shop," Kate smiled, exhibiting packages. "Have you two been swapping tall tales?"

"That we have, lass," Nathaniel greeted her with a broad smile and a rum punch. "That we have."

Lovey joined her husband behind the bar and immediately set to disposing the impressive pile of dead soldiers. "I can't leave you children alone for a minute, can I?"

Nathaniel ignored her with equanimity. "So tell me," he said instead, leaning over to where Kate sat across the bar. "What does Detroit have my Nevis don't?"

"A baseball team," Kate answered between sips. The breeze had found her through the open windows, and the sun cast dramatic shadows on the whitewashed walls. The little room was so cool. So quiet. So timeless. Kate was tempted to sit here forever contemplating the trade winds and sharing Jack's friends.

"Jack here was tellin' me you ran into dolphins yesterday."

Kate's eyes lit with the memory. She'd always dreamed of experiencing something like that. She'd actually touched one, stroked his smooth, cool back as he'd flashed by, chattering at her as if they'd been friends gabbing over coffee.

"Can't see those in Detroit," Nathaniel was saying. "Least not anyplace but a tank, poor beasties."

Kate found herself chuckling at the grizzled old man. "You're a little late, Nathaniel. Jack's tried that argument, too. In fact, he's tried everything short of promising me the fountain of youth." Kate thought of his most persuasive argument, the one he waged with silent lips and clever hands, and caught herself just shy of a delicious blush.

"I'm afraid I have to get back to my family," Kate assured Nathaniel. "At least for now. It's . . ."

She stopped, suddenly shaken.

From the other side of the bar, Jack lifted his head. "Kate?"

"The date," she stammered, looking around for clues. "What day is it?"

"The twelfth," Lovey offered.

"The twelfth?" Kate closed her eyes, her betrayal horrifying her. "Oh, God, I missed it."

"Kate," Jack persisted, already at her side. "Missed what? What's wrong?"

"My father's birthday," she admitted in a small voice, seeing that old man waiting by a phone that didn't ring. "I need to call."

A few moments later Kate stood alone in Nathaniel and Lovey's tiny kitchen trying to concentrate on the bisque figures Lovey collected and scattered over her rooms like a party of cherished friends. Spare, clean and decorated in Lovey's little people and Nathaniel's Navy momentos, the bungalow was separated from the street by a small garden that looked suspiciously English for being on a Caribbean island. At this time of the day, it was cool and quiet.

"Katie? Is that you?"

Kate closed her eyes against the pain ignited by the eager anticipation in her father's voice.

"Hi, Daddy," she sang out, eyes still closed. "How was your birthday?"

"Fine. Fine, honey. I missed you. We waited to hear from you."

"I know, Dad. I'm sorry."

"When are you coming home, Kate?"

"Soon, Dad." The echo seemed to lodge in her chest, knotting up and catching fire. She could feel that the bright sun outside had already started to dim. The world was beginning to close in on her again. "Listen, Dad, I got some wonderful news. A man here in the islands wants to sell my paintings. Isn't that great?"

"Your what? Paintings? Are you still doing that, honey? Well, that's fine. Maybe you can do that sometime."

The knot in her was cancerous now, eating at her insides until she was hollow. Hollow and hot and empty.

Don't, Daddy. Please don't. You're robbing me again and you don't even know it.

"Kate?"

"I'm here, Dad."

"Listen, honey, Harry Milton called here looking for you. He says he knows about the hurricane, and that you'd better be back here to see him Saturday or you're going to lose that big account. Does that make sense to you, hon? Should I tell him I found you? I can give him your number, you know. You don't want to jeopardize your job."

The big account. Harry's way of telling her he'd found out. He knew she was hiding from him, lying to get time away. If she didn't show up in two more days, her job, her prospects—when word got out about it— were down the tubes. The big account was what Harry called work.

Even if she did try to come back down here, she'd have nothing left to fall back on. Somehow the air had all been sucked out of the cool little rooms.

"Daddy, what if I told you I wanted—"

"Wanted what, Kate? Kate, I can hardly hear you. Why don't we talk when you get home, honey. When we have the party. We saved cake, okay?"

The fire died with his words and she was left with nothing.

"Okay, Dad. See you Saturday."

"And call Harry. Make sure everything's okay at work."

Jack was waiting in the garden. When he saw Kate stride from the little house, he straightened, wondering what he was about to face. Kate's eyes were brittle, but her gait was determined.

"How'd it go?" he asked as she reached him.

She laughed, but the sound was as brittle as her eyes. "Just great. Unless I go home tomorrow, I lose my job. In effect, my career."

Jack faltered, her words chilling him. "You have a new career here," he offered.

Whirling around, Kate faced him with tear-bright eyes. "I have a promise to try from a man Sam probably owes dinner."

Jack's silence was enough to send Kate on her heel and walking again.

Jack caught up with her down by the wharf. He tried to be patient. There was an awful lot he was forcing on this woman in a short time. He had to make her willingly risk everything she had for the promises of a man she'd only met eleven days ago. But he knew that if he didn't at least give her the yearning to open the doors she so feared, she'd never come back.

Jack saw the wind take her hair and scatter shards of ruby through its dancing lengths. He saw the strong, straight set of those small shoulders and ached to take them to him. She'd already made her decision, and he couldn't abide by it.

"You don't reach very far, do you, Kate?"

Kate looked out to the brilliant, gleaming sea where pleasure boats bobbed like large, brightly colored sea birds on the waves.

"Jack, there's a wonderful quote. By Shaw, I think. He said, "'If you don't get what you want, you'd better damn well settle for what you have.'"

"And you live by that?"

She turned on him, eyes glittering more brightly than the sea. "It's etched on my bathroom wall so I can see it every morning."

"And rather than take a chance and lose, you'd rather not try at all."

He saw the torment in her eyes, heard her ragged effort to breathe.

"Jack," she retorted with a half sob. "It took me fifteen years to learn to live without my dreams. I don't want to spend another fifteen years with a new set of regrets. That's my world back there. Not this."

He walked right up to her, careful not to touch her so that she could answer only to his logic. "Don't you wonder sometimes, Kate, just what would have happened if you'd been given the chance to go after those dreams? If even though you'd lost, you'd at least have had the satisfaction of trying?"

He saw her sway, as if buffeted by a great wind. Her eyes grew stark. When she answered, it was in a very small voice. "All the time."

"You have a second chance, Kate. Take it."

"How?" she demanded in no more than a whisper. "Just stay? Call work and quit? Sell my car, cancel my lease and telegram my father goodbye for the promise of a man I've known less than two weeks?''

He did touch her then, as if that could convey the truth of what he said. ''A man who loves you, Kate.''

Kate couldn't see anything but Jack's eyes, the sparkling life in them radiating like a hot sun that lit only her. Trapped in the steel and glass canyons of Detroit, she'd never known anyone with eyes so full of life.

Didn't the psychologists say that if people had the choice between known comfort and the chance of freedom they would choose the comfort? Kate understood why. She looked up at that vast, endless sky in Jack's eyes and was terrified.

It was too late to try. She had too much to give up. And she couldn't know, even when he promised to follow her, that he would.

''What are you going to do?'' Jack prodded gently.

''Do?'' Kate demanded, tears spilling over. ''I think I'm going to get very, very drunk. And then I'm going home.''

Chapter Eight

Oh, God, Jack, is this what a hangover's like?''

''Mmm hmm.''

Kate resettled herself into the crook of Jack's shoulder and opened her eyes. Maybe if she found some definite landmarks she could quell that awful spinning, tilting sensation.

There were no landmarks. For a minute she thought she'd gone blind. It would have served her right. She had done her very best to match the yearly national alcohol consumption of the entire island of Nevis in one night. She started at Nathaniel's and ended up with half the population of Charlestown out on the streets, where Jack had joined in and bettered her. The last thing Kate remembered was the very drunken armada that had accompanied them back to the *Mandalay* when they'd finally given up and gone home.

Ah, there she was. In the cabin. Kate could barely make out the lanterns that hung alongside the portholes in the little kitchen area. It was difficult to make them out in the gloom. And there was the tiny bathroom with a shower and toilet, which was something she might soon be in need of.

What was that whining sound? Probably her stomach, crying out in protest to what she'd inflicted on it. On her brain, which had grown to twice its size sometime during the night and didn't fit inside her head anymore.

It couldn't be her dreams, she thought with enough clarity to feel the sharp stab of grief. She'd drowned her dreams last night so that she shouldn't feel anything but relief when she walked away to that plane today. For some reason, it still hurt. It hurt badly.

The next groan was definitely her own.

"Jack."

"Mmm."

Taking a deep breath, Kate closed her eyes again. "Is that the boat moving so much, or me?" Suddenly it seemed important.

It took him a minute to consider. Probably trying to stuff his own brain back into place, she thought. Kate lay as still as she could waiting for his answer. She wasn't prepared for all the action when Jack lifted a hand and peered at his watch a moment. Suddenly he was bolt upright.

"Damn!"

Kate only just managed to stay off the deck. Regaining her precarious position, she glared suspiciously at his sudden burst of activity. "Damn what?"

He was already out of bed and struggling into slacks and shirt. "Get your life jacket on," he snapped, suddenly all business. Turning on her, he leveled a warning finger. "And stay down here."

Reaching into one of the lockers, he pulled two jackets out and tossed one to her. Then he headed up the steps.

"Jack?"

Kate had gained an upright position by the time Jack managed to get the door open. It slammed in on him, the wind howling and full of rain. It reminded Kate of Dorothy's farmhouse when the tornado struck. She landed on the deck after all, clutching the jacket and fighting twin demons of terror and exhilaration.

"A hurricane!" she crowed, staring stupidly at the maelstrom outside and laughing like a child let out of school. "It's a hurricane! I don't have to go home tomorrow after all!"

"Kate," Jack warned, turning on her one last time before heading out. "You might be feeding the fish tomorrow if you don't get your bloody life jacket on. Now, do it!"

Jack was furious. How could he not have known? Dammit, he'd been on the sea too long to let a storm like this sneak up on him. He should have at least heard something on the weather band. After all, he'd only been drinking since seven o'clock the night before. Someone should have seen this mess form before that.

Hanging on to railings and masts, he battled his way back to the wheel where he kept the barometer—29.1 and falling like a rock. Damn. He looked up into the hellish night that should have been breaking day soon. The rigging shrieked already, a few hardy birds still clinging to it before the storm swept them away. The *Mandalay* bucked and rocked in the bay, the spray already blinding before the wind. Force six. And it was from the south. Kate had been right. It *was* a hurricane.

They were in trouble.

Jack rigged the safety lines and hoisted the fore-sail. More than that would be suicide in wind like this. Already the boat was kicking like a bronc, the wind torturing what canvas was up, the boat dragging at his sea anchors. He had to try a broad reach. There wasn't any way in hell he was going to be able to turn into the wind. He was too close to a lee shore. And if he tried to run north before the wind, he would slam smack into St. Kitts. He had to get out to sea.

By the time he winched up the anchors, Jack felt as if his shoulders would pull out of their sockets.

"What's going on?"

Jack looked up to see Kate before him, both hands tight on the lifeline. Her hair was plastered to her head, and her shirt molded to her slight frame.

"I told you to stay below!"

She grinned brightly and lifted a hand to push her hair out of her eyes. "And miss my first hurricane? What can I do to help?"

He shook his head, hands on her arms to propel her. "Go below!"

Kate didn't budge. "Jack, you don't expect me to wait down there in the dark and not know if you're okay. Now, what can I do?"

Jack pulled harder on the wheel to try and ease the strain on the sail a little. He had to get the auxiliary engine going to give them a little help. He had to check the sonar. There was no way to see what was coming beyond that boiling, shrieking mess.

"If I tie the wheel, can you help hold it?"

Kate nodded. "Sure."

"I mean hold it. I'm going to tie you to it if I have to."

Kate grinned again. "Kinky! I love it!"

Jack tied her himself. The seas were breaking hard over the bow, and he didn't want to suddenly lose her to the darkness.

It took Kate all of thirty seconds to realize what a mistake she'd made. There was no way she could hold the wheel, even with help from the rope. The pull against her arms was brutal, yanking viciously every time the boat slammed into a trough. The sea rose before her in writhing, wind-whipped mountains that should have engulfed the little boat. The wind shrieked like a host of demented banshees, tormenting her ears and flaying her skin with the salt spray that whistled through it.

She'd never seen the world in convulsions before. It made her glad Jack had tied her in place. Each wave that crashed over the deck threatened to snatch her feet out from under her. A couple put her head briefly underwater, and that was bad enough.

Even worse was that she couldn't always keep an eye on Jack. She saw him stagger beneath tons of roiling water, his arms wrapped around a mast as he passed, shaking it away as he struggled by. Then he disappeared into the cabin.

At least she wasn't down there. Kate couldn't think of anything worse than being trapped down below, not knowing what was going on, whether Jack was safe.

"How ya doin'?"

He was back, his face creased and strong, water streaming from his hair. Kate thought he somehow looked in his element in a hurricane—him against the sea in pitched battle. The keen challenge that emanated from his tense stance, the taut slant of his muscles and fierce determination in his eyes made him all the more handsome. Kate knew she'd always remember him like this.

"I'm fine," she lied, leaning harder in her effort to keep the nose pointed northwest.

"I can take it for a few minutes," he offered with a smile, and suddenly her shoulders were free of the strain. For the moment the pain was worse. Then she felt the warmth of Jack next to her and found her comfort.

"I thought that was a pretty bad hangover," she said, peering up into the tortured clouds that should have bumped the mast on their way by. "This is turning into a real beast."

She saw Jack take his turn to consider the storm. He doesn't even look like he's putting any effort into the wheel, Kate thought with some envy.

"It does look like we're in for a bit of a blow," he finally admitted.

Kate stared at him a moment and then found herself laughing. "That's what I love about you English. You're so melodramatic about everything."

Jack looked down at her with dry amusement. Another huge wave caught the boat and heeled it over, throwing him against her and drenching them both. Kate came up from the onslaught of water laughing.

"Well, that's what I like about you Irish," he countered in wry amazement. "You have no respect for disaster. You should be below cowering in a corner."

"And miss this?" she demanded with a sweeping gesture. "Never! It's breathtaking."

"Kate," he retorted, laughing. "I don't think you understand. This boat could end up a pile of kindling. While we're on it. That should be some cause for concern."

"I'm terrified," she assured him in a scream above the wind, then gave him a giddy grin. "But Jack, I've never been so excited in my life! Or alive! This is incredible!"

Jack couldn't believe he'd just heard his own conviction come from those lips of hers. It was true. It was the times like this, balanced on the brink of disaster when one mistake or mischance could forfeit your life, that the adrenaline honed the senses to such a breathtaking edge—when the fear and excitement tasted the same.

"Your turn again!" he yelled, dropping a kiss on her slick lips and thinking how beautiful she looked. "Don't let the rope break!"

When Jack came back from checking the sonar, he wasn't as happy. The hurricane was beating them, beating his *Mandalay*. He hadn't had enough time to get to the open water, and now the rocks of St. Kitts were looming before them.

"Kate?"

She looked away from the storm to see the fear reflected in Jack's eyes. It was all for her.

"I can swim!" she assured him with a big smile.

He took her hand and held tight. "I love you, Kate!"

Kate reached up to kiss him, the saltwater streaming from their faces and the wind lashing Kate's hair. "I love you, too, Jack."

They fought the storm for what seemed like hours. Jack thought for a few minutes that they might just make it. Might just skirt the northwest tip of the island. Then two things happened almost at once: the rudder broke, sending the *Mandalay* right around and the change on the already taut sail put too much strain on it. With a bang like a cannon shot, the canvas split. Before Jack could do anything, the boat struck ground.

Kate was thrown sideways. The boat had stopped dead, grating deep inside against something, and the maddened seas piled up against the tilting hull. Kate hung on to the wheel and searched the darkness for Jack. The terror had just overtaken her.

Then she heard him, and began to fumble with the knots that held her.

"Mayday, Mayday, Mayday. This is the *Mandalay*. My position is 17o 15'N, 62o4'W off the south shore of St. Kitts. We are breaking up on the rocks. Mayday..."

He repeated the message three times. By then the deck was on a deep slant and shuddering with the onslaught of the sea. Kate was trying her best to get herself free, but her fingers were stiff and numb. There wasn't much time. The boat was going to turtle. She wondered how far off the coast they were. She thought she heard breakers.

Suddenly two more hands were there to help her. "Come on, my lass," Jack said with a calm smile. "We have a bit of a trip to make."

"Well," she answered with a weak grin as the boat shook again and listed a little more. "I did want to see St. Kitts before I went home."

"Can't think of a better time to look." He smiled back. Finally getting the ropes free, he took her by the arms. "Now, we should have swung back around to the beach, so landing shouldn't be too traumatic. You will be tumbled around a bit. Stay calm and hang on to me." For a moment the storm lashed at them and the crippled boat writhed in the storm. Jack and Kate considered each other with rare honesty. Then silently Jack drew Kate into his arms and kissed her.

"Ready?"

She shouldn't be so giddy, Kate thought, wanting to giggle and sing. She shouldn't want to stay where she was, but she did—just she and Jack, storm racked and clinging to life like limpets. She wanted another kiss just like that one, warm and wet and desperate, sealing and inviting and bidding farewell.

Instead she nodded her head. "Last one to shore's an English dog."

And then she followed him into the water.

The only good thing about being in the water was that it was warm. The current quickly pulled them from the *Mandalay* so that within minutes the boat disappeared beyond a solid wall of water. Kate had a death grip on Jack's hand and spent all her energy just trying to breathe. She couldn't seem to keep her face above water. Her limbs felt leaden and her chest hurt.

Only the solid feel of Jack's grip kept her kicking toward the growing thunder of the surf.

She saw the breakers only when they were on them. Huge, crashing waves that consumed a hazy shoreline with awesome fury. Kate thought in passing that they were things of immense beauty. But she didn't have the time to appreciate them. Within seconds of topping a crest and sighting the white maelstrom, she was pulled under and summersaulted.

The tumbling started. Kate's legs slammed into the shallow seabed and she slid along rocky sand. The waves whirled her again, scraping her face along the same way. As she struggled to get up for air, she lost Jack's hand.

Kate's lungs were bursting. She was bruised and battered and still in the grip of those waves. Every time she thought she could get her head up, the undertow yanked her back down. Her ears pounded. Her chest was in agony. She had to breathe. Had to get her head up. She was damn well not going to drown off some lousy little island two thousand miles from home. She still had vacation time left.

Then, without warning, the sea gave up and tossed her away. Sailing through the air, she landed with a thud on the beach like an empty beer bottle.

It took a few minutes to realize where she was. The rain was coming down so hard she could barely differentiate it from the sea. Palm fronds hurtled through the air like artillery shells. Another wave swept over her, trying to reclaim her, and Kate crabbed further up the beach.

She was crying and laughing and sick from the seawater in her lungs, gulping air like it was going to be taken away from her again. She'd made it. Terra firma.

That was when it hit her. Whipping around, she searched the beach.

"Jack?"

Kate turned around. She was alone on the beach, and that terrified her even more than dying.

"Jack!"

She was on her feet now, stumbling, falling, searching the sand, the waves, the treeline.

"Jack, God, please, where are you?"

And then suddenly, he was there.

"Kate! Oh, God, Kate!" Kate turned to find herself pulled into his embrace, his arms frantic, his face so tight against hers.

The storm howled. The trees whistled and shrieked in agony. For a long moment Kate and Jack just held each other on that beach, oblivious to it. Then Jack pulled back to get a good look at her.

"Are you all right?" he demanded, his eyes fierce. He was as bruised and battered as she, a cut running watery blood along his cheek. He had never looked happier.

"All right?" she countered with her own version of his suddenly silly grin. "I'm fine. What a hell of a ride, Jack. Let's go on it again!"

The sun rode high once again over a shimmering sea. The trades swept in through open windows and cooled whitewashed rooms. There was bougainvillea in the air, and frangipani and mock orange. And beyond the luscious green hills, a new sailboat waited with the name *Mandalay* painted on the hull. A perfect day in paradise.

"You sure didn't wait long," Sam beamed as she helped Kate adjust the circle of island flowers in her tumbled, glimmering hair.

"Just long enough to be presentable for the pictures," Kate admitted with a grin. She felt giddy again. This was so out of place. Hippies wore flowers in their hair, not brokers. But then, she wasn't going to be a broker after all. Making a final pat at her hair, she got to her feet, the simple gown of palest green swirling around her ankles. Sam, in a flower print version of the same dress, ran inspection. Her resulting grin was a dead giveaway.

"You look just like—"

"Sam," Kate interrupted with a scowl. "Don't ruin my wedding."

That seemed to be a point of great satisfaction for Sam. "I knew all along."

"Of course you did."

"So, what was it finally that made you decide to come back?"

They stood together in the bedroom before a view of the bay. Out in the other room were the sounds of gathering people.

Kate looked out into the perfect morning. "A hurricane and a waterfall."

Sam looked a little confused. Kate found herself smiling.

"Remember when we met Mr. Brenner on the way to the Great Alps Falls?"

Her friend nodded.

"Well, he'll never see those falls. He waited too long. When I was sitting on that beach with Jack, I realized that I didn't want to find myself at eighty with nothing to look back on and nothing to look forward to. If I didn't take some big chances, I'd never have anything to show for it."

"Besides," Sam finished with certainty. "You love Jack."

Kate nodded with a smile. "Besides," she echoed. "I love Jack."

"Were you so afraid of dying in that hurricane?"

For a moment Kate thought of those long, lonely days in Detroit as she'd prepared to come back. It should have surprised her, really, but that was when the matter had been settled. She had spent her time thinking of that hurricane, of the wild, howling night she'd fought alongside Jack and how alive she'd felt.

She'd never felt that alive in Detroit. She never would. But when she had stepped off that plane on St. Maarten to return to him, she had felt the life return. And now, waiting for her wedding, she knew it would never leave her again, simply because she'd taken that chance.

"Actually," she admitted. "I had so much fun in that hurricane."

Behind them the door opened. Kate looked up and smiled. Only Jack would have seen the pain and its depths.

"Ready, Katie?" the old man asked. He was gray and worn and a little stooped. There was still a sad surprise in his eyes.

Kate walked up and slid her arm through his. Only Peter Manion would wear a suit on St. Maarten. "Yes, Daddy," she smiled up at him. "I'm ready."

She knew he'd come to give her away, no matter what. But the first time she'd had to face him, that day he'd cried for the battered body she'd brought back to him, that day she'd given him her decision, that day had been the most painful of her life. Her sisters had argued and clucked and chastised. But her father, who in his quiet way knew her better than anyone but Jack, had bottled up his grief and given her her freedom.

"I suppose we should go. Your young man is waiting for you."

Jack had won him over when he'd come to Detroit himself, still as battered and bruised as Kate, to formally ask Peter's permission for marriage. And then, he'd invited him down to stay. Peter had compromised. He had decided that winters in St. Maarten wouldn't be all that bad.

Jack stood between Nathaniel and the black priest. He couldn't ever remember being more nervous. Bloody hell. His shirt was too tight. He wanted to run his finger in under the collar. The whole ship's crew was crowded in here, along with half of Nevis and most of Phillipsburgh. Probably here just to verify the whole thing. Nobody had thought he'd go through with it. If he could face that sad-eyed old man and tell him he was taking his daughter away, he could bloody well do this.

"Steady on, mate. She's closin' fast now."

Jack heard Nathaniel's warning and turned. Sam was already down next to them. There was Kate, her arm through her father's, her head high. Smiling. God, he thought, his heart jumping, she's not just pretty or beautiful, she's glorious. She glows like a sunrise.

As she passed, one person after another turned to watch her, eyes wide, voices hushed. They saw now what Jack had seen all along. That special insatiable spirit that set her apart. Hair like bloodstone, eyes like a Caribbean sky. She was a creature from fantasy.

And then they stood together, their eyes only for each other. The world had fallen away. The little priest waited for them.

"You look like you just stepped out of a forest," Jack said very softly, eyes crinkling.

"Shut up," Kate retorted with a smile that glowed. "All I want to hear from you is 'I do.'"

Ten minutes later Jack turned to her, her hands in his, her dreams the gift he gave with his love, and he smiled. "I do."

* * * * *

Kathleen Korbel

Kathleen Korbel remembers what she said at the age of five years when somebody asked her what she wanted to be when she grew up. The answer was a roller-skating, scuba-diving, singing, acting nun. Well, she came close. Instead, she's an author-nurse-singer-photographer-teacher-columnist-wife-mother. In moments of megalomania she calls herself a Renaissance woman. Most of the time, though, she says she should just try one career at a time for a change.

A confirmed bookaholic, she first thought to write her own stories when she ran out of Nancy Drews to read at age ten. It wasn't until twenty years later, however, that she decided to formally take up pen and paper and establish herself as an author.

Since her first Silhouette Book, *Playing the Game*, in 1986, Kathleen has established herself in the category field with seven more Silhouette titles, a *Romantic Times* award for Best New Category Romance Writer and a Waldenbooks romance bestseller, *Worth Any Risk*. She still continues her work as an R.N. in one of St. Louis's trauma centers and manages, between her family and her two careers, to squeeze in time for all her other interests, which have now grown to include traveling, genealogy, film and theater, and history. She plans to continue her category work while branching out into historicals and mainstream. At the present time she's also negotiating to write the screenplay for *Worth Any Risk*, which is being optioned for a feature film.

Kathleen is a firm believer in what she calls the *Mame* school of philosophy: "Life's a banquet, and most poor fools are starving to death." But she doesn't see that ever happening to her.

Kathleen Korbel

Silhouette Special Edition

presents

LOVE AND GLORY

from
Lindsay McKenna

Introducing a gripping new series celebrating our men—and women—in uniform. Meet the Trayherns, a military family as proud and colorful as the American flag, a family fighting the shadow of dishonor, a family determined to triumph—with **LOVE AND GLORY!**

June: **A QUESTION OF HONOR** (SE #529) leads the fast-paced excitement. When Coast Guard officer Noah Trayhern offers Kit Anderson a safe house, he unwittingly endangers his own guarded emotions.

July: **NO SURRENDER** (SE #535) Navy pilot Alyssa Trayhern's assignment with arrogant jet jockey Clay Cantrell threatens her career—and her heart—with a crash landing!

August: **RETURN OF A HERO** (SE #541) Strike up the band to welcome home a man whose top-secret reappearance will make headline news . . . with a delicate, daring woman by his side.

Three courageous siblings—
three consecutive months of

LOVE AND GLORY

Premiering in **June**, only in
Silhouette Special Edition.

Coming in July from

Silhouette Desire®

ODD MAN OUT #505
by Lass Small

Roberta Lambert is too busy with her job to notice that her new apartment-mate is a strong, desirable man. But Graham Rawlins has ways of getting her undivided attention....

Roberta is one of five fascinating Lambert sisters. She is as enticing as each one of her three sisters, whose stories you have already enjoyed or will want to read:

- Hillary in GOLDILOCKS AND THE BEHR (Desire #437)

- Tate in HIDE AND SEEK (Desire #453)

- Georgina in RED ROVER (Desire #491)

Watch for Book IV of Lass Small's terrific miniseries and read Fredricka's story in TAGGED (Desire #528) coming in October.

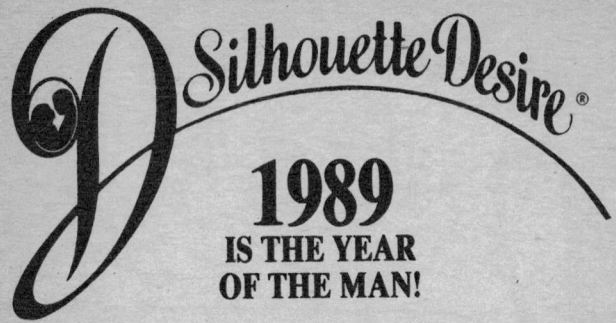

1989
IS THE YEAR
OF THE MAN!

What makes a romance? A special man, of course, and Silhouette Desire celebrates that fact with *twelve* of them! From Mr. January to Mr. December, every month has a tribute to the Silhouette Desire hero—our **MAN OF THE MONTH!**

Sexy, macho, charming, irritating . . . irresistible! Nothing can stop these men from sweeping you away. Created by some of your favorite authors, each man is custom-made for pleasure—*reading* pleasure—so don't miss a single one.

Mr. July is Graham Rawlins in ODD MAN OUT by Lass Small
Mr. August is Jeremy Kincaid in MOUNTAIN MAN by Joyce Thies
Mr. September is Clement Cornelius Barto in BEGINNER'S LUCK by Dixie Browning
Mr. October is James Branigan in BRANIGAN'S TOUCH by Leslie Davis Guccione
Mr. November is Shiloh Butler in SHILOH'S PROMISE by BJ James
Mr. December is Tad Jackson in WILDERNESS CHILD by Ann Major

So get out there and find your man!

Silhouette Desire's

MAN OF THE MONTH . . .

SCORPIO
24 OCTOBER – 22 NOVEMBER

First published in Great Britain 2013
by Mills & Boon, an imprint of Harlequin (UK) Limited,
Eton House, 18-24 Paradise Road, Richmond, Surrey TW9 1SR

HOROSCOPES 2014 © Dadhichi Toth 2013

ISBN: 978 0 263 91101 5

Cover design by Anna Viniero
Typeset by Midland Typesetters

Harlequin (UK) policy is to use papers that are natural, renewable and recyclable products and made from wood grown in sustainable forests. The logging and manufacturing processes conform to the legal environmental regulations of the country of origin.

Printed and bound in Spain
by Blackprint CPI, Barcelona

Dedicated to

The Light of Intuition

Sri V. Krishnaswamy—mentor and friend

Special thanks to

Nyle Cruz for her tireless support and suggestions

Thanks to

Joram and Isaac for hanging in there

Additional appreciation to

Devika Adlakha for her excellent editorial support

⊛ ABOUT DADHICHI ⊛

Dadhichi is one of Australia's foremost astrologers and is frequently seen on television and in other media. He has the unique ability to draw from complex astrological theory to provide clear, easily understandable advice and insights for people who want to know what their futures may hold.

In the 29 years that Dadhichi has been practising astrology, face reading and other esoteric studies, he has conducted over 10,000 consultations. His clients include celebrities, political and diplomatic figures, and media and corporate identities from all over the world.

Dadhichi's unique blend of astrology and face reading helps people fulfil their true potential. His extensive experience practising Western astrology is complemented by his research into the theory and practice of Eastern forms of astrology.

Dadhichi has been a guest on many Australian television shows, and several of his political and worldwide forecasts have proved uncannily accurate. He appears regularly on Australian television networks and is a columnist for online and offline Australian publications.

His websites—www.astrology.com.au and www.facereader.com— attract hundreds of thousands of visitors each month and offer a wide variety of features, helpful information and services.

MESSAGE FROM
⊚ DADHICHI ⊚

Hello once again and welcome to your 2014 horoscope!

Time and Speed are the governors of our lives these days. There's *never enough* time, and the hectic pace at which we move is getting *too much* to handle. So we oscillate between never enough and too much. We are either too slow in finishing our tasks, or the hands of the clock appear to be whizzing forward, especially when we're under pressure. We are constantly trying to create more time just to keep up with everyone else. And all those people are rushing out of control. What is this madness? We need to reclaim control of our lives and bring these terrible twins of speed and time under our control if we are ever to master our destinies.

According to Einstein and his incredible theory of relativity, speed and time are related. The faster we move, the quicker time flies. As we crank up the pace of our lives, time is impacted upon even more. You don't need me to tell you that; your experience will remind you of this fact every day, especially when you look in the mirror and see an additional wrinkle or two from time to time. Age is the favourite child of these two parents: speed and time. In the old days, it used to be the elderly who complained about the pace of time. But now, everyone, even youngsters, grumble about how little time they have and how they are forever trying to cram as much fun and experience into the moment. This attitude seems to be the order of the day, yet it will never, ever be enough.

The planets also operate on the same principle of speed and time, and this is how we generate astrological forecasts. Speed is related to the distance these planets traverse around the Sun, and the time it takes for them to do their celestial dance around the Sun is referred to as a planetary cycle.

We often talk about being in harmony with our environment and leaving as invisible a carbon footprint as we can, thus re-establishing natural equilibrium on earth. But our larger celestial environment is something we've overlooked. Ancient astrologers, however, knew the secret of our interconnectedness to the greater environment, and they gave us esoteric spiritual techniques for tuning in to these controllers of our fate. But how do you control the planets, let alone speed and time? It is through intuition, perception and self-awareness. By developing your perception and intuitive faculties, you will be one of the survivors in this brave new world.

If you're up to the challenge, this will increase your psychic abilities, thereby helping you surmount the obstacles of speed and time. You will bring yourself into harmony with your own physical, mental and emotional needs, and you will be able to tune easily in to your environment and fellow man. You will sense what these planetary energies are doing to you and can adjust yourself accordingly. This requires the subtle art of spiritual listening. This is not the hearing that is done with your ears. This is listening done with the heart. Through these simple techniques you *will* conquer time!

Our frames of reference are changing, and our ability to adapt to the light-speed pace is demanding refinements and adjustments in perception. In 2014, take the time to move at your own pace and look at what it is *you* want to achieve, not what is foisted upon you by culture, family and the establishment. Run your own race, and even if you are moving in high gear, at least you will be the one in control, not the clock. Use the transits and forecasts in the last chapter to help you gain an overview of the likely time of events. By taking control of your time and slowing the pace of life, you begin to control your destiny. In doing so, you rediscover the pleasure of your own self and the talents that you have been endowed with. This will then be a time of self-empowerment and great fulfilment.

Your astrologer,

Dadhichi Toth

◎ CONTENTS ◎

⊚ CONTENTS ⊚
CONTINUED

◎ CONTENTS ◎
CONTINUED

SCORPIO
PROFILE

LIFE IS TRYING THINGS TO SEE
IF THEY WORK.

Ray Bradbury

SCORPIO SNAPSHOT

Key Life Phrase		I will
Zodiac Totem		The Scorpion, the Grey Lizard and the Phoenix
Zodiac Symbol		♏
Zodiac Facts		Eighth sign of the zodiac; fixed, fruitful, feminine and moist
Zodiac Element		Water
Key Characteristics		Cagey, obsessive, determined, callous, dedicated, scrupulous and obstinate
Compatible Star Signs		Taurus, Cancer, Virgo, Scorpio, Sagittarius, Capricorn and Pisces
Mismatched Signs		Aries, Gemini, Leo, Libra and Aquarius

Ruling Planets		Mars and Pluto
Love Planets		Venus, Jupiter and Neptune
Finance Planet		Jupiter
Speculation Planets		Jupiter and Neptune
Career Planet		Sun
Spiritual and Karmic Planets		Moon, Jupiter and Neptune
Friendship Planet		Mercury
Destiny Planets		Jupiter and Neptune
Famous Scorpios		Ryan Gosling, Danny DeVito, Bill Gates, Joaquin Phoenix, Gerard Butler, Matthew McConaughey, David Schwimmer, Leonardo DiCaprio, Ethan Hawke, Sean 'Diddy' Combs, Owen Wilson, Jodie Foster, Anne Hathaway, Hillary Clinton, Demi Moore, Jenny McCarthy, Meg Ryan, Calista Flockhart, Björk, Julia Roberts, Kelly Osbourne and Grace Kelly
Lucky Numbers and Significant Years		2, 3, 9, 11, 12, 18, 20, 21, 27, 29, 30, 36, 38, 45, 47, 48, 54, 56, 57, 74, 75, 81, 83 and 84

Lucky Gems	Red coral, garnet, red spinel, ruby and yellow sapphire
Lucky Fragrances	Cinnamon, pine, cypress, lime and black pepper
Affirmation/Mantra	I don't need to control *everything*. I am free and peaceful.
Lucky Days	Monday, Tuesday, Thursday and Sunday

⊚ SCORPIO OVERVIEW ⊚

❝ IT IS NEVER TOO LATE TO BE WHAT YOU MIGHT HAVE BEEN. ❞

GEORGE ELIOT

∽

Scorpio is the undisputed spectacle of the zodiac. Your passion and vigour are universally admired, which is why few require an introduction to your star sign. You possess some remarkable qualities that are worth describing, especially for the benefit of those who may be unaware of the mysterious essence of your birth sign.

As the eighth sign of the zodiac, Scorpio rules birth, life, death and, most importantly, revival and self-transformation. Customarily, Scorpio is represented by the Scorpion. However, astrologers may also assign the Grey Lizard or Phoenix as possible totems. This indicates the multitude of dimensions that fall under your Sun sign.

The Phoenix is emblematic of your ability to transform or change, to cut through and rise above limitations, and to seek death before revival. But don't mistake this for physical death. What I'm referring to is your ability to completely discard your former self and become self-actualised. This happens to be the true significance of being a Scorpio.

It is not without reason that Scorpios are commonly perceived as secretive. This is not just guardedness, but a secrecy that relates to the universe, nature, life and spirituality. Because your birth sign is in a position that is receptive to the marvels of life, you are fascinated by aspects of psychology, religion, meditation and other forms of evolutionary self-development. It is through these interests that you try to self-reform and go beyond yourself. If this describes you, Scorpio, then you're definitely reflecting the element of the Phoenix.

There are other individuals who may symbolise the element of the Scorpion, and you can be identified by your not-so extraordinary qualities of envy, selfishness, dominance and vengefulness. These are just a few of the damaging traits associated with the Scorpion aspect of your Sun sign.

Regardless of whether you hail from the totem of the Scorpion or the Phoenix, you're blessed with an extraordinarily powerful tongue, and your speech can uplift or destroy. You can be highly critical of others, particularly those you take a dislike to.

The third totem, which is not as widely known, is that of the Grey Lizard. This type tends to withdraw into itself and may have addictive tendencies. Since Scorpio is usually intense and impulsive, this unruliness can reveal itself in gluttony, alcoholism, smoking and even drug abuse.

Sexual Scorpio

Independent of your totem is your sex drive, Scorpio. Sex will always be an integral component of your life, and you express yourself best through the act of lovemaking.

Another driving force in your personality is the will to succeed. You derive immense contentment from achieving success in your chosen field of work. You have indomitable willpower, which means that you are not easily rebuffed by circumstances. Once you decide on a course of action, your valour breaks through any obstacles that get in the way. You are also cautious, headstrong, vigorous and compelling.

Your disposition can be mystifying, and people often perceive you as enigmatic. Your eyes and speech add to your sexual appeal, and you use them as a bait to dominate others. Indeed, your Sun sign is gifted, but how the gift is used is entirely up to you, Scorpio.

⊙ SCORPIO CUSPS ⊙

ARE YOU A CUSP BABY?

Being born on the crossover of two star signs means you encompass the qualities of both. This can get tricky, and sometimes you will wonder whether you're Arthur or Martha! Some of my clients are continually mystified at whether they belong to their own star sign or the one before or after. Experiencing such feelings is nothing out of ordinary. Being born on the borderline means that you take on the qualities of both signs. The following outlines show the subtle effects of these cusp dates and how they can affect your personality.

Scorpio-Libra Cusp

If you were born between the 24th and the 30th of October, you fall in the area that is mutually governed by Libra and Scorpio. Since these two star signs are influenced by Venus, Mars and Pluto, you are bound to exude traits from both signs.

Libran traits beautifully counteract the intensity of Scorpio, thereby escalating your attractiveness and charisma, especially with the opposite sex. Blessed with impressive people skills, the desire to help others pulsates within you. Libra's sociability adds colour to your inherently pleasure-seeking nature, giving you a dynamism that attracts friends from all walks of life.

You reveal the best and worst of both star signs and display an impressive degree of fortitude, self-discipline and remarkable telepathic and instinctive skills. The perky and flippant attributes of Libra are offset by the staid and thoughtful qualities of Scorpio.

Though you possess innate insights regarding human nature, your piercing tongue and up-front beliefs can often intimidate and offend others. Clearly, you don't mince words, and though people often whine about your colossal ego, you're not bothered by this perception. You're aware of your charm and have immense confidence in your ability to win friends over. Unsurprisingly, your friends irrefutably outnumber your foes.

You are blessed with the gift of gab and can reason remarkably well. A steadfast pillar of support for the people you love, you forsake everything in the quest for sustaining their security.

Scorpio-Sagittarius Cusp

If you were born between the 15th and the 22nd of November, both Scorpio and Sagittarius govern your personality. Some astrologers may contest these dates, but the point I would like to underscore is that you will manifest qualities of both these star signs.

The intensity of Scorpio is daintily balanced by the lenient and big-hearted spirit of Sagittarius. Those born under the influence of this combination are ruled by Mars, Pluto and Jupiter, the ruler of Sagittarius. Though you're innately sanguine by nature, you can be rather aggressive in the pursuit of your goals. You like to lock your gaze on your dreams and work towards them with passion and fervour.

Your magnetic personality is accentuated even further by the well liked and gregarious Jupiter. You enjoy a near-perfect sense of timing in life and have a way of meeting the right people at the right time, all of whom enable you to get where you need to go in life.

You're sensitive and love to ruminate, and when these qualities are imbued with Sagittarius's sincerity and munificence, you can hypnotise people into trusting you even when they don't know you. You ensure your support heals all, and you are even considered mentor-like by many who are your age, younger or even older.

You're forever playing the muse and advising friends or strangers about the way they should best proceed in the midst of their life problems.

An Independent Spirit

You are an extraordinarily independent person and abhor being restricted or contained by anyone. Your early years are marked by fun-loving adventure, but these will peter out as age catches up with you.

Though you work, live and lark about, you tend to be inordinate in your ways and must avoid excess. Be especially attentive to your physical needs as they can bear the brunt of your overindulgence.

SCORPIO CELEBRITIES

FAMOUS MALE:
DANNY DEVITO

As the old saying goes, big things come in small packages, and this is true for Danny Devito, who was born on the 17th of November, 1944.

Danny's size has in no way obstructed his becoming a world-famous, first-class actor, producer and director. Scorpios are always exceedingly focussed on attaining their goals, irrespective of the handicaps they face in life. Danny is no exception. In 1970 he made his first appearance as a thug in a rather obscure movie called *Dreams of Glass*. As with many actors, he was discouraged by the meagre success of the film. But true to his Scorpio nature, he continued to chase his dream, and it wasn't long before he appeared in Milos Forman's now-famous film *One Flew Over the Cuckoo's Nest* (1975).

In 1978 he won a role on the sitcom *Taxi* (1978–1983), and it was through this show that he finally attained the success he had hoped for. The odds he has overcome have helped him become one of the world's most versatile actors. Like most Scorpio individuals, he continues to perfect his art and passionately pursues his dreams.

FAMOUS FEMALE:
BJÖRK

Björk is a rather unusual performer who has made her name by being completely different and pushing the boundaries of what is acceptable.

Women born under the sign of Scorpio have a unique intensity and depth of feeling. Coupled with their extra-ordinary intuitive abilities, they are able to tap the universal consciousness. When we look at Björk, it is obvious that she is channelling something very different and progressive in her music. Scorpios also like to add shock value to their lives. In 2002, MTV banned Björk's music video for *Pagan Poetry* because it showed images of her breasts and body piercings.

Scorpio women can sometimes be a little aggressive. This may explain why Björk once punched a reporter for stalking her. Scorpios need to bring their emotions under control, but at least Björk is directing this energy in a productive manner through her music. In fact, as a reward for her significant contribution to music and the promotion of her homeland, the Icelandic government has gifted her the island of Elliday.

As with typical Scorpios, Björk likes to maintain an air of secrecy and mystique. She says: 'What probably confuses people is they know a lot about me, but it quite pleases me that there's more that they don't know'.

SCORPIO

AT LARGE

PEOPLE OF MEDIOCRE ABILITY SOMETIMES
ACHIEVE OUTSTANDING SUCCESS BECAUSE
THEY DON'T KNOW WHEN TO QUIT.
MOST MEN SUCCEED BECAUSE THEY
ARE DETERMINED TO.

George Allen

⊙ SCORPIO MAN ⊙

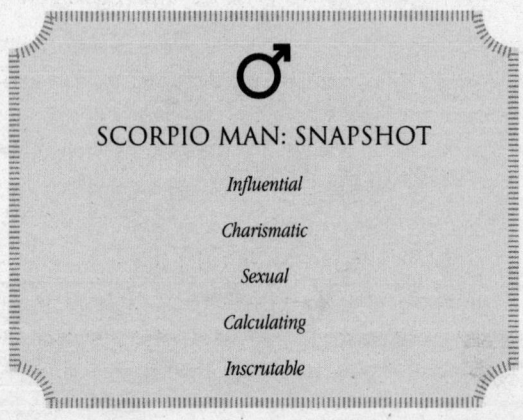

SCORPIO MAN: SNAPSHOT

Influential

Charismatic

Sexual

Calculating

Inscrutable

The Scorpio man appears to be an enigma, not just to the world at large, but also to himself! The power inherent in this star sign is tricky to fathom, and Scorpions reading this will probably understand what I'm talking about better than anyone else.

From birth, Scorpio men have evolved instinctive responses, preferring to rely on their gut rather than worldly logic. They may take a sudden dislike to someone for no apparent reason, and no matter how hard you try, changing their opinion is not easy. Their heightened sensitivity overrides mental reasoning, making it difficult to get close to them.

If you are a Scorpion male, you can be self-absorbed and have an obstinate ideology that you create and abide by. You can be uncompromising in your expectations, both of yourself and others, and you're forever trying to top the impractically high standards you set for yourself.

While you remain an enigma for most, it is this mysteriousness that attracts others to you. Regardless of whether people grasp the real you, they burn with a desire to get up close and personal with you.

Scorpio, you have the ability to shine and succeed, but I'd like you to remember that professional triumph may not guarantee true happiness. Rather, it may leave you dreadfully forlorn and lonely. You're cautious in relationships, and while your younger years were full of friendships, with age you turn into a bit of a cynic.

DRIVEN SCORPIO

You have incredible drive and patience, Scorpio, and you never fail to amaze people. With your vision set squarely on realising your goals, you pursue your dreams without resigning, even if it means toiling for years. This holds true for your vengeful streak as well. In short, a Scorpio man never forgets an act of kindness or forgives being hurt.

Sexual expression forms the core of your personality, and you have an insatiable yearning for passion, affection and attention. Anyone seeking a romantic engagement with you must come to terms with your complex motivations. For an in-depth explanation of this, refer to the section on Scorpio and romance.

Though you may appear reticent, the intensity and articulateness of your thoughts and ideas often leaves others flummoxed. It is through your style of communication that you reveal your leader-like qualities. You are clearly not fit to be a follower.

You're a phenomenal storyteller, which stems from your intrinsic desire to make an indelible impact on people around you. Your popularity gives your ego a persistent high, and in your pursuit of the limelight you can subconsciously dismiss the opinions and needs of others. Nonetheless, you remain the undisputed people-charmer, forever enthralling people with the world you create and the words you use to paint it.

Your over-possessiveness towards loved ones can often sour a relationship, especially if your partner doesn't reciprocate with the same intensity. You are unable to share your loved ones and often blur the line between loyalty and control. Endeavour to respect all energy levels, Scorpio. Not everyone is perfect, nor does a lack of passion equal a dearth of love or commitment.

Often you may find yourself torn between the philosophical and sexual aspects of your personality, seeking expression through both. On the one hand you fancy sexual intimacy and demonstrativeness, but on the other you yearn for spiritual awareness through meditation, self-awareness and sacrifice. Interestingly, even this kind of stress works in your favour as people are attracted to the complexities of your mind.

Scorpio men have supremely agile minds and commit to memory even the most insignificant details, much to other people's surprise. They fiercely guard their self-respect and highly value respect from others. In short, they aspire to be admired—and they are.

You like to be excessive in countless ways and display an obvious gluttony, as well as an immoderate craving for sex. Remember, all's well as long as it is under restraint.

Never become the object of a Scorpion's rage. Their temper can be explosive and merciless, and when a Scorpion strikes, it strikes to kill. They detest being proven wrong and react fiercely to confrontation. Though you're a man who cares little about others' perceptions, at times you should mellow out and toe the line, even if you have differences of opinion.

⑤ SCORPIO WOMAN ⑤

SCORPIO WOMAN: SNAPSHOT

Devoted

Realistic

Sensual

Persistent

Unique

Scorpio women are possibly the most attractive and sexually alluring of the zodiac. You express yourself with your captivating body language, especially your eyes, which reveal the intricacy of your feelings and state of mind.

The air of mystery you exude can be a magnetising force, though not for those who prefer uncomplicated and simple personalities. But you're not in the least disconcerted by this. You possess innate self-confidence, and the phrase 'Take me as I am or take a hike' sums up your life motto.

Your buoyancy stems from painful life experiences. Throughout your childhood and early adult years you were probably exposed to a multitude of events that tested your resilience and conviction. Coupled with this are your own innate instinct, insight and reasoning, which you creatively exploit to steer ahead in life. No wonder you grew up too quickly and with unshakable self-belief.

At the same time, possessing such a wealth of experience is counterproductive. You can exhibit an intense pride in your abilities and ideology, and you can be fiercely independent by nature. These traits make you difficult to deal with, but this is cathartic for you because it makes you feel that you're in perfect control.

While expressing yourself socially, you certainly put your best foot forward. You're adept at concealing the turmoil within and can present a seemingly innocuous front. Little do others know!

On the whole, you're sceptical of people, and your temper can erupt in the blink of an eye. You can mope for aeons over inconsequential things, leaving others scratching their heads over the possible reasons for your moroseness. Try to let go, Scorpio, as such negativity can erode even your best relationships.

You work hard and earn good money. Being independent by nature, you seek bliss by lavishly spending the money you earn. You like to live life on your own terms, and you work hard to achieve your dreams. Your social standing, character and high self-esteem make you shine among many others.

Scorpio women are the seductresses of the zodiac because they perpetually feel that the world fancies them. This self-belief enlivens your inherent charm and attracts all kinds of people to you.

You respect other people's privacy and closely guard the secrets that loved ones confide in you. Even if you choose to listen instead of give advice, you can heal people by your presence alone. Your aura exudes a therapeutic quality that attracts people who like to draw on your energy. With your clear and evolved intuition, you can offer reasonable solutions without intellectualising.

A TRUE HUMANITARIAN

Although you are possessive, you are also generous to a fault.
You give the world to people, even if they don't demand too much
of you. When you sense someone in distress, you go out of your
way to provide support. You're a true humanitarian at heart.

But your most notable quality reveals itself in romance. When it comes to lovemaking, you know exactly how to woo your man in bed. You're a gifted lover—and an exceptional one at that!

You also like to exhibit masculine qualities to prove that you're as powerful and threatening as a man. But in your quest to prove yourself, try to use your delicate feminine traits of charm, poise and seductiveness. Believe me, this works better than any other strategy you may employ.

With a remarkably precise psychic ability and a well-honed sixth sense, Scorpio women don't need to do in-depth research to understand a person or situation better. You rely on your gut. It may defy reason and common sense, but it is usually fairly accurate.

SCORPIO CHILD

Scorpio children are born with incredibly intense characters, and unless you draw clear parameters when it comes to their activities and habits, they may grow up to be more difficult than you can imagine.

Being under the planetary influence of Mars and Pluto, the young Scorpio child exhibits immense dynamism, intelligence and curiosity. From early on they love to assert their superiority over others, and for this reason they often plunge into sports and other competitive opportunities. In order to feed their self-confidence, they are constantly engaged in an inward battle to prove their worth by being the best at all they do. And they usually succeed.

Though Scorpio children are robust and physically resilient, parents must employ caution during sports and outdoor activities. They are often prone to injury because of their daredevil nature, which gets a high from dangerous sports, skylarking and other wild, outdoor activities.

Their magnetism starts at childhood when Scorpio kids wield their charm and find themselves flocked by a bevy of friends. Due to this high self-image, their ego often clashes with others as they like to be in control. Such tendencies transform into undue pride during adulthood, and it is critical for you to educate your little one on the significance of serving others as well.

They also dream of exploring terrain that is untouched by others, and they idolise heroes such as Superman. As parents you must be able to sense such desires and divert them in a constructive fashion. How about giving them a chemistry or electronics set instead? All they need is an avenue to play out their fantasies through invention and discovery.

Scorpio girls love being lady-like and one can often find them nestled in the kitchen making up new recipes along with their parents. As always, Scorpio boys take to the fields to test their competitiveness and stamina, and they work hard to be the best.

Due to their innate sense of loyalty and dedication, Scorpio kids make excellent friends. Of course, their need to be the centre of attention is high, and if they can't succeed at being the favorite in a group, they move onto another and then another until they are crowned the undisputed chief.

Scorpio children are clever and intuitive learners, and they should be encouraged in subjects they have a natural inclination for. Unless you support their interests, indolence may creep in and they will gradually resort to cutting corners, which only undermines their inborn ability.

EXCELLENT COMMUNICATORS

Scorpio children have agile minds and they are effortless, almost adult-like communicators. Their reasoning and logic make perfect sense, and you'll have no choice but to heed their demands!

Lastly, you must bear in mind that children of this sign are tempted by the darker aspects of life, such as drugs, sex and alcoholism. As teens, they derive an unusual thrill from venturing into zones that question norms, and unless forewarned, they can get miserably trapped into such intemperance. Make sure that you educate your child using reason and dialogue to ensure that they're aware of the consequences of their actions.

SCORPIO LOVER

PURPOSE DIRECTS PASSION AND PASSION IGNITES PURPOSE.

UNKNOWN

Scorpio happens to be the eternal lover of the zodiac, and this holds true for both men and women. You're the iconic epitome of seduction, and once you choose to give your heart to someone, you love them to no end. This I can vouch for, and so would peers and laypeople alike.

When you're in love, you treat it like a celebration. Far from seeming like a routine, the essence of love is a transformative creative desire that inspires you to bond on an almost spiritual level. You want love to permeate your mind and body and reach the heights of ecstasy.

Scorpios get their ultimate thrill from testing their ability to charm. They do this by assessing how many people they can seduce. In short, romance is a way of measuring your magnetism and appeal. Even if you are in a devoted relationship, you're constantly probing to see whether or not you've maintained your 'edge'.

Though Scorpios are generally secretive, love and romance are altogether different. You're an enormously demonstrative lover and demand reciprocation. Being the most 'sexual' sign of the zodiac, you possess innate vitality and enthusiasm and can be emotionally tumultuous in love—factors that must be borne in mind by your prospective lover. Though your personality may throw up some exciting challenges, love can be immensely cathartic for both you and your lover. In short, there's never a dull moment with you, Scorpio. It's one heck of a joyride!

The intensity with which you plunge into love affairs may terrify potential lovers. You make a commitment only when you've assessed all angles and know exactly where you stand, and if you sense unresponsiveness on the other end, you waste no time in moving on. Superficiality is not your thing.

Scorpios are charming and flirtatious in a very suave way, and when it comes to commitment, their devotedness is hard to beat. Scorpion lovers exhibit superlative sincerity and adoration, and they celebrate their lovers completely. They do all in their power to see their partner contented. Consider yourself fortunate if you are in a relationship with a Scorpio, and ensure that you honour their commitment just as they do.

If you take their fidelity for granted, rest assured that grave consequences will follow. Not only will Scorpio withdraw their love, they can be vengeful ex-lovers as well. Irrespective of how much they invested in the relationship, they will find a way of getting back at you. Unfortunately, you'll just have to deal with these darker elements of your Scorpio ex-lover.

SCORPIO'S DARK SIDE

When we delve into the deeper, darker elements of Scorpio's personality, traits such as jealousy, possessiveness, manipulation and domination appear. The degree to which such influences surface depends on how evolved your Scorpio lover is.

When it comes to envy, you'd better be careful. Jealousy fuels your inherent insecurities and vulnerabilities. Unless you find creative ways of plugging this emotion, your relationship is bound to collapse right before your eyes. True joy in love stems from trust. Allow your partner some breathing space and bestow on them the same independence that you demand from them.

You partner must envision growing in love with you. You expect them to be at their best, look their best and gratify all your desires. If your partner respects this about you, you too should reciprocate their commitment. When real, Scorpio love is supreme.

Your sullenness may often be over the most inconsequential and inexplicable reasons. You like to withdraw silently and mull over the past without verbalising your thoughts. Under acute stress you may collapse emotionally, suffocating those you care about. Learn to initiate dialogue and vent a fraction of what you feel. Allow your partner to be a part of your life; reach out to them and show that you believe in them.

Other water signs like Pisces and Cancer exhibit similar moodiness and can cope with your emotional shifts. However, your opposite star, Taurus, which is an earth sign, can balance your extremes by mellowing your overall intensity.

⚲ SCORPIO FRIEND ⚲

Scorpios make great friends and usually enjoy a multitude of acquaintances that stimulate their intellectual and emotional interests. However, the presence of Scorpio may be somewhat overbearing for some. You're unusually passionate and straightforward in relationships, and you can dissect a person's character and emotional needs. Unless people get a chance to bond with you, your intensity can be confronting. However, once your intentions are clear, your friends are forever looked after and well supported.

As a friend you're big-hearted, courteous and enjoyable to be around. Contrary to the perception that you have a serious disposition, you have a knack for entertaining and storytelling. In fact, you entertain others with your past experiences, and you like to embellish the finer details to make the story even more fascinating.

You're also an excellent listener and a psychologist at heart. You possess acute insights and a refined intuition that enables you to perceive what is really going on. You like to play the healer and resolve as much as you can, which is why you're forever blessed with people in your life.

Superficial or lukewarm associations do not fascinate you as your soul beats for richer, deeper relationships. You prefer to indulge in a friendship only when you sense a similar inclination in the other person. Like Japanese business relationships, you're in for the long haul!

Because you're a high achiever, Scorpio, you like to engage with people of similar calibre and self-worth. You constantly seek inspiration from friends and lovers alike, and have no room for obtuse conversations or people. If someone fails to impress you, Scorpio, they need to go back to the drawing board to chalk out something valuable that will add meaning to their conversation (and relationship) with you.

The best way to foster a friendship with Scorpio is to engage them in outdoor activities, competitive sports or intrigue them with novel topics of interest. Getting them to connect with new friends and visiting unique places with cultural or intellectual relevance are sure ways to boost companionship. Scorpios are young at heart, and music, rock concerts and similar events are avenues you could explore with them.

Scorpios are extraordinarily loyal and dedicated as friends, but only if their care and commitment is reciprocated. If they sense hostility or their enthusiasm is being taken for granted, they are quick to withdraw and redirect their passion elsewhere.

⦿ SCORPIO ENEMY ⦿

Scorpios are exceptionally adept at portraying a composed exterior, even if they're erupting with fury within. You can live your entire life misinterpreting their silence and calm-headedness, hopelessly oblivious to their true feelings. There's never a way of knowing if you're hated. Such is the perplexing nature of Scorpio's wrath—it fumes without giving you an inkling of what is going on. This makes them dreadful enemies indeed.

Scorpios have an enormous degree of self-esteem and innate vanity. They regard acts such as knavery, wrongdoing, betrayal or perfidy as a direct assault on their pride, and they attack as a result. However, their style isn't noticeably impulsive or predictable. Just like the scorpion, they wait for the appropriate time and strike when you least expect it.

Being an enemy brings out Scorpio's worst. The determined, compulsive and obstinate facet of their personality makes them an incredibly overpowering foe. To overcome this, they need to work at calmer ways to tackle their adversaries without undermining their own psychological and physical wellbeing.

SCORPIO

AT HOME

HE WHO LEARNS BUT DOES NOT THINK
IS LOST! HE WHO THINKS BUT DOES
NOT LEARN IS IN GREAT DANGER.

Confucius

⊚ HOME FRONT ⊚

Your home décor offers insights into the secretive aspect of your personality, Scorpio. You vehemently guard your territory, which is suggestive of your extreme desire for privacy and the need to shield your loved ones. Your mind is rather hostile to the concept of outside intrusion, and even with friends, you demand some sort of forewarning before they casually drop in.

Scorpios love to tease and seduce, and their home styling reflects this. You have a penchant for opulence, romantic artefacts and luxury, and you are known to spend extravagantly. This splendour is beautifully reflected in your furnishings and colour schemes, creating a sensual yet uplifting feel. You like the colour palette to set the right mood and help everyone unwind, but you also want the styling to inspire you to creatively indulge in emotional and mental stimulation.

House-Proud Scorpio

Possessions are a measure of your success, and you like your house and styling to be talked about. You invest money in doing up your space and derive enormous pride and inspiration from it.

Your house is usually spotless and meticulously organised thanks to your obsessive nature. In fact, you exhibit some Virgo traits in this area. Even your bookshelves are pretty, with each book stacked according to height, and, like Virgo, any change in this order stresses you out.

Notwithstanding your investments towards building the perfect home, you still want to create a liveable space. You like your furniture and fittings to exude an element of practicality and functionality. With water as your zodiac element, creating a pond or mini fountain would help boost your energy levels and provide a sense of being close to nature. What would be even better is a house facing a lake or the sea! Pot plants are bountiful in your home, and a fish tank may also soothe your temperament and encourage you to reconnect with yourself.

Scorpio favorites are darker shades of purple, blue and black, which allow you to create an air of mystery, which is one of the signature traits of Scorpio. You also do this by mixing exotic and passionate shades of crimson, burgundy and red. Added to this is your distinctive taste in lighting, which accentuates the mystifying feel and lends a dramatic contrast to the shading. A night at your house is bound to be remembered. You also love to entertain by wining and dining your loved ones in the comfort of your abode.

KARMA, LUCK AND ⊚ MEDITATION ⊚

'I will' is your life phrase, Scorpio, and this makes you the most determined of all the star signs. When you set yourself a challenge, you almost always achieve it. This is due to the influence of your ruling planets Mars and Pluto, the epitome of indomitable will and persistence.

You're blessed with psychic insights and an enormous degree of sensitivity, all of which you have developed and honed over your past lifetimes. Cancer is the ninth sign from yours, which is indicative of your thoughtful and affectionate nature.

Your future karma is indicated by the sign of Pisces, the fifth sign from Scorpio. This is the third water sign of the water trine, signifying your movement towards a more unconditional way of loving. Though your current stage of evolution finds you preoccupied with sensuality, possession and power, this will change for the better over time, Scorpio.

Lucky Days

Monday, Tuesday, Thursday and Sunday are most auspicious for emotional healing and self-development. If you invest a little time each day attempting something you wouldn't normally do, it will certainly augment your luck.

Lucky Numbers

Lucky numbers for Scorpio include the following. You may wish to experiment with these in Lotto and other games of chance.

9, 18, 27, 36, 45, 54

3, 12, 21, 30, 48, 57

2, 11, 20, 29, 38, 47, 56

Destiny Years

The most significant years in your life are likely to be: 2, 3, 9, 11, 12, 18, 20, 21, 27, 29, 30, 36, 38, 45, 47, 48, 54, 56, 57, 74, 75, 81, 83 and 84.

HEALTH, WELLBEING
◉ AND DIET ◉

Scorpio is the eighth sign of the zodiac and closely aligned with body parts such as the urinary tract, reproductive organs and the organs of excretion. These areas are constitutionally weak and susceptible to infection. Other vulnerable body parts are the liver, skin and, by virtue of being the sign opposite Taurus, which rules the throat, the larynx.

Just like your personality, your lifestyle is highly passionate and intense. You often find yourself overworked and anxious, even without trying. This has natural repercussions on your overall wellbeing, and if you're fond of alcohol and cigarettes, the aforementioned body parts will be enormously affected.

Aries rules the head and is in the sixth zone of health and disease from Scorpio. During your younger years, which can be quite challenging and consuming, some Scorpios may suffer recurrent headaches due to stress or suppressed emotions.

On the whole, you're blessed with a robust immune system and resilient recuperative powers, both of which enable you to withstand illness and health hazards. In spite of this, your diet should be rich in calcium, vitamin B and health supplements to boost your overall health.

In terms of daily consumption, vegetables such as asparagus, cauliflower, onions, tomatoes and figs are most advantageous, while black cherries, whole grains, seafood, green salads and nuts are excellent sources of antioxidants.

FINANCE FINESSE

Scorpio works to earn a living, and money is definitely a mark of the success you achieve in life. Scorpio also rules the eighth sign of the zodiac, which relates to shared money such as inheritance, joint investments, annuities and taxes.

SUCCESSFUL SCORPIO

During your younger years you pride yourself on the amount of cash you stack up in the bank. You have a proclivity for materialistic luxuries and symbols of prestige, such as cars, brand-name clothing, jewellery and mansion-like houses—all indicators of your overall accomplishment and success in life.

The second sign to Scorpio is Sagittarius, which governs the manner in which you earn your money and, to some extent, how you spend it. The ruler of Sagittarius, which is the magnanimous planet Jupiter, explains your karmic ability to earn pots of money and the generous way in which you spend it.

Though most Scorpions are capable of earning well, I have encountered some who capitalise on their talents only when they are considerably older. This is because you do not compromise on your goals and aspirations and prefer to stick to engaging but poorly paid jobs. It is only when you carve a place for yourself and garner respect that you demand better remuneration for your services. For you, money signifies integrity, and you're not one to beg financial favours from people. You like to be self-reliant and create a sparkling life from whatever you have.

SCORPIO

AT WORK

THERE'S NO SENSE IN DOING A LOT OF
BARKING IF YOU DON'T REALLY HAVE
ANYTHING TO SAY.

Charles M. Schulz

⊚ SCORPIO CAREER ⊚

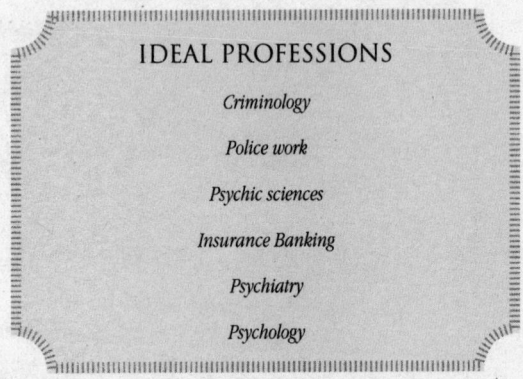

IDEAL PROFESSIONS

Criminology

Police work

Psychic sciences

Insurance Banking

Psychiatry

Psychology

You're like a machine at work, Scorpio—tireless and relentless. People often wonder where all that incredible energy comes from. This is particularly evident with Scorpio mothers who can effortlessly balance a full-time job and the needs of their family and friends. But it doesn't stop there. Scorpio draws vigour and force from the distant planet, Pluto, the ruler of their Sun sign.

Scorpios like to do everything perfectly, and they have zero tolerance for anyone who hinders that. Their rage can surface at such moments, but Scorpios can choose to be composed and calm and take full control, even if he or she is not the boss.

Scorpio, you love to be challenged, and competition inspires you immensely. As long as you're constructively engaged and making a contribution, you feel a sense of passion towards work. Unless you love what you do, you're likely to move on to greener pastures. You believe that passion towards work is part of the universal process that provides you with overall success and fulfillment.

You are exceptionally focussed and don't take your eyes off a task until you have achieved the desired end. You're intelligent and acutely aware of your responsibilities, and you detest having anyone suffocate you with their own approach to getting a job done. People who work with you must understand that your competitive spirit hides an extremely honest person who expects the same level of honesty in return.

Innately Confident

You possess innate self-confidence that doesn't stem from your ego or false notions about your self-image. It is a conviction that you develop through years of experience and painstakingly mastering your craft.

Due to your inherent competitiveness, you unhesitatingly take the initiative and are a reliable worker, thereby garnering respect from colleagues, employers and clients alike. Your love for power is best utilised in professions such as the police force, criminology, insurance, banking, investment, stockbroking, market analysis, psychology, research, science and astrology.

With such intense energy levels, only a few can keep up with you, Scorpio. The enormity of your force can only be explained by the influence of your ruling planets Pluto and Mars, which make you impulsive and tireless. However, try to avoid overwork and moderate your working hours. If you don't, your health will spiral downwards and your personal relationships will follow. Needless to say, 'workaholic' is your second name.

Having the Sun as your career planet also speaks volumes about your professional success. Because the Sun is bright and warm, you're likely to be admired and accomplished in your chosen line of work. This is also indicative of your ability to win the adulation of others.

⊙ SCORPIO BOSS ⊙

Loyalty is all-important for a Scorpio boss. For you, nothing supersedes commitment, and you demand it from your business partners or employees. They must all be prepared to stand faithfully by you and dedicate themselves to realising your vision and goals.

This may sound like a tall order to most, but those who stick by you are fortunate. If they succeed in winning your trust, you will become a staunch ally who stands by them, even in the worst crisis.

Scorpios—and Scorpio bosses in particular—are hugely competitive and hate to lose. Their competitiveness at work manifests as aggression, energy, power, authority and determination, all of which makes them highly successful in the workplace. You're an honest, hard worker, and you demand Herculean efforts, not just from yourself, but also from those in your professional circle.

EXCELLENT SERVICE

Your enthusiasm and dedication is contagious, and your clients
always feel that they receive the best possible service from you.
At the same time, you expect a similar standard of service
from those you employ.

Scorpios are usually suspicious of others and appear guarded until someone successfully proves their worth to them. There are those who tend to feel left out and discriminated against, mistaking your lack of communication for harsh judgment. However, this is your way of assessing the inherent shortcomings in people so you can use their abilities better.

You work hard to create a well ordered company and expect everyone to be aware of their rightful place. Loyalty, devotedness, timing, punctuality and meticulousness are key factors that enable you to feel secure and motivated in the workplace.

Because Pluto is your ruling planet, Scorpio, you'll often struggle with the concept of trusting others and letting go, and you'll end up cramming too much on your plate instead. You must understand that there are people like you who seek challenge and growth. Unless you're able to delegate these tasks to them, you'll lose support and impair your own success

⊚ SCORPIO EMPLOYEE ⊚

Scorpio employees are highly intelligent, self-motivated and determined. Wherever you work and regardless of the profile, you're vastly capable and understand your role and requirements perfectly. Once you're assigned to a job, you're like a dog with a bone, skillfully pouring your energies into it.

You display a remarkable work ethic and are loyal, honest and punctual. You work with careful precision, accountability and meticulousness, and you have a way of developing systems that make you much more efficient than others.

GOAL-ORIENTED SCORPIO

You're highly focussed on your vision and devote yourself to achieving your goals—both long-term and short-term. The accomplishment of these goals serves as a barometer of success in your life, which is something you hold dear.

Because you believe in laying out clear objectives and aspirations, you're attentive and have an inherent respect for time. You're not one to encourage or enjoy social gossip in the workplace, and you refrain from getting personally involved in anything except work. As a result, you may not enjoy flattery or popularity amongst your colleagues, but this doesn't bother you because you're entirely devoted to your aims.

At times you're detested for your sincerity, as some regard it as a threat to their lackadaisical and sluggish nature. My personal advice would be to maintain a low profile at work and avoid revealing your true abilities to others. If the best of you incites jealousy and hate, it would be wiser to play it down and fulfil your responsibilities instead.

Scorpio employees are bold, ingenious and eager to skate on thin ice. Courage is your mainstay, and you wield it swiftly, especially if you are discontented in a particular workplace. You're the last person to stick to a job for money alone, and if you're not engaged and constructively occupied, you move on to better opportunities.

Like the Scorpio boss, the Scorpio employee is extremely loyal. Even if opportunities come knocking on your doors, promising a flourishing career, you prefer to happily stand by your employers and the people you work with.

You're blessed with a sharp mind, and when it is supplemented with your shrewd reasoning and intuitive abilities, it makes you an incredibly gifted worker, which is something that your employers are quick to notice.

You're an individual of high principles and cannot stomach unfairness and inequality. If you found yourself or someone else being treated unfairly, you would ruthlessly voice your opposition, regardless of hostile reactions. This is because you're fearless, courageous and righteous.

PROFESSIONAL RELATIONSHIPS: BEST AND WORST

BEST PAIRING:
SCORPIO AND SAGITTARIUS

From a business perspective, this partnership couldn't be better. The most advantageous aspect of this combination is your respective ruling planets, which are deemed bosom buddies by astrologers. The Jupiter-ruled Sagittarius falls in the finance sector of Scorpio and this brings great prospects for profit and augmenting your income stream.

Scorpios work best with people who are equally intelligent and love to explore. What you benefit from and appreciate about your Sagittarian business partner is their broad range of knowledge and the open-mindedness they display when it comes to business expansion. At times they may seem unusually liberal and carefree, which makes you feel somewhat anxious. As a result, trust is critical for the success of this partnership. As long as you maintain a tight rein on the finances, the emotional and mental compatibility between you will make this partnership a walk in the park.

My professional experiences with Sagittarians have been very pleasing. They are positive, liberal-minded and imaginative in their approach. They're also quite self-assured, so you mustn't dominate if you really want them to manifest their best. Scorpios are deep thinkers while Sagittarians are adept at managing money, which shows how the two of you can balance each other.

When it comes to professional duties, the relaxed Sagittarian thrives best in an environment of diversity, free will and individualism. If you can afford them this little luxury, Scorpio, you'll be pleased at the results. Not only will your Sagittarian business associate perform brilliantly, the company will benefit hugely in terms of reputation and profits. In short, allow Sagittarius some latitude and watch your partnership and business prosper.

Spendthrift Sagittarius

Both Scorpio and Sagittarius swear by loyalty and integrity. The only failing in Sagittarius is their spendthrift nature. They are simply too generous with money. Here is where your judiciousness comes into play, Scorpio. Warn them against being too quick to trust others.

By carefully considering your respective attributes and drafting out the parameters of your association, you can both be inspired to focus and support each other productively.

I consider this combination to be one of the best, if not the best, in the zodiac spectrum. Even though you are highly compatible with water signs, when it comes to business expansion and making money, Sagittarius will stand you in good stead.

WORST PAIRING:
SCORPIO AND TAURUS

Like you, Scorpio, Taurus is a fixed zodiac sign. This puts you at loggerheads with each other right from the word go. In matters of finance you are like chalk and cheese. You perpetually stress over Taurus's tendency to probe your finances. Their tight-fistedness will also make business with them a living nightmare. While you feel that your expenses are justified, Scorpio, your Taurus associate will question every cent.

Scorpios are progressive thinkers and doers who continually sniff out new avenues to inspire and grow the enterprise. With Taurus, however, the tried and tested is a much safer bet, which is another basis for head-on confrontation. You'll always find yourself being examined and reasoning your way out, only to find that your Taurean colleague has scraped together even more accusations. Taurus is not adventurous or a risk taker. If life ever inspires them to open up, they will. Until then, this business relationship will stay put.

If you involve yourself in a partnership with them, it may be difficult for you to break apart. I say this because there's a bit of you in Taurus, Scorpio. You admire their drive, dependability and meticulousness, and because you're a profusely loyal individual, the thought of severing ties would make you feel horribly guilt-stricken. But if you take a bird's eye view of the scenario, Scorpio, you'll find that the frustration is mutual.

Your partnership is characterised by power and control. When one of you dominates, the other retaliates by taking over, which creates a cycle of mistrust. Although there are astrologers who consider this a remarkable partnership in the context of friendship or romance, I'd strongly advice against a professional partnership.

Communication is important for the health of any relationship. It thaws differences and builds understanding. Silence, on the other hand, can be almost catastrophic. When things get rough, both of you go into 'shutdown mode'. This cripples you personally and professionally. You both dig in your heels, and when saturation point is reached, an explosive and acrimonious end may occur.

Where business with Taurus is absolutely unavoidable, my suggestion would be to clearly lay out your terms of agreement and make sure you have mutually acceptable exit clauses. This should help, but the grim reality of this partnership doesn't change.

SCORPIO
IN LOVE

BEFORE YOU CRITICISE SOMEONE, YOU
SHOULD WALK A MILE IN THEIR SHOES.
THAT WAY WHEN YOU CRITICISE THEM,
YOU ARE A MILE AWAY FROM THEM AND
YOU HAVE THEIR SHOES.

Jack Handey

ROMANTIC
◎ COMPATIBILITY ◎

Are you compatible with your current partner, lover or friend? Astrology reveals a great deal about people and their relationships through their star signs. In this chapter, I'd like to show you how to better appreciate your strengths and challenges using Sun sign compatibility.

The Sun reflects your drive, willpower and personality. The essential qualities of two star signs blend like two pure colours producing an entirely new colour. Relationships, similarly, produce their own emotional colours when two people interact. The following is a general guide to your romantic prospects with others and how, by knowing the astrological 'colour' of each other, the art of love can help you create a masterpiece.

The Star Sign Compatibility for Love and Friendship table rates your chance as a percentage of general compatibility, while the Horoscope Compatibility table summarises the reasons why. Each star sign combination is followed by the elements of those star signs and the result of their combining. For instance, Aries is a fire sign and Aquarius is an air sign and this combination produces a lot of 'hot air'. Air feeds fire and fire warms air. In fact, fire requires air. However, not all air and fire combinations work.

When reading the following, I ask you to remember that no two star signs are ever *totally* incompatible. With effort and compromise, even the most 'difficult' astrological matches can work. Don't close your mind to the full range of life's possibilities! Learning about each other and ourselves is the most important facet of astrology.

Good luck in your search for love, and may the stars shine upon you in 2014!

STAR SIGN COMPATIBILITY FOR LOVE AND FRIENDSHIP (PERCENTAGES)

	Aries	Taurus	Gemini	Cancer	Leo	Virgo	Libra	Scorpio	Sagittarius	Capricorn	Aquarius	Pisces
Aries	60	65	65	65	90	45	70	80	90	50	55	65
Taurus	60	70	70	80	70	90	75	85	50	95	80	85
Gemini	70	70	75	60	80	75	90	60	75	50	90	50
Cancer	65	80	60	75	70	75	60	95	55	45	70	90
Leo	90	70	80	70	85	75	65	75	95	45	70	75
Virgo	45	90	75	75	75	70	80	85	70	95	50	70
Libra	70	75	90	60	65	80	80	85	80	85	95	50
Scorpio	80	85	60	95	75	85	85	90	80	65	60	95
Sagittarius	90	50	75	55	95	70	80	85	85	55	60	75
Capricorn	50	95	50	45	45	95	85	65	55	85	70	85
Aquarius	55	80	90	70	70	50	95	60	60	70	80	55
Pisces	65	85	50	90	75	70	50	95	75	85	55	80

HOROSCOPE COMPATIBILITY
FOR SCORPIO

Scorpio with		Romance/Sexual
Aries		Aries boosts your desire to explore new possibilities, and sex between you is fiery
Taurus		Tremendous sexual passion, but Taurus requires a lot of emotional indulgence
Gemini		Sexually fascinating, though you may stifle Gemini with your dominating ways
Cancer		Great chemistry, even though Cancer demands more emotion while you yearn for passion

Friendship	Professional
✔ A remarkable friendship as you both share strong emotional and karmic kinship	✘ A catastrophe as you are both dominating and opinionated, which will lead to an obvious clash of wills
✘ Beset with challenges intrinsic to the game of power and control	✘ Somewhat rough; outline your goals, and financial needs at the start of this partnership
✘ Your respective planets do not enjoy affability and they will eventually create agitation and anxiety in your friendship	✘ Gemini may appear too unfocused, but a fine blend of your determination and their flair can bind this relationship
✔ Their presence is comforting and you can easily let down your guard with them	✔ There is potential as long as you curb your dominating instincts and unrealistic demands from the sensitive Cancer

Scorpio with		Romance/Sexual
Leo		As long as you respect each other's individuality and temperament, happy times will roll
Virgo		A marvellous combination that brings out your best, but you must be more sensitive towards them
Libra		Mutually electrifying in bizarre ways; you find Libra sensually appealing while they enjoy your fiery temperament
Scorpio		Excessive passion creates more misery than joy; both of you are acutely protective, dominating and suspicious of each other
Sagittarius		An energetic and vibrant combination that can greatly inspire; sex is hugely fulfilling

Friendship	Professional
✔ Mutual respect goes a long way in strengthening this friendship	✔ Many life lessons unfurl during your financial relationship with them; you are both highly obstinate
✔ Virgo balances, admires and stimulates you; a fun partnership provided Virgo remains less critical of you	A practical and efficient partnership that is also intellectually stimulating and financially rewarding
✔ They inspire you to thaw emotionally and learn to trust; a socially vibrant match.	✔ A beneficial partnership in which Libra encourages you to think outside the box and look at probable opportunities that expand your venture
✔ Great kinship and a comforting friendship; you can read each other's mind and trust blindly	✔ A highly rewarding match, you both work tirelessly to pursue your mutual objectives and vision
✔ With your respective ruling planets enjoying such great affinity, the two of you are destined to be best friends	✔ Both are extravagant and like to overindulge, which may prove professionally detrimental; Sagittarius will have to abide by the ground rules you set

Scorpio with		Romance/Sexual
Capricorn		You're too intense for the slow and conventional Capricorn; invest time and patience and see the relationship prosper
Aquarius		How about foreplay with words, Scorpio? Unless you do this, you'll never inspire Aquarius to reveal their passionate side
Pisces		A near-perfect match, though you may encounter extremes in passion; both balance each other seamlessly

Friendship	Professional
✔ The two of you enjoy long lasting friendship as well as an active social life together	✔ A favourable match; both of you are assiduous, tireless and attentive workers who are committed to achieving their desired goals
✘ They demand intellectual stimulation and liberal thinking; your guarded ways will need to be thrown away	✘ A weak combination even though Aquarius inspires innovative possibilities in your life (provided you're open to them!)
✔ Pisces can read your emotional undercurrents and know how to comfort your senses; you also have a way of bringing out the best in them	✘ Their compassionate, idealistic and dreamy personality is not beneficial from a business point of view

SCORPIO
 ## PARTNERSHIPS

Scorpio + Aries

This combination is characterised by a battle of wills, as both of you are dominating and determined in nature. As a fire sign, Aries reacts quite strongly to your watery influence, Scorpio. After all, water extinguishes fire. Compromise will make this partnership work, but neither of you is prepared to do it.

Scorpio + Taurus

Your desire to express yourself through sex will flatter Taurus at first, but they need a lot more fondness, compassion and warmth if they are to feel secure about the relationship. Taurus is extremely affectionate and demonstrative by nature, but they desire emotional security over sex.

Scorpio + Gemini

Gemini is too easy-going and fun-loving to have the patience to get to know you, Scorpio. You're a deep thinker and you unnerve the social Gemini; they prefer happy conversations instead of debates on life and other phenomena. You also push them away with your overprotectiveness and dominating nature.

Scorpio + Cancer

Both of you hail from the same zodiac element—water. Although this signals astrological compatibility, there is a sexual disparity between you. You are driven by the purely sensual and sexual aspects of a relationship, and you demand a lot more passion than Cancer. Conversely, Cancer desires emotional bonding and affection before they can express unbridled passion.

Scorpio + Leo

Obstinacy rules the roost in this partnership as you are both quite intractable and opinionated. However, your spirit thaws under Leo's warm rays of sunshine. You are sensual and highly intense, which is the kind of energy that Leo finds attractive. Together you are a powerful force.

Scorpio + Virgo

This happens to be one of the friendliest and most compatible combinations of the zodiac. The two of you exude phenomenal attraction, not just physically, but also emotionally and mentally. Virgo is capable of calmly handling your stern and sometimes brutally frank retorts, and together you create a sensible, practical and efficient partnership.

Scorpio + Libra

The probability of being at loggerheads is high. Your suspicious nature and controlling instincts do not impress your Libran partner. They will need to dig deep into their arsenal of diplomatic weaponry to manage your bossiness and inflexibility, Scorpio.

Scorpio + Scorpio

Interestingly, a relationship between two Scorpions is far removed from the utopia one imagines. Undercurrents of emotional turbulence and the fight for control rupture the basis of this companionship. Unless you commit to unconditionally care for each other, these incompatibilities will not be easy to overcome.

Scorpio + Sagittarius

The two of you enjoy remarkable understanding and an electrifying sex life. However, there is a chance that the affair will be one-sided unless you loosen up and learn to trust them, Scorpio. When your reserved and suspicious nature thaws, however, you will attract Sagittarius as if exerting a magnetic force.

Scorpio + Capricorn

Your ruling planets differ greatly from each other. For this reason, it takes time for this relationship to prosper, and the initial stages progress slowly. While you are hugely inventive and sexually outgoing, Capricorn is far more reserved and conventional. Your fiery passion may completely overwhelm Capricorn.

Scorpio + Aquarius

Like a dog with a bone, you're both highly determined to fulfil your goals, fearless of the possible pitfalls or challenges you may encounter. Though this sounds pleasing on paper, the reality may be quite the opposite. The more you dig in your heels, the less chance that it will work.

Scorpio + Pisces

This is a peerless combination in which you complement each other wonderfully. Scorpio is able to creatively soothe the emotional strife that Pisces experiences. By the same token, Pisces can use their compassion to manage your intensity and sarcasm. A cathartic combination.

PLATONIC RELATIONSHIPS: BEST AND WORST

BEST PAIRING:
SCORPIO AND VIRGO

You both share similar temperaments and even certain mannerisms. The pooling of your respective intellectual, social and emotional resources generates a balance that enables you to create a joyful, contented and fulfilling life together. Your stability rates quite high due to your practical and efficient nature, and this makes you satisfied in each other's company.

Scorpio's ruling planet, Pluto, exhibits a challenging, confrontational spirit, whereas Virgo approaches conflict with rationality, courteousness and modesty. Though you're diplomatic and poised, you would definitely need lessons in tactfulness and subtlety when dealing with Virgo. You can be brutally straightforward, which Virgo takes gracefully in their stride, winning your respect in the process.

In a commitment, Virgo may often feel rebuffed by your callousness and sharp tongue, and let down by your apathy towards their basic emotional needs. At the same time, you can lose your mind over their hypercritical nit-picking nature, even over inconsequential matters. Scorpios are critical, but Virgos even more so. Strangely, these apparent incompatibilities only improve your character and relationship.

You may find yourself experiencing Virgo's silent scrutiny and their demand that you prove your worth to them. They're never vocal about it, but you will sense their watchfulness nevertheless. This stress will lurk in your mind, stirring you to better yourself. Consequently, you'll end up developing certain facets of your personality, talent and skill that would otherwise gather dust. In the long run, this friendship will bring out the best in both of you.

On the whole, Virgo offers you emotional and intellectual security, and the two of you work very well towards securing financial stability as well. Jupiter is your planet of luck, Scorpio, and this has implications for your romantic life as well. The two of you pair up best as lifelong friends due to the favorable influence of this planet on your respective destinies. But weigh up your options before exploring a sexual relationship with them. Virgo is co-ruled by Mercury, a planet that is contradictory to your nature, Scorpio.

WORST PAIRING:
SCORPIO AND ARIES

This combination is caught in the web of supremacy and domination, and the manner in which you deal with this will determine the degree of happiness you experience. In this case, the result is damaging. Aries is as intense and aggressive as you are, Scorpio, and a battle of wills is likely.

Your zodiac element is water, while Aries is a fire sign. A fusion of these elements generates heat and steam, thereby impairing the relationship. You would think that water and fire create a sizzling combination, which explains the immediate attraction and enthusiasm that you share. Realistically, however, water extinguishes fire and you must bear this in mind at all times.

On a positive note, your elemental presence stirs up the hot-headed Aries, and they, in turn, boost your yearning to explore new possibilities. But you both hail from such different elements that your attempts to dominate the fiery Aries will fizzle out, and Aries will be rendered powerless when trying to manipulate your watery nature. In this battle of wills, the big question is: who will bow down?

This relationship is beset with a number of barriers that can be crippling in nature. Scorpios are innately cagey and tend to withdraw into secrecy, unlike Arians, who are gregarious, candid and overtly probing. Temperamentally, this puts you in limbo as both of you struggle to find ways to build an understanding without communicating.

Aries dislike mentoring of any kind, and they believe their stance on things to be second to none. Even when they lack the basic skill sets or know-how, they still boast that their opinion is correct. This obstinacy and ego will leave you exasperated, Scorpio, and you'll find them feigning wisdom on subjects they know nothing about! In my opinion, your future together is far from placid.

SEXUAL RELATIONSHIPS:
⊚ BEST AND WORST ⊚

BEST PAIRING:
SCORPIO AND PISCES

From an astrological perspective, the two of you tick every box. Your planets enjoy tremendous affability, and your star signs are favourably positioned in the propitious triangular form. Indeed, this is a truly magical love match, and some may even say that it is a match made in heaven.

Certain elements of this relationship draw attention to a karmic connection between you. You both exude similar emotional energies and innate sensitivity that create a rather cathartic effect. Another wonderful aspect is how you both exhibit forceful psychic vibrations. This heralds deep understanding, and it means that you can communicate effortlessly, even in silence. Pisces seems to understand intuitively the complex undercurrents of your personality, and you're receptive to their emotional and physical needs as well.

Unsurprisingly, Scorpio and Pisces fall head-over-heels for each other when they first meet. After all, there's always so much more than meets the eye. For those already enjoying a relationship with Pisces, I'm sure you know exactly what I mean.

A warning, though: Pisces is a dreamer at heart, and even though they appear engaged and attentive, they can silently fly the coop. However, they rarely enjoy the kind of rapport that they do with you, Scorpio. You're one of those rare star signs with the power to anchor the dreamy Pisces and creatively manage their detached manner.

MUTUALLY SUPPORTIVE

You're exceptionally adept at handling the emotional upheavals and temperamental mood swings of your Piscean partner. Fortunately, they also come to your aid each time you find yourself overwhelmed by circumstances or feelings.

The greatness of this combination lies in how appreciative you are of each other. This feeling of contentment and gratitude forms the nucleus of your relationship and makes it special.

Taking all of this into consideration, there is no doubt about the quality of intimacy you share. Sex is extraordinarily gratifying and healing, and it's no wonder that many Scorpio-Pisces relationships go the distance. This is an unsurpassed match.

WORST PAIRING:
SCORPIO AND GEMINI

This combination is an astrological mismatch, and your future is bound to be demanding and intense. The first impediment is your approach to communication. The fun-loving and playful Gemini doesn't venture towards the darker zones of life, preferring to keep the dialogue light and breezy, and touching on a variety of themes instead. You, Scorpio, prefer in-depth discussions and getting to the heart of a matter.

In terms of planet positioning, there's little compatibility, and romance will be punctuated by anxiety and agitation. The free-spirited Gemini may be unnerved by your cageyness and probing mind, and remain oblivious to your feelings. It may be hard for them to understand that your staid disposition can give way to a deep thinker who relies on intellectual stimulation for personal growth. As a social butterfly, Gemini lacks patience and is bound to flutter off to happier and more vibrant pastures, thereby depriving the relationship of genuine sexual compatibility.

QUIZ: HAVE YOU FOUND YOUR
⊚ PERFECT MATCH? ⊚

Do you dare take the following quiz to see how good a lover you are? Remember, although the truth sometimes hurts, it's the only way to develop your relationship skills.

We are all searching for our soul mate: that idyllic romantic partner who will fulfil our wildest dreams of love and emotional security. Unfortunately, finding true love isn't easy. Sometimes, even when you are in a relationship, you can't help but wonder whether or not your partner is right for you. How can you possibly know?

It's essential to question your relationships and work on ways to improve your communication and overall happiness. When meeting someone new, it's also a good idea to study their intentions and read between the lines. In the first instance, when your hormones are taking over, it's easy to get carried away and forget some of the basic principles of what makes a relationship endure.

You're probably wondering where to start. Are you in a relationship at the moment? Are you looking for love but finding it difficult to choose between two or more people? Are you simply not able to meet someone at all? Well, there are some basic questions you can ask yourself to discover how suited you and your partner are. And if you don't have a partner, consider your previous relationships to improve your chances next time.

The following quiz is a serious attempt to take an honest look at yourself and see whether or not your relationships are on track. Don't rush through this questionnaire. Think carefully about your practical day-to-day life and whether or not the relationship you are in genuinely fulfils your needs and the other person's needs. There's no point being in a relationship if you're gaining no satisfaction out of it.

Now, if you aren't completely satisfied with the results you get, don't give up! It's an opportunity for you to work on the relationship and improve things. But you mustn't let your ego get in the way as that's not going to get you anywhere.

Being inherently cagey, reticent and suspicious of others, it is hard for Scorpio to commit to someone and bare their soul. Their intuitiveness is highly evolved, and they find it difficult to settle down. Their lifestyles are demanding and they seek unconventional inspiration from both life and love. Added to this is their demand for undying loyalty, obsession and intellectual stimulation. So here's a check list for you, Scorpio, to see if he or she is the right one for you.

Scoring System:

Yes = 1 point

No = 0 points

❓ Is your partner perceptive enough to understand what's on your mind?

❓ Is he/she a Pisces, Taurus, Cancer, Virgo or Capricorn?

❓ Is he/she inspired and strong-willed enough to keep up a tempestuous lifestyle?

❓ Is he/she interesting enough to remain challengingly enigmatic?

❓ Is he/she devoted and faithful to you?

❓ Do you feel content and in high spirits when you're around him/her?

❓ Are you passionately stimulated by his/her presence, in spite of years of companionship?

❓ Does he/she shower enough attention and care on you?

❓ Is he/she honest with you?

❓ Does he/she listen to you and give you an honest opinion?

❓ Does he/she understand and accept you for who you are?

❓ Can he/she cope with your demanding lifestyle?

❓ Does he/she respect your sense of privacy and give you time and space when you need it?

? Does he/she respect your belongings?

? Do you feel wholeheartedly attracted to him/her?

? Is he/she equally fascinated by the mysteries of life and spirituality?

Have you jotted down your answers honestly? If you're finding it hard to come up with the right answers, let your intuition help you and try not to force the answer. Of course, there's no point in turning a blind eye to treatment that is less than acceptable, otherwise you're not going to have a realistic appraisal of your prospects with your current love interest. Here are the possible points you can score:

 8 to 16

A good match. This shows that you and your partner enjoy a healthy understanding and reciprocate just the way you need. However, this is no reason to be slack out of complacency. You must continue working and improving your bond to make it shine more brilliantly than it does now.

 5 to 7

Half-hearted prospect. You need to work hard at building your relationship and engage in honest self-examination. It takes two to tango, so you're obviously aware that you are both to blame. Go through each question systematically, making notes of areas where you can improve yourself. Undertaking this self-examination will guarantee favourable shifts in your relationship. But if things don't improve in spite of the effort, it may be time for you to rethink your future with this person.

0 to 4

On the rocks. I'm sorry to say that this relationship is completely devoid of basic mutual respect and understanding. It's likely that the two of you argue a lot. Your partner is also completely oblivious to your emotional needs. This is the perfect example of incompatibility. The big question is: Why are you still with this person? This requires some brutally honest self-examination on your part. You need to see whether there is some inherent insecurity within you that is causing you to hold onto something that has outgrown its use in your life. You may also be a victim of fear, which is preventing you from letting go of a relationship that no longer fulfils your needs. Self-honesty is the key here. You need to make some rather bold sacrifices to attract the right partner into your life.

2014
YEARLY OVERVIEW

DO NOT GO WHERE THE PATH MAY LEAD,
GO INSTEAD WHERE THERE IS NO PATH
AND LEAVE A TRAIL.

Ralph Waldo Emerson

⊚ KEY EXPERIENCES ⊚

You have been more cautious in the way you live your life, and you have probably felt jaded by your professional and personal relationships. But the excellent influence of Jupiter brings a positive new spin on your life in 2014.

Unlike the last year or two, you will be more likely to open up to new social opportunities, travel and communication. This Jupiter aspect is also influenced by Mars, and it warns that you shouldn't invite too many people into your immediate circle until you adequately size them up.

The very important transit of Neptune continues in your zone of creativity and love affairs. It indicates the beginning of new creative adventures and a deeper, inspirational attitude to life.

ROMANCE AND
◉ FRIENDSHIP ◉

You may begin to idealise love due to Neptune's extraordinary influence on your life, but this could come with pitfalls. Firstly, you may meet people who are very much in tune with your spiritual ideals and who truly understand where you are coming from. To be able to share these deeper values in life is not always easy, and when you do come across someone who resonates with you, it's like finding a needle in a haystack. The downside, however, is that you may project your dreams and fantasies onto anyone and everyone, and you may believe that the person you have met is 'the one'. Try not to put people on a pedestal until you find out more about them.

Jupiter and Neptune dominate your horoscope during 2014, and being in the triangular direction of the zodiac, they talk of the deep need for spiritual connectivity in love, romance and intimate relationships. You also have a very powerful conjunction of five planets in your zone of communication as the year begins, but this conjunction is adversely affected by Mars and Uranus. While you may be communicating on one level, believing that you are making incredible inroads into a deep and meaningful relationship, the other person may not be on the same page. Stop, listen and try to understand where your partner is coming from, or you may make the mistake of assuming that you both have the same goals in your relationship.

Mars in your twelfth zone of secrets and, to some extent, sexual activity, doesn't pull any punches in the bedroom. You want a more sensate expression of your feelings and reciprocation from your partner. With Mercury and Mars making a hard aspect in January, this sets the trend for some rather unpredictable and possibly even negative discussions surrounding this very sensitive area of your relationship.

 Relationships on the Rise

As well as desiring deep intimacy throughout the coming 12 months, having a happy family life and a space where you can share your romantic ideals will be equally important, especially between the 12th and the 18th of January. Venus and the Sun produce magnificent effects, and up until the 22nd you should be reasonably happy. But don't forget to air your grievances after the 22nd, as you may start to feel that there is a creative block between you and the one you love.

Venus, the planet of love for Scorpio, spends the first part of the year in the lower part of the horoscope, which means that the predominating influences are family and domestic issues. After the 6th of April, however, you will find a renewal of feelings for your partner and a strong creative urge, particularly when Venus comes into contact with Neptune at this time. As a result, you can share your creative and spiritual endeavours with the person close to your heart.

The transit of Venus to your zone of marriage and public relations on the 29th of May indicates powerful feelings of love. Around this time there will be dynamic physical and emotional energy thanks to the combined influence of the Sun, Mars and Pluto, and this influence should bear upon you until the 9th of June. You can expect a more physical, lusty appetite during this phase of the year. Your feelings could be much cooler due to additional responsibilities around the 13th when Venus is challenged by the Sun and Saturn. Mars and Pluto also indicate intense power struggles, and this could cause you to retreat into your shell. You will need time to reappraise your feelings and gain a better perspective on love.

Another peak period is after the 12th of August when Venus transits the upper part of your horoscope. This is a time when you can showcase your finer attributes and make a greater impression on the world around you. This will continue to bring benefits until the 6th of September, and then more strongly until the 15th, when the favourable influence of Pluto makes you magnetically powerful and attractive to the world at large.

SEXUAL MAGNETISM

Venus enters your Sun sign on the 24th of October, which is always a good period to 'bring it on'. You will be feeling charming, magnetic and easily able to sway members of the opposite sex. Use this power to attract the right sort of people into your life until the 17th of November.

Lucky influences on the 5th of December are noticeable because Venus and Jupiter bless you with gifts, opportunities and a feeling of wellbeing, which should continue until the end of the year.

WORK AND MONEY

Harness Your Moneymaking Powers

Making money can be summed up in an equation:

$$m \ (\$ \ money) = e \ (energy) \times t \ (time) \times l \ (love)$$

If one of these factors is not present—for example, energy or love—you could still make money, but you won't be ideally fulfilled in the process.

It's important to grasp the universal laws of attraction and success when dealing with money. It is also necessary to understand that when you love what you do, you infuse your work with the quality of attention, love and perfection. With these qualities you endow your work with a sort of electromagnetic appeal, a power that draws people to your work and makes them appreciate what you do. This generates a desire for people to use your service, buy your products and respect you for the great work you do. This will elevate you to higher and higher positions because you will be regarded as someone who exercises great diligence and skill in your actions.

Becoming less distracted will be one of your key challenges in 2014. You have a tendency to say yes to too many people, which depletes your energies and fails to achieve what your Scorpio destiny has intended for you. This is a year of focus, as shown by the transit of Saturn and its extraordinarily strong influence on your zone of career. This means that your concentration will be a force to be reckoned with.

GOOD KARMA

Because your finance and future karma planet, Jupiter, is transiting your zone of past karma this year, you will be able to capitalise on lucky opportunities, and this will be noticeable on and off throughout the year. Due to your good actions in the past, people will remember what you have done.

To tap your moneymaking powers, you must also learn the art of knowing what to discard and what to keep. This year you will be inundated with brilliant new ideas. But be careful, Scorpio, because not all of them will yield positive results, and the return on investment may not be as good as you expect. Neptune in your fifth zone of creative power, and Mars, one of your ruling planets, in the zone of waste, shows that you may exert a lot of energy trying to get projects up and running only to find that your good intentions amount to nothing. Carefully plan your work before investing time, energy and love into something that may be a waste of time.

This wastefulness may also come in the form of people who want to use you to achieve their ends. This is shown by the hard aspects to the sixth zone of servants, helpers and contractors. Those of you in business may find that you are too trusting. Some people need to be scrutinised before you pay them for work that is going to be less than adequate. This will save you a lot of time and money.

With Jupiter in the upper part of your horoscope and the most spiritual direction of the zodiac, there is every reason to believe that your work should contain some element of spiritual energy. Don't let your job become a purely a mechanical, material activity.

Make sure that you discriminate between deserving individuals and those who are trying to use you for their own selfish ends.

Unfortunately, some of these people may come in the form of good friends. The moral of the story is that you can tap your best money-making powers by choosing activities that will pay off and people who will be worth the investment of your love and energy.

 **Tips for Financial Success**

The overriding factor throughout 2014 is the lucky transit of Jupiter in your zone of good fortune. As your finance planet, Jupiter spends considerable time in this lucky part of your horoscope, and for the first time in 12 years it offers you the opportunity to capitalise on your talents and moneymaking opportunities.

On the 31st of January, there is a hard relationship between Jupiter and Pluto, which means that communication needs to be clear if you want to understand the nature of your work and any business deal that emerges at this time.

Unexpected opportunities around the 26th of February and the 20th of April require strong intuition to weed out the men from the boys. While there will be some scintillating gems of professional opportunity, there will also be some clods of earth that need to be thrown out. Knowing the difference will be your task this year.

Politics after the 21st of April may be a problem for you, and unexpected disputes or emotional blackmail will tie you up and limit your ability to achieve as much as you would like.

You have a settling period from the 25th of May when Jupiter and Saturn provide you with energy for consolidation and a calm and relaxed method for achieving it. Opportunities offshore, or at least from a distance, mean that you shouldn't discount business deals that involve travel. These could be some of the best opportunities you encounter this year.

An important transit takes place as Jupiter moves into the apex of your horoscope on the 16th of July. This hails the commencement of another one-year cycle where work, business and professional prestige will be paramount, and it's likely that you will move forward in leaps and bounds. Some further unexpected opportunities occur after the 26th of September when Jupiter and Uranus once again conspire to bring you luck and assistance by way of employees and helpers.

The excellent aspect of Venus and Jupiter on the 5th of December indicates some sort of pay-off or a sense of accomplishment for your hard work throughout the year.

 ## Career Moves and Promotions

Although the period of the 1st of April indicates a strong and possibly unexpected professional move, I'd advise you to think things through before making a decision. When Uranus is involved, impulse may prevail, and the ensuing result may not be what you expect.

One of the best transits for a positive and satisfying outcome is after the 16th of July when Jupiter transits your tenth zone of professional activity. As mentioned earlier, this is a significant transit that occurs only once every 12 years, but as one of your most beneficial planets, it will certainly bring a sense of expansion, confidence and good fortune. At this time you also have the favourable influence of Venus and Mars in the eighth and twelfth zone of your horoscope, which can show help from hidden sources.

This favourable time is further enhanced by the conjunction of the Sun and Jupiter in your career zone, and your ruling planet Mars finally making its entrance into your Sun sign around the 26th. It appears that July is going to be the best period for you to make a transition, if that is what you choose.

Increased income and the fulfilment of your desires can take place when the Sun moves to the eleventh zone and is in good aspect to other planets. This occurs around the 23rd of August, the 4th of September and up to and including the 14th of September when Mars, your favourable co-ruler, enters your zone of finance.

 **When to Avoid Office Politics**

Try to eliminate gossip and other workplace problems early in the year, as the strong congestion of planets in January can adversely influence your working environment. There may be people, possibly new co-workers, who are not exactly your cup of tea and who may even openly challenge you as the year begins. You need to be one step ahead of these adversaries or they could cause trouble for you throughout the coming months.

The Sun enters your zone of enemies on the 21st of March, and because this is your career planet, it shows that your employer or someone in a higher position may openly undermine you. Around the 1st of April, when the Sun adversely aspects Jupiter, conjoins Uranus and squares Pluto, proceed with considerable caution. You may have to deal with political manipulation and enemies who will try to undermine you at any cost.

After the 23rd of April, however, you may have to secretively plan your attack on someone, possibly a pre-emptive one. By showing force, courage and willpower you can undermine those who are trying to beat you down.

AN UNHOLY ALLIANCE

The planet ruling your enemies, as well as your Sun sign, is Mars, which shows that you may have to enter into an unholy alliance with the enemy of an enemy after the 5th of October. By aligning yourself with this individual you can short-circuit someone's negative intentions and come out on top.

The final difficult aspect is on the 15th of December when the transpersonal planets Uranus and Pluto square each other. This may cause problems, mostly due to economic trends rather than any individual who is out to get you, but you should still be cautious of people who are expressing their own personal biases.

HEALTH, BEAUTY AND LIFESTYLE

 Venus Calendar for Beauty

You'll have too much of a good thing after the 17th of January when Venus and Mars are at right angles. Burning the candle at both ends may affect your body, such as the condition of your skin and your countenance. If you are not getting enough sleep or hydrating properly, your natural beauty will suffer. Apart from your usual makeup, makeovers and other treatments can go a long way to ensure that you remain beautiful from within.

The type of people we associate with can sometimes drag us down and make us feel and look bad. On the 3rd of March, Venus at a right angle to Mars may cause this to happen. Choose your friends wisely.

Venus in Pisces

The entry of Venus into the sign of Pisces is excellent and shows a better period when you are likely to feel creatively uplifted. This is going to produce more endorphins and show on your face. Try to be happy at this time and don't be afraid to attempt something creative, even if you are not that good at it. It's the feeling it generates that counts.

Some key dates for feeling uplifted and looking more beautiful are the 22nd of April, the 29th of May—when Venus enters your marital zone and makes you feel attractive—the 23rd of June and the 13th of July. At this time, your sexual energy and animal magnetism will predominate, and you will feel that you have an advantage over others. Use this power wisely.

Excellent transits to the Sun on the 2nd, 12th and 18th of August will give you the chance to showcase your beauty, elegance and fashion taste as your professional planets will be involved in the mix.

According to Hindu astrology, the second zone of the horoscope has to do with one's face, and on the 17th of November, Venus enters this zone and creates favourable aspects to Jupiter. This will give you an inner glow or radiance that others will find hard to resist.

 Showing off Your Scorpio Traits

With Saturn continuing to transit your Sun sign and being an enemy of your ruler, Mars, you may find it difficult to express some of your talents. This may be due to difficult circumstances or because you have become a little lazy. Either way, you are going to have to work a bit harder to show the world what you are really made of, and this is where your tremendous willpower will come to your rescue. Scorpio often needs a challenging situation in order to rise to the occasion, and this year you'll get a chance to do this.

Although you are considered secretive, deep and at times mysterious, there is no doubting that Scorpio has excellent powers of communication and persuasion, and with so many planets in this secretive eighth zone of the zodiac, you can make a wonderful impression on others through the way you communicate your ideas.

But communication is not always verbal, and many astrologers and lay people acknowledge the power that Scorpio exudes through their silence, facial expressions and, most importantly, their eyes. Don't forget these important Scorpio traits and use them to your advantage. One look can say so much, and with perfect timing you can achieve more through this method than though a thousand words.

 Best Ways to Celebrate

Your celebrations this year will be a result of overcoming bad habits and finding the ability to consolidate your energies, both internally and externally. For example, quitting the habit of smoking will bring with it increased health and a bigger bank balance. Although most people celebrate with some form of party or group gathering, this year you will understand that celebration can be personal and bring greater benefits than simply going out on the town.

You will be comfortable in your own skin this year, and you will be quite content to stay at home and celebrate this feeling. Being alone doesn't necessarily mean being lonely. This gem of wisdom will become clear to you and make you happy. It won't be an effusive, jumping-for-joy type of energy, but you will feel an inward satisfaction and happiness. Enjoy this without asking yourself where this happiness has come from or why.

As mentioned earlier, the transit of Jupiter to your zone of professional activities means that something truly remarkable may happen at work, which should give you cause for celebration. For those of you who have been systematically working towards a goal in an independent line of work, this could mean the acquisition or selling of a business. For down-to-earth individuals who are working for someone else, this could mean a promotion. All of these things are cause for celebration. Look forward to this after the 16th of July when Jupiter transits the pinnacle of your horoscope.

KARMA, SPIRITUALITY AND EMOTIONAL BALANCE

Your future karmic planet, Jupiter, moves into the zone of past karma, which is an excellent omen for your spiritual wisdom and the development of deep inner insights. With this rare transit you should investigate deeply why you are here and how you can improve your life and happiness.

Jupiter is influenced by many planets as the year commences, and the diversity of your interests will be a forum in which you can express some of your spiritual insights this year.

Unfortunately, most people limit spiritual activity to meditation, prayer or church-going. What becomes evident this year is that every aspect of your life can be touched by your spiritual awareness, and this doesn't need to exclude mundane activities, such as washing the dishes. Awareness is the key word for you this year, and bringing this awareness to everything you do will open up a vista of new spiritual opportunities that will carry you into the years to come.

You are putting a tight rein on your feelings this year, and although you will have some intense responsibilities, as shown by Saturn moving through your Sun sign, you will still feel in control and able to use this as fuel for spiritual growth. Jupiter has a very balancing influence on your emotions, especially in the second half of the year when it influences your domestic and family life. During this phase of the year, you will realise that you need to make peace with relatives and people you have become disconnected from. By making peace with them you can achieve even more emotional balance and, through this process, deep spiritual satisfaction.

2014
MONTHLY & DAILY
PREDICTIONS

IT IS BETTER TO BE HATED FOR WHAT YOU
ARE THAN LOVED FOR WHAT YOU ARE NOT.

André Gide

☺ JANUARY ☺

 Monthly Overview

The New Moon occurs in your zone of short travels and communication, and it is powerfully connected to the deep and intense Pluto, your ruling planet. Superficial answers won't be satisfactory at this time, and after the 18th, Venus will cause you to challenge others, which will be to your advantage. Contracts also favour you.

1 In your desire to get to the bottom of a problem, you may tread on other people's toes today. Be diplomatic in the way you approach them.

2 Your imagination is fired up today, and you have the ability to express yourself clearly and concisely. Others will respond eagerly to your communication.

3 Your mind is on family matters today, and you may need to address domestic issues. Allocate enough time.

4 Communication with people who are unavailable can be frustrating. Don't get worked up if you can't make contact with someone today.

5 You feel amorous at present, and the Moon and Neptune are making you feel idealistic about someone. Try to keep things real.

6 Health matters are on the agenda today, so take care of those little twitches and pains that have been bothering you. A full check-up is not a bad idea.

7 Unexpected changes in your work environment could obstruct you and make you feel on edge. Learn the art of relaxation.

8 Don't be obsessive today, particularly in matters of love. Your communication may be misconstrued.

9 You have far-reaching ideals today and want to achieve more than circumstances allow. Patience is your key word.

10 You may not be satisfied with the performance of your spouse or partner. You need to address the issue but could feel obstructed from doing so. Timing is everything.

11 Your warmth and sociability could help you make new friends just now, but if you're attached you may have to deal with moments of envy and possessiveness.

12 Younger members of the family may seem unhappy. Give them a little love and affection to help them through this tough time.

13 You are keen to understand the nature of things, and philosophical and meditational insights will be available to you. You may want to attend lectures and be with like-minded people.

14 If you plan to plan to take legal action, bear in mind that costs may escalate over time. Don't make decisions in the heat of the moment.

15 You'll be surprised by the response of a co-worker today. Retaliation is not the way to win them over. Understand that there are underlying motivations for their behaviour.

16 Your emotions are cooler today, but that should help you prepare yourself for important business or professional activities. Being rational is important now.

17 You are clearly focused on your professional objectives and must be careful not to mix business with pleasure. This could be a distraction.

18 Your mind and heart are not in sync today, so it's not a good time to share your feelings or ideas with others. Wait until more inner harmony prevails.

19   You have a strong desire to be with friends and expand your social circle. Make yourself available.

20   Your desire to understand your social circle continues today. You may have some profound insights and realise the ramifications of being involved with someone. Continue to appraise the situation.

21   You need to be alone now to reappraise your life and its direction. Others may feel as though you are blowing them off, so explain exactly what is happening.

22   Miscommunications are quite likely now. Make sure you reiterate your intentions or plans so that others don't point the finger of blame at you.

23   You could be overemotional in responding to someone today, especially if it relates to politics or religion. Keep a calm mind, if possible.

24   You have a strong sense of identity at the moment and you want to show it to others. What you're presenting, however, may not be what others perceive. Try to be more consistent.

25   Others are not pulling their weight, so you may have cross words with someone in the family circle. Put your foot down and ensure you are being respected.

26 With the Moon and Saturn connecting, you may feel a little down today. Although you may be in a serious mood, there's no need to be depressed. Try to be clear about your plans.

27 A financial opportunity may arise through work or someone associated with your profession. Maintain a positive attitude and this will become a source of increased income.

28 The written and spoken word takes precedence today. Communicating ideas will be of paramount importance. Make sure your grammar and spelling is correct.

29 Investigate contracts and agreements now, making sure that you haven't left anything to chance. Someone may chastise you for nitpicking, but the devil is in the detail.

30 You're angry now and may be reactive to anything and everything. Continue your exercise routine for best results.

31 Your key phrase today is 'be yourself', so don't pretend to be something you're not. You may feel a little intimidated in a new circle of associates, but stand firm and you'll be respected for maintaining your integrity.

◉ FEBRUARY ◉

Monthly Overview

Domestic issues will be high on your agenda. You may be working on creating space and solving problems with relatives and children. Important communications occur between the 7th and the 13th of February when Mercury transits your fifth zone of children and creativity.

1 You feel creative but blocked today. It's best not to force the issue. Wait for a more conducive time when your creative juices are flowing.

2 Good karma is likely to come your way just now as an opportunity, unexpected gift or pleasure may fall into your lap. Be grateful.

3 You feel dull or bored with your routine today. Do something to mix up the schedule and make it more interesting.

4 Someone will irritate you, but you won't have the courage or energy to speak up and say how you feel. The choice is yours.

5 Marriage and commitment are high on your agenda. You need to discuss issues surrounding these matters today.

6 Your vitality may be blocked because you're focusing too much on something else. Balance is essential at this time of the year.

7 You need greener pastures or some time away from family to rediscover your true self. Don't be afraid to make time to ensure your personal and spiritual growth.

8 Your imagination is powerful today and you're able to investigate some of the deeper emotional issues that have been affecting you. It's best to keep these discoveries to yourself for the time being.

9 You can balance some financial affairs in your domestic life by looking closely at where the money is being spent. It looks like a budget may be in order.

10 You're emotionally warm and expressive about your feelings, and it's quite likely that the feeling is being returned. Now is the time to share love with the person you feel closest to.

11 Trust your insights today as the Moon in Neptune indicates powerful vibrations and gut instincts that are likely to be true.

12 Educational pursuits dominate your mind and you will want to expand your understanding and sphere of influence. You should do so.

13 Tying up loose ends and getting through paperwork that has been building up on your desk will give you a sense of relief. Don't postpone these mundane tasks.

14 You want to exert some influence in your place of work, but you may be blocked or undermined by someone in a position of authority. Don't let this get you down. Go back to the drawing board and find an alternative plan.

15 There may be an older female in your life who may not be well or who simply needs a shoulder to cry on. Be there for her.

16 An excellent arrangement of planets marks a satisfying period for friends and relatives. Your domestic sphere will also be a meeting point for activities today. Remember to plan ahead.

17 You could receive some praise or a gesture of affection from someone unexpected. You may not know how to take this.

18 Attending to unfinished emotional business is tedious but essential. You need to let go of past hurts and memories.

19 Don't spend time with people who don't appreciate what give them. You may be casting your pearls before swine.

20 You need to spend money to beautify your home, even though you feel that it's a waste of time. If it will make you and your family feel more comfortable, do it in the spirit of creative excellence.

21 Travel may not be possible now, but at least you can start to plan. You are drawn to foreign cultures and the mysterious. Adventure is your key word now.

22 Think through what you have to say to someone or you could get tongue-tied and lose your train of thought. Practise makes perfect.

23 Gambling is not a good idea now, and there's an element of risk-taking reflected in the planets. Unless you're well informed, it's best to side-step any form of speculation now.

24 Your sense of self and your relationship may be blurred right now. You need to fine-tune and refocus the purpose of your relationships.

25 You'll be busy today with the Moon in your third zone of short journeys. The hard aspects from Uranus and Pluto may not be able to counteract the benefits of Venus. Make sure you don't waste time doing nothing.

26 Changing your philosophical beliefs on a whim or because you are impressionable is not advisable. Deep and protracted self-analysis is the only way to determine true philosophical conviction.

27 You want to feel happy, but certain thoughts will prevail and not allow this. The secret is to engage in a fun activity that will help you forget.

28 You know you have some tasks and errands to perform, but you may be too lazy to tackle them today. Get some smaller chores out of the way so you won't feel mentally restless.

☉ MARCH ☉

Monthly Overview

You want to take your relationships to a new level this month, but confusion may abound. Rein in your emotions and listen to the advice of family members, especially around the 6th. Health issues may take precedence after the 21st when the Sun enters the sixth zone of health and work.

---

1   You are worried about finances today, but this is not going to solve the problem. Try to think clearly about your objective and how you can improve matters.

---

2   You are hell-bent on helping someone, or perhaps several people, but this will only undermine your own commitments and responsibilities. You can't save the world in one day.

---

3   It's time to take a closer look at your diet and how this may be affecting your thinking and performance. Keep a food diary to analyse its effects on your mental and physical wellbeing.

---

4 There may be elements of power and control operating in your work place or social group. This will make you feel highly suspicious, but don't let this arouse other people's concerns.

5 A friend may not be listening to you, which could upset you right now. This will be reminiscent of past relationships that did not fulfil you.

6 You're more capable of getting to the truth today, and you are not afraid to be direct. As a result, people will be forthcoming in revealing their innermost secrets to you.

7 Sharing your money and resources with someone requires careful analysis and monitoring. Discussions may centre on these issues.

8 You want to exert your will but may feel powerless to do so. It's not so much a matter of controlling others as controlling yourself.

9 A private project or hobby can make you feel more alive today. Dedicate more time to this activity if it affords you the satisfaction you seek.

10 Bureaucracy could bother you and punch a hole in your time. If you're doing this on behalf of others, you may need to delegate part of this problem back to them.

11 Your thinking is slow, muddled and imprecise. You may lose things and be forgetful. Try to jot down reminders for yourself.

12 You have to continue working behind the scenes and planning your strategy, especially if you are a professional. Shooting from the hip will only ruin the good that you have done.

13 You must improvise and be quick off the mark today. Thinking on your feet will help you achieve solid results and get a good response from your superiors.

14 You may not have the drive and energy you normally do for work, but that's okay. Take some time out and balance this with other activities. Don't run yourself into the ground.

15 You can act as a mentor to others and steer them in the right direction. Younger people may feature more strongly in your life right now.

16 To achieve your goals, you must have firm willpower, which must be developed now. Having the ideas is not enough. Look for ways to implement your objectives.

17 Sleep will take precedence now, but you should pay close attention to the messages you're receiving from the other side. You intuition and dreams should be very powerful.

18 You can take up creative writing or jot down your ideas and start a diary. This is an excellent way to clear the emotional and mental cobwebs.

19 You could be angry at someone, but you realise that you have to bite your tongue. Unless you have a way of letting off steam, this could adversely affect your health.

20 The Moon, Jupiter and Neptune are once again in excellent positions. Use these energies to develop your individuality and spiritual ideals in a way that can enhance your life.

21 The Sun moves to your sixth zone of health and vitality. Recommit to the process of improving your health and youthfulness.

22 The Moon in your zone of finances could make you rather emotional about your income. There may be problems associated with receiving the right money, bonuses or other money that is owed. Keep accurate records.

23 You need to clarify several aspects of your plan or creative activity. You could be confused about how to proceed with a new interest. Ask those who know.

24 Your attention may be on a younger sibling or close relative, but this person may be obstructive, even though they are asking for your help. It's best to listen rather than advise if you want to help them.

25 With Venus in your zone of property and home, you have an urge to improve your bank balance through real estate and other land transactions. You must first improve the quality of the house you live in if you want to increase its value.

26 Further discussions and issues surrounding your home will come to the fore now. Get the blessing of the matriarchs and patriarchs within your domestic circle. This will ensure fewer disputes down the track.

27 Mercury and Jupiter, the planets of communication and expansion, are well placed to help you in any form of study, education or even competition. You should be successful in all of these areas at present.

28 You have a strong need for love and possibly even sex, but make sure that this doesn't override your common sense. Satisfy your needs but don't compromise your integrity.

29 You may need to be evasive just now as a planned surprise may be jeopardised if you say too much. It could be a little nerve-racking holding back.

30 With Venus and Mars strongly connected in a positive way, your emotional and sexual expressions should find an adequate outlet right now. The problem, however, is that Venus is challenged by Saturn, which means that you may not be particularly satisfied with your chosen partner. Be patient as this will pass.

31 You feel as if you're giving a lot to your work and not receiving much back. Continue to do your best and the universe will look after the outcome.

❀ APRIL ❀

 Monthly Overview

A new regime of diet, health and workplace activity is important if you are to find balance. Life may be edgy and your nerves shot. An eclipse on the 15th indicates the need to regenerate your spiritual energies, which is best done alone. The additional eclipse on the 29th brings to the fore your relationships, and with Mercury involved, important communications emerge, especially after the 23rd.

1 Business negotiations do well, but dealing with the truth or someone's deception may push you to your limits. You need to be on your toes when dealing with others today.

2 You're feeling cramped in your relationship, and someone's obsessive approach will push you away. You need time alone.

3 Your thinking is clear, slow and methodical. Don't let anyone rush you into a decision.

4 You may feel emotionally drained because you are taking on the problems of others. Know when to draw a line in the sand.

5 You are excited today but need to contain your joie de vivre. Others may not be able to keep up with your pace.

6 You may be imagining things that aren't there, particularly in matters of love and intimacy. Seeing things as they are will be your challenge.

7 There's an improvement in your general affairs, and your health will see a turn for the better.

8 Your mind is on matters associated with work and the methods you are employing to perform your tasks. You have an opportunity to change and improve them.

9 You have flashes of brilliance today, but do you have anyone to share them with? Seek out like-minded people who can act as catalysts for your ambitions.

10 Your finger is on the pulse today and you can connect with the public at large. In matters of business, this will be fortunate.

11 You may be invited to a special outing with close, intimate friends. You mustn't be critical of others today.

12 You may find it easier connecting with a close associate and sharing deep secrets from your past. There will be a strong connection made at this time.

13 You have a strong sense of compassion today, and something in your environment may trigger this. You will want to do more to help the world at large.

14 Your expenses may outstrip your income just now, but it may be too late to do anything about it. Start a budget.

15 You may have vague feelings of inferiority or an inability to get the job done today. If you're feeling lazy, wait for a more appropriate time.

16 The past may come back to haunt you, but you mustn't allow depressive feelings to overtake you. Let bygones be bygones.

17 You want to connect with someone who is unattainable just now. Don't make too much of an effort. Allow your charm to attract them.

18 You may be feeling torn about the work you do and the money you earn from it. Re-evaluate what you're getting paid for the job you're doing.

19 Not all debt is bad debt. Today you have the opportunity to establish which debts will offer you a return on your investment and which won't.

20 Someone may put the hard word on you to borrow something, possibly a book, some CDs or money. You may be torn between saying yes and trusting your instincts, which is to say no.

21 You're disturbed by your environment and need to move to a quieter location today. People may assume that you are irritated or angry with them, but you just need space to complete your tasks.

22 Your thinking is progressive at present, but those in your close-knit circle may think you're a little crazy. Keep your ideas to yourself until you can prove their merit.

23 You may enter into lively discussions that could border on dispute. A friendly exchange of ideas is fine, but don't let differences of opinion destroy a friendship.

24 You need more time to live your life the way you want, but you feel obstructed by others. It's simply a matter of saying no to their requests.

25 An interest in photography or the visual arts can trigger a sense of peace within you today.

26 You feel as if you need to be more responsible in certain areas of your life. A discussion with someone experienced will help you see the light on this matter.

27 Office politics may be a problem now, and others may be trying to undermine you. Unexpected events may catch you off guard.

28 Excessively long hours will erode your time and peace of mind. Managing your diary and schedule is essential now.

29 The eclipse this month can influence your relationships in a big way and reveal some unpleasant truths. Use this as a learning experience.

30 Try to develop a more conciliatory tone in your communication. You will understand something new at this time.

✺ MAY ✺

 Monthly Overview

The Sun, Mercury and the Moon further accentuate relationships, putting a focus on your partner or spouse. Venus also shows that love will be the key issue this month. Favourable influences from Jupiter to the Sun on the 16th of May ensure that any difficulties you experience will be smoothed over through conciliatory discussions and an open-handed approach. Sexual and intimacy issues may cause a few hiccups between the 21st and the 29th.

1   It's time to look more closely at your finances. Turning a blind eye will only create further confusion. Seek professional advice if necessary.

2   Someone may demand more accountability over financial matters, which will make you angry. It may be necessary to have a family discussion regarding everyone's role in managing the household accounts.

3   You will be disappointed to find that a friend has now become an enemy. This may not be permanent, but it will make you reconsider many of your friendships.

4 You could be inspired by the Divine or Nature, and this will cause you to rethink your life strategy. Consider what's valuable and what isn't.

5 Connecting with someone from your past will be important now. An upbeat exchange and comparison of life events will be very entertaining.

6 You have much work to do, but you also feel drawn to a series of social events. This could result in divided loyalties; you won't be able to do both well or fully.

7 Working with technology can benefit you now, but you must be brave enough to accept that things must change. Take the plunge.

8 Your communication is deeper now, and you're not interested in superficial relationships. You may have to discard some people in favour of a new set of associates. Don't be afraid to continue developing your psychological skills.

9 You can tell when someone's lying—you're a Scorpio! You may have to call someone out on the fact that they're not being completely honest with you.

10 A friendship could develop into a mutually beneficial business arrangement. If you don't end up going into business, you'll help each other in some other way.

11   You could be dealing with phobias, irrational fears and other inexplicable states of mind. Try to study the causes rather than the effects.

12   You can find a solution if you dedicate time to solving your financial problems. Direct your energies and communication into curtailing extraneous costs.

13   You could be aggressive about improving your health in half the time, but don't injure yourself. Take your time and your efforts at self-improvement will pay off.

14   You have the opportunity to re-establish an emotional or romantic link with someone. The initial meeting may be emotionally overwhelming; try to contain yourself.

15   Someone may be showering you with unwanted attention, which may cause you to lash out. Take this as a compliment, even if you don't want it to go any further.

16   Your tiredness may have to do with one or two people who you are consistently hanging out with. These energy vampires are subtly draining you of your life force.

17   Don't react to someone's recurrent flare-ups of antagonistic energy. Maintain your silence as a way of buffering yourself against these aggressive tendencies.

18 You may impulsively take time off work, only to find that you've made a rod for your own back. If you must take time off, make sure your work is up-to-date.

19 Extravagance, waste and an excessive lifestyle could lead you to regret your actions. When it comes to food and drink, being frugal will help.

20 You may get the green light to do some groundwork for a dream that you've had for some time.

21 You can make an impact on others by showing them how steady and reliable you are. The desire to win freedom at all costs will not help your cause right now.

22 Food allergies, environmental factors and even reactions to pharmaceuticals need to be investigated to see why you're experiencing physical problems right now. Attention to your diet can fix this.

23 The planets are producing some very favourable energies now and you should capitalise on these while they last. A desire for advancement in your career will be met with positively.

24 You can confront an enemy today, so don't back down! By showing them that you're fearless you will teach them a valuable lesson.

25 Generosity is your key word today. You may give someone time and energy, or even a gift. Your magnanimity will be reciprocated.

26 You're nostalgic and want to reminisce about the past. This is okay as long as it doesn't interfere with your work. Try to balance your daydreaming with what's expected of you.

27 Your spouse or partner may be secretive about their intentions to change some aspect of their work. But don't try to crack the walnut with a sledgehammer. Do it gently.

28 You may be fearful of something but are unable to define what it is. Look deeply into what is causing this feeling. The discovery could be a spiritual opening for you.

29 You may lose money today as a result of taking your eye off the ball. Check your change and study the people you interact with more closely.

30 You have some bright ideas today, but don't share them with people you don't know or trust. Listen to your instincts on these matters.

31 The month finishes with a rather hard aspect from the Moon to Mars. You may be irritable and impatient about getting things done. Try to be patient with others.

❧ JUNE ❧

Monthly Overview

You may need to stimulate your mind this month as the Moon, Mercury and Jupiter all transit your ninth house of higher education and spirituality. This is accentuated by the Sun's transit into the same zone on the 21st of June. Travelling for the purposes of broadening your horizons is also on the cards.

1 Trying to fulfil too many obligations is the cause of your distress today. Try to relax and don't do more work than you have to.

2 You should try to shock others with your beauty today. Acting in an unexpected way will give you an edge in your negotiations.

3 You may have to bend over backwards to please someone today. If you bend too far, however, you may break. Know when enough is enough.

4 You have excess emotional baggage right now. The challenge is to offload this additional weight and move more freely.

5 You may have to deal with an embarrassing financial situation with friends. Don't lose your wallet or get caught without enough cash. Be more aware just now.

6 You may feel tempted to go along with the crowd, but you realise that individuality will win out at present. Maintain your position, even under pressure.

7 You may find yourself dealing with a 'dirty' manager. Knowing other people's secrets gives you an advantage over them, but will you choose to use this knowledge?

8 You may try to make an impression today, only to find that it is negligible. Perhaps you're putting energy in the wrong direction.

9 You've become hooked on a promise, but you may be disappointed to find that it is hollow. Trust your instincts in this matter.

10 You may have to represent someone, but doing so may require a re-education of sorts. Be frank with them if you feel unable to do it.

11 You're drawn towards making more money, but you may not have the correct motivation. Don't try to keep up with the Joneses as you won't be able to sustain it.

12 You may divert your attention away from your usual source of making money, only to find that it has not given you any real advantage. Stick with what you know for the time being.

13 You have to be tolerant of others today. This will clear your conscience of some guilt that has been hanging around. Patience will assist you in other areas as well.

14 You are extremely vital today, and you may even feel that you are walking on clouds. Try to keep things real and practical.

15 You may feel that you've aged ten years due to the excessive demands that people are making of you. Try to take comfort in the one you love and don't be afraid to share your feelings with them.

16 You could be overly sensitive to others, and you may attack them even though you have nothing against them. Redirect these reactions to people who have done the wrong thing by you.

17 If you're too eager to please, it will devalue you. Be helpful but not overly enthusiastic, otherwise it will set a precedent for others to take advantage of you.

18 You don't have to rip into someone to get your point across today. Slow, steady and respectful conversation will achieve much more.

19 You may have to control your impulses for the sake of approval. Either way, there are some benefits to this, even if you feel frustrated in the process.

20 You need to liaise with an attorney or legal representative to help you through a current problem. You're concerned about paying money for this service, but you will spend much more if you try to get to the bottom of the problem yourself.

21 You are trying to decode some information, but it will be hard if you're a novice in the subject. Once again, you need to consult someone who has the expertise to help you.

22 Someone who had been keeping their cards close to their chest my surprise you today. This is not necessarily a bad thing, but it may concern you that they haven't been open with you.

23 You've been ignoring nature and not giving it much thought. Today you have the opportunity to connect deeply with it and rejuvenate your spirit.

24 You need to redefine the rules of engagement in a relationship now. The saying 'all is fair in love in war' is not necessarily true.

25 It may be someone's anniversary, so don't forget to make a point of celebrating it with them or at least making a friendly comment. You may be too busy to remember.

26 You have a short fuse and may bite someone's head off today. This could be an expensive error as the person you attack may be able to help you in some way.

27 Allocate enough time if you are planning a journey. That way you won't have to deal with trivial inconveniences.

28 Comedy, laughter and a little light-heartedness will help reduce tension in your environment today. Have a few jokes up your sleeve.

29 Your amateur input may not be as amateur as it seems; it may have an element of practicality to it. Don't be afraid to offer advice.

30 Don't cut corners now. Be comprehensive, especially if you're studying or making a presentation. Any form of apathy or laziness will show.

◎ JULY ◎

 Monthly Overview

As mentioned earlier, this is an important month. The key dates are the 16th, when Jupiter enters your career zone, and the 19th, when Venus enters your ninth zone of good fortune. Many good things are likely to occur at this time. Intense communications on the 25th and 26th, when Mars enters your Sun sign, should make it a very busy period.

1 You may be recovering from retail therapy and realise that you've overspent. The reasons may have been justified, but now you have to suffer the karma of excessive bills.

2 You don't believe everything that's being told to you at the moment. People's words are not matching their actions. Your intuition is correct.

3 You want something recreationally exotic at present, so make every effort to satisfy this desire. The mundane can become a little wearying.

4 Browse online and investigate different topics you don't understand. This will be enlightening.

5 You have an innate pride in your current circumstances and deserve to feel this, but be careful you don't incur the displeasure of others by appearing too smug about it.

6 Because you see troubling times looming, you may take a pre-emptive stance on someone in order to defuse or even sabotage a situation. Wait a little longer before you attack.

7 You might decide to take up a new sport, but this cycle brings lowered vitality that could end up impacting on you. Wait till your body is more capable.

8 You can look more elegant by paying attention to your hair. With the Moon and Saturn connected to your Sun sign, it's an excellent time for a makeover.

9 You're unrealistic in trying to achieve perfection just now. Do things in measured steps.

10 Sometimes you have to do things in reverse, which requires you to be a little sneaky. Getting to the truth will be an interesting exercise today.

11 A rush of work and demands is not catastrophic, Scorpio. Keep planning your work in an intelligent way, and if you haven't got a diary yet, get one!

12 The greater part of 'doing' is doing nothing at all. Rushing to rectify something may only make it worse. Bide your time and wait for the appropriate time to make your move.

13 Someone is abusive today, so don't get anywhere near their orbit or you could be on the receiving end of their wrath.

14 You're starting to understand that difficult experiences in life are just nature's way of preparing you for bigger and better things. Try to see the good in the unpleasant experiences at hand.

15 If you've been dumped or you're feeling hard done by, you could be frothing at the mouth right now. Prepare your response or attack before lashing out.

16 Now is the time to reform yourself, especially if you're habituated to alcohol, cigarettes and poor dietary habits. It's time for enlightenment.

17 Red will impress others today, so use this colour for maximum impact. If you're dealing with aggressive people, this colour can help you control their behaviour.

18 Pets and smaller animals may feature around this time. If you have pets, one of them may have some health problems and you could incur some additional expenses.

19 Don't allow pride to get in the way of meeting new people. If you humble yourself, you may learn something of vital importance.

20 You can refresh your finances, but you mustn't do this without consulting your partner. This decision needs to be a joint one.

21 A series of coincidences may seem like an avalanche of problems, but this is a blessing in disguise. Try to see the silver lining.

22 You must detach yourself from the idea that your salary defines who you are and how good you are at your job. You'll be tested to see whether you have the creativity to produce work of the finest calibre.

23 The Sun enters your zone of career, which gives you the edge over others due to your high energy, self-confidence and expertise.

24 Someone may not say hello or offer a courtesy that is customary. Take this in your stride and don't let it ruin your day.

25 You may have difficulty adjudicating a matter involving two friends. Remaining impartial will be a big test for you.

26 Don't project your expectations on others as this is bound to create disappointment. Listen to the full story before drawing your conclusions.

27 You're trying to do everything in your power to keep the peace in a certain situation, but you may have to sacrifice this for peace of mind.

28 Someone has a vice that is bothering you. It's up to you to say something, as long as it's done in a polite way.

29 You need mental stimulation now, so it's likely that you'll spend more time with friends. Some of your discussions may be rather unusual—even a little uncomfortable.

30 You may need to coax a friend into taking action that they find difficult. Your encouragement will be a great help to them.

31 You could be competing with a section of your peer group, but you needn't regard it as competition. Someone may challenge you, but if you take the bait all is lost.

◎ AUGUST ◎

 Monthly Overview

The Sun and Jupiter bring incredible good luck, and around the 2nd or 3rd, Mercury's conjunction with these planets should indicate good news regarding your work and profession. Income should increase, but you may need to wait awhile before you actually see an increase in your bank balance. The 16th of August is excellent for connecting with friends and discussing commercial ventures. By the 25th you may have that long-awaited pay rise, but be careful on the 26th when relationships and work could be in conflict.

1 You have to find some alternate way of dealing with debts. Reducing your interest payments is something that can be managed by changing your monthly payments to bi-weekly or weekly. Consider new approaches to reducing your debt.

2 You have strong beliefs, but they could be challenged today when you interact with others who have a different perspective on life. This will be an eye-opener.

3 First impressions are everything. Try to ensure that you have covered all bases if you are attending meetings or seeing new people today. Clothes maketh the man (and woman).

4 The Moon and Neptune indicate that you're extraordinarily creative. You may even feel that an expensive production is necessary, but that isn't the case. Start simply if you are embarking on a new hobby or activity.

5 You need to renew your vows now, and it will be easier to do because you have strong feelings of love and affection for someone. Make sure it is not a one-way street.

6 Sometimes it is a delightful joy to be inconsistent and keep others on their toes. Today you have the opportunity to do this and come out on top.

7 You need feedback from others now, so get them to tell you exactly what they feel. Bear in mind that the truth is not always pleasant, so be prepared for a few shocks.

8 It is possible to create variation in your lifestyle, but not without jettisoning some of your old habits and activities. By doing this you can create fertile ground for new growth.

9   Someone distinguished may make an appearance, but you will be less than impressed by them. You'll see through the facade and straight into their heart. Don't be deceived by the glitz and glamour.

10   There is propaganda around you and the truth is not too clear. This could make you angry, but it's not the right way to deal with the situation. Finding the source will be a great help.

11   If you are pleasing others today, it's because you are working to someone else's standards. It's time to develop your own skill set and follow your own creative impulses.

12   It will be much easier to orchestrate events in your workplace as you may have the opportunity to lead others. A pay rise or promotion is likely.

13   Being a revolutionary can be tedious, but mixing things up and challenging others to do their best is on the cards.

14   Enhance things a step at a time. You can apply this principle to yourself or things in your environment, including relationships. You don't have to do everything straight away.

15 Easy tasks should be attacked first today. Leave the difficult problems for later. Conserve time—that is the trick just now.

16 Saying yes to too many people is the reason for any illness you are experiencing right now. Work and health go hand in glove.

17 You may feel ill-equipped to deal with work. Are you out of your depth at the moment? There are ways to remedy this, but you need to acknowledge the problem in the first place.

18 Today is a casual sort of day, and this will be reflected in the company you keep. Stressful associates or friends need not apply!

19 People will exploit you only if you allow them to. It is up to you to stop this sort of behaviour.

20 If you are aiming for money and achievement, don't overlook some of the basic principles of success. The spirit of achievement has more to do with loving what you do than with being concerned about the outcome.

21 You could be fooled by someone just now, but with the Moon and Neptune in favourable aspect, this needn't happen. Falling for a sob story could be part of the problem.

22 You must go solo today rather than joining the crowd. You will feel as if your identity is lost if you don't take more control of where you want to go.

23 Someone is constantly asking you for assistance because they are not up to the task. This is not helping them in the long term. Help them to help themselves.

24 Hanging out with someone who wants to be silly is not a bad idea today. If life has gotten too serious, it is time to let your hair down and have a bit of fun.

25 Your in-tray is getting congested with work that you've been avoiding. The wisest course of action is to do tomorrow's tasks today and today's tasks immediately.

26 Reserve your judgments today, even though people will prod you for an answer. You need to sleep on the question.

27 You may be developing some sort of irritation, perhaps on your skin. This is a direct response to emotional activities. Look at what is bothering you, as this is being reflected on your body.

28 You may feel out of step with others. In matters of sexuality and dating, this could cause you some problems. Don't let your emotions run away with you today.

29 Someone may be unconsciously killing your fun and style. If it happens to be your spouse or partner, this could create a rift between you. Address the issue immediately.

30 Don't let your pride get in the way of your relationships today. Remember, this quality could lead to a fall. Remain humble and listen to the other person's viewpoint.

31 Do you have a good attorney or legal advisor? If you are not happy with the quality of advice you are receiving, get a second opinion.

⊚ SEPTEMBER ⊚

Monthly Overview

Dealing with a sick or downtrodden friend after the 2nd may occupy your mind, and you may need to set aside considerable time to help them. This is a time of compassionate work, helping others and working behind the scenes. A better social period occurs after the 20th of September with the fine aspect from Venus to the Sun. Fun times can be expected on the 28th with Mercury entering your Sun sign.

1 If you have gained momentum in your life and work, you need to make this a repeatable action. Weaving a system into your daily madness is essential now.

2 A seminar to help you increase your awareness and expand your financial horizons would be very useful right now.

3 You may be thrown into a state of wonder by simple, everyday things like nature. This is excellent for opening up creative channels within you.

4   You may find yourself attracted to someone cute. But the question is: do they have substance?

5   Someone may be twisting your arm to do their bidding. You may yield under pressure and regret this afterwards.

6   It is okay to correct someone if you find that they have made an error in judgment. The trick is how you present your case.

7   If you are working through your budget, make sure that you allow for sundry items. Those small costs can add up to a lot of money.

8   The need for amusement may be pressing now. Don't ignore the inner signs of joy, laughter and inner contentment.

9   It always helps if you're in a similar mood to someone. That way you can resonate with each other. This is one of those days when you will click with another person.

10   The architecture of modern life has been built on a biblical foundation. You may question this and rub someone the wrong way.

11   If you clarify your thoughts out aloud, you have a better chance of securing a business deal or a new friendship. Asking questions will put you in the driver's seat.

12 You're reaching your peak socially, and others will be drawn to you. Make sure you have a plan for how you can utilise these opportunities. Don't fritter away these powerful universal energies.

13 Once you are possessed with the energy to complete some job or activity, don't stop. Don't waste the opportunity to achieve as much as you can.

14 Mars moves to your second zone of finances, so don't let material things trigger arguments and disagreements.

15 You need to beat someone back if they're encroaching on your space and time. The issue of respect is paramount here.

16 Are any of the commandments disposable, such as 'Thou Shalt Not Kill'? I mean this in a humorous way, but you may feel like killing someone today. Try to find a conciliatory approach rather than exploding.

17 Connecting with someone from your past may be tough, probably because they don't have the will and heart that you do. Leave it well alone.

18 You want to tend to mankind. This could take the form of community service or making a regular donation to a charity organisation.

19 There are excellent opportunities for work, money and personal effort to yield good results right now. Just remember what I said earlier: don't make money a source of debate.

20 You may be compelled to ditch your work in favour of something better. This is okay as long as you do your research first.

21 The truth will set you free. If you've been holding on to a situation, particularly with one of your parents, now is the time to eliminate it. Speak your mind without fear.

22 You can't dodge someone else's criticisms and judgment at present. Old habits die hard, so you may need to do something alone and secretively before revealing your intentions.

23 Paying attention to your typing today could save you a lot of worry and bother. Once you have sent an email, it is impossible to take it back. Write your thoughts down and hold onto them until your mind is much calmer.

24 Public opinion may weigh heavily on you, but if you stand up to the group you'll be respected. Your way of seeing things may win a few people over.

25 Guard your reputation as some inadvertent blunders may cost you dearly. This is not something you are doing out of malice; it's simply an oversight.

26 Confidentiality is a forgotten art. If something is revealed to you now, keep it in the strictest of confidence.

27 You are feeling fulfilled now, mostly because you are reaching deep within yourself and doing things that satisfy you. Continue on the road to self-discovery, Scorpio.

28 You must disguise some of your emotions today lest you bring others down. Once again, humour is an excellent way of defusing those negative emotions.

29 You may notice some corruption around you. Should you speak up or keep it to yourself? Let your inner voice guide you.

30 Unless you want to provoke a controversial situation, you may need to be secretive about a relationship. The way you live your life is no one else's business.

☉ OCTOBER ☉

 Monthly Overview

The Full Moon around the 8th is important and shows that your work or work practices will get a new lease of life. You may be emotionally involved in what you are doing and need to remove your heart from some of the tasks at hand. Increased energy is likely when the Sun and Venus move to the sign of Scorpio on the 23rd and 24th of October respectively. You will be attractive and likely to experience success in both your work and social environment.

1   Making radical adjustments to your life is not easy when you have repressed feelings or grudges. Get together with the person involved to resolve this once and for all.

2   You probably think that half-hearted love is better than no love at all. This couldn't be further from the truth. If you are single, try to find solace in your own company until the right person comes along.

3   Wasting time and resources is the last thing you need to feel happy. Don't let external circumstances dominate your life. Take control of your time.

4   Friendly play can deteriorate into aggressive arguments. Being a good sport is the moral of the story today.

5   Your magnetism and fascination for love and people is not very strong today. Try to lie low until positive feelings re-emerge.

6   The karma from your past is returning in a good way now. You'll start to experience the truth of this universal law by 'paying it forward'.

7   You may be feeling imprisoned by someone or a situation, but this is purely a state of mind. You need to realign your thinking to more positive energies.

8   Your popularity and influence will start to increase, especially in your work. You may have thought that everyone had forgotten you, but that is not the case.

9   Be prepared for an unusual event with someone. If this happens, adjustment and greater flexibility will be necessary on your part.

10   Someone in your workplace may be ill or unavailable, and you'll have to cover for them. This means readjusting your schedule.

11 Unannounced departures are better in some cases. Stop trying to ingratiate yourself with someone who doesn't really care.

12 There is a certain degree of suspicion within you today, and you may feel that others are talking behind your back. Redirect your thinking to things that are more worthwhile.

13 Although you are surrounded by friends, you may be in a rather unusual environment. This will be a novel experience for you.

14 You'll be curious about someone's personal affairs, but you may be treading on their toes. Know where to draw the line and respect their privacy.

15 Health matters are spotlighted just now. As mentioned earlier, your mental and emotional states are causing this. Address these issues to improve your life.

16 Although the planets are stimulating your creativity, you may not an adequate outlet for it. Seeking an appropriate partner may be a disappointing experience.

17 You have intense feelings for your work at present, but you may be short-changed by those around you. Try to establish whether you are being given the best chance to do your best.

18 Sometimes an unholy alliance is the best way to get a job done. You may find yourself thrown into the pit with someone you don't necessarily like, but their professional activities will be able to assist you right now.

19 You need some peace at the moment, and you can get it by connecting with a close and trusted ally. Take some time out to recharge your worn-out batteries.

20 There is a degree of selfishness in the air, but sometimes it's necessary. Take hold of this opportunity, as it may not present itself again. Cast aside your feelings of pity, especially in the dog-eat-dog game of business.

21 Disguising your weakness is important, otherwise competitors and adversaries will cut you down. Work away from the crowd today.

22 If you follow someone else's lead right now, they may steer you into a dead end. Monitor their directives on a regular basis.

23 You can surmount your negative emotions today. If you don't feel happy, try smiling anyway. The change in your body chemistry will make you feel better.

24 Your intentions will be closely aligned with those of your spouse or partner. Finding a common goal will strengthen your emotional ties.

25 If you procrastinate now, you will lose a vital opportunity. This may refer to a job offer or similar opportunity that is ripe for the picking.

26 You may have no desire to work or exert yourself at present. Rather than making excuses, be honest about it.

27 It is time for a new makeover—on the inside. Changing your behaviour and attitude will make a world of difference, and you'll achieve your objectives more quickly.

28 Even if you have let go of a relationship, there may be moments of regret or the desire to reconnect with that person. Hopefully, you are not too emotionally entangled. A quick chat with them may help.

29 This will be an extremely busy time. Try to establish guidelines and protocols for dealing with others. You could find yourself doing their work if you are not careful.

30 Your mind is on faraway things and you can't connect with the issues at hand. If this is the case, take a few days off and come back when your mind is in a higher gear.

31 Using silence as a weapon is important now, especially in your family life. The less you speak, the more power you will have.

❀ NOVEMBER ❀

Monthly Overview

Dealing with your partner after the 7th may be difficult as they could be suffering health problems or doubts about their future career direction. Listen to them rather than talking. With Venus moving to your zone of income on the 17th, this could be a time of increased income and the resolution of your spouse or partner's problems. Don't let the Sun cause you to overspend on the 22nd.

1   Confrontation may be looming because someone believes you have a debt. This could be money or a favour, so try to settle the score.

2   If you're in a relationship, it's time to bring out the more adventurous and romantic side of your partner. This will require considerable creative effort on your part.

3   You're favoured by Lady Luck just now, but only because you've worked so hard. Don't be emotional about business decisions or your relationships. Both of these areas will naturally improve and grow better with time.

4   You have a particularly powerful imagination today, but you may be projecting some of your feelings onto others. Keep your discussions upbeat and don't dwell on your negativities or problems.

5   You're not feeling all that domesticated at the moment, but domestic issues may be demanding. Finding a balance between your social and marital life will be a challenge.

6   You are very excitable today, and you will be able to excite others as well. Don't confuse friendship with romance.

7   Self-control will be easy just now. If you've been suffering from signs of excess, now is the time to turn over a new leaf.

8   Playing mind games seems to be part of your destiny at present. You don't like mind games, but they may be necessary to counteract other people's manipulative thoughts.

9   Disagreements over your job description or role may stop you from feeling happy at work. Speak up and be counted.

10 You're in a powerful phase of emotional and sexual attractiveness. New relationships can start and end quickly.

11 Don't forget important occasions. You may be so overloaded with work that they could slip your mind.

12 It's time to enjoy culture, art and other aesthetic activities. Mercury, Neptune and your fifth house are activated today.

13 You're wearing a lot of caps right now. Let's just hope you're being paid for those additional responsibilities. Others will give you more work if they see that you're capable.

14 An impromptu meeting or outing is just what the doctor ordered. This is a time when something unconventional and out-of-the-ordinary can lift your spirits.

15 You don't feel particularly good today as the Moon is in difficult aspect to Saturn and Venus. Once again, work could be getting the better of you, and you may have to grin and bear the additional responsibilities.

16 You will get noticed today, but this is not the sort of attention you want. Your personal and professional activities are at odds with each other. Try to keep them separate.

17 Friends may try to aggressively change you or sway your opinion, but you're not in the mood to be coerced. You need to pretend to agree with them in order to allay their fears.

18 Don't share too much of your good news with others or they may become envious. Be measured in sharing your news with friends.

19 Your mind may glimpse the larger possibilities of life. If ideas come to you, be quick to jot them down, as you could forget them very quickly. You have high energy and drive today, but you may also be somewhat accident-prone.

20 The transits of the Moon can indicate emotional change for you right now. This is because your attitudes are changing. Don't keep these a secret. If you do, your changed perceptions could confuse the ones you love.

21 Your lover may not make much sense right now. Don't read too much into this or you'll make matters worse. Try to be compassionate as they could be going through some problems.

22 If you're feeling down, you may try to overcompensate through excessive use of fragrances, makeup and other fashion statements. This will be a mistake as overcompensation can mask dissatisfaction or insecurity.

23 Bold activities are what you want right now, but you may not be emotionally or physically up to it. You need to prepare yourself for intense sports and other physically demanding activities.

24 Your intuition is strong at present, and you should seize any opportunity that is in your best interests. Work should go well, and you may have something important to contribute on this front.

25 Contractual negotiations are highlighted today as the Moon and Pluto connect in the third house. Push your agenda and you'll get what you want.

26 You have a really great rapport with others today because you're able to listen to what they have to say. This makes them feel good about you and sets the trend for mutual support.

27 The Moon in the fourth zone of domestic circumstances gives you the energy to improve your life situation. As long as you don't become too aggressive about it, you'll receive support from your family.

28 Mercury transits your zone of finance, which makes you clever in earning more and coming up with brilliant schemes for improving your future security.

29 You're nostalgic today, but are you remembering the right things? Focusing on negativities and hard times will only undermine your present happiness. Be balanced when it comes to recollecting the past.

30 Don't rush into a relationship that is not going to fulfil you in the long term. Enjoy it for what it is, but don't place too much faith in it.

⊚ DECEMBER ⊚

Monthly Overview

You'll have fewer responsibilities, or at least a more relaxed approach to things, as Saturn moves to the edge of your Sun sign. You are likely to enjoy some pastimes or hobbies that you have postponed for a while. There may still be some business or professional issues stopping you from fully enjoying yourself, but the period of the 11th, 17th and 22nd bring to the fore perfect opportunities for travel, fun and adventure.

1 A change of environment will do you the world of good today; it's exactly what you need. Plodding will pay off and give you the best results.

2 You may accept an invitation to a theatrical event or unusual type of entertainment, but you may be disappointed if this is not your cup of tea.

3 You need to express what you want today because others are not capable of deciphering how you feel. If you talk about your needs, you're more likely to have them met.

4   You won't be satisfied until you have the biggest and best of everything today. Your appetite is huge, so the best advice is to moderate it.

5   You could come out the victor today, but this may cause other problems. You must understand that every situation has its ups and downs.

6   You need to be more objective about your romance because you're seeing the world through rose-coloured glasses. Try to give others a chance to make decisions.

7   You can share ideas with others today and feel as if you're contributing in a way that helps everyone.

8   Your work with others will yield positive results. As a result, you are prepared to allocate more time and energy to them, knowing that it's a win-win situation.

9   You could feel restless and defensive when others try to cramp your style. Discipline is important if you wish to control your feelings and achieve some measure of success.

10   You may have an unconscious reaction to work, the direction in which its going and your sense of identity. Nip these feelings in the bud and you will augment your professionalism.

11 A deal based on a handshake is not advisable at present. Signatures are necessary, and even if the atmosphere is congenial, it's best to formalise the deal.

12 If there's rigidity in your philosophical viewpoint, you won't grow. Today is an opportunity to open up and take in what others are saying. You may resist it, even though you feel intuitively that it is true.

13 You could be challenged to try new cuisine. This will help you grow in your general understanding of things.

14 Discretion is essential in your discussions today. Someone who is hypersensitive could make it somewhat awkward for you to share your feelings.

15 Don't take your health for granted today. If in doubt, seek the assistance of a specialist to address this problem.

16 There could be some fear surrounding your sense of security for the future. Look carefully at what suits your budget without cutting into your lifestyle.

17 If you need to settle a score with someone, discussions may not be enough. You need to put pen to paper or send an email to indicate the gravity of the situation.

18 Overindulgence may cause you problems now. Eat less and rest more. There may also be some problems associated with punctuality, either with you or someone else.

19 Now is not the time to push a friendship or relationship to the next level. You must be sensitive to the other person's needs and understand that they may not be available or ready to move forward with you.

20 Being forgetful about money is not always of great consequence, but today the risks are high. Hold on to your purse and don't sign on the dotted line too quickly.

21 You want romance, but you may be preoccupied with other things. An admirer could be on the horizon, but you may have to let them go.

22 If deadlines are overwhelming, ask for someone's help. They'll be more than happy to assist you.

23 Both pleasure and pressure are squeezing you from both sides today. Don't worry; a brief journey or weekend away will relieve you of these 'see saw' experiences.

24 You want to give to others but may be hamstrung by financial constraints. Remember, it's the thought that counts.

25 Merry Christmas, Scorpio. You could be completely scattered today as Mercury is in Uranus. If you've landed a job where you do absolutely everything, you've got only yourself to blame. Today's key word is delegation.

26 It's a day of creativity, and although you may have had a frenetic Christmas Day, today should be much more relaxed and enjoyable.

27 Frustrations are likely with Mars and the Sun in a hard aspect. Don't let this get you down. Be the calm one in the group.

28 You can assert yourself in a quiet and unassuming manner. You'll even surprise yourself with how much you can get done and how well you can convince others to follow your lead.

29 Although your friendships are being tested, you'll be able to sift the wheat from the chaff and finally get to a smaller and more loyal group of friends. This is essential as you move into the new year.

30 You needn't deal with others in a heavy-handed way. People will be civil and peaceful in the way they receive your requests and demands. Sharing is also an important component of your relationships today.

31 You have a strong urge to educate yourself and study something unique. There may be a deepening attraction to psychological or detective novels.

2014
ASTRONUMEROLOGY

THERE IS NO ONE ELSE WHO CAN EVER
FILL YOUR ROLE IN THE SAME WAY,
SO IT'S A GOOD IDEA TO PERFORM IT
AS WELL AS POSSIBLE.

Humphry Osmond

THE POWER BEHIND
⟲ YOUR NAME ⟳

Everything in nature is ruled by numbers, including your name and birthday. By simply adding up the numbers of your name, the vibration and ruling planet of this number can be calculated, and through that we can study the effects on your life and destiny. There is an ancient system of numerology that originated in Chaldea. It is somewhat different from the system devised by Pythagoras, but it is equally, if not more, powerful and takes into account the planets and the effects on your name and birthday. Here is a table of the letters, numbers and ruling planets associated with them.

AIJQY	=	1	Sun
BKR	=	2	Moon
CGLS	=	3	Jupiter
DMT	=	4	Uranus
EHNX	=	5	Mercury
UVW	=	6	Venus
OZ	=	7	Neptune
FP	=	8	Saturn
—	=	9	Mars

Note: The number 9 is a spiritual number and, according to the ancient tradition of Chaldean numerology, is not assigned a letter. It is considered an unknowable number. Once the name or birthday numbers have been calculated, the number 9 is used as a sum total number for interpretation.

Throughout history, many people have changed their names for good luck, including actors, writers and musicians. They have done this in the hope of attracting good fortune by using the numbers of the planets connected with that birth date. If you look at the following table of numbers and their meanings, you will have a greater insight into how you can change your name and use this to your own advantage for more fulfilling relationships, wealth, general happiness and success.

Here is an example of how you can calculate the number and power of your name. If your name is Barack Obama, you can calculate the ruling numbers as follows:

B	A	R	A	C	K		O	B	A	M	A
2	1	2	1	3	2		7	2	1	4	1

Now add the numbers like this:

2 + 1 + 2 + 1 + 3 + 2 + 7 + 2 + 1 + 4 + 1	=	26
Then add 2 + 6	=	8

You can now see that the sum total of the numbers is 8, which is ruled by Saturn, and that the underlying vibrations of 2 and 6 are ruled by the Moon and Venus. You can now study the Name Number table to see what these planetary energies and numbers mean for Barack Obama. We can see from Saturn that he is an extremely hard-working and ambitious person with incredible concentration and the ability to sacrifice a lot for his chosen objectives. From Venus and the Moon, we see that he is a person possessing a delightful, charming and persuasive personality, and that he has a strong love for his family.

Name Number	Ruling Planet	Name Characteristics
1	Sun	Being ruled by the Sun means you possess abundant energy and attract others with your powerful aura. You are bright, magnetic and attractive as well. You are generous and loyal in disposition. Because of your high levels of energy, you need sport to make you feel good. You succeed in any enterprise you choose.
2	Moon	You are emotional and your temperament is soft and dreamy, but you must be careful of extreme mood swings. You are psychic and can use your intuitive hunches to understand others and gain an insight into your future. You have strong connections to your mother, family and women in general. Your caring and compassionate nature will make you popular with others.

Name Number	Ruling Planet	Name Characteristics
3	Jupiter	You seem to attract good luck without too much effort, but you must be on guard as you are likely to be excessive even when you are generous. You have strong philosophical instincts and wish to understand why you are here. Travelling is high on your agenda and you will explore many different facets of life and culture. You are a perennial student who wants to learn more about yourself and life in general.
4	Uranus	The number 4 is an unpredictable number, so you need to plan adequately for your life. It will have many unforeseen twists and turns, but you are extraordinarily innovative in the way you deal with life issues. You need unusual friends as you get bored easily, and it's quite likely you will take an interest in technological or scientific things. Learning to be flexible will go a long way in helping you secure a happy and fulfilling life.

Name Number	Ruling Planet	Name Characteristics
5	Mercury	Speed and accuracy are the key words for the planet Mercury and the number 5. You love communication and connect with people easily, but you need to be on guard against dissipating your energies into many frivolous activities. This is a youthful number, and you never grow old. You will always be surrounded by youngsters and people who make you laugh. You have a great sense of humour and will always be successful as you have the gift of the gab.
6	Venus	You have a natural inclination to love and be loved if you are ruled by the number 6 and Venus. Having a delightful personality, you attract many people of the opposite sex. You are successful with money and take great pleasure in working towards your future security. You will have many love affairs, and at some point you may even be torn between two lovers.

Name Number	Ruling Planet	Name Characteristics
7	Neptune	With the number 7 as your ruling number, you have reached a very high level of evolution. You are gifted with premonitions, intuition and clairvoyance. Health and healing are also gifts that you have been endowed with. Learn to discriminate when giving yourself to others.
8	Saturn	You have incredible focus and an ability to achieve anything you set your mind to, no matter how long it takes. You sacrifice for others as your loyalty is highly developed. You work hard to achieve things you believe are worthwhile, but sometimes this overshadows your personal life. You demand that things are done properly, which is why others may not be able to live up to your expectations. Learn to relax a little more.
9	Mars	You have a hot nature and need an outlet such as sport and other physical activities to balance your life and improve your health. You are not afraid of challenges and can be confrontational. Learn to listen and accept that others don't have the same attitudes as you. You are a protector of the family and loyal to the core. You are an individual and never follow another's lead.

YOUR PLANETARY
⟨ RULER ⟩

Numerology is intimately linked to the planets, which is why astrology and your date of birth are also spiritually connected. Once again, here are the planets and their ruling numbers:

1   **Sun**

2   **Moon**

3   **Jupiter**

4   **Uranus**

5   **Mercury**

6   **Venus**

7   **Neptune**

8   **Saturn**

9   **Mars**

Finding your birth numbers is simple. All you have to do is add each of the numbers of your date of birth to arrive at a single digit number. If you're born on 12 November 1972, add the numbers of your day, month and year of birth to find your destiny number, like this:

1 + 2 + 1 + 1 + 1 + 9 + 7 + 2 = 24

Then add   **2 + 4 = 6**

This means that the number 6, which is ruled by Venus, is your destiny number.

YOUR PLANETARY
◎ FORECAST ◎

You can even take your ruling name number and add it to the year in question to throw more light on your coming personal affairs, like this:

B A R A C K O B A M A	**=**	**8**
Year coming	**=**	**2014**
Add 8 + 2 + 0 + 1 + 4	**=**	**15**
Add 1 + 5	**=**	**6**

This is the ruling year number using your name number as a basis. Therefore, you would study the influence of Venus (number 6) using the Trends for Your Planetary Ruler in 2014 table. Enjoy!

Trends for Your Planetary Number in 2014

Year Number	Ruling Planet	Results Throughout the Coming Year
1	Sun	**Overview**

Overview

You are now ready to move forward in a new cycle and create something wonderful for yourself and your loved ones. Your career, finance and personal reputation will improve considerably and your physical health should also be much better. Although there may be some challenges, you're able to meet them head-on and come out a winner.

Love and Pleasure

You can attract anyone you want throughout 2014 because your energy and aura are so strong. You will need many friends and will find yourself doing creative activities alone and with others.

Work

You will have no problem getting a better job or some sort of promotion in your current line of work. More money can be expected, and any changes you make in your life should bring you great satisfaction.

Improving Your Luck

Good luck is on the cards, with July and August being especially lucky for you. The 1st, 8th, 15th and 22nd hours of Sundays are lucky.

Lucky numbers are 1, 10, 19 and 28.

Year Number	Ruling Planet	Results Throughout the Coming Year
2	Moon	

Overview

Although you will feel emotional this year, it's time to take control of yourself and change your personality for the better. Working through issues with females, both at home and in the workplace, may be the key to your happiness and success this year.

Love and Pleasure

Domestic affairs and relationships at home will take centre stage in 2014. Your marital relationship or important significant friendships are high on your agenda of things to improve. You are sensitive and intuitive, so trust your gut feeling when it comes to making decisions in this area of your life.

Work

Make your decisions based on rational thought rather than impulsive emotional reactions. Draw a clear line in the sand between work and leisure for best results. You are more creative this year, so hopefully you will take the opportunity to move along that path rather than doing something you are bored with.

Year Number	Ruling Planet	Results Throughout the Coming Year
2	Moon	**Improving Your Luck** Mondays will be lucky and July will fulfil some of your dreams. The 1st, 8th, 15th and 22nd hours on Mondays are fortunate. Pay special attention to the New and Full Moons in 2014. Lucky numbers are 2, 11, 20, 29 and 38.

Year Number	Ruling Planet	Results Throughout the Coming Year
3	Jupiter	

Overview

A number 3 year is usually a lucky one due to the beneficial influence of Jupiter. New opportunities, financial good fortune, travels and spiritual insights will be key factors in the coming year.

Love and Pleasure

You have a huge appetite for love, and bond easily with others to fulfil this need. Try to clarify your feelings before investing too much energy into someone who may not be the best choice. This is a year of entertainment and pleasure, and one in which generosity will bring good karma to you.

Work

You can finally ask for that pay rise as this is a lucky year when money will naturally come to you. Promotions, interviews for a new position and general good fortune can be expected.

Improving Your Luck

Don't let harebrained schemes distract you from the practical aspects of life. Good planning is necessary for success. March and December are lucky months. 2014 will bring you some unexpected surprises. The 1st, 8th, 15th and 24th hours of Thursdays are spiritually very lucky for you.

Lucky numbers are 3, 12, 21, and 30.

Year Number	Ruling Planet	Results Throughout the Coming Year
4	Uranus	

Overview

Expect the unexpected with this ruling number for the coming year. If you have spread yourself thinly, then you may lack the requisite energy to handle the changes that are coming. Independence is your key word, but impulse is also likely. Take your time before making important decisions, and structure your life appropriately.

Love and Pleasure

The grass may not be greener on the other side, and if you're feeling trapped in a relationship, you will want to break free of the entanglements that are strangling your self-development. You need to balance tradition with progress if you are to come out of this period a happy person.

Work

Innovation will help you make good progress in your professional life. Learn something new, especially in the technological arena. If you have been reluctant to improve your skill set, you are shooting yourself in the foot. Expand your horizons, learn new tasks and improve your professional future. Group activity will also help you carve a new niche for yourself.

Year Number	Ruling Planet	Results Throughout the Coming Year
4	Uranus	**Improving Your Luck**

Improving Your Luck

Try not to overdo things this year, and learn to be more forbearing with others. Slow and steady wins the race in 2014. Steady investments are lucky. The 1st, 8th, 15th and 20th hours of Saturdays will be very lucky for you.

Lucky numbers are 4, 13, 22 and 31.

Year Number	Ruling Planet	Results Throughout the Coming Year
5	Mercury	**Overview**

You want to socialise and communicate your feelings this year because you have such a creative and powerful imagination, and it is likely you will connect with many new people. Try not to spread yourself too thinly, as concentration levels may be lacking. Don't be distracted by the wrong crowd.

Love and Pleasure

Reciprocation is important for your relationships in 2014. Variety is the spice of life, but also ensure that your key partnership will weather the storm and get stronger with time. Talk about your feelings, even if this is difficult. Don't be too harsh and critical of the one you love; instead, turn the spotlight of criticism on yourself to improve your character.

Work

People will look up to you in the coming 12 months, which is why new contracts will be drawn and doors will open to provide you with a bright new professional future. You are quick and capable, but try not to overdo things, as this can affect your nervous system. Travel is a great way to balance these energies.

Year Number	Ruling Planet	Results Throughout the Coming Year
5	Mercury	**Improving Your Luck**

Improving Your Luck

Expressing ideas is essential and it will help you come up with great plans that others want to help you with. By being enthusiastic and creative, you will attract the support of those who count. The 1st, 8th, 15th and 20th hours of Wednesdays are your luckiest, so schedule your meetings and other important social engagements at these times.

Lucky numbers are 5, 14, 23 and 32.

Year Number	Ruling Planet	Results Throughout the Coming Year
6	Venus	**Overview**

Overview

A year of love. Expect romantic and sensual interludes or a new love affair. Number 6 is also related to family life. Working with a loved one or family member is possible, and it will yield good results. Save money, cut costs and share your success.

Love and Pleasure

Love will be important to you, and if you are in a relationship, you can strengthen the bonds with your partner at this time. Making new friends is also on the cards, and these relationships will become equally significant, especially if you are not yet hitched. Engagement, marriage and other important celebrations take place. You will find yourself more socially active.

Work

You have a desire to work on your future financial security, so cutting back costs would be a key factor in this. You may find yourself with more money, but don't let false illusions cause you to spend more than you earn. Developing your part-time interest into a fully-fledged career is also something that can take place this year. Your social life and professional activities will overlap.

Year Number	Ruling Planet	Results Throughout the Coming Year
6	Venus	**Improving Your Luck**

Improving Your Luck

Developing a positive mental attitude will attract good luck and karma that is now ripe for the picking. Enjoy your success, but continue to work on removing those personality defects that are obstructing you from even bigger success. Balance spiritual and financial needs. The 1st, 8th, 15th and 20th hours on Fridays are extremely lucky for you this year, and new opportunities can arise when you least expect them.

Lucky numbers are 6, 15, 24 and 33.

Year Number	Ruling Planet	Results Throughout the Coming Year
7	Neptune	

Overview

You have the power to intuitively understand what needs to be done in 2014. Trust your instincts and make greater efforts at your spiritual and philosophical wellbeing. This is the time when your purpose becomes crystal clear. You can gain a greater understanding of yourself and others and have the ability to heal those who need your help both within and outside your family.

Love and Pleasure

If you can overcome the tendency to find fault with yourself, you will start to truly love yourself and attract those who also love you. This is the key law of success in love, and you will discover this in the coming 12 months. Don't give more than others are prepared to reciprocate. You need to set your standards high enough to meet someone who is worthy of your love.

Work

This is the year to stop watching the clock and produce incredibly wonderful work. No matter how menial the task, you can experience the spiritual significance of work and how this can be used to uplift others. The healing, caring and social services professions may attract you just now.

Year Number	Ruling Planet	Results Throughout the Coming Year
7	Neptune	**Improving Your Luck**

Be clear in your communication so as to avoid misunderstandings with others. If you have some health issues, now is the time to clear them up and improve your general vitality. Sleep well, exercise and develop better eating habits to improve your life. The 1st, 8th, 15th and 20th hours of Wednesdays are your luckiest, so schedule your meetings and other important social engagements at these times.

Lucky numbers are 7, 16, 25 and 34.

Year Number	Ruling Planet	Results Throughout the Coming Year
8	Saturn	

Overview

This is a year of achievement, but it will require discipline and a removal of all distractions to achieve your goals. Eliminating unnecessary aspects of your life that constrict your success will be something you need to pay attention to. Your overall success may be slow, but it is assured.

Love and Pleasure

By overworking, you deny your loved ones the pleasure of your company and emotional support. Take the time to express how you feel. Remember that love is a verb. Spend more time with your loved ones as a countermeasure to excessive work routines.

Work

This is a money year, and the Chinese will tell you that the number 8 is very lucky indeed. But remember that money can't buy you love. Earn well, but also learn to balance your income potential with creative satisfaction.

Year Number	Ruling Planet	Results Throughout the Coming Year
8	Saturn	**Improving Your Luck**
		If you are too cautious you may miss wonderful opportunities. Of course, you don't want to make mistakes, but sometimes these mistakes are the best lessons that life can dish out. Have courage and don't be afraid to try something new. The 1st, 8th, 15th and 20th hours of Saturdays are the best times for you in 2014.
		Lucky numbers are 1, 8, 17, 26 and 35.

Year Number	Ruling Planet	Results Throughout the Coming Year
9	Mars	

Overview

This is the last cycle, which means that you will be tying up loose ends over the coming 12 months. Don't get caught up in trivial matters as this is the perfect time to redirect your energy into what you want in life. Don't be angry, avoid arguments and clearly focus on what you want now.

Love and Pleasure

You want someone who can return the love, energy and passion that you have for them. If this isn't happening, you may choose to end a relationship and find someone new. Even if you need to transition to a new life, try to do this with grace and diplomacy.

Work

You can be successful this year because of the sheer energy you are capable of investing into your projects. Finish off what is incomplete as there are big things around the corner, and you don't want to leave a mess behind. You can obtain respect and honour from your employers and co-workers.

Year Number	Ruling Planet	Results Throughout the Coming Year
9	Mars	**Improving Your Luck**
		Don't waste your valuable energy this year. Use it to discover the many talents that you possess. By doing this you can begin to improve your life in many different ways. Release tension to maintain health. The 1st, 8th, 15th and 20th hours of Tuesdays will be lucky for you throughout 2014.
		Lucky numbers are 9, 18, 27 and 36.